ENLIGHTENED

ENLIGHTENED

R. WILLIAM PLUME

Published 2025
by R. William Plume

ISBN 978-0-473-76611-5 (International Edition)

© Copyright R. William Plume 2025

COPYPRESS

Designed and distributed in New Zealand by CopyPress, Nelson, New Zealand.

www.copypress.co.nz

CHAPTER 1

Homecoming

For Germans, discontent and resentment are the mood. The humiliation of defeat is the cause. Bitterness towards political and military leaders and animosity towards returning veterans are the result. There is disapproval in every glance and vitriol in every remark.

Loser. We have paid for your failure over and over again. First, we paid through the nose for the war. Then, we paid in misery. You try eating pig food, bleedin' turnips, every meal, every day, while all the real food goes to the Front. Now, we're paying the fucking Treaty of Versailles reparations.

And, mate, there's salt in the bleedin' wound. Our money is worthless. A loaf of bread costs a cartload of Deutschmarks. Wait until tomorrow; it will be two cartloads for the same loaf of bread, bucket of coal, or rent.

Hungry, cold, homeless. Thanks for nothin'.

Loser.

JULIUS STREICHER RETURNS FROM THE WAR

Julius Streicher, aboard a troop transport train, has arrived in Nuremberg.

Still dressed in his military fatigues, Streicher steps down onto the platform. Looking in both directions, he sees a solid mass of uniformed German soldiers, the survivors, shuffling silently towards the station.

This is no happy homecoming. The few civilians who are waiting to meet someone are subdued. Greetings are quiet and tearful.

Streicher, jostled along by the lumbering crowd, struggles to sling his kitbag over his shoulder. Here and there he sees faces he recognises. Those he acknowledges return acknowledgement stripped of enthusiasm.

He is standing in the hallway outside his apartment.

Inside, Kunigunde, Streicher's wife, is working at withdrawing the bolt on the apartment door. Over time, the door's hinges have worn. The door sags. The bolt is wedged.

With both hands free, the difficulty is easily overcome by lifting the door handle with one hand and withdrawing the bolt with the other. But Kunigunde is encumbered by her two young sons, Lothar and Elmar. And she is none too happy about opening the door.

Lothar, though just three, senses her hesitancy and clings more tightly to her. He wraps himself around her right leg and presses his head into her thigh. Drowsy Elmar, barely beyond infancy, rests on her left hip with his head drooping against his mother's large, warm breast.

There is a third knock, more insistent, louder than the first two.

Kunigunde flinches. She is thankful the war has ended. It has been difficult, but with her husband away, she has shared a gentle maternal time with her two children, which has pleased her.

When the door opens, that too will end.

'Kunigunde, it's Julius. *Open the door!*'

Kunigunde begins to work at the bolt again. Moderate thumping with an open hand on the bolt's handle has no effect. She intensifies her efforts.

The bolt slams open. Her palm slides over the jagged edge of the barrel. It cuts deeply into the heel of her hand. Blood spatters the door.

Now she must turn the key in the lock. Kunigunde is left-handed, but Elmar is sleeping so peacefully she does not want to wake him. So she must use her bleeding right hand, which forces her to reach around Lothar's head. A trivial business at all other times is now clumsy, untidy, and painful.

When Streicher hears the lock release, he completes what is for him a weightless task. He heaves the door open. He is drunk. A dense alcoholic haze is drawn into the room by the movement of the door.

Ignoring her blood, Kunigunde moves her hand to shield Lothar's back. As one, Streicher's family backs away from him.

A smouldering cigarette hangs from Streicher's mouth. He drops it to the hallway floor and grinds the butt out with his boot. Hoisting his kitbag, he hauls himself into the apartment. Ignoring his family, he scans the room with sullen indifference. He allows the kitbag to slide from his shoulder, to fall where it will.

Flakes of dried mud spill onto Kunigunde's spotless floor.

Closing the door, Streicher orders, 'Put them in the cot. Come to the bedroom.'

STREICHER'S CONFUSION

Streicher is bewildered by civilian life.

He is a nightly regular at his local beer hall, where he has acquired a fearsome reputation as a violent drunk easily provoked into brutal fighting. Every morning after, he goes to Café Grün for his breakfast.

On one of these furry mornings, Streicher leaves his apartment and steps out onto the footpath. He removes the roll-your-own from his lips, hoicks up a glob of phlegm, and spits it into the gutter. Abdominal throat-clearing produces more gunk, which he adds to what is already in the drain.

With the back of his hand, he wipes away the spittle that remains on and around his mouth. Scrubbing his hand on the leg of his trousers, he continues on his way.

When he is prodded from behind, his battlefield alertness triggers an instant and ferocious response. He spins around, left arm set to parry the next blow, right arm fisted and cocked back.

'So, you gonna punch me, Herr Big Man? Well, get on with it, Herr Big Brave Soldier Boy.'

Streicher is facing an elderly woman. She is pointing at Streicher with her cane, ready to jab at him again.

'I don't know where you think you are,' she says, 'but this is not some battlefield somewhere. Spitting may have been what you did there, but here, you do not spit on the street. Do you understand? Are you listening? You DO NOT SPIT on the street! You men didn't just lose the war; you forgot your manners as well. I've had it up to my back teeth with you, all of you!'

The cane underscores every phrase with another jab at Streicher's stomach.

He has two options. He can shove an old woman down onto the footpath, or he can step away.

'Now get out of my way!' the woman growls. As she passes Streicher, she shoves him aside with a closed hand.

Streicher stands motionless, watching the woman muttering along, punctuating every few steps with another jab at the footpath.

Streicher is dazed. A reaction, a first emotion, a first word, a first thought – all abandon him.

He looks behind, beside and in front, seeking a point of reference.

He fixes on his expectoration. He steps back, looks down at it, points to it.

'What's wrong with that?' he yells along the footpath.

'Don't ask me. Ask your mother!' the woman shouts over her shoulder.

❮━━━❯

Streicher arrives at Café Grün, his mother front of mind.

Herr Grün, the café owner, greets Streicher affably enough and asks, 'Coffee and the usual breakfast, Herr Streicher?'

Streicher nods, says nothing, and makes his way to his usual table, a booth near the back of the café. He sits and waits.

R. WILLIAM PLUME

His mother – forced into his mind by an unknown, aggressive old woman – now dominates his thinking.

Streicher was the youngest of nine children … *always on the short end of her attention and her food. She tried. She did her –*

'Herr Streicher?'

Have I done something wrong? Why is my mother speaking to me as 'Herr Streicher'?

When he opens his eyes, the image of Fleinhausen, his childhood home, shrinks away, and he returns to the Nuremberg of today. He sees that his hands are intertwined before his face.

'Your breakfast?' suggests Grün.

'Yes, of course. I was lost in thought,' says Streicher as he leans back from the table, making room for the breakfast.

'I gathered. But here we are. Your usual breakfast, porridge. Like everybody, we're having difficulties getting supplies of more appetising foods, but the price of porridge is coming down, and that's a good sign.'

Grün adds a reasonable, '*Bon appétit,*' and returns to the kitchen.

Perhaps he thought I was saying grace, thinks Streicher.

His mind is now occupied with the cane woman.

She's had a gutsful of us soldiers? I've got news for you, lady. I've had a gutsful of your ingratitude! And there we were, thinking we were fighting to save her country. For her! I never expected to be paraded through the city, but the shortages of everything, the worthless money, and the reparation payments are not my fault. And by the way, Cane Lady, we did NOT lose the war! We were winning the war. If it hadn't been for the fucking Jews in Berlin …

He begins scrabbling through the papers, looking for a recent edition of the *Völkischer Beobachter, The People's Observer,* the city's popular tabloid newspaper. When he finds last week's edition, he accepts it as close enough.

Adolf Hitler's speaking engagements – venues, dates, times – are prominently displayed on the front page.

Streicher attracts Grün's attention with a raised hand.

'Herr Streicher. The breakfast is to your liking? How may I help?'

'The breakfast is fine. Do you know anything about this Hitler guy?'

Streicher taps the banner photograph showing Hitler, mid-speech, in full voice, before a rapturous crowd.

'I've been to two of his speeches. He's very persuasive.'

'What did he speak about?'

'The prices of everything – beer, sausages, eggs. And the Bolshevik menace, the Jews, the November Criminals … and the Dolchstosslegende – you know, the stab-in-the-back by the Jews and the Communists. Those bastards' betrayal caused us to lose the war. And the usual – his plan for an Aryan future for Germany.'

'I see here,' Streicher says, 'that he's speaking tomorrow at the Bürgerbräukeller in Munich. What do you think? Should I go?'

'Well, Herr Streicher, you … you have a lot in common with Herr Hitler.'

CHAPTER 2

Life in Munich

MOVING INTO THE MUNICH HOUSE

'Schatzi, darling, I need help with the piano. In the parlour, please.'

Thomas Schroeder is shaving using a cut-throat razor.

'A moment, dear. Doing around the mole.'

'That mole of yours. Why don't you have it removed? Just be done with all that mess that spills out if you cut it.'

'All that mess is avoided if I'm careful not to cut it. Be there in a moment.'

When he arrives in the parlour, Lillian Annegret – Lilli to family and friends – is waiting, standing next to the piano, a petite grand, holding caster cups.

'We need to put these under the wheels. You lift, I put,' she says.

When the cups are in place, Lilli opens the fallboard and plays the opening bars of Mozart's *Sonata Semplice*.

'Oh, ouch! The G is flat. Many others as well, no doubt and no surprise. We've been moving this beast. Now that it is where it will stay, I'll have it tuned.'

Ruffling Eleonore's hair and brushing Lorenz's cheek, she adds, 'And we will start your lessons again, my darlings. But now it's bedtime, my lovelies. Come, Schatz, let's finish with the cot and get these two into bed.'

Later, after stories, prayers, and goodnight kisses, Thomas and Lilli sit facing each other across the kitchen table.

'Nearly done,' Lilli says.

She reaches over the table and covers Thomas' hand with her own.

'Thank you,' she adds.

'For?'

'Thomas, don't be coy. It doesn't suit you. I know how much you enjoyed living at Brightstone in your mother's cottage. All that work you did to bring the garden back to life and to preserve the charm of the house. And there was your relationship with Elisabeth. For me, moving to Munich is like coming home, but for you … well, it must have been difficult.'

Thomas thanks Lilli with a smile and says, 'It wasn't my first choice, but realistically there wasn't a choice. Once Herr Telgen had joined the Nazi Party and then had fabricated the idea that I am Jewish, his poison had worked its way into the school. Moving was the only sensible option.'

'Yes and no …' says Lilli.

'Which means …?'

'Telgen is a very stupid man, and his interference in our life by way of Eleonore, our daughter, a child, makes me very angry. What happened to her was bad enough, but it's dreadful to think of what could have happened. I marvel repeatedly, daily, at how well she handled it.'

'And we removed her from the threat by moving here.'

'Or you could say that we have turned our lives upside down to avoid him. Challenging him might have been a better approach. What are we going to do when other Nazis appear in our lives? This is Munich, after all, Hitler's home base, for heaven's sake.'

Thomas shrugs and looks towards the back door.

'A shrug? A shrug is your answer?'

'It means I don't know.'

'Schatz, I know how much you dislike confrontation, but when your children, your family, are placed in danger, a more forceful response is required. We cannot just up stakes and move every time things get uncomfortable at the hands of people like Telgen.'

'Lilli, you are the only person, apart from myself, who knows the full story of why I was in Meersburg and why I was working in such an unpleasant job. My concern was that confronting Telgen too bluntly could have compromised my cover.'

'So your cover was more important to you than the safety of your daughter? That's your excuse for not confronting him?'

'No. It was my reason.'

'Or avoiding your obligations as a father?'

'Perhaps you've forgotten, Lillian, that losing my cover could easily have led to me being *entirely* removed from Eleonore's life, from Lorenz's, and from yours. Sometimes, discretion is the better part of valour.'

Lilli's right hand runs through her hair and finishes supporting her chin.

'Clichés … A refuge of sorts. You are right, of course. But give it some thought. Think about what we'll do if it happens again.'

Lilli stands and heads up the stairs that lead to the bedroom.

———

A fortnight later, Sunday midday, four adults and four excited children overflow the vestibule inside and out. Johannes and Joachim squeeze past Traudl's legs and gaze up, smiling, at Lilli. She leans forward, over the boys, to hug Traudl.

Reinhard, seeing Thomas encumbered with two children, detours around an awkward handshake and embraces all of them.

'Thomas, my friend, I cannot tell you how pleased we are that you and Lilli have brought the family to Munich. Traudl tells me that the move is permanent. That is wonderful, and we are delighted to see you all. Welcome!'

Later, the wreckage of an exuberant luncheon covers the dining table. Lorenz makes his way through the legs of people and chairs, eating the debris, some of it edible, that has found its way to the floor.

The other children have drifted away to the parlour. Eleonore, indifferent to the out-of-tune G, is playing *Little Adagio in C*, a key signature guaranteed to involve the faulty G.

Lilli's ear finds the offending note unbearable.

She goes to the parlour and says to the room, 'Children, would you like to see a card trick?'

'Ah, Mutti, yes, yes! I love your card tricks,' Eleonore replies.

'Then come to the kitchen.'

As the children gather in the kitchen, Lilli shoves her sleeves up beyond the elbows and slowly extends her hands upward, fingers spread.

'Now, everyone look closely! Notice that at no time do my hands leave my body. Do you see a deck of cards in my hands or up my sleeves or anywhere?'

'No!' says everyone.

'Then what is *this*?' Lilli flicks her left hand over. And there, in the palm of her hand, is a deck of cards.

'Now, my darling Thomas, shuffle this deck to your heart's content.'

Reinhard objects. 'But what if he's just shuffling it the way *you* want it shuffled?'

'Ahh, Herr von Mörsbach, I am deeply wounded, pierced through by your scandalous suggestion. You'd prefer to do the shuffling?'

'Thomas. Darling. Dearest husband ... Please ... the deck.'

Lilli circles the table until she is standing beside Reinhard's chair.

'Now watch very carefully, Herr Suspicious. This is called a card fountain. It is the method used in the finest casinos everywhere to guarantee thorough shuffling.' Holding the deck in her right hand, Lilli arches the deck and then allows the cards, one by one, to fly upwards out of her hand. The flurry scatters cards everywhere. The children giggle and scurry around picking them up.

Lilli presents the reassembled deck to Reinhard. 'Shuffle? Herr Doubting Thomas. Not you, my love. Biblical Doubting Thomas …'

'Now, Eleonore, take a card. Keep it. Remember it. Don't show me. Now it's your turn, Joachim. Or are you Johannes? Which one are you? You twins. It's so hard to tell which is which. Whoever you are, take a card. And now your brother.'

The cards are replaced in the deck. Lilli shuffles again. She then begins moving the cards one by one, face down, onto an adjacent pile. Occasionally she puts a single card face down in front of each child. 'Alright, all together now … Turn them over!'

'Are those your cards, children?' Lilli asks.

The children are already giggling and nodding.

A round of applause goes around the table.

'And you, Herr von Mörsbach, you will be wanting your wallet back,' Lilli says, sliding it over the table towards Reinhard.

Reinhard is dumbstruck.

'Now, Eleonore, no more piano, please. Take Johannes and Joachim to see your new castle in the backyard.'

Traudl blurts out her surprise, 'How did you do that? The wallet? That trick with the cards? How did Joachim get the King of Diamonds? And Johannes, the King of Hearts? And Eleonore, the Queen of Hearts?'

'Ahh, well, it's magic. But there might have been some sleight of hand and a little misdirection.'

'Whatever it is, your talent for that sort of thing is phenomenal. You should be on stage somewhere.'

'Ah, thank you, Traudl. Coffee, everyone?' Lilli asks. And soon it appears.

'Now,' says Traudl, setting the teaspoon on the saucer, 'what are your plans?'

Lilli looks an unspoken *Me first?* question at Thomas. He agrees with a nod, a gentle smile, and an easy gesture of his right hand.

'First, we settle. When that's done to a sufficient extent, I will get the music school going again. Soon, I hope. Eleonore is doing so well. Lorenz can't reach the keys yet, but he is happy around the music and the piano. He will be a good student when he's a little older.'

'And you, Herr Schroeder? What about you?' asks Reinhard.

'If you cast your mind back a few years –'

'I'll do my best,' says Reinhard.

'– you may remember that I once told you about my father's skill at breeding Percherons. I'm sure you will remember Elisabeth Prime.'

'I certainly do. Hard to forget such a magnificent piece of horseflesh.'

'She was certainly special. She was my father's last foal. He was very highly regarded in the draught-horse community in Essex. One reason he was so successful was that he recorded every detail of the pedigree of the horses he bred. He once said that perhaps he should have done the same sort of genealogical work for his own family. "But I'll leave that to you," he said to me. And now, it is my turn. I'm going to start with my mother. She was English, of course, but I don't know anything beyond that. When things are a little more settled here, we will be going to London, and I'll start looking into our genealogy.'

'Perhaps you'll find that you're related to Jack the Ripper,' says Reinhard, smiling.

'Surprises are always in the cards,' replies Thomas.

A LONDON REGISTRY OFFICE

'A registry office?' Lilli asks. 'The Registry of Births, Deaths, and Marriages? The first place you want to visit is the Registry of Births, Deaths, and Marriages?'

Thomas raises his hands, palms upward. 'Isn't that why we came here?'

'We come all the way to London from Munich, and you want to go to a registry office? Truly?'

Thomas shrugs a yes.

'Thomas, mein Schatz, you are my treasure. I love you dearly and forever, but it seems that this morning you have left your imagination in your bed.'

'Wh—'

'Hush. Listen. I know you grew up in London, and you know the city like you were born here, which you were. But I'm a country girl from Friedrichshafen, and this is the first time I've been outside of Germany, my first time in England. Instead of a registry office, let's make our first stop Buckingham Palace or … Tower Bridge or … the Royal Albert Hall, shall we?'

Pointing vaguely eastward with his right hand, Thomas says, 'We are in South Bank, Waterloo. Tower Bridge is that way.'

Swapping to westward, he adds, 'Big Ben, Westminster Abbey, Buckingham Palace, and the Royal Albert Hall, in that order, are that way.'

'Left it is,' says Lilli. 'First stop, Big Ben. Come, children. You too, Schatz.'

———

'Yesterday we stayed far too long in Buckingham Palace, so we're going left again this morning. First stop, the Royal Albert Hall. Schatz?'

'Thank you, but no. I'll be going to the registry office. After that, I'm going to pay a visit to Brewster.'

'Ah, Seamus Brewster. Your partner in … your … youthful enterprise. Say hello for me. Right, meine Kinder. We're off.'

Thomas, now alone, makes his way to the Waterloo Registry Office. A records clerk appears behind a long, broad counter.

'May I help you?' he asks.

'I'm looking for information about my mother,' says Thomas.

'I'll do what I can to help you with that, sir. Is that a German accent I hear?'

'I am German.'

'You speak English very well for a native German.'

'My father was German; my mother was English. She was most insistent that her children be proficient in both languages.'

'She certainly succeeded in your case. But now, please, what was your mother's full maiden name?'

'Elisabeth Eileen Wyatt-Sterling,' replies Thomas.

'And your father's name?'

'Konrad Maria Berthold Graf von Stauffenberg.'

'And your name, sir?'

'Thomas.'

'Thank you,' says the clerk. 'Wait here, please. I'll be back in a few minutes.'

He goes to the stacks, soon returning with a registry ledger that he places, open, on the counter.

'In London, von Stauffenberg is not a common family name. This registry has only one family so named. I must inform you that your parents' marriage certificate records the bride's name as Sarah Michaela Goldsmid, not Elisabeth Eileen Wyatt-Sterling. Sarah and Konrad von Stauffenberg had one child, a son, whose name was Philip. Would I be right to guess that you are related to Philip?'

'We are, indeed.'

'You and Philip are brothers?'

'A very reasonable presumption.'

'Our records show that Philip was born in London. As a matter of interest, is he still in London?'

'Yes, he is alive and well and in London even as we speak.'

Thomas, keen to avoid any further conversation about Philip, immediately changes the subject.

'If we may back up a little, you identified Philip's mother as Sarah Michaela Goldsmid. If I remember correctly, the Goldsmids were a London banking family. Jewish, as I recall. It seems very odd that the

R. WILLIAM PLUME

Goldsmid name is somehow connected to my mother. Is there some sort of clerical error?'

'A clerical error is unlikely, and there are penalties for falsifying information on birth, death, and marriage records. What we know is that Sarah Michaela was married to your father. And we know from the birth certificate that she is Philip's mother. Are you certain that she is your mother?'

'As certain as is possible, but I never knew her by that name.'

'There is the possibility of circumstances that may be relevant in this case, but I must advise that the information may be difficult to hear.'

'Go on,' says Thomas.

'Before the war, certainly last century, it was quite common for Jewish people to disguise their Jewish ancestry by changing their names. Some families made the change by deed poll, but others simply began using a different name.

'But most people are reluctant to lie on official documents like a marriage licence. Goldsmid is, as you have noted, a Jewish family name. I'm as certain as I can be that your mother was Jewish.'

'That's news to me. Is verification possible?'

The clerk opens a file drawer and withdraws a large, well-worn address book. He flicks through it with the familiarity of frequent use.

'Here we are. Write to this address,' he says, putting the open book in front of Thomas and pointing to the address. 'Give them your mother's details. The Jewish clerks maintain their records – if I may say so – religiously. They will be able to confirm – and probably add to – what I've told you.'

Thomas notes the address:

Congregation of Jacob Synagogue
Stepney Green
London
Attention: Records & Archives

'Or you could just go to their offices. It's not far from here, an easy walk if you're so inclined. Is there anything else I can help you with?'

Thomas thanks the clerk and leaves. First, he takes care of family business at the Congregation of Jacob. Then, a little further on, in Tower Hamlets, he deals with personal matters.

He knocks on the door of First Impressions Ltd – on which a sign proclaims, 'Seamus Brewster, Proprietor' – then lets himself in.

The opening door dingles a bright little bell. When Brewster hears it, he puts down his tools and removes his loupe. Raising his head, he looks across the workbench and sees Thomas closing the door.

'Well, well, well. Look what the cat dragged in! If it ain't Mr Smooth in the bleedin' flesh.'

'Mr Brewster, how nice to see you again.'

'And you, me ol' cobber. What brings you back to London?'

'My ancestors –'

'And where's the lovely Lillian?'

'She's at the Royal Albert Hall today. You might remember that she's a pianist? She thought it would be an inspirational place to go.'

'So instead of musical inspiration, you thought to come see me instead. Ahh, that's so sweet.' Brewster mimes playing a violin.

Thomas acknowledges the thought. 'It would be very rude, would it not, to come to London and fail to say hello?'

'Well, it's bloody *mahvellous* to see you, me old mate. And it's wonderful that you have come here. First Impressions has been stepping up in the world. Just you look at this, mate, if you will. It's a telephone, mate. I have a bloody telephone! First Impressions is listed in the London telephone book! How's that for advancement?'

'You *are* doing well, Mr Brewster. But you shouldn't be so surprised. Your work is without peer. What are you working on these days?'

'Mostly calling cards, business cards, identity cards. That sort of thing. Everybody wants 'em engraved with the family crest or some such thing and done with every detail and curlicue. A bit of a comedown from treasury bills and chain-of-custody documents – if you take my meaning – but it pays the bills.'

'And paid for a telephone.'

'That too.'

Brewster reaches out to a small box of First Impressions Ltd business cards and hands one to Thomas.

'Ring my bell – the telephone bell, not the doorbell – sometime, just for the helluvit. And, by the way, the Credit Suisse arrangement is working wonderfully well, mate.'

'Pleased to hear that, and before I forget, Lilli asked me to pass on her regards.'

'Ahh, that is so sweet,' Brewster replies with mild sarcasm. 'Send my best wishes back!' he adds as genuine salutation.

THOMAS AND LILLI BACK IN MUNICH

The heavy brass cover of the front-door mail slot snaps shut.

Mail plops onto the floor.

'Mail!' yells Eleonore. She swings around on the piano stool, leaps off, and runs to the door.

Lorenz pushes himself up to wobbly standing and waddles after his sister.

Eleonore is returning with the mail as Lorenz approaches her. She gives him one of the envelopes and carries on towards her mother.

Lorenz turns around and follows her.

'There is mail!' she calls out as she sweeps into the parlour and puts the mail into Lilli's lap.

'Oh, look!' Lilli says, 'There's a card from Aunty Traudl. And what have you got there, my darling boy?' She takes the letter from Lorenz. She sees that it is addressed to Thomas and says, 'Lorenz, darling, this is for your father. He's in the kitchen. Take this to him, please. There's a good boy.'

The children are in bed. Thomas and Lilli are seated at the kitchen table.

Thomas is holding the letter from the Congregation of Jacob Synagogue. He folds it open. 'In summary, my mother is descended from an unbroken succession of Jewish women reaching back to the earliest of their records. I have an impeccable Jewish pedigree.'

Thomas hands the letter to Lilli, who reads it and returns it to Thomas.

Lilli turns sideways in her chair. 'So it seems.' She shakes her head slightly, baffled. 'You are a faithful, practising Roman Catholic and have been from birth. You are a cradle Catholic, as the saying goes. Perhaps you haven't noticed that you are uncircumcised? Amounts to an endorsement at least, and beyond that, a confirmation, does it not? How can you possibly be Jewish?'

'My father was Roman Catholic. My mother changed her name and professed Anglicanism to conceal her Jewish ancestry. She adopted Catholicism because she loved my father. I was raised, from birth, uncircumcised, as a Catholic. But none of that changes her Jewish origins. Nor does it change mine. In the Jewish world, if your mother is Jewish, you are Jewish regardless of your religious affiliation – the specific religious group or tradition with which you choose to identify.'

'Roman Catholic Jew? Jewish Catholic? Extends the mind a little, does it not?' says Lilli.

'Shatzi, I cannot just say, "I'm not Jewish," and make everything go away. That does not erase *my* Jewishness nor that of my mother. It does not make her or her ancestors somehow disappear.'

Lilli swings around to face Thomas directly. 'Your mother, Thomas, did exactly that!' Lilli begins jabbing a finger into the tabletop. 'Your mother said *I'm not Jewish* by changing her name and her religious affiliation, not just once, but twice!'

Thomas leans forward over the table.

'Yes, she obscured her background from the outside world, but I'm sure she understood doing so didn't change who she was. She made some choices of which, seemingly, you do not approve. Are you suggesting that I should do the same?'

'And did your father know that the woman he married was Jewish? Did he understand that any children he fathered with her would be Jewish? Did he know you were Jewish, and did he withhold that information from you?'

'I do not –'

'So besotted was he with your mother and her charms that he took pains to ignore her real name on the marriage licence?'

'Lilli, not so long ago you faulted me for leaving my imagination in my bed. Now, I want to know, what has happened to your generosity? You, yourself, have had a very personal experience of love overlooking difficult boundaries, or else you wouldn't be here now. Why should it not be so for both of my parents?'

'For heaven's sake, Thomas, he kept such detailed records of the pedigree of his horses. Anyone might think that he would be equally attentive to the pedigree of his own offspring.'

'Perhaps that's why, Lilli, he confined his genealogical endeavours to horses. That's breeding without baggage. Perhaps that's why he left it to me to deal with the humans.'

'And with that in mind, what about your offspring? Are they Jewish?' Lilli asks.

'Are you Jewish?'

'No. Though I now sense the possibility of doubt, seeing that you can suddenly turn up with a Jewish mother. But, no, I'm not Jewish.'

'Then they are not Jewish. Not, at least, as far as the Jewish community is concerned,' Thomas says.

Lilli stiffens. 'And what does *that* mean? Is there some world in which they could be considered to be Jewish?'

'Yes. Unfortunately, there is such a world. The Nazi world. I fear they won't be constrained by fine distinctions like matrilineal descent nor cultural versus religious Jewishness. Their attitude in respect of our children may yet make your hair stand on end. Like it or not, you are married to a Jew. I don't yet know how the Nazis view our children's pedigree, nor yours, for that matter, but I intend to make it my business to find out.'

———

Later, waiting for sleep to put an uncomfortable day behind him, Thomas wonders, *What is … what are the differences between Catholic and Jew?* He has never thought about it, and that prompts a twinge of embarrassment.

I could have done more for Eleonore …

Thomas is lying on his back.

Is she asleep?

Lilli is facing away from him, lying on her side.

Hesitantly, gently, lovingly, he places a hand on Lilli's waist. A touch, the warmth, an image of their first intimacy …

Lilli is upon him.

     R. WILLIAM PLUME

CHAPTER 3

The Jewish Issue

LILLIAN CONSIDERS THOMAS AS JEWISH

Preoccupied, Lilli is clearing away breakfast.

Synagogue on Saturday? Which starts on Friday? At sundown? Holy Mass on Sunday? Which begins with a Vigil Mass on Saturday. All those dietary things and strange customs. But we don't eat meat on Fridays. Will he be an Orthodox Jew or some other kind of Jew? There are different types of Christians. All those variations on Protestantism. Some of them … interesting. I do love him, but this is such a shock. But I'm not anti-Semitic. Then why is it such a shock? I'm only not anti-Semitic as long as I don't personally have to face any anti-Semitism? Am I tainted by association? Tainted?

Will our children carry this forward even though I'm not Jewish? Am I tolerant of anti-Semitism only by omission? It is absent from my own life, so it doesn't exist? Will he want a menorah in our house? How is that different from a crucifix in the house? And I insisted on that. And do we still say grace on Sundays? I struggle to think of him as Jewish. But I've never once, ever, stopped to think of him as Catholic. He is what he is. May the good Lord guide us towards each other. What now? Do something. Do it now.

She walks to the conservatory where Eleonore is playing.

'Eleonore, my darling, we're going for a walk. Be a good girl. Put your shoes on and your greatcoat.'

'And my gloves?'

'And your gloves.'

'And my hat?'

'And your hat.'

'And my nose?'

'Oh, you little scamp. Go!'

Thomas is in his study writing when Lilli appears at the door.

'Eleonore and I are walking to the council office. Lorenz is asleep in the conservatory. Back soon.'

A quick kiss on the top of Thomas' head, and she is gone.

She has never kissed me like that before, he thinks.

———

'I'd like to register a sole trader business, please.'

'Of course, madam. I will need a few details. First, the name of the enterprise, please.'

'The Lillian Piano Academy.'

THE PIANO COMPETITION

'Nikolaus, the triplets on beats one and two change to triplets on beats one and three. The rhythmical transition needs to be crisp and marked. I think that's what Herr Mahler had in mind. Practise the transition this week, and I think you will be ready for your first competition. What do you think?'

'Oh, I'm a little nervous, Frau Schroeder, but excited as well.'

'You will be fine, Nikolaus. Your first competition is always a little stressful, but I think you are ready. I will get you registered tomorrow.'

———

The signage, in austere Fraktur black-letter type, declares, 'The Munich School of Music. Piano Competitions, 1923. Registrations: Room 3.'

'Student's name?'

'Nikolaus Stenmann.'

'Teacher's name?'

'Lillian Schroeder.'

'Affiliation?'

'Lillian Piano Academy.'

'Competition grade?'

'Level Five.'

'Composition student will play?'

'A piano arrangement of the *Adagietto*, Symphony No. 5.'

'Composer?'

'Gustav Mahler.'

The registrar removes his spectacles and looks up at Lilli.

'This competition has a strong preference for the works of Mozart, Beethoven, and Bach. Is it possible for your student to present a piece by one of those composers?'

'No. He's quite taken with Mahler's music and would prefer to play that if you don't mind.'

'Well, you see, there is the problem. We do mind. We do not accept applications that include the degenerate music of Jewish composers.'

Lilli's hand comes to her mouth. She chokes down an abrupt nausea. *Stand up straight. Breathe. Slowly.*

She reaches over the desk, scrunches the application into her hand, and rips it from the pad.

———

'Lilli, darling. What's wrong?'

Lilli is seated at the kitchen table, weeping, pulling at the border of her handkerchief with both hands.

'Oh, it's nothing. It's … the piano competition. Poor Nikolaus.'

'Did he not play well?'

'He didn't play.'

'Why ever not? Did he get competition nerves?'

'He wasn't *allowed* to play,' Lilli says, brushing away a sniffle.

'I will never forget the way he looked at me when I told him that he had been disqualified. He was crushed.'

Thomas withdraws a chair at the table and sits. He puts his hands on Lilli's.

'Tell me, please. What happened?'

'Nikolaus is very fond of Gustav Mahler's work. You may not know – but the competition organisers certainly do – that Mahler was a Jew. The registrar described his work as "the degenerate music of a Jewish composer". Why, on God's green earth, would I ask, are there composers whose work is *not* acceptable? How is that possible?'

Thomas listens, waits, gently clutching Lilli's hands.

'I'm a woman, and women see our own version of this sort of thing every day. This is the same and yet somehow different. Today was the first time I've had my nose rubbed in the cat shit of anti-Semitism. It is so very cruel. I nearly lost my breakfast. It does make me wonder if I've ever dished it out without thinking about it, without even realising that I'd done it. And this is in no way connected to you, Schatz. Your Jewishness had nothing to do with this, but now, perhaps, I'm a little more aware of what it means to be Jewish.'

CHAPTER 4

Turmoil

THE CRAMPTON BROTHERS. SOUTH BANK, LONDON

'How's Mum?'

'Not well. She's coughing up blood –'

'Bloody hell –'

'Don't start, Derek,' says Martin.

'We won the war, didn't –'

'Do not start, Derek. If you do, I'm out of here. I'm not stumping up for another of your pub smash-up sessions. Just sit there, enjoy your stout, and tell me about what you're investigatin' these days, Mr Detective Inspector, if you please, down there at Scotland Yard. Page three, *Evening News*, you were. You'll be Commissioner of Police one of these days *if* you can keep that temper of yours under control.'

Derek slides his butt forward on his chair, right hand on the stout. The left hand repeatedly clicking the thumbnail with the ring finger.

'I keep telling you this, Derek. Mum, Pop – God rest his soul – all of us, we're all very proud of you. You've made a name for our family. *Crampton* up there in lights. Well done, you.'

Derek smiles, punches his brother, and says, 'Cut the crap. Now you tell me what you're up to.'

'Usual data organisation stuff down at the registry office. I've finally managed to get people to understand why a unique numerical value assigned to each person is a good idea.'

'And why *is* that a good idea, my studious brother?'

'Because it makes it possible to keep straight those people who have the same or similar names.'

'And *you,* me luvla little brother, will be the chief registrar one of these days.'

'Maybe. But I did have a very interesting case a month or so ago where a unique identifier just wasn't required. A bloke comes to the front desk. He's tall and broad in the shoulders, looking like he knows how to throw heavy stuff around, with dark hair, big hands. I'm telling you this stuff because you're a copper and you'd ask anyway.'

Derek punches his brother again, adding, 'Yeah, and?'

'He had a slight German accent. I couldn't tell if he was English and had acquired the accent or a German who spoke English exceptionally well.'

'Yeah, okay, get to the point. What was his unique name?'

'Thomas von Stauffenberg.'

'Yeah, okay. Not the usual, but not that special either,' says Derek.

'You don't understand. His father's full name was Konrad Maria Berthold Graf von Stauffenberg. I think that may be unique in London, probably all of England.'

'German nobility, then?'

'Indeed.'

Derek begins drumming his fingers on the table.

'Stauffenberg … *von* Stauffenberg … That name has a very familiar ring to it.' Derek briefly considers the matter. 'What *was* his name?' he asks himself aloud, untying his memories by smacking his forehead.

'It was … P, P, P… Paul … Peter … Patrick … Philip! That's it! Martin, does this Thomas guy have a brother named Philip?' asks Derek.

'He does.'

Derek brings his fist down hard on the table. The stout spills to the floor. The pint bounces off the table, falls to the wooden floor, and clatters under the neighbouring table.

Derek leaps up growling, a hard-closed fist held forward. 'Got you now! After twenty goddamn years! Got you now, you bastard!'

———

NAZI PARTY HEADQUARTERS, MUNICH

Germany's seething post-war political turmoil erupts daily.

Political parties of every persuasion strive to dominate Germany's government. The National Socialist German Workers Party – the Nazi Party – and the Communist Party have very different politics but similar ambitions, tactics, and strategies.

Adolf Hitler, leader of the Nazi Party, has extraordinary aspirations for himself and his movement. He has seen an opportunity and has summoned the most senior, the most reliable, and the most loyal of the Party leadership to Munich. He is joined by Hermann Göring, Joseph Goebbels, Ernst Röhm, and Heinrich Himmler.

They sit in silence.

Hitler stands and speaks.

'I am reading in the press that the Bolsheviks have tried it on again! Another lame coup d'état, this time in Hamburg! Tell me, Herr Göring, what do you think will become of our Party if the Bolsheviks manage to force their miserable collectivist arses into the Reichstag with one of these starry-eyed coups of theirs?'

Göring says nothing. There is no need. Hitler provides the answer. His astonishing oratory fills the room.

'I'll tell you, Herr Göring, what will happen,' Hitler roars. 'We will be annihilated! Annihilated, I tell you! Pitched onto the scrap heap of history! We cannot, we must not allow this to happen! We have a destiny! We must strike!' he bellows, 'before we are struck down!'

Göring looks to Goebbels, asking with his eyes, *How much longer before he gets to the point?*

Goebbels shrugs.

When Hitler finishes, he is sweating, exhausted.

'Get it done, Herr Göring,' says Hitler, turning to look in Göring's direction. 'GÖRING!' he bellows.

Göring lurches to half awake.

'Get it done, Herr Göring! Do it now!' orders Hitler as he strides out of the room.

Goebbels smiles and says, 'Nodding off, eh, Hermann? And during one of the Führer's speeches?'

Göring rolls his eyes and says, 'Well, he does go on. What have I been ordered to do?'

'Oh, my dear boy, nothing easier! Organise a coup d'état, hijack the Bavarian provincial government meeting at the Bürgerbräukeller, seize control of Bavaria, prepare a takeover of the German federal government, plan a march on Berlin, commandeer the Reich Chancellery, and lead the Fatherland out of cultural and financial ruin! Off you go,' says Goebbels, waving Göring away with the backs of his hands.

———

One by one, Röhm, Goebbels, Streicher, and Himmler arrive and scurry into Headquarters. Göring, last to arrive, carries today's *Munich Post* folded under his arm.

He delays himself with trifles until he is certain that all his co-conspirators are waiting in the meeting room.

Göring, military-alert and grave, bursts into the room. With a sweeping gesture, he smacks the newspaper onto the table, fully spread open on page one:

Bavarian Provincial Government
Public Meeting Tonight. 8.00 pm.
Bürgerbräukeller, Rosenheimerstrasse.

He allows a moment for everyone to read the headlines.

'The Bavarian Prime Minister, the State Commissioner, the Chief of Police, and the Commanding Officer of the Reichswehr detachment will all be present. Our moment has come. Herr Röhm, outline your plans for securing the army and the police barracks.'

Röhm puts a folder labelled 'Plan Red' on the newspaper. 'As agreed, we will follow Plan Red. I will command occupation of the army barracks, and Herr Streicher will lead occupation of the police barracks. Runners will be dispatched directly to Bürgerbräukeller at the instant the barracks are secured. Runners are to arrive at Bürgerbräukeller before 2200 hours.'

'Excellent,' Göring says. 'I will lead the Kampfbund into position around the Bürgerbräukeller at 2145 hours. Our Führer will be inside the meeting, secured by the Battle League. When I have confirmation from both runners that the barracks have also been secured, I will order the closure of all exits and give our Führer the signal.

'Be prepared to face the Reichswehr and the police at any time during the night. There may be units abroad when the barracks are taken. I will send the runners back with news of developments at the Bürgerbräukeller.

'And Herr Goebbels, am I correct in assuming that you have crafted an appropriate statement to appear in tomorrow's edition of the *Völkischer Beobachter*?'

'Yes, Herr Göring, you are correct as always. It's titled "Begins the Resurrection".'

'Excellent,' Göring repeats. 'Stay strong, everyone. Tonight inaugurates our time in power. Get to your stations. Prepare your troops. We are done here. You are dismissed.'

STRESEMANN INFORMED

German Chancellor Gustav Stresemann has been summoned from his home and driven at speed, with a police escort, to the Reich Chancellery.

Half an hour ago, he was asleep. Now he is alone in his office. He searches his desk for a note, a memo, something that might explain why he has been stripped from his bed at such an inconvenient hour. He thinks, *This is so important that they can't even tell me, the Chancellor, what it is.* He chuckles.

Curving back and forth across his desk, the black wire that attaches the telephone to the handpiece captures his attention. Stresemann abruptly recalls that he was dreaming about snakes, rattlesnakes, when the nightstand phone buzzed him awake. *Snakes? Why snakes? Where did that come from? Winnetou may have had something to do –*

A knock-knock, followed immediately by the office door opening, interrupts his recollection of what are now last night's dreams. Stresemann's chief of staff comes through the door carrying an ornate, oval-shaped silver tray. On the tray is a cup half-filled with strong, black Arabic coffee. The cup rests on a matching blue-and-white saucer. Beside the cup is a teaspoon with the bust of Frederick the Great embossed on the handle. A small ceramic jug steams.

On the left of the tray is a wax-sealed dispatch envelope. The words 'For Your Eyes Only' are printed on both sides in large, red, bold-faced capital letters.

Stresemann is the consummate professional politician. He has earned his office. He knows better than anyone that Germany is in deep trouble.

In every beer hall, every market, and on every street corner, there are Germans bitterly complaining. There are shortages of everything. Rapidly

     R. WILLIAM PLUME

escalating inflation has made the Deutschmark valueless. The French have occupied the Ruhr Valley, claiming failure to pay war reparations. Political parties of both the left and the right are talking openly of civil war or a coup d'état.

The dispatch doubtless concerns something of that nature.

Stresemann also understands priorities, and he is foremost pleased to see the coffee. Before he addresses the contents of the envelope, he adds a little hot water to the cup, stirs the coffee and the water, and then sips.

'I've been Chancellor of Germany for how many days now?' he asks himself aloud. 'I make it something like ninety days. But already I've learned that when you, my chief of staff, personally bring the coffee, something important has happened during the night. What, I do wonder, is it this time?'

Stresemann picks up the envelope, admiring the double-headed German eagle, the Reichsadler, embossed into the red-wax seal. Rapping, clack-clack, the long edge of the envelope on his wooden desk, he asks, 'Do I need to read this?'

'I think you should,' replies his chief of staff.

'Summarise it for me, please.'

'Last night, Herr Adolf Hitler, the leader of the National Socialist German Workers Party, also known as the Nazi Party, besieged a beer hall in Munich where a public meeting was being held. The meeting had been organised by the Bavarian State Commissioner, the Chief of Police, and the Commanding Officer of the local army detachment. The meeting was packed with people. Late in the evening, Herr Hitler entered the hall with a pistol. Shots were fired. He declared himself henceforth the leader of the Bavarian provincial government. The three men who organised the meeting have been taken hostage. The situation at this moment is very fluid, but – and this is most important – Hitler has declared his intention to march on Berlin. His Sturmabteilung, or *SA*, the paramilitary arm of the Nazi Party will be in the vanguard.'

'And he's not dropping in to pay his respects?'

'No, Herr Chancellor. It is clear that a coup d'état of the German federal government is what he has in mind.'

Stresemann sits at his desk, pondering the matter. *Do I need to devote time to yet another loudmouth, upstart politician? There are so many of them these days, and they all have pretensions beyond their ability and resources.*

The Nazi Party and Hitler are known to Stresemann as essentially a Munich, or possibly Bavarian, phenomenon. On the other hand, Hitler's action is high treason. An overt threat to the federal government must be taken seriously, no matter its origin.

'Convene a meeting,' Stresemann says to his chief of staff. 'This office. At ten o'clock this morning. President Ebert and General von Seekt to attend.'

9 NOVEMBER 1923. THE BLOOD MARCH

In the dawning light of Friday, a large crowd of men is milling about in the street adjacent to the Bürgerbräukeller, Rosenheimerstrasse.

'What happened?' asks one.

'What now?' asks another.

Hitler's plan for an overwhelming takeover of the Bavarian provincial government has miscarried. He has lost the initiative.

Although he has an undoubted flair for turning humiliating defeat into celebrated victory, on this occasion that forte has abandoned him, taking with it his decisiveness.

Hitler is standing with Erich Ludendorff, Quartermaster-General during the war. Before them is a large, listless group of men looking for leadership.

Ludendorff sees in Hitler's face what he so often saw on the Western Front: confusion, desperation, capitulation. He, Ludendorff, now shows the command presence that made him a German hero. He simply declares, 'We march! We will march to Konigsplatz!'

R. WILLIAM PLUME

To lead this impromptu escapade, Ludendorff and Hitler walk through the crowd of men, whereupon everyone turns around and follows the leaders. Those who are armed take forward positions. Everyone erupts into song at the top of their lungs. The strident lyrics of 'Deutschland Über Alles' echo along the street.

There is no plan for what will happen when they arrive at their destination, but regardless of the inconvenient details, they hope for the best and march on in high spirits.

Approaching Odeonsplatz, their progress is constrained by a pronounced narrowing of the way. The constriction is blocked by a Reichswehr detachment, armed and resolute.

The Blood March halts.

No one moves. No one breathes.

A pause, prayerful in outline, draws the opposing groups of men into each other.

Both face comrades from the war. *I know that man*, or *I shared my last cigarette with him*. Capricious fate has cast these once-comrades into opposition.

For the briefest of interminable moments, they stand together once again, awaiting the sergeant's whistle, the piercing sound that orders them over the top, wrapped, as always, in a tense, hollow, ringing, faux silence.

Hitler, brandishing a pistol, chooses this moment to demand, 'Surrender!'

A single shot. Accidental? Deliberate? Fired by whom?

It triggers a brief and brutal eruption of gunfire. When it ends, nineteen men are dead and many are wounded.

Hitler and Göring, both among the injured, are quickly moved beyond danger.

Röhm and Streicher, a few blocks away, are both forced to surrender.

Two days later, Hitler is found and arrested. He is delivered to Landsberg Prison to await trial on charges of treason.

The Beer Hall Putsch enters history as a failure.

Heavily shielded against the weather, President Friedrich Ebert and Chief of Army Command General Hans von Seekt have arrived in Chancellor Stresemann's outer office.

Stresemann's chief of staff attends to the preliminary necessities – overcoats, gloves, hats – before ushering the two men into Stresemann's inner office.

Stresemann welcomes his two guests. His pleasantries, though genuine, are perfunctory. His mood is grim.

'Gentlemen, I know you are both aware of what has happened in Munich beginning Thursday evening. Our purpose today is to examine how the federal government should respond. General von Seekt, what can you tell us about this Hitler fellow and the current martial situation in Munich?'

'This Hitler fellow, as you call him, certainly has stirred up a hornet's nest down there in Munich,' von Seekt replies. 'He is a most interesting character, Herr Chancellor. He was born in Austria and is still an Austrian citizen. Before the war, he was an unemployed vagrant in Munich. When the war started in 1914, he volunteered on the first day and spent the entire war at the front. He was awarded several citations, among them the Iron Cross First Class.

'After the war, he joined the German Workers Party and began speaking at their beer hall rallies. He is an exceptionally charismatic public speaker. He can whip a crowd into a frenzy in minutes. He is now the undisputed leader of the party he has renamed the National Socialist German Workers Party, which these days is usually referred to as the Nazi Party.

'He has made it clear that he has – or had – plans that went well beyond Munich. But his Putsch – a term that somewhat dignifies his effort – has failed. The entire business seems to have been poorly planned and poorly executed.'

Stresemann interjects with a question, 'As I understand it, there was a skirmish this morning. What can you tell us about that?'

'There was a firefight near Odeonsplatz. Four Reichswehr soldiers and fifteen insurgents were killed. Herr Hitler was injured but managed to escape. He was run to ground yesterday and is now in custody at Landsberg Prison.'

President Ebert – who reminded Stresemann of nothing so much as a walrus – has received this information in silence.

Now, he asks, 'And what, Herr General, are your thoughts of Herr Hitler's politics?'

The question brings Stresemann fully alert. He opens his mouth to ask the point of the question, but Herr General speaks first.

'For our present purpose, my opinion of Herr Hitler's politics hardly matters. It is enough, surely, that the Bavarian Division of the Reichswehr carried out my orders to suppress Herr Hitler's amateurish coup. I might also note that the Reichswehr lost four good men to save the Republic, having to deal with a much bigger problem later. But for the record, I will say that Herr Hitler's aims and mine are alike, but our methods are different. He is too impetuous for –'

Ebert interrupts. 'Am I to understand you to mean that at some future time when Herr Hitler's aims, as you understand them, and yours are more closely aligned, that you will direct the Reichswehr to support Herr Hitler when and if he attempts another coup?'

Von Seekt's hackles rise. He bridles at the words and sits up in his chair. 'What are you suggesting, Herr President?'

'I am *asking*, Herr General, in my role as Supreme Commander-in-Chief of the Reichswehr, if the Reichswehr can be relied upon to act in a neutral manner to maintain the peace for all Germans?'

Stresemann raises his hand as a preface to changing the direction of the conversation, but von Seekt cuts him off again with an abrupt slash of his flattened hand.

Glaring at Ebert, von Seekt says, 'I don't know if the Reichswehr is reliable, but it obeys my orders!'

Ebert immediately interrupts again. 'In that case, Herr General, I must ask if *you* can be relied upon to act in a neutral manner to maintain the peace for all Germans?'

Stresemann stands and commands the floor. 'Gentlemen, gentlemen, please! Let's begin again. General, if you could, please tell us what you think the future holds for Herr Hitler.'

Stresemann settles back into his chair.

'I will grant you that his political future looks very bleak,' von Seekt begins. 'There will be a trial. We can be certain he will be sentenced to some time in jail. He has been charged with high treason, and he is Austrian. That means that Article 9 of the Crimes Act applies. Article 9 stipulates that convicted aliens must be deported and not allowed to return.

'The Nazi Party has been built around Hitler and his persuasive powers. If he is convicted, jailed, and deported, I can't imagine that the Nazi Party will survive. But I wouldn't write him off too quickly. He has shown himself to be very resourceful and astute. He may well find a way to resurrect himself.'

'Thank you, Herr General,' says Stresemann. 'We all need to watch closely how this matter develops. In the meantime, please prepare the Reichswehr to respond to any consequential actions that may arise from the SA or from other political parties seeking to take advantage of the instability Herr Hitler's actions have created.'

After Ebert and von Seekt have left, Stresemann extracts the 'For Your Eyes Only' dispatch, still unopened, from his pile of correspondence.

Adolf Hitler has become a serious political problem for Gustav Stresemann, but at this moment, it is a personal dimension that concerns him most. Käte – his wife – is Jewish. He pitches the dispatch into the confidential trash, pulls on his overcoat, and leaves for home.

     R. WILLIAM PLUME

CHAPTER 5

The Bank of England

THE SWINDLE CASE IS REOPENED

'The Panel of Inquiry is ready for you, Inspector Crampton.'

Crampton is shown into a large room. Five men are seated on the far side of a long, oval table. Commander Skinner, Head of International Crimes, is flanked on both sides by senior officials representing Whitehall agencies.

'Good morning, Inspector Crampton. Thank you for joining us. Please be seated.'

Crampton sits in the single chair placed on the opposite side of the table.

Commander Skinner takes the lead.

'Inspector Crampton, as I recall, when this case – the Bank of England Case, as it came to be known – first arose, you crawled into every corner of Germany looking for one Philip von Stauffenberg. If memory serves, von Stauffenberg was identified as the prime suspect for two reasons. First, he was the Bank of England's Berlin Office's manager of international precious metal transfers, and second, he disappeared on the day of the robbery and has not been seen since. Is that an accurate summary of the case and your role in it?'

Crampton nods. 'As a starting point, it will serve the purpose.'

Skinner continues, 'You have now asked for the case to be reopened. I should note that, on the one hand, the Bank of England is very keen to progress the case. Whitehall, on the other hand, is less enthusiastic.

There are concerns about the potential political fallout that may arise.'

'With respect, I will leave to you the competing imperatives of the Bank of England and Whitehall,' says Crampton.

'Thank you,' Skinner says.

Crampton now takes the initiative. 'I crawled into *almost* every corner of Germany. It is important to note that Philip has a brother, named Thomas, of whom we were unaware at the time of the initial investigation.'

'How does that change things enough to make it sensible for us to reopen the investigation?' asks Skinner.

'We track down Thomas, which should be straightforward enough. He may have reliable information that will lead us to Philip.'

'Do you know where to find this Thomas?'

'He is a von Stauffenberg of Nördlingen in Swabia, Bavaria. He has an uncle, Klemens by name, alive and resident there. I will start with him.'

'Do you have anything more substantial than *maybe* leads from a family member who may not be inclined towards co-operation?'

Crampton moves forward a little on his chair. 'Once again, with respect, what you just said describes almost all of our investigations. We must start somewhere, and frequently, we find that something that seemed trivial in the early days of an investigation can turn a case over.'

'And if Uncle Klemens does not wish to see you?'

'Refusal to co-operate is a fact in itself. And, as you very well know, we can force him to answer our questions if we think it's warranted.'

'Inspector Crampton, as I've already said, the Bank of England is eager to have this case reopened, but our government is less than thrilled about the eventualities that may arise. Not least, it complicates politics with the German government. But, as you are aware, the Bank of England has hinted that they may take matters into their own hands.'

Skinner stands and clasps his hands behind his back. 'You must understand, Inspector Crampton, that we, England, are walking a very fine line between outright interference in the internal politics of Germany

     R. WILLIAM PLUME

and ensuring that Treaty of Versailles reparation payments continue. Political parties, the Nazis in particular, are agitating very strongly for unilaterally terminating these war compensation payments.'

Crampton raises a hand, signalling interjection. 'Once again, I defer to your leadership in the area of those politics, but be assured that I understand the delicacy.'

Skinner inclines his head as acknowledgement and begins to circle the table, speaking as he walks. 'At the same time, we have a powerful interest in not compromising the reputation of the Bank of England. A failure by Scotland Yard – England's pre-eminent law enforcement agency – to resolve this mystery would certainly be embarrassing.'

Now standing adjacent to Crampton's chair, Skinner offers his closing remarks. 'You, Inspector Crampton, have a well-deserved reputation for bringing difficult cases to a satisfactory conclusion. The Prime Minister is pleased that you are the lead investigator in this case. But he is also aware that you have a reputation for being, shall we say, unorthodox in your methods. He has judged that your ability as a detective outweighs the risks presented by your sometimes unfortunate behaviour.'

For his final directive, Skinner leans over Crampton. '*Don't* let him down.'

CHAPTER 6

Hitler is Imprisoned

Approaching midnight, a raw nor'easter has worked itself into a fury.

A downpour alternating between rain, sleet, and snow lashes the copper-clad, onion-domed towers that flank the entrance to Landsberg Prison. The banging of the iron gates and the cacophony of wind add points of anxiety to an already tense setting.

Tonight, at an unspecified but late hour, Landsberg Prison will receive its most notorious inmate: Adolf Hitler.

Landsberg is on high alert.

Prison Warden Herr Otto Leybold paces the lobby. Chief Guard Herr Franz Hemmrich, whom Leybold has assigned to be Hitler's personal guard, is watchful but relaxed. He waits with hands joined behind his back, rocking from heels to toes and back again.

The headlamps of a Reichswehr troop transport truck appear at the paired main gates. They screech open. The truck moves forward and stops in front of the main prison doors.

Moments later, the legendary Adolf Hitler is hauled, staggering, through the doors. He is flanked by two armed Reichswehr soldiers. Both men release their grip on Hitler's arms but remain beside him.

Hitler, dripping wet and shivering, holds his manacled hands to his chest. His hair is smeared over his forehead. He is still wearing the clothes he had on three days ago when he hijacked the public meeting at the Munich Bürgerbräukeller. Tired, bedraggled, and subdued, Hitler could not look less like some liberating Wagnerian saviour of Germany.

Hemmrich steps forward.

In the mannerly way of a hotel concierge, he says, 'If you would, please, Herr Hitler, follow me.' It is an order spoken so smoothly that it sounds optional. Dazed and wretched, alone and bereft of alternatives, Herr Adolf Hitler, Führer of the Nazi Party, slouches along behind Hemmrich, leaving a trail of small puddles as he drags himself into prison.

The next morning, Hemmrich arrives at Hitler's cell with breakfast. As a precaution, he peers through the small observation window in the cell door. Hitler is lying on the bed, drawn into a knot, facing the wall.

Hemmrich unlocks the door and enters the cell. Hitler ignores him.

The simple nourishments that Hemmrich left last night are untouched. Hemmrich replaces them with breakfast and says, 'Herr Hitler, you haven't eaten anything.'

Hitler now spins over and shoves himself up with his right hand. In a single forceful and irrevocable motion, he sweeps everything from the table, smashing crockery and food into the wall.

'Get out! Leave me alone! I'm finished with eating. Get out!'

HITLER'S EARLY DAYS AT LANDSBERG

Hitler, perpetually curled into a foetal ball, is fixed on a martyr's doom. Days pass into weeks.

Hitler has not bothered to remove his shoes nor even his overcoat. He has hardly bothered to move. There has been no repeat of the destructive tantrum of the first morning, but he ignores both Hemmrich and the meals Hemmrich brings without fail.

Hemmrich is summoned to Warden Leybold's office.

Leybold opens the conversation bluntly. 'And how, Herr Hemmrich, is Herr Hitler today?'

'He is taking water, Herr Leybold, but he's not eating, and he stinks to high heaven.'

'A starving body, consuming itself, does indeed begin to emit a strong aroma,' says Leybold. 'I don't know what good it might do, but have you spoken to Herr Ott? He is the nearest thing we have to a psychologist, chaplain, confessor, or what-have-you.'

'I spoke with Herr Ott yesterday,' replies Hemmrich. 'He will visit Herr Hitler today. There is one other issue of which I must inform you, sir. Yesterday Herr Hitler asked me to bring him a pistol so he could have done with it.'

Leybold rolls his eyes. 'Overdoing the tragic hero thing a little, isn't he? I'll make this clear, Herr Hemmrich, this institution will not allow that man to die – by any means – before he finishes his trial. After the trial, he can starve himself into oblivion or splatter his brains against the wall if he wishes, but not before. How long has it been since he last ate?'

'Two weeks and a couple of days, Herr Warden.'

'Enough is enough,' says Leybold. 'Herr Ott is his last chance. If he hasn't eaten by tomorrow morning, you will start synthetic nutrition.'

'Synthetic nutrition' is the Landsberg Prison euphemism for gavage.

The following morning, Hemmrich arrives at Hitler's cell, not alone as usual, but with two assistant guards. Hemmrich brings an ordinary breakfast, and the two guards stand by with synthetic breakfast.

Hemmrich enters the cell expecting to see yesterday's evening meal of rice and vegetables still on the table, only to find that Hitler has consumed it. Gavage is gruesome, painful, and always ghastly for everyone involved.

Hemmrich is much relieved. 'Herr Hitler, you've eaten your dinner!' he says with a little too much enthusiasm. Hemmrich has children, now adults, but he remembers using the same phrase years ago, always followed by 'Good boy!', and it pops out. *Damn*, he thinks, hoping it won't go any further.

'Don't you dare "good boy" me, Herr Hemmrich!' growls Hitler. 'And who are these gorillas, and why are they here?'

'These two gentlemen are here to help with the dishes, Herr Hitler. Now if you'll excuse us.'

The three guards leave Hitler's cell, taking last night's dishes and the synthetic breakfast with them as they go.

HITLER PREPARES FOR HIS TRIAL

Hitler's rapid recovery from his determined effort to end it all coincides with the arrival at Landsberg Prison of a letter from the Justice Department.

The letter informs Warden Leybold that Hitler's trial for high treason has been set down to begin on 26 February 1924. For security reasons, the trial will be held at the Reichswehr Infantry School, Blutenburgstrasse, Munich.

Herr Hemmrich delivers Hitler to Warden Leybold's office, where Hitler is informed of his impending trial. Hitler sits impassively for a moment, shrugs, and then changes the subject entirely. He asks Leybold if there are any Karl May books in the prison library. Leybold, who had thought that Hitler might show more interest in his trial, finds the seeming indifference irritating.

'Do I look like a librarian?' he says.

Hitler shrugs again.

'Herr Hitler, perhaps it hasn't been made clear to you, but this is not a hotel. It is a prison. You are an inmate. I am neither librarian nor butler. If you want to find out about the contents of the prison library, there are ways for you to do that for yourself. Does that clarify things for you?'

Hitler says nothing.

Leybold raises his hands in mild exasperation. Turning to Hemmrich, he says, 'Herr Hemmrich, please escort Herr Hitler back to his cell.'

As the two men are making their way to the cell, Hitler asks, 'Could we go to the library, Herr Hemmrich?'

There, to Hitler's evident pleasure, is a large collection of Karl May's pulp westerns. They feature Old Shatterhand – a German who becomes a cowboy and frontiersman in the American West – and his companion, Winnetou, a Mescalero Apache chief.

Hitler, running his finger along the spines of May's books, turns to Hemmrich and asks, 'Have you read any of these books, Herr Hemmrich?'

'No, I can't say that I have. What's the author's name?'

'May. Karl May. He wrote the Old Shatterhand and Winnetou series of books. Beautifully well-told stories set in the American West.'

'You'll have to forgive me, Herr Hitler. I've never heard of him.'

'Forgiveness is something that I struggle with, Herr Hemmrich, but you have been very decent to me during my time here at Landsberg, so for you I'll make an exception. But perhaps you should try reading one to see how you like it.' Hitler plucks out a volume, hands it to Hemmrich, and says, 'Read that!' in a tone that is pleasant enough but unmistakably directive.

Hemmrich has been around prisons a long time. Any and every vile thing happens in prisons, and he has seen it all. Most of it is grim. But now, he is standing between the stacks in a sad, musty, unused prison library, alone with none other than Adolf Hitler himself, who has just ordered him to read a book: *Black Mustang* by Karl May. The scene strikes him as near farcical. He chuckles and says, 'I will, thank you, Herr Hitler.'

Hitler, too, grasps the agreeable quirkiness of the moment. His bearing is open and affable. He says, 'I can tell you for a fact, Herr Hemmrich, that our own German Chancellor, Herr Gustav Stresemann, is himself a great fan of Karl May. Were it not that his wife is a Jewess, I could warm to him because of his impeccable taste in literature. Apparently, May's books are his bedtime reading. You are in good company. Tell me what you think in the morning.'

But Hemmrich hasn't forgotten another scene, the one in Leybold's office. The incongruity of Hitler's casual reception of the news of his upcoming trial and his curious interest in something entirely different begs a question.

'Herr Hitler, you've just been told by Warden Leybold that you're about to be tried for high treason. You could end up spending a lot of time here at Landsberg or somewhere else much worse. You could even be deported back to Austria and never see Germany again. I'm intrigued why it is that you are now so interested in these books of fiction about a German cowboy and his Indian sidekick somewhere in America.'

'Strategy and tactics, my friend. Shatterhand and Winnetou were masters of both. Whenever I'm in a tight spot, as I am now, I read these books again, and the way forward becomes clear to me.'

'You read all of them?'

'Yes! All of them.'

'Well, that is fascinating, Herr Hitler, that your guidance and inspiration come from pulp fiction.'

When Hemmrich looks back at Hitler, he sees that Hitler's open and receptive mood has been withdrawn. He has thought through Hemmrich's question, and in a much more subdued voice, he asks, 'I can be deported? You said I could be deported and never allowed back into Germany. Is that true?'

'Yes, Herr Hitler, it is true. You are a citizen of Austria, not Germany, and if you are convicted of high treason, Article 9 of the Crimes Act requires that you be deported.'

'And never allowed back?'

'No, Herr Hitler, never.'

A full understanding of the possible consequences facing Hitler descends upon him with devastating emotional impact. The blood drains from his face. His knees give way. As he begins to fall, he reaches out to steady himself, but he succeeds only in stripping an entire row of books from the shelf as he collapses to the floor.

For Hitler, being bound to Germany, being loyal to it, is the *sine qua non* at the innermost core of his soul. He could face with dignity a sentence of life in prison with no parole, hard labour in some nameless, merciless pit, or even a firing squad. But to be forced from Germany with the door slammed and locked behind him would be unendurable.

Hitler scrambles to his knees, Karl May books scattered all around him. Desperately, he gathers the books together. As he adds one book to the disorganised collection in his arms, two fall away. Nearly incoherent, he babbles, 'Help me, Franz. You must help me. I must get these books to my cell.'

Hemmrich kneels, putting his hands on Hitler's shoulders.

'Breathe, Adolf. Put the books down. Sit. Breathe. In through your nose, out through your mouth. Just breathe. Slowly. Calmly. Relax.'

With regular, normal breathing, the colour begins to return to Hitler's face. He leans against the shelves, embracing his knees. Hemmrich sits on the floor facing Hitler.

'Franz –' says Hitler.

'How do you know my given name?'

'I know everything,' replies Hitler with a pale smile.

'Except about Article 9?'

'Yes, that's a new one, Franz. That *is* a new one. And it paints a whole new scene. Because of that – as I was about to say – I need your help.'

'What could I possibly do to assist the great Führer of the Nationalsozialistische Deutsche Arbeiterpartei, the Nazi Party?' says Hemmrich with a gentle smile.

'First you can help me gather up these books and then guide me and the books back to my suite.'

'We refer to it as a cell, Adolf.'

'You mean to say this isn't a hotel?'

Both men chuckle at the aside.

'I still need your help getting back there,' adds Hitler. Then, imitating Warden Leybold, Hitler rolls his eyes, makes a sweeping, exasperated gesture towards the door, and says, 'Herr Hemmrich, please escort Herr Hitler back to his apartment.'

 R. WILLIAM PLUME

Hemmrich's smile opens. With twinkling eyes, he allows himself another chuckle.

'Ah, well then. *Black Mustang* for me. All the rest for you. Hardly seems fair, but I need *Black Mustang* only for enlightenment. You need the rest for salvation. Come, my friend. Your rooms await!'

A clear understanding of what might happen to him if his trial doesn't go his way brings Hitler's full attention and prodigious energy to preparation for the trial. And prepare he does.

On the morning of 26 February 1924, Adolf Hitler is delivered, under heavy guard, to the Reichswehr Infantry School, Blutenburgstrasse, Munich, for his trial on charges of high treason.

On 1 April 1924, Herr Georg Neithardt, the presiding judge, delivers the verdict: Hitler is guilty as charged. Neithardt sentences Hitler to five years' imprisonment with the possibility of parole in six months and excuses him from the requirements of Article 9 of the Crimes Act.

Hitler is returned to Landsberg Prison to begin his sentence.

HITLER IS SCHOOLED BY HEMMRICH

Chief Guard Franz Hemmrich waits at the main doors of the prison just as he did and just where he stood last November when Adolf Hitler was first presented for incarceration.

Hitler arrives. He strides through the main door dressed in military worsted serge, complete with his Iron Cross on his left breast pocket. Relaxed in familiar surroundings, he scans the lobby, sees Hemmrich and smiles.

The two men approach each other. They shake hands. Hitler puts his left hand on Hemmrich's shoulder. Hemmrich puts his left hand over their clasped hands.

'Herr Hitler,' says Hemmrich, smiling, 'I know that "welcome back" doesn't seem the most appropriate thing to say when you are returning to prison, but I am pleased to see you again.'

Smiling, Hitler says, 'You are a very decent man, Herr Hemmrich. I welcome your friendship and thank you for your greeting. But now, if you would, please follow me. I think I know the way.'

———

'How is our number one prisoner settling in, Herr Hemmrich?' asks Warden Leybold.

'In a word, Herr Warden, he is seething.'

'Oh, is that so? More or less every prisoner we have proclaims their innocence. This indignation of Herr Hitler's, is it of that sort?'

'Oh, no, sir. He doesn't deny his role in what happened. He is annoyed that he made a tactical blunder on the night. He is rebuking himself for the failure of his coup. He has it that it failed because he trusted people. He already has vengeance in mind. The news he gets from the people who visit him and from the newspapers is that without his leadership, the Nazi Party is already falling apart.'

'First and foremost, Herr Hemmrich, Herr Hitler is in this prison because he attempted an armed takeover of the state. *That* is a coup d'état, a very serious crime better known as treason. Second, what you have said tells me that now he is distressed because he won't be able to have another go at it when he leaves this prison.'

'That's a very accurate summary of his thinking, Herr Warden.'

Leybold rises from his chair and walks to the window, his hands clasped behind his back. The branches of an alder brush against the glass panes. Its spring twiglets are swelling emeralds. A few days hence, the vivid greenery of this fabled tree will be the only thing Leybold will see beyond the glass.

He considers the weight of having a person of Hitler's notoriety in his prison. Turning to Hemmrich, he says, 'I must tell you, Herr Hemmrich, that I have a certain degree of admiration for Herr Hitler.

He has transformed himself from a street urchin into a very potent political force, and that is no mean feat. But I, too, have a job to do. The sentence he was given falls well short of what was expected. That light-handedness includes the possibility of parole in six months, but you may be sure that Herr Hitler won't be going anywhere until his attitude changes for the better.

'His parole is, to all intents and purposes, *my* prerogative. I am under no obligation to parole him, even if he turns himself into a haloed choirboy. Moreover, as you very well know, Herr Hemmrich, there are ways to extend his incarceration if I deem it necessary, and you may be sure that I will take the necessary steps if he doesn't shape up. That means showing some understanding that what he did was unacceptable, regardless of his half-baked personal ambitions. Make that clear to him the next time you see him.'

———

Hemmrich is a careful man. His long occupational history in prisons has sharpened his meticulous approach to situations like the one he now faces. But Hemmrich also realises that he must examine his own relationship with Hitler. There is the jailer and the jailed, but there is also an undeniable personal closeness. *Too close? Am I compromised?* Hemmrich wonders.

On the day he has chosen for their conversation, Hemmrich gathers a few things – a foolscap legal pad, a few pencils, a towel – into a small satchel and walks to Hitler's cell. He peeks through the observation window, knocks, and then unlocks and opens the door.

Hemmrich has never felt that he had anything to fear from Hitler, but today he sees Hitler at a level of intensity beyond anything he has seen before. Hitler is seated at the small table, his eyes directed at the bare white wall with a fixed stare. Both hands on the table are clenched into fists. Hitler's face is drawn into a mask radiating a fury so extreme that Hemmrich can feel it.

Hitler is facing Hemmrich obliquely and seems unaware that the cell door has opened. To gain Hitler's attention, Hemmrich says, 'Herr Hitler…?' This mild remark fails to penetrate Hitler's deep introspection. Hemmrich repeats the words a little louder.

Now, Hitler's head comes around to face the source of the sound directly. So etched with rage is Hitler's entire body that Hemmrich wonders if he should back out of the cell, close, and lock the door.

Instead, he says, 'Come with me, please, Herr Hitler.' Hemmrich stands aside, allowing Hitler to leave the cell. Hemmrich locks the cell door, steps around Hitler, and says, 'Follow me, please.'

Hemmrich leads Hitler to the prison library, where he first checks to ensure that it is unoccupied. He closes the door and bolts it. Hemmrich approaches a table on which are placed a typewriter and a large, neatly stacked supply of foolscap paper. Pulling back a chair from a reading table, he points to the chair and says, 'Sit, please, Adolf.'

Hemmrich takes a seat on the opposite side of the table, facing Hitler. He removes the pad and the pencils from the satchel and places them on the table.

He then turns his attention to Hitler. *If he is left to it, will he open a conversation?* Hemmrich wonders.

He waits.

Hitler sits in rugged silence. His teeth are clenched, the tendons in his neck stand out rigid, his eyes are bulging, and his fists are waxy white.

He is a pulsating weapon, loaded, hair-triggered and cocked, thinks Hemmrich.

He waits. Hemmrich considers how best to start. *Let him start, or shall I begin?*

He chooses ordinary. 'How are you feeling, Adolf?'

Hitler explodes from his chair, bellowing at the extreme limit of his powerful voice, 'Treachery! Foul, obscene, unforgivable treachery! They know who they are, and I' – he says, thumping his chest – 'I will not forget! They will learn the hard way that there is a heavy penalty for betrayal!' The sound penetrates into every corner of the room.

The round has left the barrel, and nothing short of assassination will stop him now. Hemmrich makes no attempt to do so. He has come to hear what Hitler has on his mind, and now Hitler lays it before him, chapter and verse.

What Hitler sees before him are not stacks of unused books. His vivid imagination sets before him the Berlin Sportpalast. It is packed to the rafters with cheering fanatics, all hanging on his every word. He enumerates in excruciating detail every slur, every slight, every cheap remark that has stung him. Disloyalty, tepid commitment, and half-hearted devotion are all damned as capital crimes. The Aryan Ideal is glorified; all else, vilified.

Armed insurrection is the surest path to an Aryan future for all Germany. He sets all of this before his audience of one, without the slightest reduction of intensity or volume, and with continuous, unrestrained, unstoppable physical presence. Hitler works himself into a frenzy. Soon there is spittle flying from his mouth and sweat pouring down his temples.

How long can he keep this up? wonders Hemmrich.

Just as a Nordic berserker must eventually stop, so too must Hitler stop.

He does so mid-sentence. He has exhausted every reserve. Sweat is drenching his face; his breath is rasping. He stumbles into the table, supporting himself with both fists planted on the tabletop. He leans forward, bringing most of his weight onto his arms.

For a few moments, Hemmrich watches, aloof. Then he begins slow clapping. After a few indifferent pitty-pats of applause, he drops his hands to the table. 'Feel better now?' he asks.

Hitler's breathing is blowing strings of saliva from his mouth. Sweat drips from the tip of his nose onto the table.

Hemmrich pulls the towel from his satchel. Handing it to Hitler, he says, 'Take it, Adolf. Wipe your face. You have saliva all over that silly moustache of yours, and you are sweating. And sit down before you fall down. You're a mess, and if you do fall, I am not going to pick you up.'

Hitler slouches into his chair, exhausted. When his breathing has subsided to something approaching normal, he wipes the sweat and saliva from his face and neck. Craning his head forwards, he looks down the front of his clothing. Spotting a few dribbles of wayward body fluid, he wipes them away. Now satisfied enough with his appearance, Hitler pushes the towel across the table towards Hemmrich. Hemmrich pushes it back, saying, 'Keep it, Adolf. You may find you need it.'

Abruptly, Hitler stands. He jerks the towel from beneath Hemmrich's hand and flings it into the stacks. It fetches up sagging over the motor maintenance manuals. He turns to face Hemmrich, puts his fists on the table, and leans towards him.

'What's your game, Hemmrich?' he growls.

'*Herr* Hemmrich, to you. Sit down, Adolf.'

'*Herr* Hitler, to you,' he says, mimicking Hemmrich.

'I'll sit, *Herr* Hemmrich, when I'm damn good and ready!' Underscoring the point, he slams the chair under the table.

Extending his right arm, he joggles his index finger up and down while pointing at Hemmrich. 'You owe me!' he declares. 'You owe me a great deal, Herr Bloody Hemmrich! You owe me, and I *demand* loyalty! I've made this prison famous! I've made *you* famous, Herr Personal Guard to the greatest leader Germany has ever seen!'

'Greater than Frederick the Great? Greater than Otto von Bismarck? Greater than Paul von Hindenburg?' Hemmrich asks, raising a hand to forestall an answer. 'Herr Hitler, let's set a few things straight before we go any further. I have a certain fondness for you, but you are not entitled to my attention. Under different circumstances, perhaps, but not now and not here. Outside of this prison, you are, for many, the Great White Hope – as you have just reminded me – but inside you are just another prisoner. I will *not* make exceptions for you. I will *not* bend the rules to

          R. WILLIAM PLUME

suit you. It is the other way around, my friend. You do the bending, or you are here for the long haul. Is that clear?'

Hitler shuffles around a little and then directs an ambiguous nod towards Hemmrich.

'Good. Then we understand each other. Now, sit down,' says Hemmrich, delivering the final words as an emphatic, unmistakable, direct order.

It is a premeditated watershed moment that obliges Hitler to stake out the shape of their relationship.

Each watches the other, intent, unblinking, motionless.

The calculus plays out quickly.

Nice move, Herr Bloody Hemmrich. That's check. Forces me to take the next move. He's sharp, I'll give him that. Why isn't he the warden? Why the ultimatum? Why now? He's interested in me; that's clear, but he can walk away whenever he likes. He has nothing to lose. But I … I could lose everything. I could end up back in doss houses, selling crappy paintings on the street, living hand-to-mouth. He wants to know if his interest in me is worth pursuing, and I need him. Have I overplayed my hand?

Hemmrich's thoughts are no less scheming: *I am his best chance for an early release. Will he see that? Will he see that if he starts shoving chairs around, walloping tables, and behaving like a child, it will be the end of my interest in him? Will his need to dominate every circumstance stand in the way of his masterful intuition? I'll know soon enough.*

They wait. Each assessing the other.

Hitler puts his hand on the back of the chair. Hemmrich now knows that Hitler has made the right choice.

But when Hitler tries to withdraw the chair, he finds that it is stuck. He has slammed the chair into the table with such force that it has tilted forward and the armrests have jammed under the table.

Hemmrich sees this as just the light touch that's now required to release the tension. 'Sit there, Adolf,' he says, pointing to the next chair along.

'Thank you, Franz,' says Hitler. He sits, putting his hands – right over left – on the table. He looks towards Hemmrich. 'Now what?'

'For a start, my friend, you will have to be more respectful of the furniture.'

Hemmrich goes to the library kitchenette and returns with two glasses of water. He sets one before Hitler and puts the other one aside for himself. Hitler fiddles with the glass only because it's there. He neither refreshes himself nor thanks Hemmrich for the courtesy.

'Why was Leybold promoted to warden in preference to you? Why aren't you the warden?'

'Well now, there's a question from the other side of the road. Interesting that you, of all people, would ask such a question. But we're not here to discuss my career. We're here to discuss yours.'

'Me? Me … of all people? Me? Why is it so odd that *I* should ask you such a question?'

'Because you, Adolf, are all about *you*. That speech that just erupted from you was about *you*, how *you* have been insulted, how *you* have been defamed, how *you* have been betrayed. Makes a question about me something of a non sequitur, wouldn't you say?'

'Ha! *Non sequitur*. Big word for a small idea. Franz, tell me, why aren't you the warden?'

'You're very insistent, Adolf,' Hemmrich says. *Too insistent*, he thinks.

Hitler shrugs.

Hemmrich ignores the question, instead asking, 'Are you going to spend your time here at Landsberg shadowboxing with everyone who hasn't been completely supportive of you?'

'Perhaps. What does it matter to you? I might have thought your main concern would be that I don't sneak out of Landsberg when you aren't looking!'

'Do you even know why you are in this prison? *As a prisoner*, I feel I need to add.'

'I wouldn't be here if those men hadn't betrayed me.'

'I take it from that remark that your moral compass points to *Acceptable*, provided you succeed in incitement to riot, sedition, and treason.'

'Ahh, shove your moral compass up your arse, Herr Bloody Hemmrich! My compass has two cardinal points: *Succeed*, which moves me into the halls of power, and *Fail*, which flushes me down the sewer. Have you got an alternative to that?'

Hemmrich has woven his fingers together. His arched hands support his chin. 'Yes, I do. But if you don't refine your thinking, it's going to be the sewer for you.'

Once again, the two men stand off, each watching the other, both motionless.

Check. Again. My move. He's very good, this one. What has he got? What does he think he has? Still, I need to get out of here as soon as possible. If it helps me do so, maybe it's worth listening. One way or another, he's got me.

'Alright, I'm listening,' Hitler says.

'Excellent. Since you are listening, here is a metaphor for you. With your amateurish coup d'état, you have tried to storm the Gates of Heaven. That approach will avail you nothing. To announce yourself to St Peter, you first must knock.'

'What does that mean, Franz? What are you? Some kind of jailhouse missionary?'

'Oh, for Heaven's sake, Adolf, leave it outside. You remember Winnetou and Old Shatterhand?'

'Of course. The greatest tacticians of the American Wild West. Revered by all and with good reason. Yes, of course I remember them. I think it was me who introduced them to you! And you haven't answered my question! Why aren't you the warden?'

'Do you think, Adolf, that those great tacticians of the American West just walked out onto the prairie as heroes revered by everyone? No. They had to earn that respect. They had to earn their reputation step by step over the years.'

'The warden, Franz. Why aren't you the warden?'

Hemmrich stops and breathes deeply, seeing that an answer is required.

'I had an inappropriate liaison with the wife of the Commissioner of Prisons before he was promoted to that position. When he became the Commissioner, he divorced her, and he demoted me.'

'You *were* the warden?'

'Draw your own conclusions, Adolf. That topic is now closed. Instead of pursuing the details of my private life, you need to turn your attention to your own future, or you won't have one. You don't seem to understand that your political career hangs by a gossamer thread. I remind you that your prison sentence is six months minimum, five years maximum. But if Warden Leybold deems you a public threat, he can apply for an extension of your sentence. Beyond that, the federal government could appeal your verdict and re-impose Article 9. If they succeed, you will be on the quick train to Austria with no hope of a political career in Germany.

'Your problem, Adolf, is that you see only the result. You have had a dazzling rise to a very powerful position in German politics. Along the way you have seduced yourself into thinking it will continue to be one success after another. All you ever see in the Shatterhand books is the climax. I have watched you "reading" them. You're not reading them. You page through them until you find the part where Old Shatterhand and Winnetou prevail. And they always prevail. It's always made to seem like an easy win.

'All of that are fairy stories for boys. Now you get this straight – this prison is no fairy story, and you are not a boy. From here on, it's hard work and a long road for you. What it comes down to, Adolf, is this: if you triumph by way of the electorate, your government will survive. But if you gain your way through a coup d'état, you will never have a legitimate government, and you will be hindered and undermined by a constant expectation that there will be another coup d'état right up your back passage!'

        R. WILLIAM PLUME

The room falls silent.

Hemmrich waits.

Hitler lowers his forehead onto the back of his overlapped hands. After a pause, he mumbles, 'Well, I don't have much of a future anyway. Everything I'm hearing from outside the prison is that the Party, my party, is falling apart. It is disappearing. There won't be anything left, never mind *when* I get out of here.'

'Oh, Adolf!' growls Hemmrich, slapping the table hard. 'Now you are just whining! I marvel, Herr Adolf Hitler, glorious Führer of the Nationalsozialistische Deutsche Arbeiterpartei, that your imagination fails you so completely when you need it most. Have you ever stopped to *think* about who you are up against politically? In the last federal election, there were thirty, yes, *thirty*, political parties involved. All the usual ones, including the Communist Party – the Bolsheviks, as you insist on naming them – but there were also the Wendish People's Party, the Schleswig Club, the Re-Evaluation and Reconstruction Party, the Polish People's Party – in Germany, for heaven's sake! – and a Tenants' Party!'

Leaning over the table, Hemmrich again slams the table with an open hand.

'There might have been a Mad Hatter's Tea Party in there as well! If you cannot overcome that, Adolf, then go back to painting! I hear you're pretty good at it! Now, cut the *woe-is-me* bullshit!'

Hitler looks up at Hemmrich. *Check and mate.*

'Let the Party go, Adolf. Let the Bolsheviks do their worst. Your party was built around you, and if you cannot rebuild it, no one can. But first you must think clearly about a more enlightened approach. To help you with your thinking, I have a gift for you.'

Hitler has been outmanoeuvred for the first time since the war ended. He's come up against opposition that has cornered him. His speaking presence alone has not produced the desired result.

Hitler is confused, but his mind opens. *He's right. I've been an idiot. Storming the Gates of Heaven! Hah! Nice metaphor, Hemmrich. And he's right again. I am the only person who can rebuild the Party. Keep your head down. Be a model prisoner. Don't prompt an appeal on Article 9. Get beyond Leybold's reach as soon as possible. You will be Chancellor, and when you are, you will do as you please.*

'And what might that gift be, Herr Hemmrich? The keys to the Reichs Chancellery?'

'You could see it that way. It's that typewriter and the paper.'

Hemmrich extends his arm, palm open and upwards, towards the typewriter.

'Write your ideas and your aspirations. *Write a plan.* Write like your life depends on it because it does.'

Hitler rises and stands in front of the typewriter. He twiddles the 'A' key with his index finger. He draws himself into a chair and strokes the keys with both hands.

Looking up to Hemmrich, he says, 'I will. Thank you, Herr Hemmrich.'

'I'll leave you to it then, Herr Hitler,' Hemmrich says as he moves towards the door.

'One last thing before you go, Franz.'

'Yes, of course, Adolf. What's on your mind?'

'Whatever happened to the Commissioner's wife? Ex-wife?'

'We married,' Hemmrich says with a sly smile, 'and lived happily ever after!'

CHAPTER 7

Streicher is Engaged

THE PRINTING INDUSTRY DELEGATION

As Reinhard crosses the street and approaches the entrance door, it opens. Herr Erler emerges from the doorway and meets Reinhard at the bottom of the stairs.

'Herr von Mörsbach, I am most relieved that you are able to be here tonight,' Erler says. 'Herren Schäfer, Klein, and Koch have agreed to your request. You will be head of delegation. Herr Schäfer will lead on finance. Herr Klein will lead on supply. Herr Koch will lead on transport. Your delegation is expected in Berlin the day after tomorrow, so your motion to accept the terms must conclude successfully this evening. You have widespread support among members of the Bavarian Printing and Publishing Association, but it is not universal, and passage is not assured. Chairman Bosen has agreed to expedite the formalities. Do you have any questions?' asks Erler.

'Yes. First, is the Nuremberg Nazi in attendance this evening?' Reinhard asks.

'No. We deliberately scheduled this meeting to conflict with a high-level Nazi Party meeting being held in Nuremberg tonight. Herr Streicher will be there.'

'And second, Herr Bosen is a stickler for following the rules. Does he understand that "expedite" means to move things along, speed things up?' Reinhard adds.

'Almost certainly not. But if things look like they're bogging down, we've arranged for a motion from the floor for you to chair this part of the meeting. If necessary, I will give the signal.'

'Will the motion pass? Will Herr Bosen even call for a second?' Reinhart follows up.

'We don't know. We're doing everything possible to get you and the delegation on your way to Berlin tomorrow. Beyond that, we can't guarantee how members will vote. They attend with voting instructions, and we don't know what those instructions are.'

'No, of course not. I'm grateful to you, Herr Erler, for your service to Germany, to the industry, and to me. It won't be forgotten. Shall we go in?'

◆

After the formal meeting concludes, Reinhard is surrounded by members thanking him for his leadership, congratulating him on the success of his initiative, and wishing him well in Berlin.

Abraham Rubenstein stands aside waiting. And fretting.

Preoccupied though Reinhard is, he sees Rubenstein's agitation, and he thinks, *Well, finance, transport, and supply are not top of mind for Abraham.*

When the crush of people has drifted away, Reinhard approaches Rubenstein and says, 'Abraham, if you don't mind my saying so, you do not look well. Is there something wrong?'

'A week ago, my friend, we had a visit at the plant from some drunken Nazi stormtrooper thugs. There was a rally in Weimar, but the brutes here in Munich got liquored up just the same. It wasn't really a visit. They straight-out attacked us, smashed up a lot of equipment, and threatened me and some of my people. Their leader, that … that … that Julius Streicher, yelled at me when they were leaving, "Get out, Jew! Get the — out." I can't use that word. But he kept shouting, "Get the … uh … swear word … out of my country, Jew, or next time it will be you and your family!"

 R. WILLIAM PLUME

'I come from here, Reinhard. I was born right here in Munich. So were my parents and theirs. This is my home. This is my country! What am I to do?'

REINHARD'S BUSINESS PROPOSAL

Frau Gretel's Gingerbread Café is a street-front business. The building is otherwise completely occupied by the Mörsbach Schreiber Printing Company.

Frau Gretel's persona and the name of the café originated, naturally enough, with the Brothers Grimm's fairy tale *Hansel and Gretel*. The story – and a particular illustration of the cottage, the witch, and the two lovely children – had captured her imagination when she was very young. She had grown up surrounding herself with memorabilia of the story.

As a child, she had adopted the name Gretel and insisted that everyone use it. Even as an adult, she refused to reveal her real name to anyone. The one and only exception to her ruling was a marriage registrar who had laid down the law: real name or no licence.

And what more congenial way to spend her adulthood than to surround herself with the appealing charm of a gingerbread house reconceived as a café, one that bestowed upon its patrons the wholesome goodness of delicious pastries, Kuchen and coffee? The parts of the story that involved the wicked, cannibalistic old crone were deftly overlooked.

Frau Gretel's café enjoys a regular clientele, many of them employees of Mörsbach Schreiber. She is well known and well liked, a part of the local scene. Like everyone, Reinhard is fond of Frau Gretel and always found the ambience of her café relaxing and conducive to clear thinking. And it also provides a place to meet that, by its very nature, avoids the formality of a professional office setting.

———

'Thank you for meeting me here, Thomas,' says Reinhard.

'Oh, that's no difficulty at all, my friend. Frau Gretel's is very agreeable, and she does the best cinnamon apple galette in all of Munich.'

'Lilli has settled so well into her life with you, Thomas. She is radiant. I must add that you look very pleased with yourself as well.'

'I'm very content, Reinhard. I had forgotten how pleasant social life is. But I know you well, Reinhard. We are not basking in the warmth of Frau Gretel's for idle chit-chat. What's on your mind?'

'To come straight to the point, Thomas, a printing business in Munich, owned by one Herr Abraham Rubenstein, has been attacked.'

'By whom? Or what? And why?' asks Thomas.

'Herr Rubenstein, as you may have surmised, is Jewish. The attackers were a mob of drunken Nazi hooligans. They were organised – if you could call it that – by a man called Julius Streicher. It was a spur-of-the-moment, torch-and-pitchforks mob. They made an ugly mess but fortunately didn't do any real damage to the main equipment, the presses and such. Streicher threatened Rubenstein's family, and Rubenstein wants out.'

'What do we know about this Streicher character?'

'Where do we start with a thug like Streicher?' says Reinhard. 'He's a small-time rabble-rouser out of Nuremberg. He is a very active and committed member of the Nazi Party. He publishes an inflammatory, off-colour, anti-Semitic rag called *Der Stürmer*. Because of that, he is also a member of the Bavarian Printing and Publishing Association. He comes into contact with industry people in Munich regularly, including, unfortunately, me, from time to time. Herr Streicher is belligerent, overbearing, and very threatening. In short, a most unpleasant person.'

'Another one,' Thomas says to himself. 'Why are you telling me this?' he asks Reinhard.

'That will become clear in a moment. As for the Rubenstein family, we are going to move them to Zürich. I have offered Herr Rubenstein

     R. WILLIAM PLUME

a senior position, which he has accepted. And as for the Rubenstein printing works in Munich, that's why I'm here,' says Reinhard.

'I'm listening,' says Thomas.

'I think you, Thomas, using your full acquired name, would be the perfect new owner of Rubenstein's Printing Works.'

Thomas feels his gut stirring in that shimmering, compulsive, pressing way that prompted him into his youthful indiscretions.

'And if Thomas Hedwig Reichey Schroeder is attracted by ownership but repelled by management?'

'In that case, Mörsbach Schreiber Printing and THR Schroeder Printing will enter into a management contract.'

'That makes some sense to me, but I don't understand why Mörsbach Schreiber doesn't buy out Rubenstein's,' Thomas replies.

'To come straight to the point, like many Germans, we are concerned about the demonisation of Jews by the Nazi Party. The Rubenstein family's history in Germany goes back for many, many generations. Abraham Rubenstein is as German as any of us, and his positive contribution to the community cannot be faulted.

'Although we are moving the Rubenstein family to Zürich, we cannot pick up all the slack. In the Rubenstein case, that means the printing plant. What we don't want is for that equipment to fall into unsympathetic hands.

'If Mörsbach Schreiber Printing appears as the new owner, and it becomes known that Herr Rubenstein is working for Mörsbach Schreiber in Zürich, it will compromise our ability to assist other Jewish families. But if THR Schroeder appears as the new owner of the Rubenstein plant, it will divert attention away from what we are doing.'

After a time, Thomas says, 'I must tell you that I am as concerned as you are about the thuggish behaviour that we are seeing in this country, the destruction of private property, the attacks on opposition politicians, and most of all, on the Jewish community. What you are proposing, Reinhard, makes good sense to me, and provisionally, I accept.'

'Provisionally?' Reinhard questions.

'Lilli must agree, but I feel sure you can take it that we accept.'

They shake hands. Reinhard says, 'Thank you, Thomas.'

Thomas sits silent and motionless, staring intently at the remains of the galette.

Reinhard looks closely at Thomas.

'Now it's my turn to say I know you well, Thomas. What's on *your* mind?'

'I, too, will come straight to the point. When we were in London, I discovered that my mother was Jewish.'

CHAPTER 8

Inspector Crampton Crosses The Ditch

CRAMPTON PREPARES TO MEET VON STAUFFENBERG

Knuckle-rapping the table, Detective Inspector Derek Crampton abruptly closes off the pre-meeting turmoil. He stands and launches into his briefing. 'Alright, everyone. Cut the crap! Listen up! The Bank of England Gold Swindle Case has been reopened –'

Symonds, the department larrikin from Embezzlement, jumps up, waving a copy of the morning paper. 'Well, how bloody appropriate is that, eh? Look at the headlines. Here we are, April 1925, and Winston Bloody Churchill him-bloody-self, Chancellor of the Bloody Exchequer, announces, "Britain will return to the gold standard!" Where they gonna get the gold, eh?'

Crampton doesn't wait for the laughter to start. He instantly shouts, 'Symonds! Put a sock in it and sit down! Now!'

He begins again. 'The prime mover in the swindle was a German employee of the Bank of England based in the Berlin office. He was the manager of the precious metals division and therefore responsible for all precious metal transfers. His full name is Philip Albrecht Graf von Stauffenberg. New information related to him has turned up, and the bank wants Scotland Yard to track him down. They are applying heavy pressure at the highest level of government. The bank wants this guy in the stocks, so we need to be on our game.'

A hand shoots up at the back of the room. 'How do we know von Stauffenberg was the prime mover in this swindle?'

'He's a high-quality suspect because he disappeared on the day of the transfer, and he hasn't been seen since. By anyone. Anywhere.'

'Maybe he was the gopher? Maybe he's dead, shot as his reward,' interjects another participant.

'Maybe he's one clever son of a bitch who got clean away. Von Stauffenberg is German nobility, and he was a ranking Bank of England employee. He was never going to be the gopher, and I'm betting he was in it up to his eyeballs. And now we have information that suggests he's still very much alive.'

'Which is?' someone asks.

'We have learned that Philip has a brother named Thomas. Brother Thomas turned up at the South Bank Registry Office looking for information about his mother. The registry official who served him found Philip – who was born in London – in the registry records, but there is no record of a Thomas. What's important here is that Thomas identified Philip as his brother. And, furthermore, Brother Thomas confirmed that Brother Philip was, at the time of the conversation, alive and well and in London. Yes, it's pretty thin, but that's what we've got.

'What we now know is the following: One, both Philip and Thomas are fully fluent in both English and German. Two, Philip was born in London. Three, Thomas lives somewhere in Germany. Four, Thomas may have been born in Nördlingen, the von Stauffenberg family seat. And, finally, it seems certain that the mother was Jewish and had changed her name, presumably to disguise the inconvenience of a Jewish background. The father was on the diplomatic staff at the German Embassy in London. He was very fluent in both English and German. And he bred Percherons as a pastime.'

'Interview the parents,' suggests a voice in the group.

'Mother and father both died in a maritime accident in the Irish Sea. They're not going to be much help. In the first round of this investigation, I went to Nördlingen, and I'll be going there again. First time around, we didn't know about Thomas. I'll be looking to find out about him. If we can track down this Thomas, there's an even chance that we'll get a line on his brother Philip.'

MEETING WITH KLEMENS IN NÖRDLINGEN

'Thank you, Herr von Stauffenberg, for meeting with us.'

'You've presented yourself as an investigator from Scotland Yard, London, and you are here with a German policeman. It would seem that I don't have a choice about meeting with you, so let's get on with it.'

'Right you are. We'll get straight into it. You are Herr Klemens Graf von Stauffenberg?'

'Yes.'

'And Konrad Maria Berthold Graf von Stauffenberg is your brother?'

'Yes.'

'And Konrad is the father of Philip Albrecht Graf von Stauffenberg.'

'Yes.'

'Which makes you Philip's uncle.'

'Of course. You came all the way from London to instruct me about genealogy, did you?'

'No, sir. These are formalities. Family relationships are important in this case. We need to be clear about this sort of thing. My apologies, but it's necessary.'

Von Stauffenberg grunts impatiently, draws on a large Cuban cigar, and says, 'You must, I suppose, but move along.'

'And you are also the uncle of Philip's brother, Thomas von Stauffenberg?'

Von Stauffenberg shifts up in his chair. 'What brother? There is no brother called Thomas of whom I am aware.'

'As we understand it, Herr von Stauffenberg, your brother Konrad and his wife had two children, at least two children. There may have been others, but the two we know about are Philip and Thomas. We know that Philip was born in London. One of the reasons we are here is that we recognised the possibility that Thomas may have been born at or near the von Stauffenberg family seat.'

'There was certainly a child named Philip born in London to Konrad and Elisabeth, if that was her real name, but this is the first I've heard of a child named Thomas.'

'You seem doubtful about her name, Herr von Stauffenberg. Why is that?'

'Well, for a start, she was English. You seem to know quite a lot about my brother, Inspector. Perhaps you've realised that he was quite the catch. German nobility, a senior diplomat at the German Embassy in London, and a multilingual, debonair man-about-town. Everything someone seeking to improve their station in life could ask for. It wouldn't be the first time a woman changed her name looking to step up … or aside.'

'Aside?' Crampton asks.

'You know better than most, Inspector, that people often have skeletons in their wardrobes. Things they'd rather other people didn't know about.'

'Such as?'

'I suppose it could be anything. Unfortunate racial connections or perhaps a religious background that's unhelpful. That sort of thing.'

'Are you suggesting that Elisabeth had something of that nature in her past?'

'In her case, I couldn't possibly say. But we all know what's possible among the lower classes, the Bolsheviks, the Jews, the Romani, and the rest. It may be that this Thomas was the issue of a previous relationship. It's a Jewish thing, you know, children out of wedlock, rampant promiscuity, that sort of thing. No one should be surprised when children pop up out of nowhere. Jews are a shameful stain on German decency. And, by the way, Germany did not lose the war. They, the Jews, engineered Germany's defeat in Ber—'

R. WILLIAM PLUME

Crampton interrupts, 'If we could, please, Herr von Stauffenberg, come back to the topic at hand.'

'My apologies. Easy to get carried away given the way of things these days.'

'Indeed. Have you had any contact with Philip in recent times?'

'None whatsoever. We don't know whether he is alive or dead. He just disappeared. It was as though he'd died, but there was no body, no death report, no killings, no mysterious circumstances. He just vanished as if he had been abducted by aliens, like something out of an H. G. Wells novel.

'People from the bank were here, investigators like you. Police, you name it. Quite the palaver it was. And poor Emmeline; she was heartbroken. She moped around here for months, getting drunk every day.'

'And who is Emmeline?'

'Emmeline von Ettingshausen. She is … was Philip's fiancée.'

'Where is this Emmeline now?'

'She moved back to Berlin.'

'Do you have her address?'

'I do, and I will give it to you as you are leaving, which will be soon.'

Von Stauffenberg arranges for Crampton and his German minder to be escorted to the manor entrance. Crampton thanks von Stauffenberg for his time and turns towards the waiting police car. As he is opening the passenger door, he hears von Stauffenberg calling to him.

'There's one more thing, Mr Crampton. Konrad and Elisabeth had a vacation cottage in Meersburg, Baden-Württemberg. I suppose it's possible that this Thomas you are looking for was born there. If you do find him – Thomas, I mean – you will let me know, won't you?'

'Of course, Herr von Stauffenberg. Thanks again for your time.'

'And if you do find Philip, tell him he's been a very bad boy.'

Crampton smiles, flashes a thumbs-up, and closes the car door.

Crampton tries his German on the Meersburg town clerk.

'I want … find house … one … the … a … house, ummm … an owning … from … close … near Meersburg …'

Crampton's German minder-cum-driver intervenes. 'We are looking for a property that is somewhere near Meersburg, owned by Konrad and Elisabeth von Stauffenberg. Can you help us with that?'

The clerk retrieves the property ownership record.

'There is a property that was owned by that couple, but it is no longer in the name of the von Stauffenbergs. It is now owned by one Herr Thomas Hedwig Reichey Schroeder. The ownership changed in 1904 by estate sale. They lived in the house until – what was it? – something like ten years ago.'

'They?'

'Herr Schroeder, his wife, and their two children.'

'Do you have an address for Herr Schroeder?'

'His postal address is given here as a box number at the Friedrichshafen Post Office. We have no record of a physical address.'

'Can you give us directions to the house?'

The clerk supplies the directions and adds, 'You might like to know that Herr Schroeder was the night-soil man for the villages between Meersburg and Fischbach.'

Crampton looks to his minder and arches his eyebrows.

When the two men arrive at the cottage, Crampton's suspicions are alerted even before he has opened the car door. 'Well, you coulda knocked me over with a feather. Look at that. It's close enough to a straight-up English manor house. How on earth did a night-soil man buy a place like that, even at a knockdown, estate sale price?'

The minder replies, 'Looks like it's been vacant for a while. Let's have a look around. And remember, we don't have an access warrant, so we can't go inside. But no doubt it's locked anyway.'

Crampton gets out of the car, goes straight to the front door, pulls out a pocketknife, picks the lock, and opens the door.

'Hey! What are you doing? You can't go in there!'

'Well, *you* may not have a warrant, but I have the King's Warrant, and I will go where I damn well please.'

All ordinary household items – books, furniture, wall hangings – have been removed. The kitchen is stainless. Every scrap of ash has been removed from the wood-burning stove, and the cupboards have been cleared of all utensils, crockery, silverware and glassware. Upstairs, everything movable is gone. The lavatory, too, is spotless. *This is no night-soil man's hovel,* Crampton concludes.

Crampton leaves the house, locking the door behind him. He turns to his minder and says, 'We must find this Thomas Hedwig Reichey Schroeder. Any ideas where to start looking?'

'We go to the Friedrichshafen Post Office and find out if they have in their records a physical address associated with the post box.'

'Good idea. You do that. I will go to Berlin and have a conversation with Fräulein von Ettingshausen.'

———

Fräulein Emmeline von Ettingshausen and Inspector Crampton are seated on the terrace before a small café in Berlin.

Seated in awkward silence.

Two coffees appear.

Emmeline spikes hers from a flask and drinks away the top half of the cup.

'Thank you for meeting with me, Fräulein. I am looking for Philip von Stauffenberg. I have spoken to his uncle, Klemens von Stauffenberg. He thought you might have information about Philip's whereabouts.'

Again opening the flask, Emmeline refills the cup. 'The only thing I can tell you about Philip von Bloody Stauffenberg is that he broke my heart. I will never forgive him for that.'

'He has made a lot of people unhappy, Fräulein, and I'm doing my best to find him.'

She shrugs, stubs out her cigarette, and looks doubtfully at Crampton. 'When you find him, Inspector, tell him from me that he's a proper bastard.'

Crampton returns a pale smile and says, 'Fräulein, do you have a telephone number where I can reach you directly?'

'Need you ask? Of course.'

Crampton gives her his card. 'Call this number if you remember something that might be helpful in identifying him, a tattoo or something like that.'

Looking wistfully along the street, Emmeline recollects, 'He had a big one.'

'A big tattoo?'

'Oh, good Lord. You English.'

Awkward silence returns.

Pointing to his card, Crampton says, 'Fräulein, this number connects to a twenty-four-hour International Criminal Police Commission answering system here in Germany. They will pass the message on to me in London. Give your name, and I will return your call.'

CHAPTER 9

The Judaica Library

THOMAS BEGINS HIS JOURNEY TO UNDERSTANDING

Approaching a Munich synagogue, Thomas suppresses an urge to turn and walk away. Were this the grandest Roman Catholic cathedral in all of Christendom, he would feel entirely at ease. Walk through the front door, find the stoup, bless yourself with the Sign of the Cross, open the inner door, enter a hallowed place of worship, genuflect before your God, and kneel in prayer before the holy altar of the Lord.

But here, before this splendid, towering building, he wonders, *Do I knock? Open the door and walk in? Then what?*

While Thomas stands puzzling over the conventions for entering a synagogue, two men leave the building, cross the forecourt, and walk away chatting amiably with each other. *Well, the door isn't locked. That's helpful,* he thinks. He moves a single step closer to the entry and pauses again. *Is there something I'm supposed to say? Do Jews genuflect?*

'Good morning, neighbour,' Thomas hears from behind.

He turns.

A man puts his hand on Thomas' elbow and, with a welcoming smile, says, 'May I help you?'

'I hope so,' says Thomas. 'I've never been in a synagogue before.'

'Ah, well, then today is your lucky day, my friend, for I am the rabbi of this humble synagogue. My name is David Feldermann. Please, come with me.'

Feldermann leads Thomas through the door and says, 'There we are. That wasn't so hard, was it?'

'No, it wasn't. I'm sure it helps if you know. But I appreciate the intervention. I was struggling. Thank you, Herr Feldermann.'

'Call me David, please. And you are?'

'Thomas Schroeder. I'm here because I'm interested in understanding more about the Jewish world.'

———

'Yours is a very interesting story, Thomas. Born Jewish, raised Roman Catholic, discovered the Jewish connection as an adult, and now looking to understand the Jewish facet of your life. Quite the challenge you've set for yourself.'

'It is, but what you have so crisply summarised isn't quite the whole story.'

'There is more?' asks Feldermann.

'I'm looking to understand German nationalism, how Herr Adolf Hitler formed his ideas, where they sprang from, and why they are so seductive.'

Feldermann squirms.

Thomas sees the response and adds, 'I've been reluctant to raise this with you because of the re-emergence of a virulent form of anti-Semitism in Germany today. My reasons are genuine. I'm concerned about the possible effects of Nazi ideology on my family. I've made it my goal to understand Nazism in general and Herr Hitler in particular.'

Feldermann again scans Thomas, assesses him, and finally accepts him as presented: genuine and sincere.

He stands. 'Today really is your lucky day, Herr Schroeder. You've come to exactly the right place to begin your journey of understanding. Come with me, please.'

Feldermann unlocks an ordinary door set into a featureless wall. Thomas sees descending stairs that fade away into blackness. Feldermann flicks on a light, a bare bulb dangling above the stairs.

'Follow me. Close the door after you, please.'

The stairs bottom out before another door. Feldermann unlocks and opens that door. He steps inside the room and invites Thomas with a gesture of his hand to follow.

'Welcome to the Judaica Library.'

Thomas steps into a very large, well-lit room with a high ceiling. Parallel library stacks loaded with books, file boxes, and papers of all sorts fill the room.

'Your aims, Thomas, and ours run hand in glove. We, too, are concerned about the effects of Nazi ideology, and we, too, have made it our goal to understand Nazism in general and Herr Hitler in particular.

'What you see before you is an extensive library of the history and practice of Judaism and of anti-Semitism in all its forms, copies of all issues of various anti-Semitic publications, such as *Der Stürmer* and the *Völkischer Beobachter*, plus mainline newspapers, periodicals, films, Nazi memorabilia, everything. We hold transcriptions of all Hitler's speeches, his political manifesto *Mein Kampf* (My Struggle), newspaper articles about him, a large collection of his paintings, detailed profiles of all the senior members of the Nazi Party, and more. Our approach here is to do the *opposite* of ignoring the anti-Semitic community. Here, we absorb everything that's produced by them, and we learn from it. Follow me.'

Feldermann makes his way through a large collection of books. He stops and pulls a book from the stacks.

'You could hardly find a more appropriate way to start your work than by reading this book. It's called *The Protocols of the Elders of Zion*. Read it carefully. It's a fraudulent document that served as a pretext and rationale for anti-Semitism. And when you've done that, come back and make use of the rest of this collection. I'll make sure everyone here understands that I've given you my personal permission. All I ask is that you stay in touch with me.'

Thomas nods, signalling his agreement with the conditions posed by the rabbi.

'Good luck to you, Herr Schroeder.'

CHAPTER 10

Facing the Nazi Party

STREICHER THREATENS REINHARD

Julius Streicher has no interest in participating in anything soft-boiled like the Bavarian Printing and Publishing Association. But the Party hierarchy has different ideas. Streicher is, after all, the publisher of *Der Stürmer*, a suitable pretext for his participation.

The Party instructed him to join and to watch. Party loyalty forced him to attend Association meetings, but he never did so without distilled fortification. Tonight, he is looking for help. He spots Reinhard and descends upon him.

Reinhard, seeing Streicher advancing, prepares for an unfriendly, possibly hostile, conversation.

'Herr von Mörsbach, I thought I might find you at this meeting. I understand that Mörsbach Schreiber is doing very well.

'Herr Streicher,' is Reinhard's flat reply

'I will come straight to the point –'

'Please,' interrupts Reinhard.

'We are looking for help –'

'Who is *we*?'

'We are the *Völkischer Beobachter*. The enthusiasm for what we produce exceeds what we can print. To be brief, we are interested in hiring Mörsbach Schreiber to help with the printing.'

'*We*, then, refers to the Nazi Party?'

'Yes. Is that a difficulty?'

'Let's just say, Herr Streicher, that our views do not align.'

'Oh, who's a clever boy, then, Reinhard?'

Reinhard recoils at the insult implied by Streicher's use of his given name. The offence is aggravated by the childish wording.

'It is customary to show the usual degree of respect, Herr Streicher. It's Herr von Mörsbach to you.'

Streicher ignores Reinhard's correction. 'Your politics may yet change. I think you will agree that the Führer can be very persuasive.'

'He is very animated,' Reinhard replies.

'Animated? Animated? Hah! He will be the salvation of this nation, my friend. Mark my words. But we're drifting away from our purpose here. Can you help us?'

'No.'

Streicher now raises his left hand, palm up, index finger pointing into Reinhard's face, underscoring that he must now pay attention.

Streicher presents his message, borderline snarling. 'Mörsbach, you're very slick at the man-of-principle routine. But you should know that we are the future. You need to think more carefully about your discomforts. You will find that soon enough, I won't be asking.

'And, by the way, Mörsbach, I have come to understand that Mörsbach Schreiber is now managing what was Rubenstein's Printing Works on behalf of its new owner, this mysterious Herr Schroeder. No one, it seems, has ever seen him or knows where he lives. No one knows his affiliations nor the source of his seemingly considerable wealth. And yet you are prepared to work for him and not for us. Why is that, Mörsbach?'

'I am under no obligation to discuss with you the commercial arrangements of Mörsbach Schreiber.'

'Your loyalties may soon change –'

'My first loyalty is to God. My loyalties in this world are to my family and then to Germany.'

'Oh, and again! Stirring stuff, Mörsbach!' Streicher leans into Reinhard.

Reinhard stands rod-rigid, glaring, teeth clamped, hands fisted, eye to eye, nose to nose with Streicher. *Do not move! Do not blink! Say nothing!*

'Let's not beat around the bush, Mörsbach,' says Streicher, his sour, alcohol-infused breath lacing around Reinhard's face. 'You need to pay more attention to whom you choose as friends. I'm told that your two children – twin boys – are very talented. Wouldn't it be a shame if anything happened to them?'

Reinhard turns and leaves the building. He goes straight to Thomas' house. Using his fist, he bangs stoutly on the door.

THOMAS RE-ENGAGES WITH BREWSTER

The White Stork, an East London pub, is Seamus Brewster's local, and he's a regular.

The Stork has a freewheeling ambience that appeals to Brewster. It's an ambience that his own engaging style helps to steamroller along.

Brewster is the best kind of pub patron. He is a dazzling card-trickster and a thoroughly engaging raconteur, the life and soul of every evening. He mimics flawlessly many of the London accents, and he improvises hilarious stories that use those accents to good effect, bringing the clientele to such fits of laughter they beg him to stop.

Cockney rhyming slang is a genuine, almost linguistic, interest for him, and he brandishes it like a 'native speaker'. To the uninitiated, Cockney rhyming slang obscures intended meaning even though it is English. That quality of hidden-in-plain-sight meaning, where words are replaced by rhyming phrases, appeals to Brewster's professional interests.

This evening, he launches into an impromptu Cockney nonsense story:

'Me an' the trouble and strife, ya know, the cows and kisses, are down at the battlecruiser, the ol' rub-a-dub, see? Celebratin' the end o' me bird lime, see? Drinkin' mother's ruin by the bucket,

kickin' an' prancing, bubble bathin', see? Soon we're halfway
up the elephant's trunk, see? Brahms and Liszt, see? Kisses says,
"I'm Adam 'n' Eve-in', mate. It's lemon and lime for the Pope in
Rome." I sez, "O' aye, good strife, but first a gypsy's kiss, the ol'
Jimmy Riddle, maybe a ripping raspberry tart, see?" And, yeah,
we're down to our last cock and hen anyway.'

The patrons are loving it so much that the publican must shout over
the laughter.

'Brewster!' Brewster doesn't hear, so the publican tries again louder,
'Brewster!'

One of the men standing near Brewster pokes him in the shoulder
and points to the publican.

'Yeah? Wazzup, then?' says Brewster.

'Your great good fortune. Someone's stood you a round.'

'Oh yeah? Whozat then? Silly bugger,' says Brewster pleasantly.

'There,' says the publican, pointing to a booth. There sits a man
dressed in a crumpled tweed jacket over a heavy, coarsely knit grey jersey,
woollen trousers, and black steel-toed boots. He stares at the glass of
wine he holds between his hands. He is wearing a thick, ten-day beard,
a cloth cap, and a neutral expression.

Brewster slides into the facing seat and wraps his hands around the
pint.

'Well, bugger me days, if it ain't Mr Smooth!'

'Hail fellow, well met!' replies Thomas.

'Hail fellow? My dyin' arse! Jesus, Mary, and Joseph, it's good to see
you, me ol' cobber!'

The enthusiastic reception brings a smile to Thomas' face.

'So then, spill the beans. Why are you here, and why are you dressed
like that?'

'I'm here on business, but I don't want to be recognised by accident
or by coincidence.'

'What business? Please tell me that First Impressions is included in your business intentions.'

'First Impressions is my only business intention this time around.'

'What do you need?' Brewster asks.

'Those wonderful hands of yours. A close friend in Munich is potentially in deep trouble with a Nazi thug, and I need your help dealing with the thug.' Thomas reaches into his case and extracts a large-format, high-resolution photograph. It is the birth certificate of Fräulein Anna Weiss, Julius Streicher's mother. Thomas places it on the table in front of Brewster.

'I need two copies of this, but with a different religious affiliation here at the top. She was, according to this document, Roman Catholic, but her new birth certificate – the one you will create – needs to show that she was Jewish. Her maiden name, Weiss, suggests a Jewish connection, but I need a birth certificate for her that will turn that suggestion into a confirmation, and it must have a rabbi's signature attached. I need top-quality work, no effort spared. It must satisfy the sharpest eyes that are ever likely to examine your work. It will be scrutinised meticulously down to the last flyspeck,' says Thomas.

Brewster scans the photo. After a few minutes, he says, 'Bavarian birth certificate. Born in 1847. I'll need pre-unification Bavarian paper and old-style ink. And don't ya know! It was done with a quill! Some of those religious clerks just wouldn't give up on those things. Good condition, too. Hasn't been left lying around in the rolltop. Never been folded. That helps. Pretty straightforward, I'd say. I can do it. For you, mates' rates apply. When do you need it? I'll start tomorrow if you're on a tight schedule.'

THOMAS SHARES HIS PLAN WITH REINHARD

The telephone on Reinhard's desk rings. The caller is Liesel, Reinhard's secretary.

'Herr von Mörsbach, there is a gentleman here to see you.'

'I wasn't expecting anyone. Does he have an appointment?' asks Reinhard.

'No, but he says it's very important, and you will want to hear what he has to say.'

'Does he have a name?'

'Herr Thomas Schroeder.'

'Ah, well then, show him in.'

Liesel guides Thomas into Reinhard's office. Thomas and Reinhard embrace, leaving Liesel a little confused.

'Leisel, Thomas and I are well known to each other. If he shows up unannounced in the future, just show him in.'

Liesel leaves the office, closing the door as she goes.

'What brings you here, my friend?'

'Symmetry is my purpose.'

'Well, as you once said to me, *that's very concise*. I hope not so much so that you cannot or should not expand on what is meant by "symmetry".'

'The serious business of this visit is Julius Streicher. He doesn't know it yet, but he will be having a meeting with me next Monday. In case you hadn't connected the date, that's the Monday after this year's Nazi Party Rally.'

'Why the Monday?'

'If history is any guide, he will not only spend the weekend trying to get as close as possible to Herr Hitler's backside but also drinking a lot of beer. He may or may not succeed at the former, but we can be sure that he will succeed at the latter. On the Monday morning, he will be very hungover, and his guard will be down.'

'Then what?'

Thomas removes a document from his briefcase and hands it to Reinhard.

'That,' Thomas says, 'is the birth certificate of Anna Streicher née Weiss. She is Streicher's mother. Look at it very carefully.'

Some moments pass, then Reinhard's eyes come up slowly.

'She's Jewish,' he exclaims.

'Think about this, Reinhard, and keep in mind all of those blond-haired, blue-eyed, Nazi Party Aryan bigots who are so common these days. What would be the most devastating thing you could take away from them? Worse than financial ruin. Worse than being tossed out of the Party. Worse than failing in your blood oath to the Führer. What would it be?'

Reinhard looks again at the paper, pauses, and, looking back at Thomas, he says, 'Of course. You take away their blond-haired, blue-eyed, racially pure, uncontaminated Aryan master race bloodline pedigree.'

'Dead right, my friend. And at this moment, what is it that Herr Streicher wants more than anything else?'

'He would move heaven and earth to be named the Gauleiter of Franconia.'

'And what do you think his promotion prospects to the exalted position of district leader would be if Heinrich Himmler were to see this document?' asks Thomas.

'Worse than nil. Are you going to give this to Himmler?'

'Oh, no. All I need to do is make Streicher *think* that I will, and his mind will do the rest.'

Reinhard puts the document on the table, sits back in his chair, and begins stroking the cleft of his chin. 'This is fascinating, Thomas, but I must say that I'm surprised to hear that Streicher's mother is Jewish. I would have guessed her to be Roman Catholic. Is it true that she's Jewish?'

'No. As you have surmised, she is – was – Roman Catholic.'

Reinhard leans forward, taps the document, and says, 'Alright. Explain, please. Where did this come from?'

'The one and only Seamus Brewster.'

'Forgery. Of course. I never would have guessed. It doesn't look like it.'

'That's Brewster for you. The best there is outside the law – well, no. He's the best there is, full stop. That ordinary-seeming piece of paper is an unparalleled work of art. Notice that he hasn't just done a masterful job of matching the main features of the document; he has observed and included every little irregularity, every flyspeck, every crease and every dimple. I have no idea how he manages to match the paper so well. Sorcery, perhaps?'

'When did you see Brewster?'

'I went to London a few days after Streicher threatened you.'

'But Brewster had to have something to work from to make this engraving. What did you give him?'

Thomas smiles at Reinhard's perception. 'Excellent question, Herr von Mörsbach. Streicher was born in 1885 in Fleinhausen, a rural hamlet – population three hundred, maybe ten more if you include the cows – not far west of Augsburg. The family was Roman Catholic. He was the youngest of nine children. Allowing about two years per child, perhaps including a set of twins, it means the mother – his mother, Anna – would have started having children somewhere around 1865 to 1870. Guessing she was eighteen or nineteen, no more than twenty years old, when the first child was born, her birth year would have been something like 1845 or 1846.

'In 1846, Jewish births, deaths, and marriages were recorded by the rabbi in their own Jewish way. But to keep the Catholic parish records co-ordinated, a copy, produced by the parish but signed by the rabbi, was placed in the records of the cathedral office.

'I went to the Jewish cemetery in Augsburg. I walked around looking at headstones to find a female born in 1846, give or take a couple of years, and I found one. I made a note of her name and went to the Augsburg Cathedral office. I introduced myself as a genealogist and asked to see her birth certificate. Ten minutes later, Father Clerk comes back with the rabbi-signed copy of her Jewish birth certificate. I took multiple photographs of both sides and headed to London. I gave the photographs to Brewster. What he had to do was reproduce the document but with Anna Weiss' name replacing the real name. He produced this in six weeks.'

'Unless I'm missing something here, Thomas, if Streicher goes to the cathedral in Augsburg and asks to see his mother's birth certificate, he will be shown a document that confirms that she was born Catholic.'

'As it happens, you are missing something. He will be shown the other copy of this,' replies Thomas, touching the forgery.

'Brewster made two copies of the document. I took the other copy to the cathedral registry, posing again as a genealogist. But this time I asked to see Anna Weiss' birth certificate. Father Clerk soon came back with a large volume already open to the page I wanted to see. I took the book to one of the study carrels, removed the real certificate and replaced it with the forgery. This is Frau Streicher's real birth certificate,' says Thomas, handing Reinhard another sheet of paper.

'I will put it back in the Augsburg Cathedral registry sometime in the future, but for now, I will keep it in a safe place.'

'I'd love to be a fly on the wall when Streicher sees that piece of paper,' Reinhard says.

STREICHER'S SURPRISE AT CAFÉ GRÜN

Julius Streicher stumbles into Café Grün.

'Herr Streicher,' says Herr Grün, the owner, 'you are early today. Are you feeling … Are you well? You don't look — Well, I mean, you look like you need a strong coffee and a solid German breakfast. Eggs. Sausages. *Pomme frites*. Ja?'

Streicher grunts, turns, and drags himself to his favourite booth. Even as he slides himself onto the seat, the owner puts a large mug of steaming hot black coffee on the table.

'Breakfast in a few minutes, Herr Streicher, but this should get you started. It's from my best African supplier. If this doesn't put your wheels back on, nothing will.'

Grün hurries away to the kitchen.

R. WILLIAM PLUME

Streicher turns his attention to the coffee. As he raises the mug to his mouth, he feels his hips shunted into the wall. The coffee leaps up from the mug towards his face. Streicher's head snaps into the wall, and the steaming coffee arcs over the edge of the table and falls into his lap.

Streicher is no longer alone in the booth.

Three men have joined him. Thomas, dressed in a business suit, sits diagonally opposite Streicher. The other two men wear the insignia of their purpose. One with gauges in both ears, a knuckleduster on his right hand, and an insolent, just-you-try-me smile; the other, a skull-and-crossbones tattoo on the back of his left hand.

'What the hell do you think you're doing?' demands Streicher. 'Get the hell out of my booth!'

'We need to talk, Herr Streicher,' says Thomas.

'I don't know you. I have nothing to say to you. Fuck off!'

Streicher heaves his right elbow towards Brass Knuckles, who is seated beside him. Knuckles parries the blow and claps the bony part of Streicher's elbow down hard onto the table. Crossbones jerks the right sleeve of Streicher's greatcoat away from him. A dagger flashes from nowhere. Slammed down, it pins the sleeve to the table.

'It would seem, Herr Streicher,' says Thomas, 'that no one is going anywhere. Not until you have heard what I have to say to you.'

Streicher grunts.

'You look like you have spent your weekend at that Nazi booze-up … get-together … thing.'

'Congress. The Third Nazi Party Congress.'

'As you wish, Herr Streicher. I must say, you do not look well. Did the Congress fall short of your expectations?'

'That's none of your fucking business.'

'Of course, you're absolutely right, Herr Streicher. If you want to go around looking like something the cat dragged in, well, that's your choice.'

'Damn right it is. I don't know why you are here, but take your knife and FUCK OFF!' Streicher lunges across the table, aiming for Thomas' throat. He misses his mark and fetches up with a handful of shirt.

Knuckles is instantly upon Streicher, cross-gripping his greatcoat collar over his throat, thrusting his head against the wall, and gouging his jaw with the knuckleduster.

'Release him!' Knuckles hisses. 'Or you have drawn your last breath, my friend!'

Streicher releases his hold on Thomas' shirt.

'Listening now, Herr Streicher?' Thomas asks.

Streicher says nothing.

'Recently, you threatened Herr Reinhard von Mörsbach –'

'What of it? He's a shitty little Jew sympathiser.'

'Herr von Mörsbach is tolerant of many things, Herr Streicher, even you, up to a point. But I'm not here to discuss Herr von Mörsbach's standard of charity. I have a document that you must see.' Thomas withdraws a sheet of paper from his briefcase and places it on the table in front of Streicher.

'Where did you get this?'

'That's not important, Herr Streicher. I encourage you to look at it with great care.'

Streicher looks back at the paper. After a few moments, his eyes widen. He stares at it. Riveted. Motionless.

A static moment envelops the four men.

Streicher thrusts the paper across the table as if it has burst into flame. 'No! NO! This is a lie!' he says, smacking the paper with an open hand. 'That is NOT true! My mother was a fine Christian woman of impeccable breeding! That is a lie! That is a fucking, bald-faced lie!'

'Herr Streicher, this is very simple. Your mother's maiden name was Weiss. That suggests Jewish ancestry, and this document, her birth certificate, confirms it. You are familiar, in your own way, with Jewish culture. I'm sure you are aware that Jewish descent is through the female line. I need not instruct you on what that means for you. But I do wonder whether Herr Himmler will think it's a lie when he sees such compelling evidence to the contrary.'

Streicher has plans. If Himmler sees or even hears of this paper … Streicher sees his future evaporating. 'No! No! Not that!' he barks, realising, as the words leave his mouth, that he has exposed his worst fear: Herr Heinrich Himmler.

Thomas reaches across the table, picks up the paper, and puts it back into his case. He leans a little towards Streicher. 'Now, Herr Streicher, you listen and listen very carefully. You will stay away from Herr von Mörsbach, his family, and his business. If I hear that you have interfered with him in any way – if you, or any of your thugs, so much as *breathe* near him, anyone in his family, or his business – this document will find its way into the hands of people who, I'm sure, will be far less lenient than I. Is that clear?'

Streicher, staring open-mouthed into the distance, says nothing.

'I'm glad we understand each other, Herr Streicher.'

The three men slide out of the booth, stand, and leave the café.

Streicher, shocked and desolate, is left pinioned to the table, trying to make sense of what has just happened. For a time, he sits motionless, seeing nothing, hearing nothing, lost in the grotesque family history that has wrapped itself around him.

He reaches across the table with his left hand and pulls at the hilt of the dagger. It doesn't budge. Streicher is right-handed, he is seated, and he is obliged to reach across his body. He cannot move the blade. Using his left hand, he undoes the buttons and wriggles out of the overcoat. He gathers it into a bundle and chucks it into the facing seat with the right sleeve still spiked to the table.

He slides out of the seat and stands. The standing brings on a faintness caused by the intensity of his emotional state and the sapping hangover gnawing at his gut. Realising that he is about to fall, he tries to sit but manages to get only half his butt onto the seat. From there he slips, pitches over, and strikes his head against the table leg. He falls to his hands and knees on the dirty wooden floor. Straightaway, he vomits, retching several times. Breathless and panting, avoiding his vomit, he crawls backwards, plops his butt onto the floor, and sags back against the seat. He wipes the strings of saliva from his chin and smears his hand down the leg of his trousers.

After a time, he gathers himself together and hauls himself up using the seat and the table as grips. Now standing, he grabs the dagger with both hands. Surely it will come away easily now that he is able to get a firm grip on the handle. He jerks on the dagger with all of his considerable strength. But it is so deeply thrust into the wood, it doesn't move.

His right hand – slick with the slime he has wiped from his mouth and nose – slips up the handle, past the sharply pointed recurve pommel. The point catches the webbing between his thumb and forefinger, ripping the skin open across his palm.

He reels back, blood pouring from his hand, and stumbles into the adjacent row of booths. The man seated there fends him off, shoving Streicher away. Now off-balance again, he steps into his own vomit, slips, and collapses onto the floor, wrenching his left knee.

Bleeding, covered with vomit, and lame in his left leg, Streicher staggers to his feet. Ignoring his coat, he limps for the door.

The owner, emerging from the kitchen, holds Streicher's breakfast. He looks towards the booth. 'Herr Streicher,' he says, 'you'll have to clean up that mess before you leave.'

CHAPTER 11

Streicher is Unhinged

STREICHER ATTEMPTS TO REMOVE A BIRTH CERTIFICATE

The days after the Café Grün incident were the stuff of nightmares for Streicher. His mind a tangle of vague memories of his mother.

In his youth, he paid little attention to her, and now, when it was of the utmost importance to remember details of her life, he realised that he didn't know much about his mother. He remembered only fragments, all of which were devoid of the information he most needed to know.

And, yes, perhaps he could remember kneeling beside his mother at St Nikolaus Church as she clicked through the rosary beads, reciting the Hail Marys and the Our Fathers reverently, rhythmically. He didn't recall her rushing along with the haste of the faithless.

But perhaps she did when I wasn't there? Did she have weekly rituals? Was she Catholic in outward appearance only? It doesn't add up! How could she possibly be a Jewess? How? But ... she wouldn't be the first Jew to marry a Catholic. She wouldn't be the first Jew to marry outside the faith and then furtively cling to the old ways, the traditions of her childhood. Did she eat the pork sausage she cooked?

How could he know? He hadn't paid any attention. She ate her meals in the kitchen, either alone or with the current youngest child. And since Julius was the youngest, he never observed the custom.

Did she light candles on Friday evenings? Perhaps she did? Perhaps not? How many candles did she light? Was it three? Or five? None?

As Streicher searched his memory, his mental gymnastics became increasingly far-fetched and convoluted.

Could it have been seven candles placed all around the house? A kind of disaggregated, disguised, and symbolic menorah? Didn't she always go out onto the road on Saturday at dusk to look up into the darkening sky? Did she do that? I think she did. Maybe?

She said once that she just liked looking at the stars. Twinkling reminders of the greatness of God. She did say that, didn't she? Does it make any difference if she did?

In lucid moments, he realises his far-fetched speculations are shifting too far from the rational, and he returns to where he started.

But, no, surely not. None of this could be true. It cannot be true. It must not be true!

As he rummages through his unclear and unhelpful memories, Streicher realises that merely asking the question is doubt enough, and the thought paralyses him. That thought alone in another mind, the wrong mind, in Himmler's mind, will spell his doom.

DO something! Go to Fleinhausen. Talk to the people at the church. That will make everything clear. Why didn't I think of this a week ago? Go now. The sooner I get this resolved, the better.

But where was she born? He doesn't know. His moment of clarity wilts away as quickly as it had blossomed.

Doubts be damned! Streicher goes to St Nikolaus Church and asks the registry priest for his mother's birth certificate. The priest looks puzzled but nonetheless fingers his way along the spines of the many large volumes on the shelves. When he arrives at the volume he needs, he opens it on his desk. Long familiarity with the contents of the registers quickly leads the priest to Streicher's parents' marriage certificate.

'Ahh, yes, just as I thought. Herr Streicher, your parents' marriage certificate shows that your mother was born in Augsburg, not Fleinhausen. If you want to see her birth certificate, you will have to go to the cathedral registry there. I'm sorry we couldn't be more helpful,

R. WILLIAM PLUME

but I'm sure they will have what you are looking for.'

Streicher manages a graceless 'Thank you'. He leaves the office with his mind on making sure he catches the next train to Augsburg.

At the cathedral, the registry priest finds the register with the document Streicher seeks and places it on the desk, saying, 'Here we are, Herr Streicher. This is your mother's birth certificate.'

Streicher's eyes sweep down the open page, and he sees that he is looking at confirmation of the disgraceful family history he saw a few days ago at Café Grün.

Sweat springs to his forehead. He stands, eyes flaring with the dread of a man mortally wounded, stroking his hands against his trousers as if to cleanse them. He looks again at the piece of paper.

Now what he sees before him is a death certificate. Rational thought deserts him, and a jumble of half-baked possibilities takes its place. *Go to the synagogue. Force them to change the record. No! Just rip this page out of the book!*

He moves to act on his panic-inspired idea, but the priest – observing Streicher's agitated behaviour and sensing the direction of his inner turmoil – has closed the register and is holding it under his arm, shielded by his other hand.

'Give me that book!' Streicher demands, grabbing the spine and pulling on it as best he can with one hand bandaged.

The noisy scuffling brings another priest into the room, and together the two priests manage to overpower Streicher.

'Go! Get out! Now!' the registry priest says forcefully, leaving no room for Streicher to protest.

THOMAS TAKES ON THE NAZI PARTY

'Table for two, gentlemen?' asks the maître d'hôtel at Restaurant Parisian, Marienplatz.

'Yes, please, Monsieur Buteau.'

'Your usual?'

'If it's available, please,' Thomas replies with a gentle smile.

Thomas and Reinhard are shown to their table by Monsieur Buteau. He withdraws Thomas' chair. When Thomas has seated himself, Buteau places a serviette in Thomas' lap and then assists with scooching Thomas a little closer to the table. In the meantime, Reinhard has seated himself, dealt with the serviette, and turned his chair a little sideways to the table. He crosses his legs and, with his hands together, places an elbow on the table.

Thomas smiles and says, 'You know, Reinhard, when my grandmama Eleonore saw any of the grandchildren putting their elbow on the table, she would reach across and whack the bony part with a fork and say, "Polite people never, ever put their elbows on the table!"'

'I had the same thing from my grandmother,' replies Reinhard, 'though she never hit me with a fork. My only delinquency as a youngster was to put my elbow on the table when she wasn't there. Proper tearaway, I was. It got to be something of a habit. Unless you're tempted to whack me with that fork, would you mind awfully if I left it there?'

Thomas laughs and concedes the point with an open gesture of his hand.

Buteau, who has waited in the background while Thomas and Reinhard agree the standards for table manners, now comes forward and places the wine list in front of Thomas.

'Good evening, gentlemen, and welcome again to Restaurant Parisian. This evening we have a lovely Rue de l'Église Pinot Gris if you gentlemen would care to try something adventurous.'

'That sounds very appealing, Monsieur Buteau. A bottle and two glasses, please,' says Thomas, handing the unopened list back to Buteau, who then continues his patter with details of the evening's menu.

'*Messieurs*, as you will surely know, we have secured ze services of a new and breathtaking *chef de cuisine* here in Munich direct from Paris.

    R. WILLIAM PLUME

So tonight, we have three menu choices instead of the normal two. Tonight, we have *table d'hôte* and *à la carte, comme d'habitude. Mes amis*, are you ready for this? We are very pleased to say, to … to announce to our patrons, our … special patrons, our new and altogether … umm … tantalising *menu dégustation*. Would you like a moment to consider your choice?'

'Herr von Mörsbach,' says Thomas, looking across the table, 'shall we try the altogether new and tantalising *menu dégustation*?' Reinhard smiles and shrugs with hands raised, palms up, to indicate unconcerned agreement.

Buteau inclines his head and departs for the wine cellar.

'You know, Reinhard, sometimes when we come here, I'm tempted to say, "Monsieur Buteau, I'll have the everlasting stew, please."' Both men chuckle.

'Now that you are living in Munich, Thomas, it makes it much easier for us to share times like this, and I'm grateful for that.'

Thomas nods his agreement. Reinhard shifts the direction of the conversation.

'Your mind games with Julius Streicher seem to have hit the bullseye dead in the centre,' says Reinhard.

'So I believe. My information has it that he's jittery and suspicious of everything and everyone, always angry and even more aggressive than he was before. His anti-Semitism becomes more poisonous with every issue of *Der Stürmer*. So much so that even some Nazis are objecting to it,' says Thomas.

'Doing everything possible to validate his Aryan credentials?'

'Yes, I suppose he is. Who knows? He may even start to deny that he had a mother.'

'You're aware, Thomas, that as of a month ago, Himmler has been elevated to Reichsführer Schutzstaffel? He joins the Nazi Party, and just four years later, in January 1929, he finds himself *numero uno* of the SS, Hitler's elite bodyguard. Well played on his part. He's been doing the rounds, making sure everyone knows there is a new boss in town. He was in Nuremberg a few days ago, and our mole in the SS was at that meeting.'

'You have a man in the SS?'

'I do, and he saw Streicher at close range, and he was … How shall I put this delicately?'

'Shitting himself?'

'That, and he was sweating profusely, eyes shifting in every direction. Turned himself inside out trying to ingratiate himself to Himmler. It looks like his difficulties with Himmler are just beginning.'

'How so?' asks Thomas.

'Have you heard the name Joseph Goebbels?'

'Gauleiter of Berlin. He is another Streicher. Smarter, smoother, and more devious perhaps, but just as drenched in the Nazi Aryan master race culture.'

'That's the man. He has an interesting and important history. You may know that he has a clubfoot and walks with a pronounced limp. Some among the master race purists think the defect disqualifies him from being considered Aryan. He was born into a Catholic family. His parents had hopes that he would become a priest. As fate would have it, he went through his Catholic catechism with none other than the man who is now the Bishop of Augsburg.'

'Is that so? Unless I very much miss my guess,' says Thomas, 'you're about to tell me that the Bishop of Augsburg has a role in our story.'

Monsieur Buteau arrives back at the table with the bottle of wine and two glasses. Without a word, he goes through the wine choreography, displaying the label to both men, withdrawing the cork, soliciting Thomas' approval by taste, and, finally, pouring. He places the bottle into the *seau à glace* beside the table, bows, and departs.

Reinhard resumes where he left off. 'The bishop does indeed have a role. Streicher did go to Augsburg to check his mother's birth certificate, just as you thought he might. When he saw the page you had inserted into the register, he became agitated and tried to rip it out of the book. He was prevented from doing so by a quick-thinking priest. The priest reported the event to the bishop, together with the presumed prompting fact that Streicher's mother was Jewish. The bishop, at a social occasion, then passed the information on to his childhood friend, Herr Goebbels.'

'And he passed it on to Himmler?'

'It would seem so. What we do know is that after that conversation, two SS men turned up at Augsburg Cathedral. They went straight to the bishop, asking – demanding – to see the birth certificate of Streicher's mother. Streicher himself has no way of knowing that somebody checked unless he staked out the cathedral with one of his own thugs. If he did, it would account for his grovelling behaviour with Himmler at their meeting in Nuremberg. If he didn't, the cringing will be the product of an over-active imagination. Either way, Himmler is now looking sideways at Streicher.'

'This is what I hoped would happen, but I'm most relieved that it seems to have removed a real threat to you and your family.'

Thomas pauses as the first of the four dégustation courses arrives by way of a waiter carrying a large ornate tray on which are placed two small plates. Monsieur Buteau carefully places the plates before the diners.

'*Maintenant, mes amis.* I know, I know what you are sinking. Zees ees four or five olives, some water crackers, and a few thin slices of cheese. But a moment of your time, *s'il vous plaît.* These olives come from trees growing in the Holy Land.' Buteau crosses himself. 'Jesus Christ himself may have slept under the tree that brought forth these succulent fruits. And as for these crackers, the flour comes from wheat grown in the shadow of Mount Vesuvius in soil distilled from the finest lava that rich Mother Earth has to offer. And, finally, the cheese was made by the Grand Fromagerie of Mont Blanc from the milk of the docile and contented cows of Vachéry Etroubles, who graze on the purest meadow grass of the high plateau.'

Thomas looks at his plate. 'Monsieur Buteau, I must say, and I'm sure that Herr von Mörsbach will agree, that you've made it sound very appetising indeed.'

Buteau smiles, bows, and returns to the kitchen.

Thomas looks at his plate, then at Reinhard. He smiles, shrugs, and picks up the conversation again.

'The way things have developed, Reinhard, has set my mind to work. At first, I only wanted to force Streicher to back off. But I have realised that what has been done to him could be done to others in the Nazi Party. Have you ever stopped to think about the effect that a single person can have on events – events that affect an entire country?'

'I can't say that I have,' answers Reinhard.

'Right here, in Germany, as we speak, we have Adolf Hitler, the leader of the Nazi Party. I have been watching him and looking into his background. He was born in 1889 in Austria. Until 1914, he lived a wasted and directionless life. When the war started, he was an impoverished street tramp in Munich. He was, by choice, a frontline soldier throughout the war. He was awarded the Iron Cross First Class, and that's no trivial achievement; I will give him that.

'Hitler knows what a single person can do. He wrote about it in his book *Mein Kampf*, where he says, "From millions of men … one man must step forward …" We should not doubt for a moment that the one man he has in mind is himself. And how has he done this? No doubt his impressive skill as a highly persuasive speaker has been helpful. He has appealed to the credulous and the gullible by presenting a corrosive mixture of nationalism, racism, anti-Semitism, and simple solutions to complex problems.'

The second dinner course arrives. Once again, Monsieur Buteau explains what a carefully crafted delight awaits the two discriminating diners.

'Once again, *mes amis*, I know what you are sinking. Thees ees a salad of coarsely chopped iceberg lettuce with a vinegar-and-oil dressing. But what you do not see ees the attention to the detail of cutting the lettuce.

　　　　R. WILLIAM PLUME

If the lettuce is cut too coarsely, the oil and salt dominate in the flavour. If the lettuce is cut too finely, the vinegar and the pepper dominate the flavour. When the cutting is done exactly right, the flavour is something to die for.'

Reinhard replaces his serviette on his lap. 'Well, I for one, Monsieur Buteau, am just dying to eat it.' Buteau retires.

'Make no mistake, Reinhard, Hitler isn't just a superb orator with a charismatic presence. He is nobody's fool and is very shrewd. People have underestimated him repeatedly, and he has outsmarted them, outmanoeuvred them again and again.

'The Nazi Party is a rigid hierarchy: rank-and-file members at the bottom and the Party leader, Hitler himself, at the top. This hierarchy, a form of personal dictatorship, has a name. It's called the Führerprinzip, the leader principle, and it is a core tenet of Nazi ideology. It is the glue that holds the Nazi Party together and the basis of executive authority underpinning its structure and governance. It dictates that the will of Adolf Hitler is supreme and should be followed without question or dissent. It means every member, every function, and every group is subordinated to a single leader, the Führer. Leaders have unfettered dictatorial power over subordinates, and unhesitating obedience is required from subordinates.

'This rigid pyramid structure looks like a miracle of administrative clarity, but in practice it is … Well, it has its drawbacks. There are very attractive benefits for individuals in leadership positions, and the competition for titles is brutal. And – this is important – the rivalry is encouraged. Conflict is seen as a kind of Darwinian sorting mechanism which, in Nazi ideology, ensures the strongest, the best, and the most capable rise through the ranks. In practice, Party members have been quick to understand that deceit and cunning are the surest path to promotion. That "miracle of administrative clarity" is a deadly jungle.

'I am concerned about the people Hitler has gathered around himself, their anger and resentment, the bigotry, the anti-Semitism, and the Aryan master race garbage. Were you aware, Reinhard, that to be a member of the Nazi Party, you must be Aryan? Herr Streicher is now very worried that he no longer qualifies. And we can assume that Himmler will have his own doubts about Streicher.'

The third dinner course arrives. Both diners expect a mismatch between the offering and Monsieur Buteau's pretensions.

Buteau stands momentarily silent. He breathes deeply. Clears his throat. Adjusts his cravat. 'I know. I do. Thees looks like a small piece of lamb over which has been dribbled a small … modest? tiny? amount of jus. But you will see that ze new and breathtaking *chef de cuisine* thinks of food as art. For your dining pleasure, he has dribbled a few droplets of jus on the plate and then swept it out into a graceful *arc de jus. Mes amies*, enjoy your meal.' Buteau departs.

Thomas points to the artistic flourish and looks across the table. Reinhard – who has already finished the third course – looks as if to say, *What? You want me to explain that?*

He reinitiates the conversation. 'Why are you telling me this, Thomas?'

'Think for a moment about what has infected Streicher. Imagine what it's like to be him now. He was a strutting, swaggering, big-mouth bully, full of his own superiority. Now he's filled with self-doubt and anxiety, petrified that someone will discover his nasty little secret, as we now know they have. Even if I went to his office tomorrow and told him the document was a forgery, he is irredeemably compromised. Eventually, his colleagues, the Nazis, not forgetting Himmler, will realise that Streicher has lost his edge.

'Watching this transformation happen in Streicher made me think: why not do it again? Infect another Streicher in the same way. There's an unlimited number to choose from. Make the next one think he has some Romani blood or a congenital mental deficiency or some other compromising non-Aryan defect – a too-swarthy visage, brown eyes, skin that's just a little too dark – and that will trigger the same anxieties and doubts.'

Momentarily Thomas stops, collecting his next thoughts. 'If this game were just aimed at finding credulous people and dosing them with insecurities, it would be a little sad. But imagine that the doubts begin to spread from an infected person to his workmates or his beer-drinking friends. Or perhaps those people are infected with suspicions about him in hush-hush beer hall conversations. Perhaps the man working next to him starts to wonder why he's behaving so strangely. Or perhaps he just *thinks* the behaviour is different and guesses at the reason.

'It doesn't matter whether the guess is right or wrong, but he starts spreading it around. He tells the shop steward. Then another person is infected, and the process starts again. It spreads by whispers and lies from person to person, working their way through the Nazi hierarchy root and branch until the suspicions and doubts start to overlap each other.

'How long do you think it might take before the process becomes self-reinforcing, and they start dosing each other with insecurities? The ambitious and cunning will see the advantage of smearing the reputations of people they are competing against for positions of rank. Doubts and fears, misgivings and apprehension will reach into every dark corner of the Nazi Party, and the rot will spread throughout the hierarchy.'

The fourth and final dinner course arrives. It is a demitasse of tepid green tea.

Monsieur Buteau puts the cups and saucers on the table. He looks from Thomas to Reinhard and again to the tea.

'I know what you are sinking. Thees ees a silly little cup of nonsense, and you are right. I offer you my apologies for the dinner. There will be no charge, gentlemen. I hope you will forgive me and come again.'

Buteau bows and retires.

Thomas looks at Reinhard. '*Chef de cuisine* a little too Parisian, perhaps?'

Reinhard rises, catches Buteau. 'Monsieur Buteau, thank you for your consideration. I assure you, we will be back.'

A disconsolate Buteau nods and continues towards the kitchen.

Reinhard returns to the table. 'Where were we?'

'We were destroying the Nazi Party,' says Thomas. 'Shall I continue?'

Reinhard rests an elbow on the table. 'I'm all ears.'

'People will start looking in every direction. They will begin to see glaring disloyalties, substandard personal qualities, incompetence, lack of dedication, deliberate interference, incomplete adherence to the Führerprinzip, failure to work towards the Führer's goals, and, crucially, failure to meet the Aryan Ideal. Question marks will begin to appear above colleagues and then above their superiors. The doubts will percolate up until, in the end, the Führer himself will be as suspect as any other party member.

'Everyone is suspicious of everyone else while not knowing what is suspected or known of them. Once the rot has set in, there will be no recovery, no way to stop it. Ultimately, it must all collapse. The emptiness and monstrous evilness of it must end with its own ruin. Think of it as a Roman colosseum where the lions are attacking each other while the Christians stand aside and watch.'

'That's a very elegant and devious idea, Thomas. When I think about the situation with our friend Julius Streicher, he created a clear problem by threatening me. You were perceptive enough to realise that Streicher's extreme anti-Semitism, together with his ambition, created the solution. Now you're thinking of applying something similar to millions of people. But how do you propose to bring it about?'

'I shall join the lions in the Colosseum.'

SELF-DOUBT EATS AT STREICHER

Streicher admits to himself that his behaviour in Augsburg has made matters worse. In a rare moment of self-awareness, he recognises that the priests involved had no difficulty discerning how distressed he was. *Did they understand why? One of them knew what I was thinking. Did*

R. WILLIAM PLUME

they look closely enough to see the reason why I was agitated? Did they look at the birth certificate after they threw me out? Did they tell the bishop? Did they tell anyone else?

If it got around that he had made such a scene over his mother's birth certificate, maybe someone else would go have a look. *That wouldn't be good. Maybe I could send someone down there to remove the page. But now they will be wary of anyone asking to look at her birth certificate. I must be more careful.*

He imagines a conversation that he might have with Himmler. *I must think about how I would answer a question about my mother and how I would behave.*

'Herr Streicher, I have received some very disturbing information about your mother.'

'Oh?' Streicher says aloud and casually. *Leave it at that. Don't give him anywhere to go from there.* But even as he says this single word, he notes the delivery, as if standing aside watching himself, and he wonders if it conveys the right shade of innocent puzzlement.

Deciding that perhaps it doesn't, he tries again.

'Oh?' he says again, and this time he imagines himself so involved in something – the papers on his desk or some such thing – that he has a plausible reason for not turning his attention immediately and entirely in Himmler's direction. Perhaps that would cover any suggestion that the articulation conveyed more information than the single word might suggest. *But Himmler is alert to every trick. He's wily that way. If I don't pull it off, he may see it as being disrespectful, insulting even, and that will just make him more suspicious. Besides, he's made it plain that he doesn't have much time for me. Seems so anyway …*

Now starting to feel more than a little exposed, Streicher tries a third time.

'Oh?' he says, smiling to emphasise how honoured he is at Himmler's visit. Streicher adds a robust version of the mandatory Nazi salute. But smiling and saluting do not go together – it makes the salute look insolent. *That will make him sceptical right at the start.*

Every way he devises to deliver this single, innocent, harmless word seems suspect in some way. He tries different words, but with the same result. He cannot move beyond the bland ritual of a simple greeting without feeling that he is announcing his guilt in the subtleties of his behaviour.

Now he chides himself. *Don't be such a fucking idiot! Don't forget; I know the secret, but Himmler doesn't!* But that isn't the least bit reassuring. If Himmler ever does become aware of the birth certificate, he will conclude that Streicher has misrepresented himself and that he is – despite his virulent anti-Semitism and his seeming hyper-energetic support of the Nazi Party – dragging it into disrepute. And presented with that, what could he do beyond insisting that he supports the Party wholeheartedly and that the birth certificate must be a forgery?

But Streicher knows from his own experience of the document what Himmler's response will be: 'I'm told, Herr Streicher, that if it's a forgery, it is a sovereign masterpiece of the forger's art, and I will be guided in my thinking by the content of that document until you can convincingly demonstrate it to be false. Besides, why would *anyone* go to all the trouble of forging your mother's birth certificate?'

I have nothing that will demonstrate it's a forgery. But if he sees it, I'm in shitter's ditch. But he doesn't know, so I'm worrying about nothing. But I still must be sure that I don't give him a reason to put a man on the case.

For now, he will make it clear where his loyalties lie. *And I'll point to that if necessary.* With the dreadful stain of his mother's provenance driving him, Streicher's version of anti-Semitism becomes ever more virulent. After a time, he begins to feel satisfied that he has laid down a convincing smokescreen. But even so, he now realises that he isn't all that sure what his own normal behaviour is. Trying to behave normally in a deliberate way is challenging, and he misses the mark. The change, though subtle, is apparent. He becomes even more aggressive and difficult.

     R. WILLIAM PLUME

'What the hell is going on with Streicher?' becomes a common question among his associates.

THE BRAIDED-WIRE FACTORY

The Nazi Party has grown. Its influence has broadened.

Support for Nazi ideology begins to extend beyond the Party itself. Some employers take it upon themselves to make Nazi Party membership a condition of employment.

Thomas presents himself at the Munich Employment Office. He insists on placement in a Nazi-only organisation. A braided-wire factory hires him.

On his first day, Thomas joins a group of workmen gathering at the factory gate. They are waiting for the shift change. A whistle blows, the gates open, and the men begin ambling through the gate and into the factory. They clock in, go to their stations, and take over from the shift replaced.

Thomas and the other new employees have gathered aside. A man carrying a clipboard identifies himself as the foreman. He calls out names and gives each new employee a card for the time clock.

'This factory makes braided wire,' he says. 'You must understand how important it is to do your work properly. The wires and cables we manufacture are used for many things: communications, aircraft engines, and manufacturing equipment. This factory is the only source of braided wire in Southern Germany, so it is vital that you don't make mistakes. Understood?'

Some of the men look around, at the floor, at each other, at the door behind them, at nothing in particular, but not at the foreman.

'Through that door,' he says, pointing, 'is the main factory floor. There are ten braiding machines. All of you are operator assistants. Each of you will be assigned to a machine operator. In this factory, pay and promotions are directly linked to production.'

Produce and prosper, thinks Thomas. *I'll remember that.*

'Here's how it works. Each braiding machine takes five strands of copper wire from five supply reels. It braids the five strands into a single strand of braided wire that winds onto an output reel. These machines run twenty-four hours per day, seven days per week. Beside each machine there's a rack that has places for six supply reels –'

One of the new men, tall and muscular, interjects, 'You said they was five wires –'

'I did say that. Just hang on, I'll exp—'

'It's only you sez they's five wires and six reel things, I don't –'

'Do you want this job or not?'

'Yeah …'

'Then be quiet and listen. Understood?'

'But –'

'No buts! Just listen!'

Thomas, who is standing next to the inquisitive man, puts a hand on his arm and whispers, 'Stay near me.'

The man looks cautiously at Thomas but nods.

The foreman completes his explanation. 'The machine operator will instruct you in everything you need to know. Now follow me.'

As the new men are moving to the factory floor, Thomas turns to the man. 'What is your name?'

'Bruno Eisen.'

'I'm Thomas Schroeder.'

The ten braiding machines are arranged in two rows of five, set cheek by jowl. Thomas, first through the door, is assigned to the first machine in the first row, and Bruno is assigned to the adjacent machine.

Thomas approaches the operator of the machine.

As acknowledgement, the operator glares. 'I'll make this simple. This machine is number one. I'm operator number one. I am your supervisor. You work for me and only for me. You do exactly what I tell

　　　R. WILLIAM PLUME

you, no questions asked. Just do your job and keep your mouth shut. Understood?'

He doesn't wait for an answer.

'This machine runs non-stop from the time our shift starts until I hand over to the next shift. You screw up, the machine stops, you're out the door, and your pay is docked to repay me for the loss of production. Your job is to keep me supplied with reels of wire.'

He points. 'They're kept in the supply room.'

'I need a new supply reel every six minutes. When one of these reels is running out, there must be a full one on the rack ready to take its place. I will be needing another one soon. Get one now.'

Thomas goes to the supply room and finds stacked reels of copper wire. He puts a reel onto a dolly and returns to his machine.

'Okay, here's how this works. I'm going to explain this just once, so listen up. This rack has spindles for six reels of wire. Five of these reels are being fed into the machine. The sixth reel will be added into the process when one of the other five runs out. When you get back from the supply room with a new reel, you put it on the vacant spindle. DO NOT forget to put the locking pin in place. If you forget it, sooner or later the reel will come off the spindle, and when it does, it makes a helluva mess. The machine has to be shut down, and my production pay goes out the window. So I'm tellin' ya, no fuck-ups, or you're a goner, and I *will* have a piece of you before you get to the street. Got it?'

Thomas nods.

In the days that follow, Thomas crosses paths with Bruno occasionally. They acknowledge each other but say nothing. On one of these occasions, Thomas whispers, 'See me outside after shift.'

Thomas is waiting when Bruno leaves the factory.

'You wanted to see me?' Bruno says.

'I'm interested to know if the job is working for you.'

'Why? Why do you want to know?'

'I have been watching the way you work. You are paying attention all the time. You always have a new reel ready for your operator. You are doing the job like you don't want to lose it even though you nearly threw it away on your first day.'

'I don't want to lose it. I cannot lose this job. On the first day I was trying to make sure I didn't do something wrong.'

'What did you do before you started here?'

'Security officer.'

'And before that?'

'Western Front. My train will be here soon. I have to go.'

———

Days later, Thomas leaves his machine to get another reel. A few seconds later, Bruno arrives at the supply room.

Thomas places a reel on his dolly and begins the return trip. As he is passing through the doorway a third man appears and the two dollies collide.

Thomas' reel is knocked off the dolly and it begins rolling across the factory floor. Thomas puts the dolly aside and pursues the out-of-control reel.

Bruno, now emerging from the supply room, sees the developing commotion and steers around it. The evasive action brings him close to machine number one.

Operator one sees that Thomas cannot retrieve the reel and be back in time to maintain production uninterrupted. He steps away from the controls and stands in front of Bruno. He lifts the reel from Bruno's dolly and places it on the vacant spindle of his machine.

'Hey! You can't do that!' Bruno yells.

'Try and stop me, arsehole!'

Bruno's machine is now moments away from being forced to shut down for lack of a fresh reel.

Thomas has recovered the errant reel, picked it up, and seeing that it is now needed at machine number two, moves in that direction. Operator two runs to Thomas, grabs the reel from his hands and returns to his machine. He slams the reel onto the vacant spindle. He feeds the new wire into the machine seconds before the fifth reel is exhausted.

He is relieved. His production figures are intact.

But in his haste, he has forgotten the locking pin.

Over the machine noise, he yells at operator one, 'Bastard! I'll be seeing you after –'

The threat is never finished nor later carried out.

A weighty reel of copper wire, spinning rapidly, flies from the unlocked spindle. It strikes operator number two on his hip. Extending his hand to regain his balance, he entangles his forearm in the wires moving into the machine.

The wires cut deeply into the flesh of his forearm. Bleeding profusely, he slips on his own blood and falls, dragging down the now-broken wires. He strikes his head on the bare concrete floor.

Precious few moments pass. His bleeding stops.

The remaining four reels, still spinning rapidly, now disconnect from the machine and fling wire into the room. Someone pushes the emergency shutdown button. A klaxon sounds. All ten machines begin a controlled shutdown.

The foreman barges into the room, yelling, 'What the hell is going on here?'

Seeing operator two lying in a pool of blood, he hastens to him. Herr Foreman checks the pulse and stands. 'He's dead.'

He turns to the man closest to him and says, 'Go tell the shift manager we need the police and an ambulance.'

'No loss,' says operator one. 'Useless operator. Forgot the fucking locking pin. Now, my production pay is flying out the window.'

'Who knows what happened?'

Silence.

'Does anyone know *where* this started?'

Silence.

'Speak!' he shouts.

Everyone is dazed. One of the operators offers, 'I don't know how or where it started. All I can tell you is one minute everything was working fine, and then it was complete chaos. Wire everywhere. And so quickly.'

There are some nods and murmurs of agreement.

'Alright! Now listen carefully! All of you! You will *not* speak of this incident to *anyone*. Understood? Operators, get this mess cleared up.'

The foreman turns to Bruno. 'You are terminated effective immediately. Get your things and leave.'

Thomas and Bruno leave the building together. Bruno, who is at the point of weeping, turns to Thomas and says, 'What am I going to do now? That's the first job I've been able to get in nearly two years. Now what? Family starves for another two years?'

Thomas removes a pencil and a piece of paper from his shirt pocket and hands them to Bruno.

'Write down your address.'

Bruno takes the paper and pencil, looks at them and, making a small, disheartened shrug, hands both back to Thomas. 'I'm not too good at writing, Herr Schroeder. You write it for me, please?'

Bruno dictates. Thomas writes.

But Bruno's mind is elsewhere. 'Two children and another on the way. Christ in heaven! What do I do now, Herr Schroeder?'

'I will contact you, Herr Eisen. Soon.'

They shake hands as Eisen's train arrives.

———

Thomas contacts Reinhard to arrange a conversation over coffee at Frau Gretel's.

At their meeting, Thomas hands Reinhard the piece of paper with Bruno's name and address. 'Please give this man a job at THR Schroeder Printing Works.'

Thomas knocks at the door of First Impressions Ltd and lets himself in.

'Blow me down, mate, if it ain't Mr Smooth again. This is gettin' to be a regular thing with you, me ol' cobber.'

'Mr Brewster, how nice to see you again.'

'You've come all the way to the Hamlets because you need some more forged documentation? I hope so. You always ask for the most interesting things.'

Thomas smiles. 'As it happens, yes, I do have another job for you.'

'Kneecapping another Nazi, are ya?'

'It's a little more subtle than that, but that's the right idea. I need a full set of identity papers as Thomas H. R. Schroeder, including a passport and a Nazi Party membership card. The passport must show my birthday as the twentieth of April 1876, and the membership card must show that I joined the Party on the twentieth of April 1921. I also need membership cards and identity papers that I can use when I don't want to be me, that is, when I don't want to be Thomas. The other version of me needs, say, three sets of papers that are the same except for the member identification number. They need to have five-digit membership numbers that are pre-November 1923. That means all of them smaller than 21,000. Give them numbers that are hard to memorise on sight. Let's use, oh … Let's use 19,303, 19,503 and 19,703.'

Brewster looks at Thomas' list. 'The numbers. They all start with one nine and end with zero three. Why?'

'Nineteen oh three. That's the year my parents died.'

'Aww, that is so sweet!' says Brewster, miming violin playing.

'Ya know, mate, I understand you gettin' all weepy about yer mum an' all, but goin' all gooey and sentimental here is gonna get you dead. I can't have clients gettin' shot up when they's using my work. Word gets around, and I'm finished. Got it?'

Thomas realises he's been too casual about the details of what he's asking Brewster to do. He tries to acknowledge Brewster's concern, but Brewster raises his hands and rolls on.

'You don't seem to understand that Nazi Party membership cards are kinda like a badge of honour. I know this because I know guys in the engravers' brotherhood in Berlin who've reconstructed Party membership cards for people who have lost or somehow destroyed their cards. And get this! The members who have been around for a while can look at your card – just your card with the membership number, the enlistment date, and the Party official who signed it – and get a pretty good idea where you fit in the scheme of things. You waltz in there with a card that has a number plucked out of the air or a signature they don't recognise, and the next thing you know, you're missing some teeth. So, we won't be guessing around on the details.

'I'll tell you what we need. We need the actual membership list, names, numbers, birth and death dates. Do you have that? Don't answer. Course you don't. Do you know someone who can get that information for you?'

'Yes, I think so.'

'Then go get it. When you've got it, come back and we'll start over.'

Thomas returns to Munich and meets with Reinhard. Reinhard gets in touch with his mole in the SS. The SS man, citing a confidential internal investigation, secures a complete list of all Party members who signed up before the November Putsch. Thomas gathers up the list and returns to First Impressions in London.

'Now this is more like it,' says Brewster and sets to work.

———

'Alright, my friend, here's how this is gonna work. I've made up a set of papers for you, for Thomas Schroeder, like you asked for. The membership number I've used for you is a number that was never assigned to anyone. In a long list of numbers like they have, there are

     R. WILLIAM PLUME

always mistakes, omissions, duplications. The number I've given you was an omission. If someone confronts you about it, you say, "Yes, I'm aware that it's an omission. I'm trying to get it sorted out with the Party clerks." Don't forget that. I have also made up ten – I know you asked for three, but you won't get far with three – sets of identity papers that you can use when you want to be someone other than who you really are. Really aren't, I s'pose … Never mind. When you get back to Germany with these things, yer on yer own, so pay attention. Each set has the name and the number of a person who is alive and who matches you more or less in age. All of 'em different, you understand?

'Now get this and get it straight: you only use each of these papers once! If someone gets suspicious and takes a number and checks, they will go off and find the real person who goes with that number. Then they will know the papers you showed 'em are a forgery. They will start looking for you, your card, and your papers. If you weren't listening before, pay attention now: you never, *ever* present these documents twice. Here's the rule: you present it, you destroy it. Are you gettin' all this? You better, because your life might depend on it.'

CHAPTER 12

The French Connection

HITLER WELCOMES RÖHM BACK TO GERMANY

Ernst Röhm and Adolf Hitler are well matched. Too well matched. Both men have towering ambitions. Hitler's are political. Röhm's are martial.

The Sturmabteilung, the formidable Storm Troopers, is Röhm's work, a work in progress as the original paramilitary arm of the Nazi Party. Röhm's objective, once Hitler has secured the role of Chancellor, is to subsume the entire Reichswehr into the Sturmabteilung, the SA, with himself, Röhm, in command.

But Hitler's path to the Chancellery is complicated by Röhm's aspirations. The difficulty is with the Reichswehr, and it starts right at the top. Field Marshal Paul von Hindenburg has made it crystal clear that Röhm's plan will not be tolerated. Full stop. No further discussion is required.

To remove the problem, Hitler removes Röhm. Röhm chooses Bolivia for his exile, leaving Hitler, the Sturmabteilung, and Germany to their own devices.

In September 1930, as a consequence of the Stennes Revolt in Berlin, Hitler assumed supreme command of the SA as its new Oberster SA-Führer.

———

But events have turned full circle. Hitler finds the additional challenges that come with active leadership of the SA are too distracting. He acknowledges that he needs his old friend back to reorganise the SA. He places an all-is-forgiven phone call to Bolivia, asking Röhm to return to serve as the SA's Stabschef, its chief of staff. Röhm accepts the offer and returns to the fold in November 1930.

On 5 January 1931, Röhm finds himself standing in a meeting room among a large group of uniformed men. They are waiting for the Führer, and Hitler always keeps an audience waiting.

A door opens. Hitler enters the room.

Everyone snaps to attention. He strides to the lectern at the front of the room. He grasps the lectern with his hands. The gesture triggers a perfectly synchronised Nazi salute and a robust 'Heil Hitler!'

The men now relax but remain standing. Hitler speaks. 'It is now my great pleasure to welcome back to Germany one of the Fatherland's most capable sons. I speak here of none other than Herr Ernst Röhm. Herr Röhm, please come forward.'

Röhm marches forward – strictly orthogonally – until he is standing in front of the Führer, facing him directly. He comes to attention, snaps his heels together, and gives the mandatory Nazi salute. 'Heil Hitler!' Hitler returns the salute and indicates to Röhm that he should stand beside him, on the right, and face the group.

'As you all know, Herr Röhm has had a distinguished military career, serving at the Front during the war, where he was awarded the Iron Cross First Class. The association of Herr Röhm and myself goes back to the earliest days of the Party. Indeed, our association goes back to the days of the German Workers' Party. In recent times Herr Röhm has been in Bolivia, assisting their government in the development of their army.

'As I'm sure you are all aware, Herr Röhm was responsible for the expansion of the Sturmabteilung, the military arm of our glorious Nazi Party, and it is for this reason, Herr Röhm, that you are here today. At my request, Herr Röhm has come back to the Fatherland to take command of the SA.'

There is the patter of applause. Hitler and Röhm turn to face each other. Hitler's adjutant comes forward carrying a tasselled satin cushion on which are the chief of staff lapel insignia. Hitler pins both insignia to Röhm's lapels, and both men turn back to face the group.

'Please join me in congratulating Herr Röhm on his past sterling efforts and on his elevation to the rank of Stabschef, Sturmabteilung!'

As the group claps, Hitler turns back towards Röhm and shakes his hand. Still holding Röhm's hand, Hitler leans forward and says, 'Welcome back, my old friend. I'm expecting great things from you.'

'I have great things in mind, mein Führer.'

Röhm steps back from Hitler and comes to attention. This signals to the group that the customary salute to Hitler now follows.

'Heil Hitler!' Synchronised to perfection.

THOMAS ALERTS REINHARD

Reinhard waits until Thomas is seated with his coffee. 'Well then, my friend, what's on your mind?'

'Ernst Röhm.'

'Why him?'

'Did you know, Reinhard, that he's back from Bolivia and now in charge of the SA? Were you also aware that the Nazi Party is moving its headquarters to Brown House on Briennerstrasse?'

'I'm aware of both, and I'd be interested to know why you are raising both in the same breath.'

'Röhm's been given an office in Brown House. At the moment, things are very chaotic in and around the premises because it's being remodelled and there's the continuous, noisy busyness of moving people and equipment here and there. Amid all that, Röhm, Hitler's current favourite, has reappeared, and everyone wants to make sure they connect with him. His appointments calendar is full.'

Reinhard nods his understanding.

'Because of all the turmoil,' Thomas continues, 'they're not being too careful about who they allow in to see him. I have managed to arrange a meeting with him. He won't recognise me as a senior party official, so it is certain that he will ask for my identity papers. This is the first of the ten Nazi Party membership cards that Brewster made for me.' Thomas places the material in front of Reinhard.

'This is the card that I will show Röhm. After the meeting, I will burn it. Note the name, "Krause", and the membership number, 13769. If Röhm's suspicions are prodded, he may also take note of the number and follow up on it. Your SS man needs to be on the alert for this.'

THOMAS MEETS RÖHM

Amid the feverish remodelling activity, Röhm has occupied his office before the dust has settled. It is walnut-panelled and decorated with the orthodox symbols of Nazi culture and ideology. The desk is mahogany, deeply and intricately carved in a Baroque style.

It is a sign of Hitler's favour that Röhm's office overlooks Königsplatz.

'Herr Krause is here to see you,' says Röhm's adjutant, holding open the door and gesturing with his other hand that Thomas should enter the office.

The adjutant leaves and closes the door.

'Good morning, Herr Krause. Please, sit down.'

'Thank you, Herr Röhm. I'm here today to speak with you concerning the Stennes Revolt.'

'Ah, Herr Stennes, the SA leader in Berlin. I know him well. His behaviour in recent months is also well known to me. But speaking bluntly, Herr Krause, you, on the other hand, are not known to me, and until I know more about you and the reasons for your presence here, this conversation will go no further. Let's begin with a look at your identity papers.'

'Of course,' Thomas says as he reaches for his breast pocket. He withdraws the wallet that holds all the expected documents. It is bound in soft red leather with the sword, oak leaves and swastika emblem, the Nazi Hakenkreuz, embossed in gold on the cover.

As he extends the hand holding the wallet towards Röhm, Thomas is acutely aware of Brewster explaining the subtleties of identity papers. Credible information isn't just what the ink presents. It is also the shape and the feel of the document. The issue date marks this membership card as ten years old. Has it been in his wallet for ten years? Is it slightly frayed? Rounded at the corners? Soft and pliable? Ripped? Coffee stained? Or is it crisp and stiff? Weighty? Has the passport been used? Has the passport holder travelled? Where? When?

Brewster knows that while the eye is scanning the data, the mind is assessing all these other seemingly insignificant details. Brewster's genius is that he understands the crucial distinction between getting the ink in the right place and getting credible information in the right place. He has, once again, done a masterful job of putting exactly the right information in exactly the right place.

And Röhm, too, did just as Brewster expected. His eyes looked at the ink while his mind was assessing the other information written *in* the paper.

Röhm flicks through the passport, looks at the photo, then at Thomas, then at the photo again. Satisfied with the passport, he turns his attention to Thomas' Nazi Party membership card.

'Alter Kämpfer, Old Fighter, eh? Signed up in April 1921. Herr Krause, I've been a member of the Party a long time, since before it was the Nazi Party, and I've seen a lot of Party members since 1919, but I have never seen you before. Now you turn up in my office wanting to talk about the Stennes Revolt, and on whose behalf I don't yet know.'

'Herr Röhm, I'm sure you remember as well as I do that the years after the war were very chaotic. Every week, two new political parties would appear and three would disappear. They were difficult times for

R. WILLIAM PLUME

everyone. I am not surprised that you don't remember me. My main concern in those days was my next meal.'

Röhm leans over his desk. 'Were you in Munich on 9 November 1923?'

'The day of the Beer Hall Putsch? Yes, I was there. I was among the two thousand who marched to Feldherrnhalle that morning. I will guess that you didn't see me there because you were at the front, looking forward, with Herren Ludendorff and Hitler and the other Kampfbund leaders. I was somewhat further back.'

Röhm makes a note of Krause's membership number on a slip of paper and hands the documents back to Thomas. 'Alright. I'll accept your credentials, Herr Krause. I'm sure you will acknowledge that a man in my position cannot be too careful.'

'Thank you, and I appreciate your candour, Herr Röhm.' Thomas is relieved. The forgeries squared up well enough for Herr Krause to be judged as valid.

'Let's get on with it then, Herr Krause. What's on your mind?'

'First, with respect to the Stennes incident, I should say that I am here on behalf of the uppermost echelon of the Nazi Party. Second, although the methods that Herr Stennes used to make his point are, shall we say, unfortunate, the content of his concern is accepted as having some validity, and that has caused some anxiety at the top table.'

Röhm's mind is bristling with suspicion. *This guy has arrived, to all intents and purposes, unannounced, claiming to represent the uppermost echelon of the Party, if you please. If he's not on the level, he's got some serious brass cajones …*

Röhm knows how the Nazi Party works. He knows that rank outranks courtesy. Never mind Röhm's long history in the Party; his conduct has been controversial. Yes, he has been summoned back into the Party by the Führer himself, and that gives him some leeway, but he is on probation, and he knows it.

Is it possible that this guy has been sent here by Himmler to assess whether

I have left my Nazi Party loyalty in Bolivia? Like it or not, I'm going to have to tread carefully with this … What's his name? … Krause?

'Please be more specific, Herr Krause.'

'Since we are speaking bluntly, I will say that the difficulty reduces to the unsoldierly and unprofessional behaviour which seems to be too common in the SA. Being more specific, I mean the heavy drinking, the pointless brawling, and – how shall I put this delicately? – the widespread and unsavoury intimate behaviour that is seen as inconsistent with the Aryan Ideal –'

Röhm aggressively interrupts. 'There's no need for delicacy, Herr Krause. I've never made a secret of my preference for males when it comes to sex, nor have I disguised that preference in any way. The Führer himself is aware of my inclinations, and he cares not one whit provided he gets the results he needs from the SA.'

'Ah, well, there is the problem in a nutshell, Herr Röhm. It is not clear that the SA can be relied upon to deliver what is required of it. The SA is seen to lack direction. Because of that, the great fear is that the SA will begin to break up. It is for this reason that the Stennes Revolt has caused so much concern.'

'I see,' says Röhm, underscoring each word with a knuckle rap.

'It is understood that you have inherited this problem, so the finger of blame is not yet pointing in your direction. Because you have been in this role only a few weeks, now is seen as the proper time for the SA, under your able leadership, to make the adjustments necessary. To come straight to the point, you must root out the Separatists and impose a clear unity of purpose on the membership.'

Röhm swivels around in his chair and stands with his back to Thomas. He gazes down into Königsplatz, noticing a man and a young boy. The boy is struggling to ride a bicycle. When Röhm realises the boy is a distraction, he turns and sits down.

He slaps an open hand down on the desk. 'Consider it done.'

Röhm now swivels his chair to the left as a prelude to standing and bringing the meeting to a close. 'Please convey to the leadership that I have the matter in hand and that I will be issuing a full report – including my plans – before the end of the month. I thank you for bringing this matter to my attention, but now, unless you have other issues that require my attention, I must ask that we draw this meeting to a close.'

As he delivers these final remarks, Röhm puts his right hand on the desk and leans forward, eyes wide and fixed on Thomas. His unmistakable unspoken directive is that Thomas is to initiate the customary pleasantries that will bring the meeting to a close.

Thomas is at the point of discharging this nicety of etiquette when some crafty invagination of his mind fabricates another issue that will require Röhm's attention.

'There *is* one other thing, Herr Röhm.'

Röhm is a little surprised, but he restrains his irritation. 'Which is?'

'There are rumours – and they are only rumours at the moment – that you have been approached, through intermediaries, by the French government. The substance of these approaches, according to the rumours, is an offer by the government of France to pay you a substantial sum of money to bring about the downfall of our Führer.'

Röhm is dazed. *Holy Mother of God!* The suggestion that Röhm is participating in something as preposterous as what Thomas has suggested knocks him to the back of his chair. He cannot disguise his horrified astonishment.

Powerful forces are arrayed against me. His mind races. *Perhaps this Krause guy is the vanguard? Sent here to test the water? Even if he is a nobody who has somehow managed to squirm his way in here, anything might happen. He cannot be ignored nor lightly shoved aside. I must choose my words carefully. He can take whatever I say to heaven knows where. And if he is who he says he is … God in heaven! This is a very serious problem!*

Thomas observes the discomfiture. 'I'm certain that these speculations are a malicious fiction, but not everyone is so sure –'

Röhm interrupts. '*I* can assure you, Herr Krause, there is no truth whatsoever to these ridiculous allegations! I am shocked to hear that someone, somewhere, thinks I would do such a thing.'

'I've no doubt that is true, Herr Röhm. But you would be wise to address this issue in your report.'

'You may be sure that I will.'

Röhm stands, strides to the door and opens it. With a sweep of his hand, he orders Thomas out of his office.

Röhm flatly orders his adjutant, 'Get in touch with the SS. Krause's member number is 13769, and his card was signed by Strasser. Get the membership list and find out if he is who he says he is.'

———

'Where did this request come from?'

'From Herr Stabschef SA, Herr Röhm.'

'He has asked the SS to check the validity of a Party membership name and number?'

'Yes, sir. The number and the name match the information of a member who is a blacksmith at the Frankfurt railway yards. We have confirmed that the Frankfurt card is valid and genuine.'

'So, the card presented to Herr Röhm is a fake?'

'Yes, sir.'

'No possibility of a misprint producing two cards with identical numbers?'

'No, sir.'

'Ordinarily, you would report this information directly back to Herr Röhm, but you are raising it with me. Why?'

'Because …'

'Don't be coy. Because?'

'Because Herr Röhm has only recently been welcomed back into the Nazi fold after having been dismissed by the Führer. If we tell Röhm that the card is fake, he will ignore the meeting, and no information will emerge.'

'And if we tell him that the card is valid?'

'We don't know what was discussed at the meeting, but a way to possibly find out is to tell Röhm that his visitor is the genuine Krause. A report of some kind is guaranteed to turn up with SS Document Detachment. Who knows how that might be useful to Herr Himmler?'

'But we know that Krause is a fraud. How useful can the information be?'

'We won't know unless we provide an opportunity.'

'Herr Stabschef, I have the information that you requested concerning Herr Krause.'

The adjutant places the list in front of Röhm, opened to the appropriate page. He points to the entry for member number 13769.

Röhm looks at the name.

'That's the right name – Krause. He's on the level?'

'Yes, sir. I've been assured by the SS that Herr Krause is who he appears to be.'

'So be it. We have work to do. Get the team together.'

'Sir!'

REPORT ASSESSOR ZEIGLER

The SS is Hitler's Praetorian Guard, and the role of the SS Document Detachment is to vet intra-Party communications, sniffing out conspiracies against the Führer. The Detachment occupies the basement of Brown House.

Though it is still early morning, the daily flow of documents has already been sorted and distributed to various assessors. Reports, proposals, and discussion papers go to Report Assessor Zeigler.

Zeigler is young, hardworking and ambitious. He is blessed with a sharp eye for detail. When he finds something interesting, he writes down his comments and recommendations and inserts them into the document at the appropriate place. The document then goes to his supervisor, Herr Goertzen, by way of the office mail system.

Goertzen has the responsibility of deciding whether the 'something interesting' should be brought to the attention of Heinrich Himmler, Reichsleiter SS. Himmler relies on Goertzen to weed out everything but those items that genuinely require Himmler's personal attention.

When Goertzen appears in Himmler's office with a 'something interesting', Himmler always takes a sharp interest. A high-level 'something interesting' will absorb Himmler's finicky attention until the underside of every pebble has been examined.

Ernst Röhm, Stabschef SA, has produced a report detailing his plans for unifying the SA. Röhm has also addressed the issue of his rumoured connection with the French government. He stoutly denies any such impropriety and challenges anyone to produce evidence that any such association exists. It is a robust self-defence.

When Zeigler reads it, he comes to full alertness. *This is dynamite! This is the mother lode!* But he resists the urge to take the document straight to Goertzen. If he overplays his hand, he's putting himself on the line.

He rereads the report. Now, there is a part of Zeigler that wants to bolt from his chair and invade Goertzen's office. That's a caution. He reads Röhm's report a third time to be sure that he hasn't seduced himself into premature conclusions about its intent. Finally, he is satisfied.

For this delicious 'something interesting', he writes neither comments nor recommendations. Neither does he rely on the internal mail system. He draws on his black SS jacket. He slips the knot of his tie back into place. He tucks Röhm's report under his arm and hurries to Goertzen's office.

He knocks and waits until he hears something from inside, which may have been 'Come in'. He bursts into the office wide-eyed, chattering as he advances on Goertzen.

'You must see this now!' he says, slapping Röhm's report on Goertzen's desk, opened to the part dealing with the French connection. 'Read this!' Zeigler orders, banging on the report with his index finger.

Goertzen knows that Zeigler would not be frothing as he is without a good reason. Read it, he does. 'I see,' is Goertzen's understated response. 'That's very interesting.'

'Interesting? *Interesting?* It's sensational! You must take this to Herr Himmler at once!'

'Calm down, Herr Zeigler. I will grant that this is extraordinary, but I must ask, Is there some sort of French conspiracy?'

'Just look at what Herr Röhm says! He says, "I am not involved in this French conspiracy. I never have been. I never will be." He doesn't say there isn't one –'

'Perhaps there isn't.'

'Perhaps there is, and if there is …'

'Perhaps this is nothing more than poor phrasing, inept wording.'

'Perhaps. And if it isn't …'

'Even if there is some kind of French conspiracy, he's made it clear enough that he's not involved.'

'Then Röhm is in the clear. But our job is to find these conspiracies –'

'You needn't tell me what my job is, Herr –'

'My apologies, Herr Goertzen, but if we let this pass and someone else turns up later involved in –'

'Nor do I need to be reminded of the consequences of failure. Do I take it, Herr Zeigler, that your recommendation is that I kick this up the chain of –'

'It certainly is, sir!'

'I note that there is none of your usual complete set of paperwork supporting your recommendation. I'll have to ask you to submit a dated, written, and signed statement to that effect. Include your reasons. Do that and I'll move things along.'

'Berlin Sportpalast, Tuesday, the nineteenth of May,' says Joseph Goebbels. 'That's the place. That's the date when the Führer will speak. We are here to ensure it goes well. Let's get started.'

Goebbels, the event organiser, has convened a meeting of the uppermost echelon of Nazi Party leaders to finalise the security arrangements for the Sportpalast fixture.

Heinrich Himmler, Hermann Göring, Robert Ley, and others are present.

Ernst Röhm, recently appointed as the Stabschef SA, is to outline the security arrangements for the event. Röhm understands the brutal realities of Nazi Party politics. He knows that preparation is the key, and prepare he has. Relaxed and confident, he joins the meeting.

The meeting room is large but is otherwise an ordinary, rectangular space. The tables and chairs are arranged in a U-shape along the walls. Goebbels, responsible for the seating arrangements, has placed himself in the centre of the base of the U. The lectern is at the opposite end of the room. There is ample space on the front wall for diagrams, maps, and so on.

Goebbels calls the meeting to order. The chatter ends, and people take their seats.

Goebbels underscores the importance of tight security for the Führer when he speaks at the Sportpalast, his first speech at that venue for 1931. Then, with hardly a pause for breath, Goebbels turns the meeting over to Röhm.

Röhm walks calmly to the front of the room and begins. A large map of the Sportpalast and environs is displayed on the wall behind him. Röhm has placed SA troops in two concentric rings surrounding the entire building, a huge indoor arena. The more military-minded around the table note the large number of armed troops assigned to the operation.

Every street and pathway approaching the venue will be blocked by placing troop trucks sideways in the streets. Röhm reminds everyone that when it comes to the security of our Führer, one cannot be too careful. Heads begin to nod, and Röhm sees, with some satisfaction, that his plan is being well received. With easy confidence, he turns his attention to the arrangements for inside the building.

As he does so, the door to the meeting room opens. An SS officer slides into the room. He is carrying a single, thickish folder which he takes to Himmler and places on the table in front of him. The officer whispers a few words into Himmler's ear and then leaves.

Disruptions like this are common in Nazi Party meetings. Everything is of the utmost importance all the time. Röhm is aware of the minor disturbance, but he is unconcerned, and he continues despite it.

Himmler, with ill-mannered haste, now dives into the folder. He begins flicking through the document, becoming more agitated with each page. The snapping of pages and the rustling of paper become intrusive.

Röhm looks to Goebbels and, by a tilt of his head in Himmler's direction, asks Goebbels to intervene. Goebbels – perhaps thinking that Himmler's rudeness can't last much longer – responds with a gentle shrug. He suggests, with a pirouette of his hand, that Röhm should carry on.

Himmler, visibly agitated, is oblivious to both Goebbels and Röhm. Now Röhm himself is agitated, and he casts a *please desist* look in Himmler's direction. The only person who does not see this pressing signal is Himmler. Röhm continues speaking, though now somewhat louder.

The ambience of the room acquires an unmistakable electricity that brings everyone fully alert. *What is this little dance between Röhm and Himmler?*

Röhm is speaking, but no one is listening.

Whatever it is that Himmler is reading must be charged indeed, for now his odour glides through the room.

Palpable tension has overthrown the meeting, and Goebbels sees that he must act.

'Herr Himmler?'

Himmler, absorbed in what he is reading, does not hear his name. Goebbels repeats his words somewhat louder, 'Herr Himmler!'

Now Himmler looks up, not at Goebbels but at Röhm, his mouth agape, his eyes flaring. Sweat has appeared on the top of his bald head. Himmler stands and turns his attention to the map. Every eye in the room is fixed upon him.

'You may know this, Herr Röhm, traitor that it seems you are –'

Röhm's head snaps back as if he has been punched.

A shocked, collective gasp arises from the room.

Goebbels bolts from his chair and barks, 'Herr Himmler! I *demand* that you retract that insolent remark!'

With airy detachment, Himmler waves away Goebbels' order. 'Demand all you wish, Herr Goebbels. I shall do no such thing.'

Directing his remarks to Röhm, Himmler continues, 'As I was saying, Herr Röhm, my SS people have been investigating Herr Stennes. We have found irrefutable evidence that he has been paid by Chancellor Brüning's government to disrupt the Nazi Party. But you, it seems, are a much bigger fish swimming in a much bigger pond. My people have uncovered your treacherous arrangement with the French government, who are paying you to overthrow our Führer!'

'NO!' barks Röhm.

'Now we can see all too clearly why you have made such formidable "security" arrangements for the Sportpalast. The provisions for inside the building are only to be guessed at, but outside – every approach cut off and two rings of shoulder-to-shoulder armed men! Your map shows them facing outwards, but all you need do to change this operation from protection to usurpation is to turn those men around.'

Goebbels sees that the meeting is now irretrievably lost, and he must act before things turn uglier than they already are.

Röhm is now circling the table, closing on Himmler. Röhm is nothing if not a fighter – he has facial scars and medals from the war to prove it.

Goebbels knows that hand to hand, Himmler – even Himmler with a pistol – is no match for an enraged Röhm. And Röhm is seething.

Goebbels sees that if Röhm is not stopped, Himmler will end his day in great pain.

'Herr Röhm!' Goebbels bawls out, 'Stop! I order you to stop! Now! Göring! Stop him!'

Hermann Göring, placed in the seating arrangements between Himmler and the front of the room, is now the only possible barrier between Himmler and the thrashing of his life.

But Göring is seated and doesn't have time to stand. With his feet, he shoves himself tumbling backwards, blocking Röhm at the last instant before he can lay hands on Himmler. Göring and Röhm fall together to the floor, with Göring's chair inverted on top of them.

So furious is Röhm that he ignores Göring's bulk covering him. Röhm has a free arm, and Himmler's feet are within reach. *I'll have this slimy weasel-fucker on the floor and beat the shit out of him with one hand!*

Göring, himself no stranger to the rough, sees what could happen and rolls between Röhm and Himmler, at the same time restraining Röhm's free arm with a half-nelson. He yells, point-blank, into Röhm's ear, 'Stop, Ernst! Stop!'

Goebbels orders Himmler to join the group on the opposite side of the table.

Göring begins to feel the tension easing from Röhm's body. 'Alright, Ernst, I'm going to let you up, but don't you do anything. Understand? And you stay on this side of the table. That's an order!'

Röhm is face down on the floor, panting heavily, but he nods. Göring slowly releases his restraint. They stand.

Göring thinks it's all over and sets about putting his uniform back into tidy order.

But Röhm, unrepentant and narrow-eyed, fixes a blood mark on Himmler, who is standing beside Goebbels directly opposite with two rows of tables and chairs between. Röhm's message could not be more plain: *I'm not done with you, shitbag!*

Everyone sees it and understands exactly what it means. Everyone, that is, except Himmler, who now fashions, with a few simple words, a masterpiece of poor judgement.

'That's just the beginning of your comeuppance, traitor –'

A red tide of murderous fury plunges through Röhm. He hurls himself *over* both rows of tables. There will be no stopping him this time, and he means to kill. In a split second, he has Himmler by the throat, slamming his head into the wall.

Röhm unleashes a thunderstorm of bare-knuckle sledgehammer blows to Himmler's head and face. So frenzied is the attack that he nearly achieves his purpose before anyone responds.

Before the death blow falls, Röhm is subdued.

WILL HE SURVIVE?

'Will he survive?' asks Hitler.

'Probably. But it will take him some time to recover,' replies Goebbels.

'He called Röhm a traitor?'

'He did. Twice. The first accusation was ill-judged but perhaps understandable. Röhm was for a moment incredulous. That turned to fury. He was going to have him, Himmler, I mean. It was only Göring's intervention that saved Himmler the first time. The second time, Himmler's remark was just reckless vanity, and he paid dearly for it.' Goebbels shakes his head in wonder. 'Who would have thought that a short, pudgy man like Röhm could move so quickly? He nearly killed Himmler with his bare hands before anyone realised what was happening.'

'Did it seem to you that Röhm's security arrangements were excessive?'

'There were some murmurs, some surprise, around the table that the arrangements were so robust. But we were also impressed that Röhm had done such a thorough job of planning every detail. Everyone knows how meticulous he can be. I'm sure there would have been equal surprise if his plans had been any less robust.'

'Tell me about this connection between the French and Herr Röhm.'

'This is most interesting. It seems Röhm was approached by one Herr Krause, who portrayed himself as representing the uppermost echelon of the Party. Röhm had his suspicions but says Krause's credentials looked impeccable. But Herr Meticulous jotted down Krause's member number and had it checked. The SS confirmed it as correct even though we now know that the real number goes with a blacksmith in Frankfurt. Eventually, Himmler will realise that he's been done over by his own people. They may have had good intentions, but … it's not going to be pretty.'

Goebbels pauses and looks at Hitler to gauge his response. 'In any case, this Krause fellow directed Röhm to submit a report detailing his plans for unifying the SA. Röhm says he thought the request reasonable given the situation with the Stennes Revolt. But then Krause raised the issue of "rumours" about a connection between the French government and Röhm, aimed at overthrowing you, mein Führer, and the Party. Röhm denied it, of course, but at Krause's suggestion, Röhm went to some trouble to address the issue in his report and, there, to deny it again. It was that denial that Herr Himmler took as evidence sufficient to label Röhm a traitor.'

'Who sent Krause to meet with Röhm?' Hitler asks.

'A very good question, mein Führer. After Himmler was sent off to the hospital in the ambulance, we discussed that. None of the Reichsleiter knew anything about Krause. It could not have been Himmler unless he had concocted some convoluted double feint, and that seemed absurd given what happened to him. With respect, mein Führer, we concluded that there was only one possibility –'

'That I had sent Krause to sort out Röhm?'

'Yes, sir.'

'A logical conclusion, I will grant you, but I can assure you that I did not.'

'In that case, we have no idea who he is or how he managed to arrange a meeting with Röhm.'

'Enough! First, find out who this Krause really is. Second, have his Party number checked again. Third, find out if there *is* a connection between Röhm and the French. Do it now, Herr Goebbels, before this gets out of hand.'

HIMMLER SENDS PEOPLE TO PARIS

Himmler regains consciousness. He is in considerable pain and a vengeful frame of mind. He summons to his bedside the SS man standing watch. The man must lean over to hear Himmler's laboured whisper. Himmler gives his instructions and sends the man on his way.

'He wants us to send two people to France to see what they can find out about Röhm's French connection."

'You mean find out if there *is* a Röhm–French connection?' asks his supervisor.

'I asked the same question. His answer was that there must be one somewhere.'

'Did he say anything else?'

'Himmler thinks there must be someone in the SS who has diplomatic experience in France, and that we should find him.'

It does not take long for the SS system to find within their ranks a person, one Herr Tillich, with a résumé that includes diplomatic service. His qualifications are suitable for what is required. His last posting before joining the SS was in Paris, where he held a mid-level diplomatic posting specialising in international travel issues. Most useful, Tillich is fluent in French.

SS Operator Herr Stübner is designated mission leader.

The Nazi Party is a domestic German entity with no international diplomatic status. Thus, Tillich cannot use diplomatic channels to contact people in French Foreign Affairs. He must do what is possible by privately contacting people he knows in or around French diplomatic organisations.

Tillich and Stübner visit Himmler's bedside as they are leaving for France.

In a low, rasping voice, Himmler issues his instructions. 'Do not fail me,' he adds as the two men are departing.

———

'Paris in spring!' enthuses Tillich. 'Delightful, isn't it?' he adds. 'Every bit as charming *as les poètes, écrivains et chanteurs* would have us believe. Is this your first time in Paris, Herr Stübner?'

'Yes, and it is delightful. I am beside – what street is this? – and if I lean into the street, I can see the top of the Eiffel Tower. Lovely.'

They have settled for breakfast al fresco at a café a block from their hotel. The aromas of *petit déjeuner*, the coffee, the eggs, the fresh croissants – all play their part in this agreeable seduction by Paris.

Tillich pulls a small notebook from his soft-leather briefcase, which he places on the table. Tapping the cover, he says, 'My diplomatic contact book when I was at the embassy here. If we are lucky and, perhaps, a little inventive, this will get us started on our assignment.'

Over breakfast, he compiles a list of people to contact in some way. The list is arranged – in order of seniority – as it was at the time of his return to Germany.

'We'll start at the top of the list and work our way down. But first we go to *trente-sept Quai d'Orsay*!'

'What or where or who is that?' asks Stübner.

Tillich chuckles in a good-natured way at Stübner's innocence. 'It's an address. The headquarters of the French Ministry of Foreign Affairs, Number 37 Quai d'Orsay. We will walk. It's not far. We're off!'

Stübner grips Tillich's wrist. 'Not so fast. If we go to the French Ministry of Foreign Affairs at 37 Quai d'Orsay and talk with your diplomat friends, won't they just deny all knowledge of a Röhm–French connection, whether there is one or not?'

'Possibly. But that's why we're here. To find out if there is one.'

Stübner places his butter knife beside the croissant. 'No. We are not here to do research.'

'What does that mean?'

'Herr Tillich, you were selected for this task because you are fluent in French and because you had experience in the diplomatic service. That's what Himmler asked for, but that is *not* what he wants.'

'Oh, is that so, Herr Mind Reader? And what is it that Himmler really wants?'

'When Himmler issued his orders, he was barely conscious and in great pain. Making some kind of diplomatic connection may have seemed to him like a good place to start, but we need to make allowance for him not thinking very clearly. For starters, Herr Tillich, as far as this task is concerned, what would you consider to be a successful result?'

'Finding evidence of a Röhm–French connection.'

'Nice try. But the complete answer is *either* finding irrefutable evidence of Röhm having a French connection, as you've just suggested, *or* establishing that there is no such connection. Yes?'

Tillich finds the logic puzzling. 'What are you driving at?'

'Think about it, my friend. We have no reliable way of establishing that there is a connection. We are not a diplomatic mission. We are just a couple of guys – German guys – off the street. Your diplomat friends and contacts will give us nothing, even if they have something. And who else are we going to contact? There isn't anything we can do that will lead to a result, reliable or otherwise. And it is flatly *not* possible for us to establish that there is no connection. So now, my friend, what would be a failure in your obligation to Himmler?'

'Not finding evidence of a Röhm–French connection?' Tillich responds.

   R. WILLIAM PLUME

Stübner nods qualified agreement. 'Again, not quite complete. Not *finding* evidence of a connection and there *not being* a connection are two very different things. But we cannot, we will not, report either of these possibilities to Himmler.'

Tillich finds Stübner's diktat disturbing. 'Why not?'

'Because, Herr Tillich, it would mean that Herr Himmler got the shit beaten out of him for a good reason, and he *will not* swallow that rat. He swallowed some of his own teeth at Röhm's hands, and he will choke on having to swallow a good reason for it as well.'

'But … but … if we *cannot* reliably establish a connection, and it's *not* possible to establish no connection, and we will *not* report no connection, and we will *not* report not finding a connection, then why are we here?'

'Good question, Herr Tillich.'

'He really dropped us in it, didn't he?'

'Yes, he did. It's a forlorn hope, isn't it?

'A what?'

'Never mind. When we're done here, he will thank us.'

'Why? What are we going to do?'

'Talk to the newspapers.'

BRÜNING AND VON HINDENBURG MEET

Reichspräsident Paul von Hindenburg strides into the office of Chancellor Heinrich Brüning.

The meeting table is covered with French daily newspapers, all with blaring headlines:

```
French Government Greases Sleazy
    Deal with Cheesy Nazi?
```

Von Hindenburg ignores the meeting pleasantries. 'What's this I hear of a French conspiracy to overthrow the Nazi Party and the Bohemian corporal, which, frankly, seems to me a good idea? What's going on?'

Brüning, with a casual, open-handed, palm-upward gesture, defers without comment to Herr Julius Curtius, the Minister of Foreign Affairs.

Curtius outlines the appearance of the Röhm French conspiracy, Röhm's attack on Himmler, and what is known of Himmler's two-man mission to France.

Curtius then plunges into the details. 'Röhm is the head of the SA, and Himmler is the head of the SS, which is a sub-section within the SA. That makes Röhm, technically speaking, Himmler's superior. Himmler is having none of that, and the standoff has ballooned into an administrative nightmare for Hitler. It undercuts the Nazi principle of Führerprinzip, and that has led to widespread and various rumours about favouritism, inconsistencies in the strict application of Party structure, and so on.'

Curtius pauses for questions. There are none.

Curtius continues, 'The two men involved in the mission to France were assigned to contact diplomatic sources to the extent that they could without a diplomatic warrant. Instead, they went to the French papers. It must be acknowledged that it was a very shrewd move on their part. Himmler, probably without realising what he was asking for, put them in an impossible position.'

Von Hindenburg wags a hand and issues a question. 'What were they thinking? The French papers, I mean. Two nobody Germans walk in off the street, and five minutes later it's an international sensation?'

Brüning smiles. 'Increased sales perhaps? Do you think that might have had something to do with it?'

Von Hindenburg harrumphs.

Curtius continues, 'What has appeared in the French press has served to underline Himmler's accusation, directed at Röhm, of treason. To be very clear, everything we have seen in these newspapers is pure speculation, nothing more than guesswork. But it's there, and people will believe what they will.'

     R. WILLIAM PLUME

Von Hindenburg turns to Brüning. 'I get the feeling, Herr Chancellor, that you are enjoying this … this …'

'Little escapade? Well, it's a light moment in an otherwise challenging life, Herr President.'

'Well, make sure you keep it private. Alright?'

Brüning chuckles. 'Shall we let Herr Curtius get on with it?'

Curtius begins again. 'The tension has caused a deep division in the Nazi Party, with those aligned with Himmler on one side and those aligned with Röhm on the other. The rift has seriously undermined the Party machine supporting Hitler, as it has exposed a serious flaw in lines of authority based on the Führerprinzip. We are aware of at least one all-in beer hall brawl spawned by these events.'

Once again Curtius provides an opportunity for questions.

Brüning asks, 'Given that glaring failure of the much-vaunted Führerprinzip, what has been Herr Hitler's public response?'

'Uncharacteristically, he has, on this occasion, remained stone silent,' says Curtius.

Von Hindenburg wags his hand again. 'How did this get started?'

'The original source of the French connection was in a report submitted by Röhm to the Nazi Party senior officials. We have no information about why Röhm thought it necessary to include the information in what was otherwise a document setting out plans for unifying the SA. As you have noted, Herr Reichspräsident, the issue has deepened into an awkward but as yet harmless international incident. As things stand, there is nothing that the German government needs to do. This is primarily a problem, and a serious one, for Herr Hitler.'

CHAPTER 13

The Indoctrination Programme Begins

THOMAS AND REINHARD MEET

'I asked you, Reinhard, to come to the Englischer Garten because we need to speak privately. Hofgarten would have been my first choice, but it's a little too close to Brown House for my liking.'

'Englischer Garten is beautiful, Thomas, and I'm pleased to be here. Most of all, though, I'm eager to hear what you've been doing for the past year and a bit.'

'I will come to that, but first, I presented – and burned – all ten of the Party membership cards I had, and I'd like to know if your mole in the SS was able to track what happened as they were used.'

'The first one you presented – the one you presented to Röhm – did the most damage. After your meeting with him, Röhm sent your card number to the SS to be verified. Whoever did the checking wasn't careful enough, and Röhm was told that you – as Krause – were genuine. That forced Röhm to address the French connection and to strenuously deny any such arrangement.'

'My apologies, Reinhard, for interrupting, but do you recognise the aroma that surrounds us?'

'It's strong, and it's lovely, but no, I cannot name it.'

'I'll give you a clue. We're in the *English* Garden.'

'It's a flower, isn't it?'

Thomas smiles indulgently at Reinhard and says, 'In the daily papers there seems to be a lot about a standoff between Röhm and Himmler.

R. WILLIAM PLUME

What's going on there?'

'That's the French connection, and you will be pleased to know, my friend, that you are responsible for that.'

'How so?'

'Röhm, of course, denied everything. But Himmler, in his usual perverse way, took denial to be an admission of guilt and flat-out accused Röhm of treason. Röhm assaulted him. Nearly killed him. Himmler sent a deputation, actually just a couple of SS guys, to Paris to find a French connection. It was a flyer, but at least one of those guys had his head screwed on facing forward, and now the entire world knows all about the connection with the French government.'

'Thank you, Reinhard. But before you carry on, I'll give you another clue. No, I'll give you two clues. It's a vine, and the flowers have a lovely lavender colour.'

'It's that cascading purple –'

'Lavender –'

'*Purple* flower … plant … covering the Dianatempel.'

'Close enough. Then what happened?'

Reinhard looks puzzled. 'With what? The flower?'

'No. With Himmler.'

'Well, my friend, the next part of this story is just pure theatre. Somebody in the SS picked a bad time to make a serious blunder. They sent back a report to Röhm to say that you – as Krause – were genuine. It didn't take long before the mistake was uncovered. But by then, to avoid copping the blame when the mistake became known, everyone in the SS hierarchy was forced to pass the details of the mistake up the chain of command. Eventually, of course, the information arrived with Himmler, who was then compelled to face the fact that his own people had created the situation that led to Röhm's attack.'

Thomas' facial expression shifts from bemusement to outright delight. 'I probably shouldn't be so pleased, but I did set out to create instability, and it seems to have been successful.'

'Thomas, what is the name of that flower?'

'Wisteria. My mother loved it. And why would she not? It's lovely.'

'Couldn't be nicer, my friend.'

'Well, yes, it could be nicer. Like many lovely plants, Reinhard, left to their own devices, they turn into weeds. Now, tell me, my friend, how does this story end?'

'The whole business turned into quite a drama. I won't bore you with all the details, but eventually Himmler ordered all membership lists to be amalgamated, centralised, and retyped. A small army of typists set to work. The process fixed some errors, preserved some errors, and introduced new errors. Those ten small pieces of paper created by Mr Brewster caused serious problems for the Party. The SS is still trying to work out what's going on.'

'Well, I'm pleased,' says Thomas, thoughtfully. 'I have Brewster to thank for this success. I'm in his debt. Again.'

Reinhard hangs an elbow over the back of the bench. 'But you haven't asked me here to instruct me about wisteria, have you?'

'Ahh, no.'

'And you haven't asked me here to be told that you have wrecked the Nazi Party membership process?

'No, Reinhard. I'm here to tell you that the "National Socialist Indoctrination Programme" is about to begin.'

A BEARING FACTORY IN MUNICH

'Herr Schroeder, what we do here is essential to the life of our great country. In this factory we make bearings of the highest quality: ball bearings, roller bearings, and thrust bearings. The bearings we make are used in virtually every machine that is manufactured in this country. You will be working in the ball-bearing section, managing the acid bath.

'You must understand how important it is that you follow the

  R. WILLIAM PLUME

procedures set out for your job. We are very particular about that, and it's why we exclusively employ men who are members of the Nazi Party.'

Thomas nods, displaying his most attentive expression. 'At the employment office, I asked for a job in just such an organisation and was pleased when a position here could be arranged. In all ways and at all times, we should, each one of us, be striving to meet the highest standards of the Aryan Ideal.'

'Of course, Herr Schroeder, but now that we have completed the formalities, it's time for you to learn your new job –'

'Please forgive me for interrupting, Herr Klausen, but there are a few things I'd like to understand before we do that.'

'Such as?'

'I'd like to understand how you run indoctrination and study programmes, such things as *Mein Kampf* reading groups for elucidating the meaning of "working towards the Führer" and for understanding Party structure and how it works for everyone. And, may I suggest, the men should start each shift singing "Deutschland Über Alles".'

'Herr Schroeder, we don't run such programmes here. We see that as the responsibility of other organisations. And as for singing before the shift starts … Well, that would have a negative impact on production, and I find it a little difficult to see how that helps us.'

'Well then, Herr Klausen, we will have to discuss this matter at greater length soon.'

'Of course, Herr Schroeder. But right now we need you to begin your training on the operation of the acid bath. So, if you'll come with me –'

'By soon, I mean later today, Herr Klausen.'

'I'm afraid that won't be possible, Herr Schroeder. So, if you don't mind –'

'I do mind, Herr Klausen. If a conversation with you is not possible, I will take up the matter with my district commander this evening, and tomorrow morning we, you and I, will have this conversation with him.'

Klausen's demeanour changes from dismissive tolerance to pale-faced attention. He manages a weak smile. 'Well then, Herr Schroeder, let's sit down again so you can tell me what you think we need.'

'At its core, Herr Klausen, what is required is the very essence of simplicity. We must identify and remove all that departs from the Aryan Ideal. Everyone must understand and apply the principles of National Socialism as expressed by our glorious Führer in his incomparable manifesto, *Mein Kampf*. Everyone must learn what it means to "work towards the Führer". Half-hearted commitment is not acceptable. Everyone must participate and devote themselves – heart and soul – to the Party, and everyone must be ever vigilant for signs of backsliding and ever on the lookout for behaviours, characteristics, or individuals who do not measure up to the Aryan Ideal.'

'That seems like a very admirable and comprehensive programme, Herr Schroeder. But let's not forget that these men have work to do, and production must not suffer.'

'Herr Klausen, you strike me as a highly intelligent and perceptive man, so I can only guess that you left your foresight and vision in your bed this morning. Surely, you must see that when these men are committed to the Party ideals, production will soar to levels beyond anything you've ever imagined. And surely you can also see that will only be beneficial to your prospects for advancement?'

'Well, yes, that would be helpful.'

'It's settled then. I'll get started organising things immediately,' says Thomas, reaching across the desk to shake Klausen's hand.

'And it would be appropriate for you, as the plant manager, to make an announcement to staff that I will be running these programmes and that you expect everyone's full co-operation.'

DEMERITS APPEAR

Klausen's announcement introducing Thomas and his intentions appears on the dayroom bulletin board. Not everyone reads it. Some, uncooperative by nature, ignore it. Some don't understand it. Some don't know it is there.

Not everyone appears for the first start-of-shift indoctrination meeting.

Thomas calls off the names on the shift roster. Silence outnumbers 'Present' responses.

'There are a lot of men missing. Where are they?' asks Thomas.

Shrugs, glances, this way and that. Questions sit foremost in the men's thoughts.

Bewilderment. *Why are we here? Who is this guy?*

'You are wondering who I am?'

Nods. Shrugs.

'I am Herr Schroeder. I am the new acid-bath operator. I also have the great honour to lead you men to a better understanding of National Socialist Germany. But before we can continue, everyone must be here.' He points to the closest man and says, 'Go round them up, please.'

The missing men arrive. Thomas starts again.

'We will meet here every morning. Attendance is mandatory. We will begin every shift singing "Deutschland Über Alles". When you get yourselves into a proper frame of mind, we will move on to group study of *Mein Kampf* and other matters that define what it means to participate in the great National Socialist movement.

'But now we sing "Deutschland Über Alles". All of it. All three verses. Ready?' He kicks off the singing with '… three, four!' and a wide, downward sweep of his right arm. Thomas begins in a robust, full voice, *'Deutschland, Deutschland über alles …'*

A few mousy, mumbling voices join him.

'Sing!' he roars and carries on, *'… Über alles in der Welt!'*

Mumble, murmur, shuffle.

Waving both arms, Thomas stops.

'I can see you men need some encouragement to sing your national anthem properly. Meet here, same time tomorrow. You are dismissed.'

At lunchtime, Klausen posts another notice. Every man has been given a demerit point for failure to participate with the proper enthusiasm in the indoctrination meeting.

The notice includes the details of a demerit system that applies to all workers.

Demerits will be levied for various infractions, such as failure to participate in the Indoctrination Programme and failure to meet production targets.

'Since when do we have demerit points?' men ask one another.

The following morning, the men have assembled for the indoctrination meeting.

Klausen stands at the front of the group. 'I understand that there has been some confusion about the purpose of these meetings, and some of you are wondering why you have been penalised with demerit points.'

Someone at the back grumbles, 'Yeah, well, some guy appears out of nowhere, and suddenly he's in charge of these, these … What are they? Propaganda meetings? And he's handin' out demerit points if we don't sing proper. Since when do we have demerit points, anyway? Looks like if I get enough demerit points, my pay gets docked, and now I'm gonna get another one when I don't reach my production target 'cause I'm here bloody singin' instead of working. And I'll tell you what, Herr Klausen, if a not-singing-proper demerit point puts me over the limit and my pay's docked, I won't be happy, and you and I will be havin' a little chat.'

Klausen is wedged between his men and Thomas, but having instigated the indoctrination meetings, he must now defend both the meetings and Thomas. He gives himself some time.

'I am working on reducing your production targets to allow for the time you spend with Herr Schroeder, so you needn't worry about that.'

Now he needs to underscore Thomas' credibility and thereby his own.

'Herr Schroeder is …' he says, then hesitates. *What? An authority? No, recognised as one.* He continues, '… a recognised authority on National Socialism and, and …' He falters. *Ah, comes recommended.* 'And he comes

     R. WILLIAM PLUME

to us highly recommended. We should all be grateful for the chance to …'
puzzled again. *Um,* he thinks. *Be thankful for the opportunity to improve
what? Our understanding of the Party? National Socialism?* Klausen forges
on, '… to improve our understanding of what it means to be part of the
great National Socialist Revolution!'

*This is why I'm the supervisor and not still operating one of those infernal
machines. I think quickly on my feet, and did you hear that? What a speech!
And impromptu!*

'We pride ourselves on being a workforce entirely made up of
members of the Nazi Party, and we should not grudge learning more
about what it means to be a fully committed member.' Now Klausen
turns the spotlight from himself to Thomas. 'But now, I think, Herr
Schroeder, you should tell the men what you expect from them.'

'That will be my pleasure, Herr Klausen. Let us begin with where we
were yesterday. We were trying to sing our wonderful national anthem,
"Deutschland Über Alles", but it seems most of you don't know all the
words. Most people don't know the second and third verses. That's not
surprising since most of the time we hear only the first verse. Some of
you don't know the words, and I am not bothered by that. You can learn
the words. You *will* learn the words.

'When we begin our study of *Mein Kampf,* you will be expected
to purchase your own copy if you don't already have one. I will expect
you to read it. All of it. You will not be penalised if you do not or
cannot understand the contents. But you will suffer if you don't *try* to
understand.

'What I will not tolerate is lack of commitment. If you cannot or will
not commit yourself to the coming order of our nation, then how can
you expect the nation to be committed to you? And a way to show that
commitment is to learn, to understand, to sing like you mean it, and
to sing in a way that shows you are devoted heart and soul to the New
Order of our nation. It means to understand the thinking of our great
Führer, to understand what it means to think like him, and to understand

his glorious vision for the future of our nation! I hope that clarifies the matter. And when you've done that, you *will* produce and prosper!

DEUTSCHLAND ÜBER ALLES

The next day, Thomas once again calls off the names on the shift roster. Only two men are absent. *Progress*, he thinks.

'Are Herr Brünner and Herr Müllner here? Has anyone seen them this morning?'

'They're both here, Herr Schroeder. Herr Brünner is in the shipping office, and Herr Müllner is fixing the conveyor belt,' says someone at the back of the group.

'Thank you. Wait here. If I'm not back in fifteen minutes, you are dismissed.'

Thomas finds Herr Müllner at the conveyor. 'Good morning, Herr Müllner. Why aren't you at the indoctrination meeting?'

'I don't need any help from you to understand why I'm a member of the Nazi Party.'

'Herr Müllner, no matter how much we think we know, we can all improve our understanding. Perhaps you don't understand that attendance at the meetings is mandatory. Please stop what you are doing and join the group.'

'And just who the hell are you? Who gives you the authority to show up here and start shoving me around?'

Thomas ignores the question. 'Join the meeting, Herr Müllner, or there will be consequences. I expect to see you there when I return.'

Thomas goes to the shipping office, a small, sparse room at the far end of the factory adjacent to the shipping docks. 'Herr Brünner, why aren't you at the indoctrination meeting?'

Brünner is organising his pencils, shoving paper around, looking grim. He is mute for a few moments.

     R. WILLIAM PLUME

'I will not beat around the bush, Herr Schroeder. Your great Führer is a repulsive monster. He is an evil liar and a charlatan. Germany is a great nation, and he is dragging it into the mud. "Deutschland Über Alles" is our national anthem, and a stirring statement it certainly is. I know all the words to all the verses. You don't yet know this – why would you? – but I am a classically trained tenor. If I sang that song in full voice, you and everyone else in the room would be knocked off their feet –'

Thomas flatly orders, 'Go to the dayroom, Herr Brünner.'

'I will do no such thing. Your little audition yesterday was textbook how-to-butcher-a-song. You started in the wrong place, with amateurish directing gestures barely connected to the actual rhythm. You were breathing in the wrong places, and your intonation sounded like you were strangling a cat. That song has been subverted to Hitler's purpose by people like you. I will not sing it again until that vile man is dust blown away.'

Expecting *I can't sing a note*, or *I don't know the words*, Thomas is caught off guard.

'And yet here you are, working in a factory that employs only members of the Nazi Party.'

'I have a family, Herr Schroeder. We don't need much, but we do need to eat. In recent years, I've been forced to swallow much of my pride, but there are limits even to that. As for *Mein Kampf*, I have read that already. I have studied every word in great detail. A clearer statement of cultural annihilation has yet to be written. I could probably teach you a few things about it. Study it here? In an absurd Indoctrination Programme run by you? Whoever you are? Not on your life.'

Thomas finds himself in a dilemma. He is facing a mirror image of himself and yet is now forced to require from him behaviour that Thomas himself finds repugnant.

'You are required to attend regardless of your personal opinions.'

Brünner scoffs. 'Really? "Working towards the Führer"? Pffft! Call the SS and order them to shoot me now because I will not! I will not *ever work towards* the fucking Führer. The Jews are his – everyone's – favourite target when they need someone to blame for things gone wrong. But Jews are not subhuman beasts. They, too, need to eat. Do as you will, Herr Schroeder. I will have no part of your squalid Indoctrination Programme.'

'Are you Jewish?'

'Must I *be* Jewish to have sympathy and compassion for them as fellow humans? If you prick them, do they not bleed?'

Thomas – again confronted with himself – is startled into silence. He stands motionless. He puts his hand on the steel of a hammer on top of the filing cabinet. He wonders for a moment, *Why is there a hammer in the shipping office?* His attention now on the hammer, he quotes, in English, Shylock's speech from Shakespeare's *The Merchant of Venice*:

Hath not a Jew eyes? Hath not a Jew hands, organs, dimensions, senses, affections, passions? Fed with the same food, hurt with the same weapons, subject to the same diseases, healed by the same means, warmed and cooled by the same winter and summer as a Christian is? If you prick us, do we not bleed? If you tickle us, do we not laugh? If you poison us, do we not die?

Brünner is himself thrown off balance, and his face softens. Now, also speaking in English, he says, 'Allow me to finish it for you.'

And if you wrong us, shall we not revenge? If we are like you in the rest, we will resemble you in that. If a Jew wrong a Christian, what is his humility? Revenge. If a Christian wrong a Jew, what should his sufferance be by Christian example? Why, revenge. The villainy you teach me, I will execute, and it shall go hard but I will better the instruction.

Brünner and Thomas gaze steadily at each other for a moment. Both silent. Both astonished.

 R. WILLIAM PLUME

'Unless I miss my guess, Herr Schroeder, it is you who has some explaining to do.'

'Join the group, Herr Brünner. Stand at the back. Mumble The Lord's Prayer during the singing if that helps.'

Leaving Brünner, Thomas thinks, *He could be a big problem. Or perhaps ... I need to meet with him somewhere other than here.*

A few days later, Thomas appears in the shipping office.

'Tuesday evening, eight o'clock,' he says, handing Brünner a small, folded piece of paper. It reads, 'Come to this address.'

THOMAS AND BRÜNNER MEET

Thomas sits near the door and waits. He is pleased – and relieved – that Brewster's work had successfully passed Röhm's meticulous examination. But now he has the opposite problem.

If Brünner shows up, Thomas must convince him that he, Thomas, is *not* the person presented in Brewster's engravings. Brünner, who should now be approaching the door, is bringing with him a mind already on full alert.

Eight o'clock arrives. There has been no knock at the door, but Thomas hears – or thinks he hears – someone outside the door. He moves closer to the door and cocks an ear.

There is someone there. Thomas can hear feet moving, scratching the grit on the concrete.

Now there are two people no more than thirty centimetres apart, separated from each other by a slab of wood. Both are assessing what is happening on the other side of the barrier.

Why hasn't he knocked? Is it who it's supposed to be? Shall I open the door? Or wait until he knocks?

There is a single, soft, almost inaudible knock on the door. Thomas waits for a moment and then opens the door just enough to see who is there.

It is Brünner.

'You're alone?' Thomas asks.

Brünner nods.

Thomas opens the door just enough to allow Brünner into the room. As he enters the room, his eyes dart here and there. He puts his hand on his head. Thomas closes the door. Almost before the door latch falls into place, Brünner, who is pale and sweating, begins the conversation.

'I'm not sure why I thought to be here this evening, Herr Schroeder. You are not my favourite person. Well, I shouldn't say that. I don't know you well enough. But I detest your politics. Why have you asked me here?'

Well, that's thrown down the gauntlet, hasn't it? Perhaps I should tell him he's in no danger? Would he believe me?

With a hand gesture, Thomas invites Brünner to sit.

'I asked you to come here tonight, Herr Brünner, because we, you and I, have more in common than you realise. Using your phrase, I will not beat around the bush. My activities these days are given over to covert resistance to the Nazi Party.'

Brünner turns paler still.

'I work as an agent provocateur, looking to incite discord by subverting faith in the Aryan master race ideology. My aim is to plant in Party members doubts and suspicions about other members. I style myself as the archetype of Aryan purity against which everyone else is to be judged. I craft my public behaviour to match that. I detest the public version of my politics as much as you do. Perversely, it gives me a way to deal with something that I cannot accept.' Thomas pauses.

'Fascinating. You still haven't told me why I'm here.'

'For a start, to give you some advice. When we spoke the other day, Herr Brünner, you were either very brave or very foolish. I could have been SS. At this moment, you could be face down in the Isar River with a hole in the back of your head. You need to be more careful.'

'Thanks for the advice. Get to the point, please.'

     R. WILLIAM PLUME

'I need your help. If I am to be the standard of Aryan purity, I cannot repeat the mistakes I have made that triggered your defiance. I need to be credible to people like you, who know enough to know when I'm making it up.'

'Why would I do this? What are you going to do for me?'

'Herr Brünner, you have failed to understand that when you take risks, as you did the other day, you aren't exposing just yourself to danger. You are putting your family at risk as well: your wife and your two daughters. Speak as openly as you did to the wrong person, and you will end up dead, and your family will end up, well, frankly, who knows where? I have ways of protecting you and your family. If you help me, that protection is available to you.'

Brünner fidgets. His hand passes back and forth over his bald spot, stopping to scratch at the dry skin near the crown.

He looks around the room. 'If I were SS, Herr Schroeder, you would be the one in serious trouble right now.'

'Your point is well made, Herr Brünner. But, in the first place, I know that you are not SS. In the second place, in matters of this nature, one must sometimes rely on good judgement and a little intuition when putting one's faith in an unknown. You are something of an unknown for me, but I'm willing to rely on my assessment of you as a fellow traveller. To come straight to the point, I need you to teach me how to lead the morning singing.'

'You want me to join with you, whoever you are, just to teach you how to conduct "Deutschland Über Alles"?' asks Brünner with thinly disguised scepticism.

'It would help if it looked like I knew what I was doing. But you have other talents as well, Professor Brünner. These may yet be useful.'

Brünner begins to fidget again. His hand goes straight to the dry patch. Thomas sees the behaviour and wonders, *Does he scratch his head every time he's uncomfortable or feeling nervous or exposed? He could turn me over to Klausen. Perhaps he's wondering if he should do that. Not likely, though, for someone who described Hitler as – what was it? – a repulsive liar. He could have had me on the floor after that first conducting episode, but he didn't.*

'You have discovered much about me in a short time, Herr Schroeder. Now I'm asking myself how you did that and if I need to be concerned about you snooping around my life and my family.'

'Take it as a lesson in how easy it is to track you down. I have offered you the opportunity to become part of my operation. I don't make such offers without knowing something about you. Yes, you could have been SS, but if you were, you wouldn't be here. I don't make assumptions about such things.'

'I suppose I should be flattered with your confidence in me, but I don't feel that way.'

'If you choose to join me, what you will be doing is dangerous. I cannot protect you from every possible peril. The possibility of death will never be far away. Perhaps the way you're feeling is a recognition of that.'

After a moment of silence, Brünner says, 'As you have done, I will take you on trust and accept your offer. What happens now?'

Right to be careful and right to accept the offer. He's going to have to learn not to show his fear the way he does, but I'll take it as a sign of his concern for his family, Thomas decides.

'Like it or not, Herr Brünner, you will have to continue to participate in the Indoctrination Programme at the plant. You will need to become outwardly committed to the Party. Hold your nose if you must, but you need to behave as if my Indoctrination Programme has delivered you into the blazing light of full understanding. Meanwhile, I also want you to watch and listen for anything of interest that might be making its way around the shop.'

'You want me to be a snitch?'

'In a word, yes.'

'That'll make the job more interesting. And you want me to teach you choral conducting?'

     R. WILLIAM PLUME

'That would be helpful. We will meet here daily until I at least look like a competent conductor. After that, as needed. I will let you know when I want you to come here.'

<hr>

The following afternoon, Thomas and Reinhard are sharing a table at the back of Frau Gretel's. Both have coffee. Thomas has supplemented his coffee with a large piece of apple and cinnamon galette.

'She does this cinnamon galette so well, Reinhard. I'm surprised you can resist it. And the name, it sounds like a medieval dance.'

'Frau Gretel does everything well, my friend. If I started eating everything she did well, I'd be in here all day. And I think the word you're thinking of is "gavotte".'

'There was a cinnamon gavotte?' asks Thomas with mock incredulity.

'You're in a very frivolous mood today, Thomas. What is going on?'

'Herr Brünner has accepted my offer. Please put a man on his family.'

CHAPTER 14

The SS Stakes Out the Schroeder Residence

LILLI AND THE SS MAN

Lilli rocks up on her toes and stretches over the kitchen counter towards the windowpane.

Turning her head hard and putting her cheek to the glass, she can see a portion of the street at the front of the house.

He's out there again. That's what? Three? Four months? Enough's enough. Today's the day. Let's hope Reinhard's information is reliable.

———

'Excuse me, sir?' says Lilli.

The man turns to face the voice and, for the first time, sees the lovely Lilli at arm's length.

His surroundings recede away. The pain in his toes and fingers disappears. His breathing stops. His voice freezes.

Lilli smiles.

'Hello, sir. You must be freezing. I've brought you a mug of hot coffee. You should drink before it freezes as well.'

Transferring the mug from Lilli's hands into the man's hands brings together a clumsy mismatch of gloved fingers and thumbs. The mug slips. A jumble of hands try to control it. They fail, and the mug falls onto the grass verge. The coffee hisses into the snow and disappears.

'Oh dear. That did not work well. Never mind. Frozen fingers don't always co-operate the way they should. Come with me. Let's go inside.

It will be warmer, and making another coffee will be easier.'

Using the back door, Lilli and the man enter the kitchen.

'Here, warm your hands over the stove while I make you another coffee.'

'Thank you, Frau Schroeder. I'm –'

Pin-drop silence envelops the room.

Lilli looks towards the man. She closes the tap and puts the kettle on the counter.

Motionless silence follows.

She points to the chair at the end of the kitchen table and, with a hand gesture, directs the man to sit.

When he is seated, Lilli says, 'You know my name.'

The man fidgets. 'Yes.'

'Well, I suppose there might be a certain justice in that. May I know your name?'

'Herr Mertz. Walter Mertz.'

'I have seen you, Herr Mertz, around the neighbourhood for several weeks. Are you spying on someone?

'I really shouldn't say.'

Lilli pushes up the bun at the back of her head and cocks herself against the counter. She has one hand on the countertop and the other on her hip.

'Herr Mertz, where did you grow up?'

Mertz is puzzled by the question but answers, 'Here, in Munich.'

'What a coincidence. So did I. Do you remember that game we used to play as children called True or False? I make a statement about something, anything, and you must truthfully answer "True" or "False". I ask questions until I get "False" for an answer. That game was such fun. Shall we do that? Very good. I'll go first. Number one: Your real name is not Walter Mertz.'

There is a brief pause, but he says, 'True.'

'Number two: Your real name is Walter Schäfer.'

'True.' *Time to go*, he thinks.

'Number three: You are maintaining a surveillance of this house because it is the Munich residence of Thomas Hedwig Reichey Schroeder.'

Schäfer stands and says, 'That will do, Frau Schroeder. Thank you for the warmth. Good day to you.'

He turns towards the door.

'That door is locked, Herr Schäfer.'

'In my experience, Frau Schroeder, when locks tangle with bullets, the locks usually come off second best.'

'Ah well, you know best. Give it a go. See how you get on.'

Schäfer reaches into the breast pocket of his overcoat and finds it empty. When he turns around, Lilli has drawn a bead on him with his own pistol.

'The coffee, Herr Schäfer. It was almost too easy. Now don't do anything silly. In my experience, when *people* tangle with bullets, the people *always* come off second best. We haven't finished our conversation. Sit down.'

Schäfer has been bested by a woman, and now he has been ordered by her to sit down. In a gutsy way, he finds the sensation appealing. He sits.

'Now, I think I was up to number five. You were sent here on the direct order of Heinrich Himmler.'

'True.'

'Number six: You are Jewish.'

Panic spreads over Schäfer's face. He puts his hands on the table, preparing to stand.

'Unh, unh, unh, Herr Schäfer. Stay where you are. True or false?'

'False.'

'Number seven: You are lying.'

'True. No. False … No … shit. True. How do you know that?'

'Number eight: You are circumcised.'

'How on earth do you know that?? How could you possibly know such a thing? Have you been sneaking into my bedroom when I'm asleep?'

'No. But you have been sneaking into my backyard to pee behind the garden shed. I can see you from the washing room. You are very well endowed in that area, which makes it easier to notice, but you are, without a doubt, circumcised. And now you've confirmed what I suspected, that is, that you are Jewish. And, in any case, Himmler would take your circumcision as ironclad proof, would he not?'

The blood drains from Schäfer's face. 'Please ...' is all he can manage.

'Walter, listen to me. You have secrets you want kept, and so do I. If we work together, we'll both get what we want. You report to the SS on Monday, Wednesday, and Friday using a post office payphone?'

'True ... Sorry ... Yes.'

'From now on, we will work together on the content of your report before you make that call. Is that clear?'

'Yes. Thank you, Frau Schroeder.'

'Please, Walter, call me Lilli unless there is someone else in the room.'

'Lilli, it is. Thank you. Now that we're working together, as you say, I'd like to have my pistol back, please.'

'Can I trust you?'

'Since you know all there is to be known about me – including the size and shape of my penis – you, at this moment, have the whip hand. But let's be straight up with each other, shall we?'

'Meaning?'

'You, too, are going to have to trust *me*.'

'Why?'

'If I go back to headquarters without my pistol, I will be in trouble, no doubt, but so will you. You can expect a squad of men around here to retrieve it, and they won't mess around being polite. And they won't forget where you live.'

CHAPTER 15

The Factory Programme Expands

THE SINGING IMPROVES

At each morning singing session, Thomas applies what he has learned from Brünner.

Soon Thomas' style coheres. The men get the idea. Things start to work. The initial reluctance is overcome; the men begin to enjoy singing. Even grumpy Herr Müllner starts to show up without being forced along.

Brünner teaches Thomas about projection. The following day he starts by saying, 'When we gather, you must arrange yourselves in lines so everyone can see me. You must stand erect with your head back a little. Like this. That is so your voice will fill the room and the words of the song will fill your heart. You must look at me at all times. No looking at the floor or over there. Look at me.'

The group of men shuffle around until they are aligned as Thomas has asked.

'This wonderful song has three verses, as you all now know. Each verse has a chorus. That's the part that repeats twice the first line of the verse. In that part, we all sing the same words a little louder, but with a different melody. When we start the chorus, I will put out my left hand like this with my palm up. When I raise my hand, it means *sing a little louder*. When I turn my hand over and lower it, that means *sing softer because we are starting the next verse*. Everybody understand?

'Alright, gentlemen. Let's do this like we mean it! Put your back into it!'

And they do. The men follow Thomas' gestures exactly. Everyone, to a man, comes in on the beat, pitch perfect and flowing into the first verse. Thomas is leading, and he knows it. As the song moves along, his gestures become more fluid and expansive. He feels the pulse; he feels his place, and the men respond.

It ends. The final notes and words resonate around the room. Every man knows that something special has happened. No one moves. Thomas says nothing. What seems like minutes passes in expectant silence.

A man in the back row raises his hand and says, 'Herr Schroeder, can we do it again?'

Thomas says, 'Yes! Yes, I think we should.' He leans forward and adds, 'Now then, gentlemen, let's raise the *roof* off this place!'

There is some whispering. Eager faces look forward, watching as Thomas raises his hands that say, *Quiet, please. We are about to begin.* The men come to attention, cock their heads back, and watch Thomas.

He nods.

Down comes one.

Eyes sweep right on two.

On the dot of three, every voice – perfectly synchronised – bursts in, shaking the rafters, rattling the roof iron.

Brünner sets oaths aside and joins in *voce piena*. Thomas hears him and smiles to himself.

They are away. Every eye fixed on Thomas. Klausen appears at the door, wondering, *What is going on?* He sees a well-disciplined group of men belting out 'Deutschland Über Alles' like he's never heard it before, all ably directed by Thomas. *Are these my workers? Seems they are.* He, too, joins in.

When it finishes, everyone claps. They turn to each other and shake hands. There are smiles all round. Klausen approaches Thomas and says, 'Well done, Herr Schroeder. I would not have thought that possible. Wonderful!'

At their evening meeting, Brünner says, 'That was a very skilful performance today, Herr Schroeder. You should be pleased with yourself.'

'Well, I have you to thank for getting me there. And now that we've set the scene, it's time to start the real Indoctrination Programme.'

THOMAS HAS SECOND THOUGHTS

'Good evening, gentlemen, and welcome again to Restaurant Parisian. It has been too long since you were here. We have missed the pleasure of your company, and I assure you it is a great joy to welcome you back. Come, gentlemen, I will show you to your table.'

After the usual preliminaries, Thomas says, 'Monsieur Buteau, last time we were here your wine cellar had a lovely Rue de l'Église Pinot Gris. Do you recall?'

'Of course. It is one of our most popular whites. A bottle and two glasses, gentlemen?'

'Yes, please.'

Thomas' mood is thoughtful.

After Monsieur Buteau has poured the wine and retired, Thomas' finger begins to trace around the rim of his glass, unaware that he is watched by Reinhard.

'You're very thoughtful this evening, Thomas. Is there something on your mind?'

'Yes. Yes, there is.' But he's not ready to elaborate, and his finger continues on its way around the rim.

Reinhard waits, and after a time he gently asks, 'You are making progress in unravelling the Nazi Party?'

Thomas emerges from his thoughts and says, 'I have yet to plant the seeds of doubt. Indeed, one could be forgiven for thinking that I have done exactly the opposite. I'm learning to be a chorister.'

'Another Russian doll,' Reinhard comments.

     R. WILLIAM PLUME

'This Russian doll has no inner successor. I can lead only when the song is "Deutschland Über Alles". If it were any other song, I'd be lost. It is so infectious, Reinhard. It is so very gripping. This morning, we did it twice. The second time, well, mein Gott im Himmel! Those men loosed the most riveting, the most … the most stirring version of that song I have ever heard. We were so pleased with ourselves. And why wouldn't we be? It was magnificent, and with Herr Brünner's behind-the-scenes help, I taught them to do that. I brought them together and inspired them to sing like that. Anybody would think that I'd been sent from Herr Goebbels himself.'

'Isn't that exactly the kind of credibility you are seeking to foster? Sounds like complete success to me.'

'Yes, of course it is. I do see that, Reinhard, but now, acting against the Party is beginning to feel like a betrayal of these men.'

'Thomas, my friend, what you are setting in motion will damage –'

Buteau is approaching the table, but Reinhard raises his hand and says, 'Give us a moment, please, monsieur.' Buteau tilts his head and returns to the kitchen.

'What you are doing will damage people, Thomas. You will be prodding people's worst fears and their deepest prejudices. Heads will be knocked together. There will be blood. People may die. If you can't live with those consequences, stop now. Go back to Lilli and the children.'

Thomas is silent.

'Tell me about Herr Brünner,' says Reinhard. 'He sounds very interesting.'

'Oh, he is indeed. He is unwaveringly opposed to Hitler. When I started at the factory, I made some stupid mistakes trying to get the men to sing. He was the only person who spotted them. He is a trained classical singer. I'm fortunate that he said nothing to Klausen. He is also an ex-professor of engineering at Munich University. He was pressured out of that position by the university, who considered him too liberal, too progressive. And he knows his Shakespeare. He quoted Shylock's speech from *The Merchant of Venice*, Act Three, Scene One, in English. He is a resistance cell of one, working to keep his family together and fed. To do that, he has been forced into the Party so he could get a job at the factory.'

'Is he doing anything more than teaching you how to teach the men to sing "Deutschland Über Alles"?'

'I need someone on the shop floor who can tell me the gossip. So far, he's given me no reason to think that he's not reliable.'

Reinhard looks around the room, spots Buteau, and signals for him to come to the table.

'Tonight, gentlemen, we have two menus: *table d'hôte* and *à la carte* –'

'Monsieur Buteau, what happened to the new and tantalising *dégustation menu*?' asks Thomas.

'Well zen, Herr Schroeder, how do we say … It has been going … gone … wiss ze … ze … ze, umm, ex … um … erstwhile! Zat ees ze word! Zee erstwhile *chef de cuisine*.'

Reinhard raises his hand. 'You know, Thomas, *table d'hôte* is as close as we will get to everlasting stew. Shall we do that?'

Thomas nods.

Buteau retires.

'This is harder than I expected, Reinhard. The men in that factory are just ordinary people who have been seduced by Hitler's charisma and rhetoric. I could feel the pull of patriotism yesterday while we were singing. This is our country, Germany, that we are singing about, hearts bursting with pride. Who can resist such stirring appeals?'

'You, for example? You're not sliding away from your purpose, are you?' Reinhard asks.

'No. But I can see how easy it is to be led.'

'The Temptations of Christ,' muses Reinhard.

'Is that a compliment or an insult?'

'Neither. It is an acknowledgement, my friend, that you have chosen a difficult path, just as Christ did. And like him, you are facing a demon recognised for his powers of persuasion. But never forget, Thomas, that Christ did not yield, and you won't either.'

Buteau appears, pours the wine, and retires.

Thomas raises his glass. 'Reinhard, I need you to do something for me, please.'

'Of course, just name it, my friend.'

'What can you tell me about Gauleiter Adolf Wagner?'

'Not very much, I'm afraid. What I do know comes from the Veteran's Association. He served at the Front until he lost part of his right leg. He is a Nazi Party stalwart, much in favour with the uppermost echelons. Why do you ask?'

'Please deliver an anonymous message to him. The message needs to say that he should make an unannounced visit to the bearing plant at the start of the day shift. It's time to make the Indoctrination Programme known at his level of the Nazi Party hierarchy. The men are very impressive when they sing, and that will make me known to Wagner in a favourable way. Spreading the programme further than a single factory in Munich is what I'm looking to do. Wagner can start that process if I make the right impression.'

WAGNER APPEARS FOR THE MORNING RECITAL

Morning. The men are preparing to sing.

A door opens behind Thomas. He hears the disturbance and turns.

Klausen is holding the door open, ushering Herr Wagner and his adjutant into the room. Thomas signals to the men to stand at ease. He turns his attention away from the workmen and approaches the group.

'Gauleiter Wagner, this is Herr Thomas Schroeder. He is an employee here at the factory. He has taken responsibility for our Nazi Party Indoctrination Programme.'

Wagner extends his hand towards Thomas and says, 'Herr Schroeder,

Herr Klausen has spoken very highly of you and your efforts here. I understand that among your other talents you are a gifted musician.'

'You are much too kind, Herr Wagner. If I am anything, it is as a humble chorister that I make my contribution.'

'I understand that you have taught these men to sing "Deutschland Über Alles" and that the result of your effort is quite rousing.'

'We gather here every morning to begin each day with singing our wonderful national anthem. The timing of your visit is most apt. We are about to start. You would honour us greatly if you would stay to hear these men at their best.'

'Not at all, Herr Schroeder. I'm looking forward to it. Please continue.'

Thomas returns to stand before the men.

'Gentlemen, this morning we have company. Please welcome Herr Adolf Wagner, the Gauleiter of the Munich–Upper Bavaria Division.' He claps and indicates the men should clap as well. They do, and with enough enthusiasm that awkwardness is avoided.

Wagner smiles, clicks his heels, and inclines his head to acknowledge the welcome.

'Now gentlemen, let us show our guests how this song should be sung.'

He raises his hands to the 'quiet please' position and begins. The German national anthem reverberates through the room, more robust even than a few days ago.

Wagner and his adjutant are overwhelmed. Wagner, who is never very secure when standing, steps back. The adjutant steadies him. Wagner joins the singing. The adjutant and Klausen follow suit. Thomas hears the singing behind him and finds it disorienting. He continues, pouring heart and soul into this moment. The men sense his commitment and find another register.

When it finishes, Wagner is speechless. He shakes his head. Once. And again, as if startled awake. His mouth open, his eyes move from the men to Thomas.

Wagner raises his hands and begins to applaud. Everyone joins in. Wagner approaches Thomas, leans forward enough to be heard over the din, and says, 'When you are finished here, I will see you in Herr Klausen's office.'

'Come,' says Klausen to the knock on his office door. 'Ah, Herr Schroeder. Come in.'

Klausen, indicating the chair Thomas should use, invites him to sit. The chair, a balloon back, has been placed facing Wagner. More than a little lower, it has been deliberately chosen to underscore Wagner's rank. There is a ladder-back chair beside Klausen's desk, which Thomas sees is near enough to the same height.

'Herr Klausen, I'm very sorry,' says Thomas, 'but I cannot sit in a balloon-back chair. They don't support the injuries in my back. If you wouldn't mind very much, may I use the ladder back?'

The chairs are exchanged. Thomas now sits facing Wagner eye-to-eye.

'Herr Schroeder, I want to congratulate you on your initiative. I'm quite sure that I have never before heard "Deutschland Über Alles" sung with such intensity, such conviction!'

'Thank you, Herr Wagner. You are very kind. If I may, I will share your remarks with the men when we meet tomorrow morning.'

'Please do so, Herr Schroeder. Herr Klausen tells me he has instigated a National Socialist Indoctrination Programme, and the singing is part of that initiative.'

'Yes, Herr Wagner. Herr Klausen is very advanced in his thinking about the future of the Party. I was honoured when he asked me to take charge of his programme.'

'Starting a programme like this is very resourceful. Herr Klausen tells me he selected you because of your deep commitment to the Party. You can be sure that the Party will hear of your achievements, and I can't help but think there's a bright future for both of you. Tell me about the singing. Are you a musician?'

'My musical training is very limited, Herr Wagner. I don't play an instrument. As a youngster, I sang in the cathedral choir. Our chorister trained some of us in conducting. When he died, the priest who managed the music asked me to take on the role.'

'Your conducting this morning seemed masterful to me. Tell me, why did you choose to start the programme with singing?'

'Because singing brings the men together. It melds them into a unit. When we move on to other things, such as the study of *Mein Kampf*, the discussion tends to be more constructive.'

'That I can understand. *Mein Kampf* can be very challenging, Herr Schroeder. It is easy for me to see other places where such an initiative would be useful. How would you feel about managing similar programmes elsewhere?'

'Well, of course, but Herr Klausen may have something to say about that.'

'Herr Klausen and I have spoken. I think he sees the benefits of using your skills more widely.'

'In that case, I would be most honoured to serve in that way.'

'Good man. We'll see you at my office first thing Monday morning.'

When the meeting finishes, Wagner himself, smiling and enthusiastic, sees Thomas from the office.

As the door closes behind him, Thomas thinks, *Well then, smart guy, there's no going back now.*

———

Meanwhile, back at his own office, Wagner has no difficulty in spotting an opportunity for self-promotion. And he is not shy about acting on the impulse.

He lifts his phone and says to his adjutant, 'Get me in touch with the *Völkischer Beobachter*.'

     R. WILLIAM PLUME

Derek Crampton, standing before his brother, Martin, smacks the *Illustrated London News* down onto the registry office counter.

The headline reads:

**German Duo Lay Groundwork for
Promotion of Nazism.**

**National Socialist Indoctrination
Programme Begins in Munich.**

On the front page is a photograph of Thomas and Wagner.

'Is that him?' demands Derek, jabbing a finger at the banner photograph. Is this the Thomas von Stauffenberg who came to the registry office wanting to know about his mother?'

'It's possible, but don't forget, Derek, that I only saw him once *and* then only briefly, *and* it was quite a long time ago. And in the meantime, everybody's been here looking into that guy. The Foreign Offices of both England and Germany have been here. Employees of and detectives working for the Bank of England. And your mates from Scotland Yard. They've all been here. Some of them multiple times,' says Martin.

'When you asked him what his name was, what was his answer?' asks Derek.

'Thomas.'

'Just "Thomas", not Thomas von Stauffenberg?'

'No. He said "Thomas", and I assumed the surname.'

'So he could be a half-brother to Philip?'

'Yes, if his mother was someone other than Sarah Michaela. But even so, he would still be a von Stauffenberg, though not necessarily Jewish,' Martin explains.

'Didn't Thomas say at the time that Philip was alive and well and in London?'

'He did.'

'Did he say where in London?'

'He did not. And before you ask everybody's favourite question, "Do you have an address for Philip?", I do not.'

'Wooo-ooo! Who's the snarky little brother? What's got into you, eh?'

'You and all your detective mates, mate. I'm going to write a little book about Philip. I'm going to put a stack of 'em on the counter here with a little sign that says, "Are You Interested in Philip von Stauffenberg? Read this. Take one. They're free." Now, brother of mine, I'm busy. I've got work to do. Have you got any more questions?'

Derek looks at his exasperated brother. For a moment he considers giving him a hug and walking out the door, but instead he says, 'Yes, I do.'

Derek flips through his notebook and says, 'I have it that his mother's name was Elisabeth.'

'That's the name Thomas gave me as well. What I know for sure is that *Philip's* mother was *not* named Elisabeth. Her name was Sarah Michaela Goldsmid.'

'Of the banking Goldsmids? She was Jewish?'

'Without a doubt.'

'So that's what Uncle Klemens was rattling on about,' muses Derek.

'Eh?'

'Never mind. It's a von Stauffenberg clan issue. So Thomas and Philip could be half-brothers?'

'Only if Konrad fathered both of them and Sarah and Elisabeth are not the same woman. But it's possible, even probable, that Sarah used Elisabeth as a pseudonym.'

'In which case, Thomas and Philip would be full brothers,' Derek remarks.

'Oh, well done, Mr Fabulous Detective! Of course. And not just full brothers but both of them Jewish. But now, returning to this photograph,

     R. WILLIAM PLUME

I note that the name given in this article is Thomas H. R. Schroeder, not Thomas von Stauffenberg.'

'I see that, brother, but ignore the name. I want to know if the person in the *photo* is the person who came here looking for information about his mother.'

'I can't be sure, Mr Persistent. I might be inclined to tell *you* that it's the same person, but if I were asked to swear on Holy Scripture, I could not do so.'

'Not enough to drag him in, perhaps, but it's a lead. That's good enough,' says Derek.

'I suggested that he, Thomas, talk to the records people at the Congregation of Jacob Synagogue. If he did as I advised, they will almost certainly have a home address in Germany. 'Now, *go!*

Derek grins and asks, 'Do you have an address for the synagogue?'

Martin punches his brother on the shoulder. Derek laughs as Martin pushes him towards the door. 'Out! … Out! … OUT!' he commands. 'And *don't* come back unless you're going to stand me a stout!'

THE REAL INDOCTRINATION PROGRAMME STARTS

After the incredible events of the previous week, Klausen is bubbling. He can't do enough for Thomas. 'You need space? Workbooks? Printed course material? Paper? Pencils? Shut down production to accommodate classes? Just say the word. And we'll have to find a more suitable role for you in the factory. The acid bath is not appropriate for a man of your calibre. I'll promote you to Chief of National Socialist Studies.'

On Tuesday morning, Thomas keeps the men back after the singing. Today, the first coursework class begins. It starts with Nazi Party history. Everyone is there. All manufacturing processes have been placed on standby.

'Gentlemen, today we are going to begin the next phase of the

National Socialist Indoctrination Programme. We have learned how to sing together, and we do that so very well! You are to be congratulated! Give yourself a round of applause!'

A cheer goes up from the men around the room. There is a little commotion near the front which attracts Thomas' attention. He sees a few men pushing another man forward.

'C'mon, Deet, go! Do it!'

A chant begins, 'Go Deet! Go Deet! Go Deet!'

Deet rises from his chair, and, awkwardly, he steps forward.

'Herr Schroeder?'

'Yes, Dieter?'

'Herr Schroeder, I want to thank you. Umm, we all want to thank you for teaching us guys to sing "Deutschland Über Alles" every morning. At first it was a little strange. Well, it was really strange and, you know, hard. But now, you know, we all want to do it. Even Herr Müllner.'

Everyone laughs. Deet laughs a little, too, and adds, 'You know what? Some of these guys only come to work so they can sing in the morning. But seriously, we all look forward to it. Now we'd all like to say thank you the best way we know how.'

He turns to face the group, and they all stand. Deet raises his hands to the *quiet-please* position, and the entire room sings, *voce piena*, for Thomas.

'Deutschland, Deutschland, über alles ...'

Thomas cannot withhold his tears. *Gracious God in heaven, forgive me for what I am about to do to these men.*

———

The following day the men gather to move into the substance of the second phase of Thomas' programme.

'Gentlemen, yesterday we were going to begin learning about our Party. But that was postponed by more singing and your gracious acknowledgement of the work we have done together. And I thank you most sincerely for the lovely gesture. We have learned how to sing together. Now we are going to learn how to think together. We will study the concept of "Führerprinzip" and what it means to "work towards the Führer". In a few weeks, we will move into a discussion of *Mein Kampf*. Gentlemen, this will be difficult, and it will take time. So, now is the time to get your own copy of *Mein Kampf* and start reading it. But today we'll set the scene for our work with some Party history. Who can tell me when our Führer was born?'

Silence.

'No one knows?'

Silence.

'Our Führer, Adolf Hitler, christened Adolphus, was born on the twentieth of April 1889 at six thirty in the evening. Can anyone tell me the names of his mother and father?'

Silence.

'His mother's name was Klara, and his father's name was Alois. These are simple, though not trivial, historical facts that you should try to remember. They help us in a small way to understand his origins. They also help us to understand the beginnings of the development of his mind and his thinking.

'Our Führer had a difficult relationship with his father. What young man does not? But he was devoted to his mother and has remained so to this day. Both his mother and his father died when he was a young man. Suddenly, he found himself alone in the world. He was thrown onto his own resources to survive.

'Our Führer is an artist of very considerable talent – decades ahead of his time in his artistic insight and expression. He applied twice to the Vienna Academy of Fine Arts and was rejected on both occasions by shallow-minded men unable to see his great artistic power.'

'Herr Schroeder?'

'You have a question?'

'Yes, Herr Schroeder. Vienna is in Austria, isn't it?'

'Yes, it is.'

'Why didn't he go to the Fine Arts Academy here in Munich?'

Another workman interjects, 'Because he isn't German. He was born in Austria.'

Thomas intervenes. 'It is true that our Führer was born in the German-speaking part of Austria. It is true, technically, that he is not a German citizen –'

A murmur of surprise runs around the room.

'But let's remember that in every other respect he is German to the ends of his toes. He volunteered to fight alongside Germans in the war. He signed up just hours after war was declared and spent the entire war at the Front, showing exemplary bravery under fire. Our Führer was awarded the Iron Cross for bravery not just once but twice. A clearer statement of his devotion to Germany, the German people, and German art and culture is impossible to imagine.'

'But he's not German?'

'No. *Technically* speaking, he is not German,' Thomas says.

And conversations among the men start bouncing around the room again.

'How can he be "our Führer" then?'

Thomas draws his papers into his chest. 'If he thinks of himself as German, then he's German.'

'That's fine if you're a butcher or … or … or a worker in a ball-bearing factory, but if you're looking to be the Chancellor of Germany, shouldn't you be German? Why isn't he leading the Austrians down the golden path to glory?'

'And what the hell's wrong with being a worker in a ball-bearing factory, Herr Vorrath?'

'Nothing. I just think that the Chancellor of Germany should be –'

The sentence is never finished. The challenger advances from the back of the room. A single blow sends the speaker sprawling to the floor.

'Gentlemen, gentlemen! Control yourselves! This is not a beer hall!'

'Yeah, well, maybe not, but that guy better watch his mouth.'

'I think we better stop for today. You and you, help me get this man to the sickbay.'

THOMAS COACHES BRÜNNER TO SUBVERT SHIPPING

'You handle the inward/outward shipping at the factory?' asks Thomas.

'And the mail. I pick up the mail from the post office every morning and post it every afternoon,' Brünner replies.

'Does the mail include such things as purchase orders, invoices, shipping manifests, and so on?'

'Almost all of it concerns exactly that. The purchase orders and invoices come from Herr Klausen. Shipping manifests, inward and outward, are handled by the floor manager.'

'Do you see the documents? Do they come from Herr Klausen or the floor manager in a sealed envelope or as an open document?'

'Most of it is just a pile of paper. I'm expected to sort it out, stuff it into envelopes, add the address, and add the postage.'

'For orders being shipped from the factory, do you know who the client is? Do you know where the bearings are going?'

'I know the destination of *all* orders. The address used depends on whether it's classified or not. If it's classified, it comes to me in a sealed envelope addressed to an anonymous post box number. If it's unclassified, it goes to a physical address with a name. The name "Krupp Industries", for example, may appear in the address. Both Herr Klausen and the floor manager tend towards carelessness about the way they handle correspondence and shipping documentation. They make mistakes regularly. That has made it possible for me to work out which company goes with which post box number.'

'If neither Herr Klausen nor the floor manager is consistent about the way they deal with the mail and documentation, then something could get lost, get put into the wrong envelope, go to the wrong address, or turn up at the post office with insufficient postage. That would be easy to do, wouldn't it?' Thomas says.

'That sort of thing doesn't happen very often because I do the job well. But if I'm getting your drift, perhaps I'm doing it too well.'

'If a purchase order for feedstock came to you from Herr Klausen, would you be able to delay forwarding it long enough for the factory's feedstock to run out?'

'Very easily. The factory will exhaust its supply of chromium steel within about twenty-four hours if a new supply isn't delivered on time.'

'And if a purchase order went to the wrong address and was then returned by the post office and sent out again to the correct address, thirty-six hours more or less could go by? What happens then?'

'If the feedstock runs out, the entire process must stop. And it takes a while to get the machines going again when the feedstock does arrive.'

'You appear to have grasped what I have in mind. Can you do it?'

'Yes, I certainly can. I'm disappointed that I didn't think of it myself.'

TRAINING SESSIONS DESCEND INTO ASSAULT

'Once again, gentlemen,' says Thomas, 'the singing of "Deutschland Über Alles" this morning was beautifully well done. You are to be congratulated. But now, we need to begin our discussion of Nazi Party structure. And who is at the top?' Thomas asks.

'Well, it's the Führer, Hitler, himself, Herr Schroeder. Did you not know that?' someone says, causing a smattering of laughter.

Thomas smiles and says, 'We are all members of the Party. Who can tell me when it started and who started it?'

'Surely it was Hitler, Herr Schroeder.'

'It seems like it should have been, but it wasn't. It was started by a man by the name of Anton Drexler on the fifth of January 1919. Can

 R. WILLIAM PLUME

anyone tell me when our Führer joined the Party?'

'I think it was September 1919, wasn't it?' says someone.

'Very good! That is correct. Between January and September 1919, Herr Drexler only managed to scrape together fifty-four members. Then in September 1919, the Führer joined the Party. Now the Party has millions of members, all due to the tireless efforts of … Yes?' says Thomas, pointing to a raised hand at the back of the room.

'Herr Schroeder, I thought the Führer was member number five five five?'

'No, he was member number fifty-five, because didn't they start the numbering at five hundred?' asks another workman.

'Then he was number fifty-six,' someone throws in.

'How do you figure that?'

'If they started the numbering at five hundred and his number was triple five, he was the fifty-sixth member. Just count starting at zero.'

'I don't get that. But why did they start at five hundred anyway?'

'To make the Party look bigger than it really was.'

'Nahh. They didn't do kid stuff like that.'

'Except they did.'

'Herr Schroeder, is that what happened?'

'What happened was that our Führer joined a rudderless and lazy bunch of beer enthusiasts, and he transformed it into the greatest political powerhouse this country, possibly the world, has ever known. Gentlemen, do not be distracted by trivia. Do not be confused by history. All of what's been said is true, but what does it matter? As far as I'm concerned, his member number is one!' says Thomas.

'With respect, Herr Schroeder, now it is you who is being distracted by trivia.'

'How so?' Thomas asks.

'We were discussing Party structure. The Führer is the leader of the party. We all recognise that. Why does it matter whether his Party number is one or fifty-five … or 3,579?'

'It matters to our Führer,' says Thomas.

'Does it?' The man glances from side to side, wondering if he should voice what's on his mind. 'Then he is the one being distracted by trivia,' he blurts out.

Thomas feigns indignation. He drops his jaw, turns a little sideways, puts his papers down on the table, and holds them down with a splayed hand. He is the very picture of indulgent disappointment. He stands motionless, silently urging someone to step into the gap. As pregnant silence begins to glide into awkwardness, someone does.

'Well, it matters to me too, and it pisses me off when people second-guess the Führer, saying stuff like he's distracted by trivia. If you think he's so silly, mister, why are you a member of the Party then, eh?'

'Because you have to be a member to get work these days.'

'Well, then, are you some kind of Party poseur? Looks like you are, so why don't you just fuck off?' snarls the man, standing abruptly. His chair clatters to the floor behind him. A half-second later, he is lifting the other man from his chair by the front of his shirt.

For Thomas, the scene plays out in slow motion. He times his intervention to perfection. He waits until the instant *after* the punch is thrown.

'Gentlemen! Gentlemen! Stop!' He orders the attacker to sit down and helps the other man, whose nose is bleeding heavily, back into his chair. 'We will continue this discussion tomorrow. Let's all go to our stations and get to work.'

———

'There was another confrontation this morning,' Thomas says to Klausen.

'That's the fourth one, or is it the fifth? You don't seem too concerned. Is this going to be a common occurrence in your meetings, Herr Schroeder?'

'I'm not concerned, Herr Klausen. And you needn't be either. What we are witnessing here is the elegant subtlety of Party doctrine.'

       R. WILLIAM PLUME

'Really? Looks like a breakdown in employee relations to me. If this keeps happening, it won't be long before they're at each other's throats and production will drop through the floor. Nothing subtle about that, Herr Schroeder.'

'Our Führer recognises that in all areas of life there must be competition. The strongest will dominate and survive; the weak will fall away. The principle applies at all levels of life, from the relations between countries right down to the interactions between individuals. What we are seeing here is the practical expression of that principle. For you, it means that what you will be left with is the best possible workforce. I'll grant that it's a little unfortunate for the person attacked, but so be it.'

Klausen is not convinced. But when it comes to trading points of Party doctrine, he knows he is out of his depth when he's up against Thomas.

He takes the path of least resistance. 'Alright, Herr Schroeder. Just don't let it get out of hand.'

THOMAS GOES TO WORK FOR WAGNER

The lunchtime indoctrination sessions continue with Klausen's enthusiastic support and encouragement. The daily singing of 'Deutschland Über Alles' settles into a pattern. The men look forward to it, and they are always pleased with the result.

One morning, after the singing, Brünner brings a hammer to Thomas' new office. He puts his head through the open doorway and says, 'You wanted to borrow this, Herr Schroeder?' and puts it on top of the filing cabinet.

Thomas takes this reversal of the usual process to mean *Meeting tonight, usual time, usual place.*

When Thomas arrives, Brünner says, 'You got the message, Herr Schroeder. I thought you would.'

'Very cleverly delivered, Herr Brünner. What news?'

'Your strategy is working. The whispers and lies are starting to anchor themselves. Cliques are forming. Herr Müllner is one demerit shy of having his pay docked, and he's not happy about it. On Tuesday, he said, "We didn't have none of this demerit bullshit before Herr Bloody Fucking Schroeder came here. Dock my pay, and I'll dock his fuckin' head!"'

'You heard him say this?'

'Yes. It was in the dayroom at the end of shift. People were milling around and looking at the demerit list to see if they had any new ones. Müllner had been given another one. He was angry and loud. Couldn't miss it. No mistaking who said it, and no mistaking what was said.'

'Well then,' Thomas says, 'it's time to put more grease on the pole.'

The following day, Thomas meets with Klausen. Thomas raises an issue of concern for him: the problem created by the demerit point plan. Klausen says the system seems to be working well enough, and, by the way, Herr Wagner approves of it. Thomas agrees that the problem is minor but thinks perhaps some thought should be given to improvements.

'What did you have in mind, Herr Schroeder?'

'Only that it has been noted that the process only works one-way. A workman can gather up demerit points, and that leads to loss of pay, and, as we've seen, there's one person who is only one point away from losing his job.'

Klausen interrupts to say, 'Have you forgotten, Herr Schroeder, that it was your plan?'

'It was a plan that I suggested, Herr Klausen, but as the leader here, you approved it, and it is you who will benefit from it. Herr Wagner was very impressed with your initiative, and you are the one who will get the well-deserved promotion.'

Klausen is keen to move up the Party ladder, and now advancement is within his reach. And it is Thomas who has made it possible. Klausen's ambition again intrudes upon his thinking. Once more, he shifts his ground.

'Let's back up a little, Herr Schroeder. Do you have a change to propose?'

Thomas begins wondering aloud, asking if there might be some way to balance things a little. 'Well, it's just swings and roundabouts. The positives and the negatives balance each other and might provide a way to even things up.'

He drops 'offsetting merit points' into the conversation but presents it as though it is one of several possibilities. He makes no mention of the others.

'I'm not sure, Herr Klausen. I bring it to you because it's the sort of problem you handle so well. Perhaps you could give it some thought. I'm sure that a good solution will sharpen people's attention, and they will appreciate the consideration. And a suggestion box might be a good idea. And one last thing, Herr Klausen. I think you must have been informed by letter from Herr Wagner that I will be resigning my post here to assist him in the Provincial Indoctrination Programme.'

Klausen interrupts not by speaking but by a startled look at Thomas.

'Ahhh,' he says, drawing the word out, for he is struggling to find words to follow. He finds one: 'Well.'

'All will be well, Herr Klausen. I wish you every success, for you deserve everything that's coming your way!'

AN AFFIRMATION BOX IS INSTALLED

Klausen does think about it. But the 'it' that he considers is more about his promotion prospects and less about solving the difficulties at the factory. His first thought is ensuring there is some scheme that brings his exemplary initiative to the attention of Herr Wagner. Then he thinks about the demerit problem.

Perhaps what Schroeder meant with all that blathering on about swings and roundabouts and balancing things is a merit programme that will offset demerits. Sounds plausible. We'll do that.

To enhance the likelihood that Herr Wagner will look favourably on the new programme, he takes pains to ensure that merit points are linked to National Socialism.

Workers earn merit points by spotting departures from the Aryan Standard or the Aryan Ideal and reporting them. They can also earn merit points by having the right attitude and identifying those who don't. They can earn merit points by reporting workers who do not arrive back at their station in a timely fashion after the lunch break or those who arrive at the plant too late or leave too early. Reporting general deficiencies, behaviours, and physical characteristics that are inconsistent with the Aryan archetype is encouraged.

Klausen has grasped the nettle. He felt abandoned when Thomas gave his notice, but now, suddenly, his ideas are flowing, his confidence is brimming over, and his future still looks bright.

Now he revisits Thomas' idea of a suggestion box. *It's brilliant!* It will make it possible for workers to report things discreetly. The box will be installed in the dayroom. Workers make their observations known to Klausen by writing them down and putting the paper into the box.

But 'Suggestion Box' gives the impression that he is acknowledging that his own ideas are somehow incomplete or inadequate. An alternative name eludes him. He tries 'Affirmation Box'. *After all, people are affirming such and such. I suppose it could be the Assertion Box — people asserting this or that. But that sounds too … What? Mechanical? Elitist? I don't know. 'Affirmation Box' it is.*

A part of Klausen cringes at the silliness of the name he selects. But that part is shoved aside by his National Socialist self, which fancies it emblematic of relentless positivity, as in '*Affirmation* Box' or '*The* Affirmation Box'. Herr Goebbels himself would approve. *Hah! Well done, you!*

The tangible box is a solid wooden container bolted to the floor. It has a hinged, lockable lid which features a narrow slot. Once things go in, there's no getting them out without the key or a sledgehammer. Klausen reviews his solution to the demerit problem and congratulates himself. *I've been working towards the Führer. Herr Schroeder would be impressed.*

Klausen comes to the morning gathering to announce the new initiative before the daily singing begins. The men are gathered, standing, and waiting.

'You all know that recently I initiated a demerit programme designed to foster a wholehearted, full-blooded commitment to National Socialism. The programme has been very successful. I can hear the singing even from my office, and I congratulate you! Your singing improves with each passing day.

'But I have decided that a demerit programme without a merit programme is too one-sided: it marks only the things you do wrong. Now I want to give you the opportunity to be rewarded for the things you do correctly: a merit programme.'

He enumerates the things that workers can do to earn merit points, which boil down to reporting failures to meet the Aryan Ideal.

'I have also had installed in the dayroom a box I call the "Affirmation Box", and, no doubt, you will have seen that the work has been done. You can write your ideas on a slip of paper, put it into the box, and it will be dealt with promptly. The number of merit points will be assessed based on the quality of the information passed on. And remember that your report must be signed, or I will have to award the merit points to myself.'

He chuckles, though no one else does, at his subtle sense of humour.

Müllner immediately spots the opportunity to reverse his demerit ranking. Others also seize on the opportunity, and before the end of shift, there are already 'affirmation notes' in the box.

Overnight Klausen's life changes.

Müllner affirms that Herr So-and-So was far longer than necessary in the toilet. His, Müllner's, demerit count is reduced by one. He lines up other infractions he can report and other co-workers he can finger. He is already thinking that when he gets points onto the merit side of the ledger, he will begin to agitate for merit bonuses. *After all, if you can be docked for too many demerits, you should get a bonus for merits, right?*

Herr So-and-So is called to Klausen's office and reprimanded for shirking in the toilet. Herr So-and-So is indignant and maintains that he has never done any such thing. 'Look at my production statistics if you don't believe me. You can't get production like that if you're jerking off in the WC.'

Klausen has blundered by rewarding Müllner the merit points before speaking with So-and-So. He attempts to reassure So-and-So, telling him that his production figures are outstanding. 'But, please, don't give people a reason to tag you.'

'Who tagged me?' he asks.

'Ah, well, of course, I can't reveal that information.'

'Well then, since you know who it is, you give him this message from me: If this happens again, I will find out who you are, and when I do, you – whoever you are – will be in serious trouble. Tell him that.'

As an afterthought, he adds, 'Am I going to get a demerit point for this?'

Klausen is cornered. 'Not this time,' he says and dismisses Herr So-and-So, hoping he will leave the office without further confrontation. So-and-So leaves, but he is muttering.

It isn't long before the Affirmation Box is full at the end of each day. It has become a big problem for Klausen. It has achieved nothing and created endless problems. But if he stops the programme, he will get hard-knuckle resistance.

Meanwhile, production is trending in the wrong direction. Klausen uses every device he can invent to make the figures look better than they are.

Then, for the first time, he misses a delivery. The buyer is furious; the delay has compromised his contractual obligations. To add to Klausen's troubles, a delivery of chromium steel has been delayed for no obvious reason, and production has ground to a halt.

And the singing of 'Deutschland Über Alles' has lost its inspirational lustre.

CHAPTER 16

31 January 1933

HITLER BECOMES CHANCELLOR

Thomas points at the Bürgerbräukeller. 'That is where it started.'

The weather is cracking cold. Both Thomas and Reinhard are exhaling clouds. They wear hats, gloves, and hefty overcoats. 'You sound like a tour guide, Thomas. Why have you asked me here?'

The two men are standing on Rosenheimerstrasse, not far from the solid masonry archway that is the main gate into the Bürgerbräukeller. Even if they wanted to, they couldn't get any closer. The beer hall is full to overflowing with boisterous revellers. The outside gardens are packed with beer drinkers, vigorously banging crockery mugs together, singing one martial song after another. They are having the time of their lives, for yesterday, Reichspräsident Paul von Hindenburg appointed Adolf Hitler to the office of Chancellor of Germany.

Thomas ignores the question. 'That is where Hitler failed for the last time. Ten years ago, hubris got the better of him. He thought he was powerful enough, smart enough, organised enough to storm the halls of power. He was convicted of treason and, all up, spent more than a year in Landsberg Prison.'

Reinhard waits, stomps his feet a couple of times, rubs his gloved hands together and jams them back into the pockets of his greatcoat.

Both men are uncomfortably cold. But Thomas is also troubled by serious challenges. He is reciting aloud his thoughts, almost unaware of Reinhard standing silent beside him. 'Something happened to him in

Landsberg. He went in there a persuasive but still run-of-the-mill rabble-rouser. But something, more likely someone, in Landsberg opened his eyes, showed him the way, and gave him the key. When he came out of prison, he had a clear plan for getting himself to where he wanted to be. And now, ten years later, he is Chancellor of Germany.'

Reinhard sees that his participation in this one-sided conversation is not necessary.

'People have underestimated him time and again. He has outsmarted everyone. Now the best the Prussian Old Guard can do is shoehorn Herr Franz von Papen into the role of Vice Chancellor, thinking von Papen will control Hitler's excesses. Small chance, I'd guess, but perhaps we shouldn't be too hasty. Von Papen may yet show there's a rod of steel up his back.'

Thomas turns and starts walking down Rosenheimerstrasse towards the Isar River. Reinhard stays with him. The rowdy crowds recede. When they arrive in the middle of Ludwigsbrücke, Thomas stops and looks up and down the bridge. The two men are alone. They lean a little over the balustrade, looking down on an Isar solidly ice-encrusted.

Thomas turns his head to look at Reinhard. 'Twenty years ago, you came to Brightstone seeking my help to commit treason. Now I need your help to commit treason.'

Reinhard stands upright. 'Tell me what you're thinking.'

'When I set out to put the skids under Streicher, my only purpose was to separate him from you. But it succeeded so well that I began to think that it might be possible to take on the entire Nazi Party. But to *strike* at the heart of the Party, I must *be* at the heart of the Party, and hence the National Socialist Indoctrination Programme. We are about to release the programme throughout Bavaria.'

'Things are working like clockwork, Thomas. What's the problem?'

'Of course, I'm pleased. It's developing just the way I hoped it would. But as of yesterday, everything has changed. Until then, I was working towards the destruction of a political party. As of yesterday, I'm subverting the government of Germany. I'm up against an altogether different beast.

'The Nazi government has all the resources, the money, and the power they need to pursue anything or anyone not in tune with their plan. They have the police, the military, the SA and the SS, both of which are now government entities. And they have a powerful inclination to snuff out opposition. The original intent of the Indoctrination Programme boiled down to political activism. Now its aim is treason at the outer limit. I need to know how it ends.'

The two men stand with their elbows on the railing, looking out over the river.

After a time, Reinhard puts his arm around Thomas' shoulders and says, 'Let's go to Monsieur Buteau's. It's not far from here. We can warm up and have dinner, and I have a thought to share with you.'

———

Buteau is fetching wine. Thomas and Reinhard are beginning to recover from the cold.

Reinhard steers the conversation in a gentle direction. 'Herr Wagner sounds like a very capable fellow.'

'He's a very skilled administrator. He's nobody's fool.'

'Except yours?'

'Ah, trust you to spot that.' Thomas is silent for a moment. 'If it were possible by some magic to lift away the Nazi influence from Germany, remove it from people's consciousness as if it had never been, there would be millions of people throughout this country with whom you could be on good terms. Polite, generous, engaging. You could go to the Gasthaus with Wagner. You'd have a few beers and share a very enjoyable evening with him. You might not believe it, but he has a sense of humour. He's the kind of person you'd want for a neighbour. You could borrow his crosscut saw and keep it for a year, and he wouldn't care.'

'And your fear is that Wagner and people like him will suffer in the conflict that you are setting up?'

Buteau returns with the wine. Thomas, pointing with a little circular motion, tells Buteau to skip the wine choreography and pour. Buteau complies with an abbreviated but graceful version of the wine ritual and retires from the table.

Two glasses clink together with a nod, and the two men sip.

Twirling his glass, Thomas says, 'When I was hiding in Meersburg, I never took alcohol. Buying it broke my little bubble of hermitage. In the early days, I didn't feel I could take the risk of discovery. As time went on and we, Elisabeth and I, settled into that life together, taking alcohol wasn't part of it. But here we are – lovely wine, good food to come, pleasant company. I didn't mean to be patronising, Reinhard, but I'm concerned.'

'I understand, Thomas, but now you're worried, and not about me, but the people who will be affected by what you're doing.'

'Of course,' replies Thomas. 'If you don't put yourself among them, it's easy to dismiss them as nothing more than a bunch of beer-swilling street thugs. True, some of them are evil bastards, but most of them are just folks misled.'

Thomas brings the conversation back to the starting point. 'You said you had an idea. How is it ended? How are things restored to normal?'

'Martial law,' replies Reinhard.

'An interesting suggestion. How do you plan to bring it about?'

'Does the name Erich von Manstein ring any bells?' asks Reinhard.

Thomas devotes a little time to dusting off memories but says, 'No.'

'He is now General Staff, Reichswehr, Berlin. He is Oberstleutnant, Lieutenant Colonel von Manstein. Erich and I were both cadets in our youth. We were at the Berlin Militärakademie together. We became close friends and have maintained contact since those days.'

'Yes. And?'

'Does the name Field Marshal Paul von Hindenburg ring any bells?' asks Reinhard.

'Ah, now we're in familiar territory. Yes, of course.'

'Since you don't know Oberstleutnant von Manstein, you won't know that Generalfeldmarschall Paul von Hindenburg is his uncle.'

Thomas' eyes widen. He places both hands on the table and leans forward.

'Is he just?'

Thomas has read Reinhard's mind and divined the direction of his thinking.

Reinhard continues, 'We know that Reichspräsident von Hindenburg has the statutory power to dismiss a government and declare martial law. We also know that von Hindenburg has, at best, an ambivalent attitude towards Hitler. Hardly surprising. Von Hindenburg, Prussian by descent – the son of a Prussian officer of old Junker stock, that is to say, aristocratic – is a field marshal to this day. Whereas Hitler was only a corporal. That is a very wide chasm to close.

'We will see how things play out, but as Germany learns what Hitler has in mind for it, we may find that von Hindenburg will review his statutory options. I will, with the greatest discretion, make enquiries with my friend, Erich, as to what might be required for von Hindenburg to take the ultimate step.'

Thomas raises his glass. 'That might work.'

'Then we will march together into the valley of death, my friend.'

27 FEBRUARY 1933. THE REICHSTAG BURNS

'Are you aware, Reinhard, of what's happening in Berlin?'

'If it is the Reichstag fire you are referring to, Thomas, then, yes. I read about it in the morning paper.'

'Yes, that. But are you aware of its consequences? The fire at the parliament building has given Hitler a pretext to request emergency powers from Herr von Hindenburg, and he has already signed the enabling legislation, the Reichstag Fire Decree.'

          R. WILLIAM PLUME

'Already? The fire was yesterday.'

'That should tell you something about what an astute politician Hitler is. He has been Chancellor for only four weeks, and already von Hindenburg has handed him sweeping powers to do, close enough, whatever he wants.'

'It does beg the question, who started the fire?' Reinhard asks.

'Hitler has already stuck the blame squarely on the Communists. What the truth is, we may never know. What we do know is that he has already used the decree to ban all political parties other than the Nazi Party. He has also suspended freedom of the press, freedom of speech, and the right to free assembly.

'Restraints on police investigations are gone. He is free to arrest and incarcerate anyone, including his political opponents. He needn't bother with charges. And he can confiscate private property. He will ignore the Reichstag – wherever it chooses to sit – from this day forward. This fire has put him squarely on the path to full dictatorship. "Marching together into the valley of death" seems a little more visceral today, does it not?'

'As if it weren't visceral enough,' adds Reinhard.

ADOLF WAGNER'S OFFICE, MUNICH

What Herr Wagner saw at the ball-bearing factory inspired him in a way that he had forgotten was possible. Yes, he knows the bearing factory is going through a bad patch, but his attention is elsewhere. The difficulties at the factory are a vague gloom, best left behind him. He will not be deflected from the satisfaction that awaits him by what is nothing more than an incompetent manager. The factory will sort itself out.

Wagner, meanwhile, is moving forward with all possible haste. His eyes and his hopes are fixed on the future. What he sees is brightness rimmed with glory.

He starts by considering his options for spreading the word as quickly and as widely as possible. A weekend Kreisleiter conference for his province is, he concludes, the standout best option. Wagner will use this meeting of the district leaders to initiate the implementation of the Indoctrination Programme throughout the province. Thomas will provide the inspiration. Wagner will set down what is required from each Kreisleiter.

An important consideration is ensuring that his name is tied to this initiative. After all, he is its champion, and he wants this known from the start to prevent ambitious others from muscling him out of his golden opportunity.

The best way to keep a firm grip on the project is to inform and solicit approval from his superior, Reichsleiter Robert Ley. Wagner sends an appropriate memorandum through the internal mail system. The request gets Ley's languid, pro forma, don't-bother-me-with-trivia, get-on-with-it agreement.

Wagner can now devote time to planning the conference. He allows his mind to wander into the details of the opening ceremony. *Will there be music? Martial music? Not 'Deutschland Über Alles' – I'll save that for Thomas. I'll surprise him. I'll ask him to lead the group in singing. Perhaps the 'Horst Wessel Song' instead?*

There is, Wagner knows, a dais. *That will give Thomas room to move around while he speaks. When all the Kreisleiter are seated, I will enter, stage left.*

Wagner is chuffed to think that he's hit upon that theatrical embellishment. *I will go out onto the dais and introduce myself, welcome everybody, and make them feel comfortable. And finally, the grand entrance! The star attraction! Enter stage right! Thomas himself! Please be upstanding and welcome –*

There is a knock on his office door.

Thomas takes the liberty of opening the door, half-entering the office, looking around the door, and saying, 'You wanted to see me, sir?'

'Herr Thomas Schroeder! Herr Thomas … Schroeder. Herr Schroeder … Yes, yes … Yes, I do, Thomas … Herr Schroeder, come in.'

'I don't often get a welcome like that, Herr Wagner. What's on your mind?'

The Kreisleiter conference is on his mind. Wagner shares with Thomas what he has organised. Wagner is buzzing with excitement.

He asks Thomas to be prepared to participate in the conference as the principal contributor. *Not writing your script for you, but do this and say that, and make sure you cover this, and don't forget that* is the substance of Wagner's requirements.

———

A large hall is full of bright, eager young men, all in uniform and all mightily pleased with themselves. Their futures could not look brighter. They have Gauleiter Wagner to thank for their good fortune, and they show it.

When Wagner appears on the dais, he is welcomed with a spontaneous, loud, and extended standing ovation. Smiling broadly, he holds both hands above his head and waves them to bring the applause to an end. He thanks the audience and plunges straight into the substance of the meeting.

'Gentlemen, we have a very special guest with us today: Herr Thomas Schroeder. Recently it was suggested to me that I should make a visit to one of our factories in Munich. I wasn't sure what to expect, but on arrival, I was introduced to Herr Schroeder, who was at the point of leading the factory workers in singing "Deutschland Über Alles"! I can tell you, gentlemen, that I have never before heard that anthem sung with more power and conviction. Herr Schroeder formed a choir from the workers at the factory and taught them how to sing, and, my God, do they sing!

'Herr Schroeder is also leading a Nazi Party Indoctrination Programme at the factory. I've asked him to come here today because I think what he is doing should be done more widely. I will come back to that after he has had an opportunity to tell you about what he is doing. Please welcome Herr Thomas Schroeder!'

Thomas walks to the front of the dais and is welcomed with a generous round of applause. 'Thank you, Herr Wagner,' he starts. 'At times like this, it can be difficult to know where to begin, so I will start at the beginning. The National Socialist Indoctrination Programme certainly began humbly and without pretension. In truth, it began before it was a National Socialist Indoctrination Programme. I have, for several years, immersed myself in the study of the dazzling genius of our Führer – the clarity of his thinking, the genius of his solutions, and the precision of his goals for Germany.

'Somewhere in that process, I began to think that everyone should have a better understanding of our Führer's ideas. That developed into the National Socialist Indoctrination Programme. And, as they say, the rest is history. But it is a history not yet complete. That is why we are here today, to begin to do our part to achieve for Germany the Aryan Ideal that our Führer has set out for us! Thank you!'

The applause for Thomas is little short of an ovation.

Wagner, smiling broadly, approaches him and shakes his hand vigorously. When the applause has subsided, he says, 'Would you care to lead us, Herr Schroeder, in the singing of "Deutschland Über Alles"?'

Thomas is genuinely and pleasantly surprised. 'I am greatly honoured to do so. Please stand, gentlemen, and put your head back slightly so your voice is aimed just above my head. Now then, let's do this like we mean it!'

They sing the anthem as they always sing it. Thomas is animated and convincing. His conducting follows rather than leads, but he knows the men will be happy with the result. They sing all the verses. When they stop, there is loud clapping and a few cheers.

'Well done, Herr Schroeder!' declares Wagner. 'And with no rehearsal!' He turns to the audience and says, 'I think you can see why I've asked

     R. WILLIAM PLUME

Herr Schroeder here today. Now, are there any questions for him?'

A Kreisleiter from a southern county, one Kreisleiter Telgen, who is seated in the front row, stands and says loudly, 'When can you start for me, Herr Schroeder?'

'Doubtless we will approach each county in turn, but I'm sure you will understand that.' He touches Wagner's elbow. 'I must confer with Herr Wagner before any specific plans of that nature are set down.'

'I quite understand, but I think you will find that of the entire district, my county is recognised by everyone as the most committed to Party ideology,' Telgen says.

'Perhaps that's a good reason to start elsewhere, wouldn't you think?'

Telgen persists. 'My thinking was that you could quickly bring my county to the point of complete understanding before you moved on to others.'

'With the greatest respect, you appear to have failed to grasp that there is no such thing as a complete understanding of the thinking of our Führer,' Thomas replies.

Wagner chuckles. 'My dear Telgen, I think he's got you there.'

Telgen bridles at the putdown.

A response is thwarted by Wagner, who overrides further discussion by holding his palms forward. He says, 'I think you are going to be very busy, Herr Schroeder!'

Wagner sees in Telgen's crude remarks the practical expression of the opportunity that Thomas has created for him. The Kreisleiter of his district are not just willing but eager to participate.

If the Indoctrination Programme is successful, Wagner has a bright future in the Party. He sees himself moving up to the exalted rank of Reichsleiter, reporting directly to the Führer. He will rub shoulders with the luminaries of the Nazi world: Himmler, Göring, Goebbels, Speer, and Heydrich, among others.

Wagner organises one-on-one meetings with each Kreisleiter. At each meeting, Wagner hints at the near certainty of his own elevation to

Reichsleiter status. His subordinate Kreisleiter all get the message, and the manoeuvring to replace Wagner as Gauleiter begins immediately.

Kreisleiter circulate around Thomas and Wagner at every opportunity. Telgen joins a group of men standing in a circle with Wagner and Thomas at its centre. Telgen makes himself the object of attention by moving somewhat within the circle. He then interrupts the conversation to order Thomas to report to his, Telgen's, county office on Monday morning, prepared to set up a programme.

Wagner ignores Telgen's loutish intervention and steers Thomas back onto the dais.

'Gentlemen,' he says, 'I think we all see the possibilities that have been presented to us by the fortuitous – one might say, providential – appearance in our midst of Herr Schroeder. There is no time to lose! We must move with all possible haste to use Herr Schroeder's considerable talents. Tomorrow, we, Herr Schroeder and I, will begin planning an Indoctrination Programme for this district. Herr Schroeder will supervise the content of this programme. I will require from each of you, by tomorrow morning, a list of all installations, factories, training facilities and the like where Herr Schroeder's programme would be appropriate.'

Telgen now makes another clumsy attempt to regain the initiative. He raises his hand but doesn't wait to be recognised. He stands and says, 'Herr Wagner, I am committed to meeting every duty that is expected of Party members, and I look forward to developing an Indoctrination Programme in my county. I do wonder, however, if you shouldn't bring this programme to the attention of Reichsleiter Ley, who leads Party organisation.'

Telgen has pushed Wagner beyond the limits of his patience. 'Kreisleiter Telgen, that is a matter that you needn't concern yourself with. I need you to do what I've asked you to do and leave all such matters to me.'

Telgen, stung yet again by another public rebuke, continues trying to establish dominance over the situation. He opens his mouth, but before he

R. WILLIAM PLUME

speaks, Thomas steps forward, both hands outstretched, palms outward, to suppress further comment, and says, 'Gentlemen, gentlemen. Please.' He turns to Wagner and asks, 'May I intervene here, Herr Wagner?'

'Please,' is Wagner's clipped reply.

Thomas says, 'Gentlemen, what we are witnessing here is a good example of why I have developed the Indoctrination Programme and why it needs to be used widely. There are two concepts that apply here: Working towards the Führer and the Führerprinzip. Herr Wagner is *working towards the Führer*, taking the initiative, stepping up and stepping out to further the goals that our Führer has set for us. He is also applying the leadership principle of *Führerprinzip* in asking all of you to assemble the lists he has requested. Thank you, Herr Wagner.'

The room is silent.

Wagner's authority – openly challenged by Telgen – has been unambiguously validated by Thomas' clear statement of Party doctrine.

'Thank you, Herr Schroeder, for that concise summary of authorities. I think we are now finished here.' He dismisses the group but adds loudly enough that everyone can hear it, 'Kreisleiter Telgen, stay.'

He turns to Thomas and says, 'Thank you very much for your time today, Herr Schroeder. Please come to my office tomorrow at midday, and we will begin our discussions. In the meantime, could you please excuse us?'

STANDARD MUNICIPAL UTILITIES

'Before we begin, Herr Schroeder, I want to thank you again for your masterful presence at the Kreisleiter conference yesterday. You are an inspiration, and I think the men saw the wisdom of what you offer.'

'You are too kind, Herr Wagner. It was a pleasure and an honour for me to assist you. I must say that I'm not sure that all of the men saw the wisdom of my programme.'

'Perhaps you are referring to Telgen. He does have a spiteful streak, but there's no doubt he is ambitious, a man in a hurry. And always so well-dressed. I don't know how he does it. Every crease is razor sharp. His shoes are always dazzling. He is perfectly groomed and perfectly presented every time.'

'Herr Wagner, you should give some thought to appointing him to a role on your staff. If you didn't want him underfoot, you could assign him to – oh, I don't know – Bayreuth, say, which is about as far away from here as you can get. You wouldn't have any trouble avoiding him, but he'd still be where you could keep an eye on him.'

'Now there's a thought! You're just full of good ideas, aren't you?' Wagner says with a smile. 'But now, Herr Schroeder, I'd like to know a little more about you. I can see that you are a capable musician and are devoted to the Party. Apart from that, you are a bit of a mystery.'

'Isn't everyone in one way or another?'

'Yes, I suppose that's true. But tell me, what did you do before the war?'

'I worked in the banking industry.'

'But you're not working in that business now. What changed?'

'The war changed everything for everyone. After the war, the country was in such a chaotic state. Nothing worked as it did before. The monarchy was gone, replaced by anarchy. And anarchy was everywhere: in the streets, in the military, in politics, everywhere. People were starving. As you know very well, it was terrible, just terrible.'

'Let's back up a little. Were you involved in the war?'

Thomas pauses and looks towards the office window. His gaze fixed, he says, 'I'm sure you will understand, Herr Wagner, if I tell you that those times are an area of my life that I prefer not to discuss.' With the back of his hand, he brushes from his trousers a speck of lint that isn't there.

'I quite understand. My experience of the war wasn't pleasant either. I lost my right leg below the knee in Belgium. The artificial leg is a constant remin—' Wagner stops himself, pauses, then hurries on. 'But we're not here to rummage around in the past, are we?'

'Indeed not. If anything, we are here to lay the groundwork for a bright future.'

'Well spoken, Herr Schroeder. Let's get started!'

Wagner and Thomas start in an unstructured way: Wagner is asking questions, and Thomas is making suggestions.

Wagner is interested in Thomas' motivation, how he came to be so knowledgeable about Party doctrine, and how he constructed the programme.

'You are a uniquely talented individual, Herr Schroeder, but you are only one person. How do you propose to manage programmes in six or eight or ten installations spread throughout the province?'

'We will need a cadre of instructors,' Thomas replies. 'We use your position in the Party to find suitable men from around the province. We send out a memorandum asking for expressions of interest in the role of Party doctrine trainer. If you give the position the status and importance it's due, there will be more applicants than we need. There will be competition for the job, and that will always result in the best person being appointed. Of course, I will train them to the standard that we need, and as things get started, I will travel the province making sure standards are maintained.'

Wagner scribbles some notes in his diary and waits. He's allowing Thomas to set the pace.

'I am concerned about which industries and sites we select to start these programmes,' Thomas says. 'I think we should concentrate on industries most fundamentally important to the efficient functioning of the economy.'

'That sounds very reasonable. What did you have in mind?' asks Wagner.

'The standard municipal utilities: energy, fresh water supply, and sewage treatment.'

Wagner is shocked. He wants industrial glamour. He wants to point to Krupp Industries and say, 'Isn't it marvellous the way these workers are so skilled in Party doctrine? You can be sure that the best-quality field artillery pieces come from that factory.'

'What about the armaments industry? What about shipbuilding? Steel? Aircraft? Automobiles? Trains? You want to start with municipal utilities? You must be joking! We start the programme your way, and one day Reichsleiter Ley, or heaven forbid, the Führer himself, shows up to see how the programme is going, and we take him to the local sewage plant to show him how well the shitmeisters can sing "Deutschland Über Alles"? Are you out of your mind?'

'Herr Wagner, calm down. Remember that we are indoctrinating the people, not the plant. It is just as important for the men at the municipal sewage plant to be as knowledgeable as the men who make tanks at Krupp Industries. And, yes, sewage settling ponds aren't as impressive as tanks, but what we will want the Führer to take away is an understanding of the commitment to him and to his plans for Germany.'

'Do you think, do you honestly think, that Herr Hitler would ever *ask* to inspect, or even agree to inspect, a sewage treatment plant?' Wagner says.

'Herr Wagner, you know very well that Herr Hitler is – with good reason – concerned about his personal security. He has mastered the art of keeping people constantly guessing about where he is at present, where he will be tomorrow, and whether what is planned for him will actually take place. If he thought it would be in his security interest to alter his plans and go to a sewage treatment plant instead of Krupp Heavy Industries, he would do it.

'Don't think for one moment that a request to inspect a sewage treatment cannot happen. And if it does, we take him there. We do so happily. When he arrives, we scoot him straight into the conference room and close the curtains and the door. There are fragrant lilies in the

     R. WILLIAM PLUME

room. We let the men talk to him about our programme. And while he is there, no one uses the words "sewage" or "waste" or "shit". No one mentions faecal sludge. If we are forced to say what the plant does, we say it's a regeneration facility or a water-cleansing plant.'

Wagner chuckles. 'Ah, Schroeder, you're good, you are. You make me angry, and then, straightaway, you make me laugh. I think that might work. Especially if it's just Reichsleiter Ley involved. He's an alcoholic. He gets himself falling-down drunk every day. Sometimes I wonder why he has the elevated status that he does. He's a Reichsleiter, for heaven's sake! Reports directly to the Führer. He's an embarrassment to the –'

Wagner pauses. Gloom sweeps over his face. He drums his fingers on the desk. He opens his mouth to speak, but he lingers, unsure. Finally, he says, 'I never would have thought of this before I met you, but I've just realised that's not up to the Aryan Standard, is it?'

'No, it isn't. And I congratulate you, once for recognising that and again for having the courage to say so.'

Wagner inclines his head to acknowledge the compliment. A moment of silence passes. Wagner brightens and raps his desk. 'You want to start with sewage treatment installations?'

'Among others, yes. Municipal utilities are not fashionable, and sewage is no one's favourite thing. But when toilets around the city start overflowing, when sewage starts running in the streets because the treatment plant has broken down, you will come to a full understanding of what a real problem looks like.'

'And what do I do when Baron von Krupp calls to ask why we are not running a programme in his factory?'

'You say, "We're expanding as rapidly as we can, and Krupp Industries won't be overlooked."'

'Alright. We're agreed. We will start with utilities.'

'Including sewage plants?' says Thomas behind a rascally smile.

'Don't push your luck, Herr Schroeder!'

The public notification seeking expressions of interest in the position 'Indoctrination Trainer' is prepared.

Wagner makes it clear that only the best of the best need apply. He requires their talent to assist him in his crusade to instil in workers' minds a proper understanding of Party history, Party doctrine, and Party aspirations. Successful applicants will be promoted to province-level staff reporting to Wagner. The position's title, remuneration, and benefits will reflect the importance attached to it.

And significant benefits certainly do attach to the position. There is the freedom to operate more or less independently of the Party hierarchy. Successful applicants are expected to operate in the best interests of the Party without constant supervision. Relocation costs are covered. Day-to-day expenses are covered. There is a clothing allowance and an accommodation allowance. There is training leave and generous annual leave.

When the notice appears, the switchboard lights up.

Party members in their hundreds, throughout the province, clamour for the positions. Applications stream through the Party's internal mail system. Wagner must leave the phone handpiece off the cradle and devote every moment to dealing with the flood of interest that swamps the provincial headquarters.

Meanwhile, Thomas compiles a list of every electricity generation station, every coal mine, every water treatment plant, and every sewage treatment plant in Bavaria. He sets out what resources he needs to create a training operation for each installation.

Wagner, his adjutant, and Thomas dive into the pile of applications. They quickly eliminate unsuitable applicants. To expedite the process, they assign successful applicants to installations.

Herr Brünner is appointed as music director. He begins organising for the training of choristers and for the purchase of sheet music. Music publishers join the melee.

Bruno Eisen is appointed security manager.

Successful applicants are summoned, at Party expense, to Munich for the first Party Doctrine Training Conference.

When Wagner looks out over the large conference room, he sees the cream of Party membership in Bavaria. All of them now report to him, and he is pleased. Most of the applicants have leapt up the Party hierarchy from obscure rank-and-file roles to senior and powerful positions, and they, too, are pleased.

Wagner's welcome is expansive. He introduces the successful applicants to Herr Schroeder, a Party devotee, musician, and brilliant mind who has seen the need for this important programme.

When the plenary session closes the conference, everyone is looking forward.

Thomas' training of trainers is consummately successful. He stitches together a disparate group of eager men with the right balance of gravity and levity.

Wagner watches from the back of the room, satisfied to think that such a capable person has fallen, seemingly by the hand of Fate, under his authority.

Wagner introduces Brünner, the programme's music director, and under his direction, they sing together – not for the last time – 'Deutschland Über Alles'.

Wagner's elevation to Reichsleiter status is all but assured.

MAY 1933. MUNICIPAL UTILITIES THROUGHOUT BAVARIA

Trainers are despatched to their assigned installations.

Thomas, Brünner, and Eisen together do the rounds. Thomas introduces the instructors to the working staff. He explains the purpose of the programme and sets things in motion. Brünner introduces the custom of singing 'Deutschland Über Alles' at the start of every shift and leads workmen in their first rehearsals of the anthem.

The roll-out goes smoothly, and soon the programme is functioning as planned in all the selected installations.

Thomas has directed that instructors must focus first on the singing. He explains that before you begin with the difficult task of imbuing the challenging principles of Party doctrine, you must cohere the workmen into a tight-knit group that understands common purpose. The best way to do this is training them to sing together.

Party membership in the province increases dramatically. It is clearly linked to the roll-out of Thomas' programme. Wagner notes the upward trend in membership with satisfaction. The figures are included, as usual, in his regular report to Reichsleiter Ley.

Ley, not one to spend his time reading dry reports from subordinates, misses the fact that Party membership in Bavaria is suddenly outstripping the membership efforts of all other provinces.

But Reichsleiter Himmler, who misses nothing, does not.

THE SS VISIT WAGNER

'I've asked you to bring your identity papers, Herr Schroeder, because we're about to get a visit from the local chapter of the SS. My monthly report has been bouncing around among the Reichsleiter, and it ended up on Himmler's desk. He called the local office, and they called me. They're on their way here now. I apologise for the short notice, but I've only just found out myself.'

Before Thomas is able to respond, Wagner's phone rings. Wagner picks it up, listens, and says, 'Thank you. Show them in.'

The door opens, and two men in glistening black SS uniforms appear, both still wearing their peaked caps and each holding a swagger stick behind their back. They stride into Wagner's office.

　　　　R. WILLIAM PLUME

'Good morning, Herr Wagner. How good of you to make the time to see us,' says the first of them.

The other SS man turns to face Thomas and says, 'And you, sir, unless I miss my guess, are Thomas Hedwig Reichey Schroeder. I'd very much like to see your papers, if I may.'

Thomas reaches into the breast pocket of his jacket and removes the red leather, gilt-embossed wallet containing his identity papers. Thomas hands the wallet to the SS man, who handles everything and examines everything with great care. He holds up the passport, looking repeatedly from photo to face.

'Ah,' he says, looking at Thomas' party card. 'Alter Kämpfer, I see. Signed up in 1921. That's impressive, Herr Schroeder, if it's true.'

'Why would you doubt it?'

'Let's just say that in my line of work it's wise to be sceptical. But this all looks in order.' He reassembles the wallet and hands it back to Thomas.

With the pause in conversation, Wagner takes the opportunity to invite everyone to sit down.

The first SS man opens the conversation. 'We've come here today because we understand that you have initiated an Indoctrination Programme throughout the province, and you have taken this initiative without telling us.'

'We are not required to tell you everything we do,' Wagner says.

'Perhaps not, but we like to know what is being done in our backyard. And when the subject matter is Party doctrine, we insist on it. Tell me, on whose authority have you initiated this programme?'

'My own. I am the Gauleiter of this province, and, as you very well know, that gives me considerable latitude to take steps, without reference to anyone, on any matters that affect the Party.'

'All the same, it does rather raise our interest when things like your Indoctrination Programme appear out of nowhere. Why weren't we told, Herr Wagner?

'In the first place, as I've already said, there was no need to tell you, and secondly, we've made no attempt to disguise or suppress or hide what we are doing. Perhaps you are suggesting that I should have put a notice in the morning paper?'

'Don't get cute with me, Herr Wagner, or there will be consequences,' snarls the SS man.

Wagner erupts. He stands as assertively as he can manage. He leans over his desk and snarls back. 'Now you listen to me, you silly little swaggering peacock! The only thing that makes you the dreadful little shit that you are is that uniform you're wearing. Without it, you are a sad, pathetic nobody. Now you listen with your brain. Production province-wide is up. Party membership is up, and the Party is richer than ever because of this initiative. So don't you dare strut in here with your snotty attitude, your shitty little innuendos, and your pathetic veiled threats. Now, both of you, get your arses out of my office!'

Wagner stands rigid, waiting until he hears the outer door closing, then he picks up his phone and punches the button for his adjutant.

'Get me through to Himmler's adjutant immediately! Call back the instant you've got him!'

Wagner looks at Thomas. 'I've just made the local SS into a wasp nest, and it's heading our way, Thomas.'

The door opens. 'Himmler's adjutant is on the line!'

Wagner calms himself, picks up the phone, and says, 'Good morning, Herr Vogler. I'll come straight to the point. I need to call in a favour. We've just had a visit from two of your colleagues, and it seems there's been a misunderstanding about our Indoctrination Programme. I need you to set up a meeting with Herr Himmler for myself and one associate.'

Wagner listens to Vogler's tart response.

'I know he's a busy man,' Wagner continues. 'Anybody who's doing their job is a busy man. But we need to get a few things straightened out with the SS, and what better place to start than right at the top?'

There is a pause.

'Yes, I'm still here, Herr Vogler.' Wagner looks at his watch and says, 'We can be on the overnight train.' Vogler issues instructions.

'Right you are, Herr Vogler, eleven hundred hours tomorrow. We'll see you then. And thank you … and may the Führer's grace shine upon you as well.'

Wagner hangs up. He urges Thomas, 'Get your things. We're going to Berlin on the overnight. We can still catch it if we hurry. Move!'

Soon they are headed north on the overnight Berlin express to a meeting with Herr Heinrich Himmler, Reichsleiter SS and Chief of the German Police.

HAUPTBAHNHOF, BERLIN

After their meeting with Himmler, Thomas and Wagner return to the Berlin Bahnhof, hoping to catch the late express back to Munich. They buy their tickets and head straight for the platform.

Departure is only minutes away. On his own, Thomas would make the train without difficulty. But Wagner, with his artificial leg, cannot manage anything better than galumphing along. He has difficulty steering between and around other people who are coming and going, which further impedes his progress.

Thomas turns at the large portal that opens onto their platform. He sees the conductor holding the flag extended in his left hand. His right hand holds the whistle to his mouth. Departure is imminent.

Thomas looks back and sees that Wagner has made it onto the platform, but he is struggling. He turns back and goes to Wagner, taking the bag from Wagner's hand, and runs to the last carriage. He throws both bags through the still-open door. He turns back to assist Wagner, who is nearly exhausted. Thomas swings Wagner's right arm behind his neck and takes as much of Wagner's weight as he can. The two men are stumping along in a kind of desperate three-legged race along the platform.

People leaving trains and people catching trains are everywhere, presenting a series of obstacles. With as much politeness as the situation warrants, Thomas urges them out of the way.

The white flag is now moving up and down; the whistle is no more than a few seconds away. Still struggling, Thomas and Wagner arrive at the carriage door at the very moment the conductor's whistle signals the driver that he is to depart. Wagner manages to grab the vertical handhold and pull himself into the carriage, but he trips over the two bags and falls face down across the narrow aisle between the opposing doors on either side of the carriage.

As the train slowly starts to move, Thomas grabs the handhold and manages to get both feet onto the lowest tread between Wagner's legs and under his heavy overcoat. But he is still completely outside the carriage.

The train gathers speed and moves beyond the end of the platform. Thomas is now committed to forcing entry into the carriage. The train is already moving fast enough that if he loses his grip or jumps from the train, the best he can hope for is a quick end.

Wagner sees Thomas' predicament and knows that he must move out of the way quickly. If Thomas doesn't get into the carriage soon, there's every likelihood that he will be swept away by a train passing on the parallel track or by some trackside equipment, a pole or suchlike.

Wagner tries to roll away from the bags, but they are still caught beneath him. Struggling against his own weight, he pulls the bags from beneath his body and pushes them into the aisle between the seats. Using his hands and his good leg, he tries desperately to slide himself across the floor away from the door, but he can find no purchase. He is as helpless as a beached whale.

Thomas, still fully exposed outside the carriage, now grabs the handhold with both hands. He puts his foot squarely into Wagner's groin and shoves him, with all the force he can muster, away from the open door.

There is now enough room for Thomas to get himself half into the carriage, but Wagner's legs prevent him from closing the inward-swinging door. Wagner is now far enough into the carriage that he can put his left foot on the aisle wall. He pushes himself away from Thomas. In the stress of the moment, Wagner overdoes it and pushes himself into the opposite stairwell with his head – on the bottom-most tread – jammed against the door.

Thomas moves completely into the carriage and quickly closes the door. Meanwhile, the conductor has made his way to the back of the train. He finds a disorganised pile of people and baggage. Thomas is struggling to lift Wagner's deadweight out of the stairwell. The conductor and Thomas together manage to get Wagner back onto his feet.

With both men safely on board, the crisis is over.

Wagner and Thomas straighten themselves up as best they can. Thomas presents their tickets to the conductor, who shows them to their seats. They put their bags in the overhead rack and sit.

Wagner pulls out his handkerchief and begins scrubbing at the dirt and scrapes on his hands. Presently he says, 'That wasn't very dignified.'

Thomas nods his agreement.

'You could have been killed, collected by an arriving train.'

'Oh, I don't know. I don't think there was much danger of that. And look at us. Here we are, a little mussed up perhaps, but otherwise fine.'

Wagner grunts and falls silent. After a time, he says, 'Thank you for coming back to help me.'

'My pleasure, Herr Wagner.'

'Next time, my friend, find another place to put your foot when you have to shove me out of the way.'

'I'll keep that in mind, Herr Wagner.'

'Call me Adolf, please.'

'Adolf it is. And, likewise, call me Thomas.'

Adolf acknowledges the courtesy with a nod but says nothing for a while. 'I share my given name with the Führer,' he eventually resumes. 'It surprises me at times how some people respond to that simple fact. I shouldn't have to say this, but it is the name my mother, may the Lord bless her soul, gave me. I've had people – more than one – suggest that I have changed my name to Adolf for the added glow or so that I may bask, in some small way, in reflected glory. Perhaps even to enhance my promotion prospects. I sometimes think that, if it weren't for the great respect I have for my mother, I would change it to something else.'

'Like what, for example?' asks Thomas.

'Fritz?' says Wagner with a grin and a shrug.

Thomas smiles at the deliberate silliness but says, 'We have no say in our own naming, and we cannot control the idle speculations of other people. Your respect for your mother should guide you. But I will guess that isn't what's on your mind.'

Wagner briefly fiddles with some dry skin on his thumb. 'I served my country honourably in the war. Got half my leg blown off for my trouble. I don't grudge that, Thomas. That's the reality of war. I'm lucky to be alive. But it's been said that I got the Gauleiter position by playing on my war wounds or because my name is Adolf. But that's all crap. I was given the job because I work hard and because I do my job.'

'You do both very well, Adolf.'

Wagner stares out of the window into the fading light. 'It's my leg. It's my useless fucking leg. When I cannot do things, simple things like catch the train, it annoys the hell out of me. And sometimes when we get that cold, damp winter weather, it aches intensely. I can tolerate the pain. What bothers me is that it comes from the part of my leg that isn't there anymore.' Wagner falls silent for a moment. Then, 'You probably wouldn't believe that a great lump like me could be interested in something like dressage –'

'As in horse training?' asks Thomas.

'There is another kind? Yes, of course, horse training. A very specific type of horse training. Some people think of it as ballet for horse and rider. Before the war, I was a dressage trainer and rider. To control a horse, you must use your legs. After the war, I discovered that my right leg, the

   R. WILLIAM PLUME

artificial one, no longer sent the right signal to the horse. It got confused. The horse couldn't decipher what I wanted from it. That's a roundabout way of saying that I could train a horse for myself, but I could no longer prepare a horse for anyone else. All of those things are annoying and disappointing, but now it's starting to worry me for another reason.'

'Which is?' asked Thomas.

'Do you recall when we were talking about Reichsleiter Ley and his excessive drinking?'

'Yes, I remember that conversation. I recall that you thought his behaviour wasn't up to the Aryan Standard.'

'That's the one. Since then that idea of failure to meet the Aryan Standard has been very much on my mind. Now I'm worried that … umm … that …'

'That your leg disqualifies you from ever meeting the Aryan Standard.'

'Yes.'

'Adolf, you lost part of your leg through no fault of your own, doing your patriotic duty. I think it's fair to say that we all have our defects. But they shouldn't stop us from working towards the ideal in the same way that we work towards the Führer. Did you know, for example, that Herr Joseph Goebbels, who is Reichsleiter Propaganda, has a clubfoot? He walks with a very pronounced limp, and yet he is a Reichsleiter and a very capable head of the Party's propaganda operation.'

Wagner looks indulgently at Thomas and says, 'And did you know that he has, shall we say, a roving eye for the ladies? That doesn't match the Aryan Standard either. You either meet the standard or you don't. And I'm beginning to think that I don't. And if I don't, I shouldn't be in the Party. And, if I shouldn't be in the Party, I shouldn't be a Gauleiter. I don't know what to do.'

CHAPTER 17

Ambition

Thomas arrives at Wagner's office first thing in the morning. He is told by Wagner's adjutant that he is expected and to go straight in.

Thomas, standing with his right hand on the doorknob, raps a couple of times with his left. The muffled sound of his knuckle striking the door brings to mind the phrase 'Men shut their doors against a setting sun.' He recognises it as Shakespeare and wonders why it has come to mind at the moment he knocks on Wagner's door. Thomas is not much given to relying on fanciful interpretations of events of this nature, but he still wonders, *Is this meant to be a sign that Wagner is closing a door? Which door? Is he having doubts? Surely not –*

Thomas is jolted from his musing by Wagner forcefully opening the door. The knob is jerked out of Thomas' hand as the door flies open.

'How many times do I have to say "Come in"?' Wagner shouts.

'My apologies, Herr Wagner. I was lost in thought. I didn't hear you.'

'Come in. Come in. Sit down. Let's get started,' says Wagner as he plops himself into his chair.

'I don't need to tell you, Herr Schroeder, that after yesterday's meeting with Himmler, we have a lot of work to do. No sooner do we get the provincial programme off the ground than we're asked – ordered – to implement the programme nationwide. You must have been pleased to see how enthusiastic Himmler was about your choice of municipal utilities as the starting point.'

Wagner doesn't wait for a comment from Thomas. He barges on.

'We will need provincial supervisors. You were the provincial supervisor here, but as of yesterday, you are the national supervisor. By the way, that reminds me that both of us will have to think about successors.'

And he ploughs on non-stop. Thomas sees he doesn't need to say anything, can't say anything. *Let his guard down a little too much on the train?* Thomas wonders. *All of those doubts about whether he is fit to be Aryan? Gone, it seems.* The next thing Thomas hears is Wagner's fist banging on his desk. The pencils are bouncing.

'What's wrong with you today? Have you disconnected your ears? What did I just say?'

Thomas shrugs.

'I said, compile a list of qualifications for provincial supervisors. We'll do the indoctrination of trainers the same way we did last time. No doubt there will be a similar response.'

Still, he steams ahead, preventing any possibility of Thomas entering the conversation.

'You must be very pleased with yourself, Herr Schroeder. Not so long ago you were teaching men in an obscure ball-bearing factory here in Munich. Ten days hence, you will be in Berlin and reporting to Reichsleiter Heinrich Himmler himself – well, through me. And that reminds me. He wants the name of the programme changed to the National Socialist Enlightenment Programme. I'd guess that's a deliberate poke in the eye for Herr Goebbels, Reichsleiter of Public Enlightenment and Propaganda. One final thing: We are scheduled to meet the Führer the day after we arrive in Berlin. Be prepared for that. That will get us started. That's all.'

Yesterday it was his life story, complete with angst. Today, I'm dismissed. Guess he wants his crosscut saw back, Thomas thinks with a small inner smile. A nationwide programme is what Thomas has been aiming for. How quickly it has arrived! There is something perversely mocking in the rapidity and ease with which it has been adopted.

Perhaps it is an orgy of self-congratulation now, after they've taken over the government. And, just like that, meeting the Führer. I will judge for myself those steely-blue eyes which, legend has it, penetrate straight into your soul. We'll see about that. But that's where we'll get approval, or not, for the whole enterprise.

He is pleased and concerned at the same time. Now that things are heading towards a nationwide programme, he feels certain that something will go wrong somewhere in Germany. *Let it be serious enough to trigger what Reinhard is setting up. But nobody dead, please.*

Outwardly though, Thomas receives the dismissal placidly, gathers up his papers, and, without a word, lets himself out.

MÖRSBACH SCHREIBER PRINTING, MUNICH

Liesel calls Reinhard to let him know that Thomas has arrived.

As he's hanging up, there is a single knock at the door.

Thomas lets himself in and closes the door.

'Don't get up, my friend. I don't have much time. Himmler, with Hitler's approval, has ordered us to implement a nationwide Indoctrination Programme. Next week, Wagner and I will be moving to Berlin. Both Wagner and I will be reporting to Himmler. We are scheduled to meet with the Führer the day after we arrive.

'My goodness! Things have moved along in great haste, my friend. It sounds like you've set the scene beautifully. What, if anything, do you need from me?' asks Reinhard.

'Three things. First, I need your men on both Wagner and Brünner. I'm confident that Eisen can take care of himself, but I'd be interested in your opinion.'

'I already have a guardian angel looking after you, and I'll do the same for Wagner and Brünner. I'm interested in your request to watch over Wagner.'

'Not so surprising,' Thomas replies. 'Wagner, more than anyone, has made this initiative possible. It's true that he's done it without realising what he was doing. But, candidly, Reinhard, I have a lot of respect for the man, though not the Party member. He's no slouch. He's very much like you. But what it boils down to is that I owe him a favour.'

'Understood. And the second thing?'

'The Enlightenment Programme – that's what it's called now – is moving into a large, vacant office building. We've been assured that everything will be ready when we arrive. Without doubt, the SS has planted listening devices everywhere and tapped every telephone. I've been assigned an adjutant, and he will surely be SS as well. When I have to get a message to you, I will do it through Eisen, and he will use a public telephone.'

'Are you sure you can trust him?' Reinhard asks.

'No. But he owes me a big one. Either way, we'll find out soon enough.'

'Alright, I'll contact him. And before we're done, I should tell you what progress has been made with the Reichswehr.'

'That's the third thing,' says Thomas.

'I've made several trips to Berlin on the pretext of a large printing contract. I established contact with Oberstleutnant von Manstein, and we've met several times over dinner. It was easy enough to steer the conversation towards the state of the nation, the thuggish, out-of-control behaviour of the SA, and the problems between the Reichswehr and Röhm's SA. To get to the point, von Hindenburg has ordered the Reichswehr to prepare for the imposition of martial law and the dismissal of Hitler's government, in case it is needed.'

'Ordered them?' asks Thomas.

'He still holds his commission as a field marshal, and he is the Reichspräsident. Hard to treat it as anything other than an order.'

'All we need to do now is push him over the line?' Thomas asks.

'It will have to be something more than a factory being closed down, but yes. If a prompting event of sufficient gravity occurs, there is now a strong likelihood of martial law.'

'Next time you see your army colleague, tell him that I expect the national programme to mimic what happened in Munich. In the initial phase, we aren't going to do much more than sing "Deutschland Über Alles". In Munich, when we did start on the actual enlightenment, the problems began on the first day, and when I added merit and demerit points, everything fell apart very quickly.'

HAUPTBAHNHOF, MUNICH. STREICHER RECOGNISES THOMAS

Thomas and Wagner arrive at the Hauptbahnhof and make their way towards the ticketing office. When they have their tickets, Thomas excuses himself to the men's room.

While waiting, Wagner busies himself with minor but necessary organisation. He encloses his ticket in his leather wallet and puts that into the inner breast pocket of his overcoat. He checks the time again. Plenty of time to get onto the platform and on the train. There won't be a repeat of that dreadful near disaster in Berlin. He shudders to remember how long Thomas stood in the doorway outside the moving train.

He checks the laces on the shoe of his artificial right foot. It gives him no sense of how securely the shoe is attached. He has learned that he must check it regularly. In the early days of his artificial leg, the shoelaces would occasionally come undone, and the shoe would fall off. Invariably, this would cause him to stumble or fall.

He puts his foot onto the lower railing of a barrier and bends over to retie the lace. This simple procedure brings to his mind his habit of watching people tie their shoes. Everyone seems to do it differently. Who would have thought that there are so many ways for Herr Bunny Rabbit – that of his mother's little shoe-tying ditty – to make his way around the tree? Is the way people tie their shoes unique to each person? Would it be, he wonders, enough to uniquely identify someone?

R. WILLIAM PLUME

Still bent over, finishing this small task, Wagner becomes aware that a person who is not Thomas is closing in on him. In his peripheral vision, he can see, more or less, the bottom half of a man – and a large one at that – now next to him. He stands and turns to his right to face the person.

'Ahh! Herr Julius Streicher! What a pleasant surprise!'

They shake hands, and the routine, inconsequential patter follows. 'What brings you here?' 'Where are you going?' Streicher is on his way back to Nuremberg. Wagner is off to Berlin, meeting with Himmler, the new Enlightenment Programme, and so on.

While this is going on, Thomas comes out of the men's room at the far end of the long, rectangular lobby. Between himself and Wagner, there is the usual noisy busyness of people coming and going, running for trains, and greeting arrivals.

Wagner is facing Thomas but is now speaking with someone who is standing with his back to Thomas. The man's head is not just balding but completely hairless.

Thomas has a fragile clue to the man's identity. *Is that Julius Streicher? If it is, will he recognise me?*

Thomas cannot avoid rejoining Wagner, but he is alert.

As Thomas approaches the two men, Wagner becomes aware of him and says, 'Ah, here he is now.' Wagner puts his left hand on the man's right arm and gently turns him towards Thomas, saying, 'Thomas, this is Herr Julius Streicher, the Gauleiter of Franconia. Julius, I'd like you to meet Herr Thomas Schroeder.'

When Streicher hears Thomas' name, he gives away a tell. Thomas sees it and senses that his name has triggered in Streicher's mind a pathway to recognition.

'And would I be right, Herr Schroeder, in supposing you are in the printing business?'

Thomas knows now that Streicher is on the right track. 'Oh, no, Herr Streicher,' chuckles Thomas, 'I know less than nothing about printing.'

But Streicher has the scent. His intuition is at work, and it tells him he's got the right idea, and furthermore, it urges him to pursue Thomas with another question.

Characteristically, he blunders into a too-hasty response. He leans forward. His eyes acquire a sparkling intensity. His tone is too assertive, nudging towards demanding. The first words that come to his mind are delivered to his tongue.

'Oh, surely not, Herr Schroeder. There must be someone among you Schroeders who is in the printing business, isn't there?'

Thomas now allows his irritation to show.

'Herr Streicher, my business and that of my family are things I would not normally discuss with someone I do not know and had only met a few seconds ago. I hope you will understand.'

Streicher is now glaring at Thomas.

It's him! Know nothing about printing, my arse! I'll bet my Gauleiter warrant that you are the Schroeder who owns the Rubenstein plant. And that voice! I know that voice! You are the fucker who did me down at Café Grün! Got your arse now! Payback time, you bastard!

Thomas sees that Streicher has made him, but he remains impassive, saying nothing, silently urging Wagner to do something to bring the encounter to an end.

Wagner sees that the conversation between two people unknown to each other mere seconds ago has taken a decidedly strange turn. He doesn't know what's causing the tension, but some sort of intervention is required.

He looks up at the large wall clock. 'Well then, Herr Schroeder, we should probably head for our platform.' He knows their train doesn't leave for another thirty-five minutes, but the move resolves the impasse.

The following day, Thomas finds a public telephone. He calls Reinhard to report the incident with Streicher. 'I'm certain he has worked out where I fit into his past. Soon enough his thugs will be following me if they aren't already. I need your help.'

CHAPTER 18

Hitler's Favour

MEETING WITH HITLER

Heinrich Himmler and ostentation are bedmates.

The office of the National Socialist Enlightenment Programme is no more than a few blocks from the Chancellery, but the distance must be covered not just by a splendid automobile but by a motorcade. Wilhelmstrasse, spacious though it is, is closed to ordinary traffic to allow for Himmler's puffery.

At precisely the appointed time, SS-1, Himmler's personal staff car, flagged and with the top down, arrives. It stops in front of the main entry of Wagner's new office. Himmler always rides in the front passenger seat. When the top is down, he can stand and strike the conquering-hero pose as the car moves along the boulevard. Today, however, he arrives seated. The motorcade comes to a halt in the street immediately in front of the Enlightenment office.

Wagner and Thomas are guided to the second car, in which they will ride together to the Reich Chancellery. The entourage travels down the centre of Wilhelmstrasse. When it arrives at the Chancellery, Himmler tells his driver to park facing the opposite direction. To do this, the driver executes a huge sweeping turn that consumes the entire width of the Wilhelmstrasse, which here is more of a plaza than a street. The turn brings them to the main entry of the seat of the German government: the Reich Chancellery.

Wagner gives Thomas one last piece of advice. 'The Führer can be quite affable and congenial, but he is easily provoked, so be careful what you say.'

At the reception area, their papers are examined by armed SS men. Because Thomas and Wagner are with Himmler, more intrusive checks are considered unnecessary. Himmler, his adjutant, Wagner, and Thomas now mount the two flights of steps that lead up to the first floor, where the Führer's office is located.

Two armed guards are stationed at the top of the stairs, and two more stand to attention on either side of the entrance to Hitler's outer office. An adjutant approaches Himmler and says, 'The Führer is expecting you, Herr Reichsleiter Himmler. He is occupied, but I'm quite certain that he will be available very soon. Would you care to sit?'

Himmler, saying nothing and not bothering even to look at the man, waves him away. The man bows and, in the customary way, clicks his heels, turns, and strides away.

Moments later, the huge double doors swing outward. An army colonel in full dress uniform steps out and invites the party to enter the Führer's outer office. He comes to attention and salutes as Himmler passes through the doors.

When the doors are closed, the colonel approaches Himmler. He salutes again and then says, 'Welcome, Herr Reichsleiter, once again to the Führer's office.' Himmler nods and turns his attention to the wall clock.

The colonel then says, 'Which of you is Herr Schroeder?'

Thomas raises his hand. The colonel faces Thomas and stands motionless and mute for a moment. The slight disruption to the otherwise smooth flow of introductions goes unnoticed by everyone except Thomas.

'Herr Schroeder, the Führer is most impressed by your Enlightenment initiative.'

'I am pleased to hear that. Thank you.'

'And you must be Herr Adolf Wagner.'

'Yes,' replies Wagner.

'You are well known to the Führer. He was also most pleased, and

          R. WILLIAM PLUME

not surprised, to find that you were the motivating force behind this initiative. He is grateful for your service to the Party.'

'Thank you.'

'Gentlemen, you are about to be received by the Führer of the German Reich, Herr Adolf Hitler. While you are with him, there are certain protocols that will govern your behaviour. During the entire audience, you will stand unless he invites you to sit. That usually does not happen. If he does invite you to sit, it is a sign of his favour. You do not speak unless you are spoken to. Finally, you are to focus your attention in his direction at all times. These are simple courtesies that acknowledge his station and his importance to the life of this nation. Now, if you would, please follow me.'

He approaches the large double doors to the inner office and knocks gently once. The doors open and swing into the room. The colonel leads the way into Hitler's office, followed first by Himmler and then by Wagner and Thomas, walking side by side.

Thomas surveys the rectangular room. It is large with a high ceiling. Hitler's desk is at one end of the rectangle and set at a considerable distance from the main entry doors.

The void clearly announces where the power resides. Guests are forced to traverse a long, empty space to approach the great leader seated at the epicentre of his domain.

A door, leading to Hitler's private apartment, is adjacent to his desk. At the opposite end of the room is an inconspicuous service entrance.

Hitler is on the phone, staring through a window. The colonel crosses the space to Hitler's desk and makes him aware that his guests have arrived. Hitler makes some terminating remark, ending his phone conversation.

He stands and moves out from behind his desk. The colonel signals the visitors to come forward. Wagner and Thomas follow Himmler's lead, and soon they find themselves standing face-to-face with Adolf Hitler himself.

Hitler approaches the group. 'Herr Himmler, it's a great pleasure, as always, to see you again. Thank you for bringing these two gentlemen with you today.'

'The pleasure is all mine, mein Führer,' replies Himmler, clicking his heels. Himmler turns to his right with the intention of handling the introductions. He is at the point of introducing Wagner, but Hitler cuts him off.

'Adolf, Adolf Wagner! My great friend over so many years. How wonderful it is to see you again!' Hitler smiles broadly.

For no apparent reason, Wagner recoils, and Thomas, without thinking, reaches out to steady him. Hitler notices the minor interaction and says, 'That leg of yours still bothering you, Adolf?' Wagner shrugs but says nothing. Hitler smiles again, slaps Wagner's shoulder, gives him a gentle shake, and says, 'Ah, the Alter Kämpfers! They never give in!' Wagner again recoils, and again, Thomas steadies him.

Thomas is now paying close attention to Hitler's mouth. When he smiles, the Führer displays a mouthful of rotten teeth. Not wanting to be seen to stare, he moves his attention to Wagner. Hitler and Wagner are, after a fashion, reminiscing about the old days.

Hitler moves along the line, and Thomas finds himself face-to-face and eye-to-eye with the most powerful man in Germany.

The room melts away.

Thomas sees nothing remarkable in the fabled 'steely-blue' eyes. He feels nothing remarkable in the hand he holds. He notes the colour of the hair – dark brown, bordering on black. The knot of the tie is loose, but the flesh of Hitler's neck spills over the collar.

Thomas is at ease.

Hitler releases the handshake. 'And you are, I believe, Herr Thomas Schroeder.'

During his time as a night-soil man, Thomas' sense of smell accommodated itself to the fearsome stench of human excrement. Hitler's breath now delivers to his nose a different but equally forceful foulness.

     R. WILLIAM PLUME

He has long experience with such aromas, and he gives no outward indication that Hitler's knee-bending halitosis has reached him.

'Yes, mein Führer, the very same.'

'I have been hearing so many good things about your Enlightenment Programme and about your determination to make it available across all of Germany. But I am forgetting my manners. Please, gentlemen, come. Sit down.'

Four plush chairs, all covered in soft leather, are arranged around a low coffee table. Three of the chairs are light grey; the fourth is bright red – the revered red leather chair, furtively spoken of as his 'throne'. On either side of the red leather chair is a lamp table, each with a single drawer. The lamps are carefully placed to illuminate the occupant of the red leather chair.

At the invitation to sit, the adjutant colonel moves to the red leather chair. His role now is to ensure that guests are adroitly steered away from sitting in the 'unofficial throne'.

Thomas sits facing the cathedra at the opposite end of the table. The chairs to his left and right are occupied by Himmler and Wagner. When everyone is comfortable, Hitler begins again, 'Tell me, Herr Schroeder, what inspired you to develop your renowned Indoctrination Programme?'

'I hail from Munich, where I have followed your career with great interest since early 1919 –'

Hitler interrupts to ask, 'When did you join the party, Herr Schroeder?'

'On the twentieth of April 1921 –'

Hitler smiles and interrupts again to ask, 'Do you know that the twentieth of April is my birthday?'

'I know that now, mein Führer, but I didn't at the time. In any case, I signed up on that day because it is also my birthday.'

Hitler slaps the broad, flat arm of his chair and turns to Himmler. 'Herr Himmler, you are the astrologist among us. Isn't the astrological sign for the twentieth of April Leo the Lion?'

'No, mein Führer, the sign for that date is Taurus. The date is on the cusp between Aries the Ram and Taurus the Bull.'

'What does "on the cusp" mean, Herr Himmler?'

'It means that you have some of the characteristics of both signs.'

Hitler abruptly changes the tone of the meeting. He shuffles forward in his chair. He leans over the table, his elbows on his knees. 'Enough of this piffle,' he says. 'Now, Herr Schroeder, who gave you the authority to start your Enlightenment Programme?'

Thomas' demeanour is relaxed. He does not move. He replies, 'With the greatest respect, mein Führer, you did.'

'Herr Schroeder, I think you may have missed the point of my question. I'll rephrase it for you. You started this programme of yours in a ball-bearing factory in Munich. Who gave you the authority to do that?'

'Mein Führer, at the risk of seeming disrespectful, I must say once again, you did.'

Hitler bristles.

Himmler shuffles a little in his chair, crosses his legs, and folds his arms on his chest.

Wagner sends a look in Thomas' direction – *tread carefully.*

Thomas says, 'I'm sure it will help if I go back to the beginning to explain how this came about.'

'It better. Get on with it!' growls Hitler.

'After the war ended in such a calamitous fashion for this country, you immersed yourself in study. You sought to understand how such a catastrophe could befall a great nation like Germany. You studied the writings of the great political and genetic thinkers. When you had developed a clear vision of how to elevate Germany from its fallen state, you began to search for a way to give voice to that vision.

'In September 1919, you joined Herr Anton Drexler's German Workers' Party. Within days, Drexler and other Party members recognised your talent and the depth of your knowledge. Less than a month later, you presented your first speech at the Hofbräukeller in Munich. A month after that, you gave a second speech at Eberlbrau, also in Munich.

'You soon became leader of the Party, and in February 1920, you changed the name of the party to the National Socialist German Workers' Party and presented, at Hofbräuhaus, Munich, your 25-Point Plan for the recovery of the German nation. You stepped up, and you shared your message with the people.

'I might now say that the rest is history, but that would be an incomplete answer to your question. You advocated for preserving and strengthening the Aryan Ideal and setting and living up to the Aryan Standard, and you shared your message with the people.

'During your incarceration at Landsberg Prison, you recovered from the shock of your defeat on the blood-stained streets of Munich. The scales fell from your eyes. You saw that defeat was temporary, and it opened the door to success. You realised that storming the gates of Berlin was a fool's errand. You changed your path, and you shared your message with the people.

'At the same time, you wrote *Mein Kampf,* and what did you do with that brilliant work when you were released? You published it. And what is that if not sharing your message with the people?

'By the time you were released from Landsberg Prison, your Party had withered away. You picked it up, breathed life back into it, and resumed sharing your message with the people.

'Since then, mein Führer, how many times have you stood before thousands of people who love you and who have come to hear your words, to hear your message for them? What am I doing? I'm doing what my Führer would do. I am continuing his great work and sharing his message with the people. I most respectfully hope that answers your question, mein Führer.'

———

Himmler's motorcade stops in front of the Enlightenment Programme office. The car door is opened, and Wagner and Thomas step onto the footpath. They walk ahead to Himmler's car to pay their respects.

Himmler looks up and says, 'Nicely done, Herr Schroeder. Now, gentlemen, let's get my Enlightenment Programme off the ground!' He signals to the driver, and the motorcade moves away.

Thomas and Wagner are left alone on the footpath. Wagner puts a hand to Thomas' elbow and says, 'May I buy you a drink, Thomas? I certainly need one, and there are some things I need to say that can't be said in the office.'

When the two men are settled at a table, Wagner begins the conversation.

'I must say, Thomas, you handled him beautifully. I can cut off fingers and still have more than I need to count the number of people who can handle him the way you did today. Congratulations, and, as Herr Himmler said, nicely done, Herr Schroeder.'

'Thank you, Adolf.'

'And by the way, Thomas, that young colonel in the Führer's office has your eyes. Quite remarkable, the similarity.'

A quiet moment passes.

'Were you really born on the twentieth of April?'

'Close enough. What is it that you need to say that you don't want the microphones in the office to hear?'

'You have risen from a nobody to front-and-centre in the Führer's office in a very short time. But don't be fooled, Thomas. You can be sure that he has been fully informed of your history. He sees your talent and your ability, but you may be sure that what he does not see is someone who will "deliver his message to the people". He is very capable of doing that himself. He sees you as a threat.'

'Thank you for the warning, Adolf.'

WAGNER AND THOMAS ARE FETED

'Come, come, come now! Herr Schroeder! Herr Wagner wants you in his office now, before now, yesterday. He is beside himself!'

As Thomas turns into Wagner's office, Wagner is pulling on his jacket.

'We have been summoned to the Führer's office. We go now. There's a car waiting. Go! Get yourself ready!'

———

Soon Thomas and Wagner are ushered into Hitler's inner sanctum once more. The office is occupied only by Hitler and his adjutant. Hitler is seated in the red leather chair, looking at state papers.

Hitler stands as his two guests near the seating area. 'Thank you both for coming at such short notice. I wanted to speak with you without other ears present. I have news for both of you that you should know before it appears in the papers tomorrow. First, I congratulate you both on your smooth and effective implementation of the Enlightenment Programme. All reports I am receiving are very positive, and, of course, I'm very pleased.'

Hitler looks towards his adjutant and, with a tilt of his head, indicates that he should guide Thomas and Wagner into the side chairs.

When they are seated, Hitler, without preamble, moves directly to the purpose of the meeting.

'Herr Wagner, I am elevating you to the rank of Reichsleiter Enlightenment. You will report directly to me, and as of now, you have full responsibility for the Enlightenment Programme. I have asked Herr Himmler to remain attached to the programme in an advisory role. You will keep him informed of your plans and take his advice as appropriate.

'Herr Schroeder, I am elevating you to the rank of Plenipotentiary Party Education. You will report directly to Reichsleiter Wagner. All reports indicate that the relationship between the two of you is one that works well. The chain of command will remain as it is.

'I want you to know, Herr Schroeder, that I am deeply impressed by your skill and by the depth of your knowledge. Your initiative, too, is extraordinary and will assist greatly in Germany's Great National

Renewal. I now leave you in the capable hands of my adjutant. Good day.'

Everyone stands. Hitler shakes hands with both men, looks to the adjutant to complete the dismissal, and walks to his private rooms.

When they are in the outer office, the adjutant leads them to his own office and invites them to sit around his table.

'You, gentlemen, both of you, are greatly favoured. I need to inform you now of events that will involve you in the coming days and weeks. The Führer has invited you to join him at Berghof next week.

'When you return to Berlin, you will be the guests of honour at a gala evening celebrating the introduction of the nationwide version of the Enlightenment Programme. You will meet later today with Herr Hoffmann, the Führer's private photographer. He will take your official photographs. One of them will appear in tomorrow's papers, nationwide.

'You have become something of an international sensation. Foreign Affairs has received numerous enquiries about the Enlightenment Programme from foreign entities. These include the American chapter of the Nazi Party. Be aware that although there are no plans to send you to America, that may change. Be prepared for it.

'Time Life Publications has also been in touch. They want to do a cover story about you, Herr Schroeder. They are planning to put your photograph on the cover of *Time* magazine. This is under discussion with Reichsleiter Goebbels. Herr Goebbels will choose the moment for this placement so that it has the greatest possible positive effect. He is meticulous about these things.

'Each of you will find the details, travel arrangements and so on, on your desk. The Führer has asked me to thank you again on his behalf for your loyalty to him and to Germany.'

As Wagner and Thomas leave the Chancellery, Wagner touches Thomas' forearm as a prelude to stopping. Thomas turns to face Wagner, obliquely. Wagner is struggling to speak.

'Herr Schroeder, Thomas, at the time we met at the bearing factory

    R. WILLIAM PLUME

in Munich, I was Gauleiter of Munich–Upper Bavaria and happily so, pleased to serve my country, my Führer, and the Party in that role. But when I met you and saw where you were headed, I, for the first time, began to think that Reichsleiter was within my reach. And now, here we are. Reichsleiter Enlightenment and Plenipotentiary Party Education. I have much to thank you for, Thomas. You made this possible. Thank you.'

Thomas smiles and says, 'My pleasure, Reichsleiter Wagner.'

'By way of thanks, the least I can do, Thomas, is stand you a drink. Come.'

When the two men are seated with their drinks, Wagner asks, 'Where did that word come from?'

'Which word?'

'Plenipotentiary.'

'Herr Goebbels?' says Thomas with a mild grin and a shrug.

'Oh, for goodness sake. You can be so obtuse sometimes. What does it *mean*?'

'Herr Know-it-All,' Thomas replies.

Wagner, laughing, says, 'Ah, *en pleine dans le mille*!' Thomas is right on target.

Later, sitting at his desk, Thomas thinks, *And now the Führer himself has compromised the Führerprinzip. Interesting.*

ENLIGHTENMENT MOVES TO ITS NEW OFFICE

A large office complex in Berlin's government operations district is made available for Wagner and Thomas. Every detail is catered for: furniture, telephones, pencils, paper, lighting, flowers, everything.

Wagner, Thomas, Brünner, and Eisen walk in on day one and get straight to work. All the applications for provincial supervisors and trainers are processed within a few days.

Thomas sets his staff to work identifying all target installations. They make start-up arrangements with all plant managers. The programme to train the trainers begins.

Trainers are dispatched to their assigned installations. Synchronised Indoctrination Programmes begin throughout Germany. Thomas, Brünner, and Eisen travel incessantly. At every installation, they support plant managers, bolster trainers, and encourage employees.

Eisen handles the usual things that a security manager would, but he is also the private conduit for communications between Thomas and Reinhard, and so, as the three men move around the country, Eisen finds public telephones and passes information back and forth between Reinhard and Thomas.

It is a cat-and-mouse game with the SS. Eisen revels in the challenge.

Throughout the country, every shift at every installation begins with a robust rendition of 'Deutschland Über Alles'. Positive results begin to flow in almost immediately.

Just as Thomas had predicted, production figures begin to rise, and operations begin to run more smoothly. Site managers report high levels of worker satisfaction. Absenteeism falls to an all-time low.

Complimentary articles and editorials begin to appear in the mainstream press. Even the international press begins to watch. Other industries begin clamouring to be included in the programme. The benefits are plainly obvious, and everybody wants to be involved.

Hitler is pleased that someone had seen the wisdom of sharing his wisdom with everyone else.

CHAPTER 19

Streicher Starts His Own Investigation

STREICHER'S STALKING

What is Schroeder doing with Wagner?

Not long after meeting Wagner and Thomas in the Munich Hauptbahnhof, Streicher begins to see irregularities.

Why were they going to Berlin? What Indoctrination Programme? Or did he call it 'an Enlightenment Programme'? First I've heard of it. Why would Schroeder be involved in something like that? Whatever it is. What the hell is going on?

While these questions swirl through Streicher's mind, he sets one of his men, Herr Wetzel, on Thomas.

Streicher's instructions are simple: 'Watch him carefully. Follow him everywhere. Don't let him out of your sight. Report back to me everywhere he goes, everything he does, everyone he sees. For starters, stake out trains returning from Berlin. Wagner and Schroeder will be back in Munich tomorrow or the day after.'

Wetzel sets himself up at the Munich Hauptbahnhof. He spots Wagner and Thomas leaving the Berlin service. He follows his quarry through the Bahnhof to the taxi rank, where they get into a taxi.

Wetzel takes the next cab off the rank. 'Follow that taxi!' he commands.

The quarry cab stops at Wagner's office. Wagner gets out and closes the door. He has a brief chat with Thomas through an open window.

Wagner punctuates a full stop with a couple of gentle raps on the roof of the cab, which the driver interprets as the signal to leave.

Thomas is meeting with Reinhard, so now the destination is the Mörsbach Schreiber plant. Following his usual practice, Thomas does not go directly into the plant. Instead, he goes into Frau Gretel's Gingerbread Café.

Wetzel returns to Streicher and reports to him, among other things, that Thomas entered Frau Gretel's Gingerbread Café at such-and-such a time and left not long after in the same cab.

To Wetzel, Frau Gretel's seems a very ordinary piece of information. He includes it in his report because he thinks the entire trip from the Bahnhof is very ordinary, and if he doesn't include it, the report will be very thin.

Streicher is listening, but Frau Gretel goes in one ear and out the other. He is hoping for something wildly incriminating, like Thomas being seen entering a synagogue. Suddenly, Streicher realises that the stop at Frau Gretel's is anomalous. Thomas and Wagner have shared a taxi to Wagner's office. So far, so good. The taxi then winds its way further across town, where it stops, not at another office nor at a hotel nor even at a train station, but at a coffee shop?

'Hold on a minute! Back up! Where is Hansel's coffee shop?'

For a moment Wetzel is confused. 'Oh, you mean Frau *Gretel's*,' he says. He gives Streicher the street address.

Streicher slams his open palm down on the desk and jumps out of his chair. 'Mörsbach Schreiber! He was going to Mörsbach Schreiber Printing! This Herr Schroeder *is* the man I thought he was!' He congratulates the tracker. 'You have done well! Very well!'

———

It is 3.00 am. Streicher is lying flat on his back, staring into darkness.

Kunigunde, his wife, is lying beside him, on her back, snoring.

What the hell is going on here? We have Mörsbach Schreiber Printing, owned and operated by two families, both with serious anti-Nazi attitude problems.

Then there's Adolf Wagner, war veteran, committed Nazi Party member, Gauleiter of Bavaria, and prime mover of this new Enlightenment Programme.

And smack bang in the middle, between these incompatible extremes, somehow connected to both, is none other than Thomas Schroeder, a smooth operator if ever there was one.

What is Schroeder's game? For that matter, what is Mörsbach's game? And why is Wagner to be involved? What is going on here?

—

Streicher has another surveillance job. This operation requires two gumshoes.

Herr Wetzel is assigned to follow Reinhard, and Herr Stoppel is to follow Thomas. The two men are issued cars, abundant cash, and a free hand to do whatever they think necessary.

After the first month or so, Wetzel reports back to Streicher that Reinhard is regular in his habits. Apart from a weekly trip to Berlin, he is always in Munich.

'And the trip to Berlin? Do you know where von Mörsbach is going and who he is seeing when he's in Berlin?' Streicher asks.

'Not yet, but he uses the same train service every time. I will stake out that service, and if he turns up, I will buy a ticket, and when he gets to Berlin, I will track him.'

Streicher approves and Wetzel carries on.

Wetzel's simple tactic works. Reinhard appears for the service twenty minutes before its scheduled departure. It's more than enough time for Wetzel to purchase a seat.

Knowing that Reinhard is on the train, Wetzel simply sleeps through the entire journey, expecting to re-establish his contact with Reinhard on the platform in Berlin.

But in Berlin, there is no sign of Reinhard. He has vanished.

Wetzel has observed every face moving off the platform, and Reinhard is not among them. Thinking that perhaps Reinhard is deliberately delaying departure to avoid prying eyes, Wetzel moves to a more discreet point of observation.

When the train begins to move away to be serviced, Wetzel knows that Reinhard cannot possibly be on it. His only option is to go back to Munich and try again next week.

On the next trip, Wetzel books a ticket for the same class in the same carriage that Reinhard has habitually used.

On arrival in Berlin, once again Reinhard has vanished. He is not in his seat, not in the toilet, and not on the platform.

On the third trip, Wetzel discreetly watches Reinhard's every move. Reinhard cannot blow his nose without Wetzel noting the movement.

Late into the night, the train makes a brief but essential stop in the rail yard of a small, rural town not far from Berlin. The purpose is to replenish boiler water. There is no platform. Passengers do not leave the train.

As the train is approaching the water stop, Reinhard collects his things and goes into the toilet cubicle at the end of the carriage, adjacent to the external carriage door.

Wetzel watches Reinhard's every move. When Reinhard jumps from the train, Wetzel notes the name of the village. When he gets back to Munich, he marks it on a map. Then he drives to Berlin.

Now staking out the rail yard where the water is replenished, he observes a car appear a few minutes before the Munich to Berlin service makes its water stop. The train stops, Reinhard jumps off the train, gets into the car, and the car leaves the rail yard.

Wetzel follows. The car drops Reinhard at a downtown Berlin hotel. Wetzel notes the name of the hotel and thereafter stakes out the hotel.

Wetzel, now fixed on Reinhard's purpose in Berlin, soon establishes that every time he travels to Berlin, he goes to army headquarters. He spends the day there and catches the late express back to Munich.

———

Meanwhile, Stoppel has a difficult time just keeping Thomas in sight. Thomas' role in the Enlightenment Programme requires him to move, daily, from one municipal installation to another.

Once a week, a man emerges from Thomas' entourage, finds a public telephone and has a brief telephone conversation with someone.

———

Streicher's men return to Nuremberg a few days before Christmas and deliver their reports. Both men present the information they have as a bland recitation of facts.

Stoppel's report is confirmation that Thomas is doing just what his job requires. But there is the peculiar public telephone behaviour of his assistant. The man makes a point of finding a public phone from which he has a brief conversation. *And, no, I don't know with whom, and, no, I couldn't hear the conversation.*

Wetzel's report is similar.

Neither sleuth sees much of anything that might cause excitement.

But Streicher, once again, picks up a scent. 'Do we know if the days that Schroeder's assistant uses a public telephone box coincide with the days that von Mörsbach is in Berlin?' he asks.

The two men look at him blankly. After a moment, one of them ventures a tentative 'No'.

'Well then, look at your notebooks,' Streicher growls with some exasperation.

It takes a while for the two men to match up the required information from two different field books.

On twenty of the twenty-one occasions that Thomas' assistant used a public telephone, it was on the same day that Reinhard was in Berlin.

Streicher doesn't wait for an explanation of the single anomaly. Just as he did last time, he slams his open palm down on his desk and jumps from his chair.

'Whatever these two guys are doing, they are doing it *together*!'

He accentuates the remark by banging his fist down on the desk. He underscores the point with another forceful thump. His eyes are shining. Quite the little puzzle! He has just fitted a most difficult piece, and he is pleased.

'You two have done very, very well! Keep up the good work!'

After the two men have gone, Streicher sits at his desk, pondering over what Thomas and Reinhard are doing.

Their activities couldn't be more different. But if they are working together, Thomas' Enlightenment Programme and Reinhard's visits with the army must be related somehow.

'But how?' Streicher says aloud.

CHAPTER 20

Demerits Added to the National Programme

DEMERITS AND THE PROVINCIAL PROGRAMME

'What demerit programme?' Himmler asks.

Thomas looks at Wagner and points to himself. The unspoken question is, *Shall I answer this one?* Wagner bobs his head a little.

Thomas says, 'The demerit programme that is referred to in the Enlightenment Programme Implementation Plan.'

Himmler doesn't know there is an Implementation Plan, but he says, 'Ah. Yes, of course. But humour me, please. Remind me why we are adding the demerit system.'

'The Enlightenment Programme, at this time, is entirely devoted to promoting brotherhood and loyalty by singing "Deutschland Über Alles". You will be well aware that all the reports we are getting from the field show that this phase of the programme has been very successful –'

Himmler interrupts to say, 'So simple, yet so effective. I think I hit the mark with that proposal.'

'– and shows inspired leadership,' adds Thomas, completing his sentence.

Himmler interrupts again, saying, 'Cream rises to the top!'

Thomas continues, 'And now that workers are absorbed in what we are doing, we will begin the actual indoctrination work. In our trial programme, we found that workers needed to be motivated to give the programme their full attention. Singing is one thing; study is something altogether more challenging. A demerit system has a wonderful way of concentrating the mind.'

'Carrot and stick, eh, Herr Schroeder?'

'Very succinctly put, Reichsleiter Himmler.'

'I see the stick, but where is the carrot?'

'Well spotted again, Reichsleiter Himmler. After the workforce has become accustomed to the demerit system, we will start a complementary "re-merit" system.'

'Why not start both at the same time?'

'Because it's confusing for people. And starting it somewhat later gives the installation management an opportunity to show good faith with the workforce.'

'Oh, Herr Schroeder, that's very wily. I wholeheartedly approve.'

Thomas smiles to acknowledge Himmler's compliment but adds, 'The re-merit programme is not meant to be in any way deceitful. It is meant to underscore the principle that hard work and adherence to the Aryan Standard have their rewards.'

Himmler decides that there is a rebuke in Thomas' comment.

'That makes perfect sense. Keep me informed of progress.'

Outside SS headquarters, Wagner says, 'Sometimes, Thomas, every now and again, you stroke people the wrong way. Let's not forget that the Enlightenment Programme is much more likely to succeed if we are not pushing uphill against Herr Himmler.'

'Of course. I understand that, Herr Wagner. But, if the programme is to have any meaning, it shouldn't depart from the thinking of our Führer.'

Wagner understands the comment as obscure but doesn't bother to pursue it.

They continue along the footpath in silence.

Presently, Wagner says, 'It seems that Herr Himmler hasn't entirely left his bucolic background behind.'

Thomas puts his hand on Wagner's back and says with a smile,

     R. WILLIAM PLUME

'Perhaps when he talked about "cream rising to the top", he was referring to you.'

'Aah, Herr Schroeder, that's such a lovely thought, but I think we both know he was referring to himself. You are, Thomas, an acutely perceptive person, and you know better than most that a Himmler reproached is a Himmler resentful and dangerous.'

Thomas allows the comment to rest for a time and then says, 'Himmler is a good example of someone who didn't depart from the thinking of our Führer. He was a chicken farmer, and now he is Reichsleiter SS and Chief of the Gestapo.'

CONFUSION RISES TO MUNICIPAL LEVEL

'It says, "Part Two: Promoting a Deeper Understanding of the Thinking of Our Führer".'

'Part two? Part two of what? What does that mean? What was part one?'

'I don't know. I'm just reading what's written in the memorandum.'

It is Monday morning. Throughout Germany, workers in municipal installations gather around their dayroom bulletin board.

'Otto, read the line at the top of the page.'

'I'm only going to do this once more, so pay attention. It says, "Part Two: Promoting a Deeper Understanding of the Thinking of Our Führer".'

'Well, yeah, okay. I still don't understand. What was part one?'

'Getting us to sing, maybe?'

Hans joins the conversation in a fluster. He is jabbing at the last paragraph.

'Look!' he says. 'We get demerits for being late and leaving early, and demerits for being too long away from the workstation. And look at this – "for attitudes and behaviours that depart from the Aryan Standard"!'

'What does that mean? What's a demerit, anyway?' asks Hartmut.

'It means you've been a bad boy, Hartmut.'

Hans is reading the end of the last paragraph, and in some alarm, he says, 'Well, yes, you've been a bad boy, but it says here "… failure to work towards meeting the Aryan Standard will have consequences …" But it doesn't say what those consequences are.'

When the trainer arrives to begin the day, as usual, with 'Deutschland Über Alles', Hans approaches him and asks what is meant by "failure to meet the Aryan Standard". He also wants to know the details of what is meant by "consequences for failure to meet the Aryan Standard".

The trainer doesn't know because he hasn't been told.

Thomas has deliberately withheld the details. He prefers to let febrile minds come to their own conclusions. The following week, the list of consequences appears. They start at a reprimand, elevate through loss of pay, and end with dismissal.

Thomas' final detail is to note that demerit points are given out at the sole discretion of the Enlightenment trainer.

Some trainers are alarmed at this stipulation, for they grasp that inevitably they will be seen as favouring some men over others. Many trainers are uncertain what to do, so they do nothing. If they ask for guidance, they are told to "work towards the Führer" and are left to decide for themselves what that means.

Some trainers simply pass on that advice to the workers they are meant to be training. Other trainers see the selective use of demerit points as an opportunity for professional advancement.

Installation managers are also concerned about the demerit system because they have no control over demerits; it diminishes their management prerogative. But complaints from the managers of municipal utilities end up with the Party-appointed mayor and not with the Enlightenment Programme office.

A workman turns up late, and someone else points this out at the morning choir session, asking, 'Shouldn't he get a demerit for that?'

The late-arriving workman says his train was late and he had no control over the situation. Furthermore, he takes exception to the first workman interfering and threatens to meet him behind the building after shift.

The trainer now has a problem on his hands. Maybe being late should warrant a demerit, but maybe that's a bit tough if the employee had no control of the situation. And maybe interfering also warrants a demerit.

With countless variations, this scene plays out throughout the country.

Hans, concerned about non-Aryan factors, approaches his trainer at the Gasthaus one evening. He asks to speak privately. When they are seated alone in a dark corner, Hans wonders aloud if the trainer needs any help.

'With what?' the trainer asks.

'With identifying substandard behaviours, infractions of the rules, and perhaps even sniffing out Untermenschen, the subhumans, in the ranks.'

The trainer, who hasn't been given any guidance on how he is meant to deal with demerits, sees that a very elegant solution has fallen into his lap. On the point of blurting out acceptance, he asks, 'And what would you be expecting in return for your services?'

'Well, let's say I accidentally, ya know, did something that might warrant a demerit point, yeah. Ya with me? Know what I mean?'

'Go on.'

'Well, you just forget to put it in the book, okay?'

The trainer has begun to comprehend that his job is far more challenging than he thought it would be. The singing is easy. But dealing with all the different personalities and viewpoints, the bloody-mindedness, and the bad-tempered grumpiness is nightmarish.

Still trying to do his best, he says to Hans, 'Isn't that cheating? And isn't cheating a failure to meet the Aryan Standard?'

'Well, yeah, alright then. I'm just sayin', it might make things a little easier for you. If ya know what I mean? But if you're not interested, that suits me fine.' With that, he moves to leave the booth.

The trainer grabs his wrist and says, 'Not so fast. I didn't say I wasn't interested. It's just that we have to understand each other. First of all, you tell no one. Not anyone, no matter what. Understood?'

'Yeah, okay. What else?'

'Don't get carried away coming to me with too many demerits. Understand?'

'Yeah, I get it.'

For what it's worth, they shake hands.

As Hans leaves the booth, the trainer thinks, *I've got him where I need him. If he starts playing rough, I'll crank up his demerit count and have him dismissed.*

Hans walks away from the booth thinking, *I've got your arse now, Herr Trainer. You do things my way, or I'll shoot off an anonymous letter to Berlin.*

Throughout the country, people see ways to use the system. A small-scale black market emerges in trading ideas on how to curl the Enlightenment Programme to advantage.

The brotherhood and cohesion promoted by the singing begin to fall away.

Every man sooner or later realises that he could be ratted out by anyone else, and suspicions begin to grow. And everyone, eventually, realises that demerits always lead to the same result: dismissal. Everyone but the most devious will end up unemployed.

Some of the workmen take up the issue with the trainer. He undertakes to pass on their concerns to Berlin, which he does. In Berlin, letters from trainers saying they are getting a lot of complaints about the demerit system begin piling up.

Meanwhile, some workmen have accumulated enough demerits to warrant dismissal. The trainer notifies the unfortunate workmen that they have been dismissed. The trainer goes to the plant manager, as a courtesy, to let him know that so-and-so has been dismissed.

Plant managers soon recognise this overarching power of dismissal is a serious problem, but there's little they can do about it.

Berlin starts receiving letters. Many letters. Some are from installation managers asking – no, demanding – to know about demarcation of responsibilities and lines of authority. Trainers, it seems, are imposing what they think is their authority to dismiss workers for having accumulated too many demerit points. The situation is impossible, say managers.

Anonymous letters from workers, and even some trainers, start appearing, filled with compromising information about participants in the programme. None is helpful, but Wagner decides it's a management problem, not a governance matter, and ignores the letters.

The singing of 'Deutschland Über Alles' loses its appeal.

Berlin begins to see an unmistakable levelling off of production. There are a few reports of minor failures in equipment. Absenteeism figures begin to rise. But Wagner sees no cause for alarm, and Himmler continues to place glowing reports before the Führer.

One day the Führer says, 'Herr Himmler, I am getting an unending stream of good reports from you about the Enlightenment Programme. Of course, I'm pleased, and I congratulate the team on its good work. But Herr Himmler, I have important things on my mind at this time. Until we have resolved the issue of Herr Röhm and the SA, I do not need any further reports about the Enlightenment Programme.'

Himmler instantly loses all interest in the programme and ceases acting as an advisor to Wagner and Thomas.

CRAMPTON RETURNS TO GERMANY

'Welcome back to Germany, Inspector Crampton. It would seem that for my sins, I am honoured to be your minder and driver again.'

'There are less pleasant ways for you to make your atonement than to be my minder.'

'Wise words. Where are we off to today?'

'The Munich City Property Office.'

As they make their way through the city, the driver questions Crampton about the details of what they are looking for.

When they arrive at the office, the driver parks the car. He moves the rearview mirror so that what he sees in reflection is Crampton's eyes. In his turn, Crampton sees the driver's eyes. For a fleeting moment it strikes him how odd it is that he is looking into a mirror seeing two eyes, just as he would see if they were his eyes. Yet they are not. *What a clever deception.*

'Before we go in there, I need to ask if your German has improved since we went to the property office at Meersburg?'

'Why do you ask?'

'Because we are here on official police business, and your bumbling around with German makes us both look like a couple of rank amateurs. Do your talking through me. Understood?'

'Understood,' Crampton confirms.

When they arrive at the public counter, the minder takes the lead. He puts his identification card on the counter and signals that Crampton should do the same. The attending clerk surveys both cards.

'We are here on official police business. We have a residential address, and we need to know the name of the owner,' the minder says in crisp German.

'Show him the address,' the minder then says to Crampton.

Crampton opens his diary and, pointing to the handwritten address, places it in front of the clerk.

The clerk returns with a large volume and opens it to the given address.

'The house is owned by Thomas and Lillian Schroeder, and it is also the registered office of the Lillian Piano Academy.'

'Do you record the full names of the owners?'

'They are Thomas Hedwig Reichey Schroeder and Lillian Annegret Schroeder, née Zaunmann.'

'Do they own any other properties in Munich?'

'Yes. They also own THR Schroeder Printing, which is at this address.'

The clerk turns the book around, pointing to the address.

———

'Good morning. You are Frau Schroeder?'

'Who is asking?'

'We are with the police. This is Detective Inspector Crampton from Scotland Yard in London. We would like to speak with Thomas H. R. Schroeder. Is he home?'

'He is not.'

'Do you know where he is?'

'No.'

'Will he be back soon? Later today?'

'No.'

'To be clear, the Thomas H. R. Schroeder who is part owner of this house and who lives here is the same Thomas H. R. Schroeder who is involved in the Nazi Party's Enlightenment Programme?'

'Yes.'

'Well then, for now, that brings us to an end. I will leave my card. If you would, please, next time you speak with Herr Schroeder, give him my phone number and ask him to call me.'

'I will tell him next time I speak with him.'

'Thank you for your co-operation, Frau Schroeder.'

When the police car has left, Lilli finds SS man Schäfer in his usual place, surveilling the Schroeder residence.

'We need to get a message to the SS immediately.'

A few minutes later, a memorandum marked 'Immediate Action Required' is put into Wagner's hands by his adjutant.

Wagner reads the message.

The adjutant waits for Wagner's instructions.

'Find this Detective Inspector Crampton. He will still be in Munich, partnered with a German Police minder. Get in touch with Immigration. Arrange to have his visa revoked and deport him. And keep him under close supervision until the vessel that's ferrying him back to London is out of sight. Is that clear? Do it now. And get in touch with Herr Schroeder – he's in Regensburg today – and let him know that London police are looking for him. Do that first.'

———

Crampton and his minder go back to the police station. The minder, on the spur of the moment, calls the Enlightenment Office in Berlin, hoping he might find out where Thomas is now.

He is told that Herr Schroeder is in Regensburg today.

'We can be there in three hours,' says the minder to Crampton.

'We're off,' replies Crampton.

———

'I'm sorry to interrupt, Herr Schroeder. Two policemen have arrived. One is from Munich police, and the other is a detective inspector from Scotland Yard. They are in the front office and would like to speak with you now.'

'Go, please. Get Herr Brünner. Bring him here now. I will wait.'

A few minutes later, Brünner arrives.

'Listen carefully. We are about to be interviewed by an English-speaking detective inspector. In this conversation, I cannot speak English. You must act as translator. I'll explain later. If something goes off the rails here, call Lilli immediately.'

Thomas and Brünner arrive at the front desk.

Crampton holds up his Scotland Yard identification card. 'Ah, here we are. And you are Herr Thomas Hedwig Reichey Schroeder?'

     R. WILLIAM PLUME

Thomas looks at Brünner, who translates the minder's question into German.

Thomas nods and says, 'Yes, I am.'

'And your companion's name and purpose here?' the minder asks in German.

'This is Herr Brünner. He is here to translate as necessary.'

'I will do the translation. He may be excused.'

'If it is your intention to translate, then he is here to ensure that you do it correctly. He will stay.'

Crampton barges in. 'Your real name is Thomas von Stauffenberg, is it not?'

'It is not.'

'You must have a Party membership card. May I see it?'

'Of course,' says Thomas and hands his card to the minder.

The minder turns to Crampton and says in English, 'This looks in order, and it is likely to be correct. The Party is meticulous about ensuring membership information is accurate.'

The minder hands the card to Crampton. Crampton looks at it and then at Thomas. 'Meticulous be damned. I think he is stonewalling.'

Crampton steps up to Thomas, bringing the two men nose-to-nose. 'There is much about you that doesn't add up, Herr Whatever-Your-Name-Is. I have a very reliable intuition, Herr Mystery Man, and it's running red hot because of you. Despite your denial, I think your name is Thomas von Stauffenberg. I think you have a brother named Philip, and I think you know where he is.'

Crampton, his posture tense, scrutinises Thomas. 'I think you speak English like a person born to the language. This translator you brought with you is just eyewash. In Meersburg, you own and you once lived in a house more befitting the lord of the manor than a night-soil man, which was your occupation at the time. In Munich, you jointly own with your wife, Lillian, another house equally refined.

'And that's not all. No, sir. You and Frau Schroeder are the joint owners of THR Schroeder Printing. Whence comes the readies – on a night-soil man's wage – to indulge your expensive tastes? And why are you getting around the place using Thomas Hedwig Reichey Schroeder as a pseudonym?

'Which reminds me to ask, how is it that a Jew is developing and running a programme promoting uber-Nazism? All of these questions add up to a real puzzle, and we're not going to get to the bottom of it here. Since you have shown no willingness to co-operate, you, sir, are coming with me. I'm arresting you in the name of the King.'

'He has arrested you!' Brünner says to Thomas in German.

Astonished by Crampton's unexpected action, Brünner steps forward and demands, 'On what charge?'

'I'll think of something on the way back to London. And you, Mr Translator, stay out of my way, or you will be coming with us.'

CRAMPTON GOES BACK TO LONDON

'You kidnapped him,' says Commander Skinner.

'I took him into custody,' replies Crampton.

'No. You kidnapped him. What are we going to do with you, Derek?'

Skinner pushes a small button on his desk. His secretary appears at the door. 'Ask Mr Pickering to join us, please.'

Skinner leans back in his chair, observing and puzzling over Crampton. Crampton begins rhythmically clicking his thumbnail. Neither man is sure of how much time has passed before the office door opens again. Mr Pickering is ushered into the room.

Skinner stands. With an open hand, he suggests a chair that Pickering could use. 'Inspector Crampton, this is Mr Pickering, Head of Operations, Foreign Office.'

Pickering wastes no time with introductory delicacies, not bothering even to sit. 'Inspector Crampton, you have created a very serious problem for the Foreign Office. I would understand if you weren't aware that Foreign Affairs has been keeping an eye on Herr Thomas Schroeder, so I'll ask.'

'No, I wasn't aware of that,' answers Crampton.

'Were you aware that his father, one Konrad Maria Berthold Graf von Stauffenberg, was a senior diplomat at the German Embassy in London?'

'Just so, his brother, Klemens, has informed me.'

'You are aware that Herr Schroeder is Jewish?

'Yes.'

'Furthermore, you are aware that Herr Schroeder is the originator of, and primary driving force behind, what is known as the "Enlightenment Programme", a training course that promotes an extreme version of Nazism?'

Crampton nods.

'Surely you would agree that when those two things are combined in the same person, it adds up to more than just a passing degree of interest. Did it ever occur to you to wonder how or why a Jew has created and runs a course that promotes uber-Nazism?'

Pickering rumbles on, not waiting for an answer. 'We, at the Foreign Office, have reason to believe that what he is doing serves our purpose. Aside from that, Herr Schroeder has committed no crime that warrants extradition, particularly if that expatriation is unlawful. We want Herr Schroeder back in Germany at the earliest possible opportunity.'

'But I have questions for him, and I will deal with that before he goes anywhere,' replies Crampton.

'You don't seem to understand, Inspector, the full import of what your ill-considered initiative has precipitated. There has been a stern response at the highest level of the German government. Herr Hitler himself has initiated Head of Government intercession. He wants Herr Schroeder back yesterday.'

'But since Herr Schroeder is here in London –'

'*Was* here in London,' says Pickering.

'As we speak, he is returning to Germany aboard RMS *Lancastria* in full, silk-sheet comfort. On arrival in Bremen, he will be escorted via private rail car directly to Berlin. From the Berlin Hauptbahnhof he will be chauffeured to the Chancellery, and from kerbside he will be "hand-delivered" directly to Herr Hitler's inner office. From this moment, you, Inspector Crampton, will stay well away from Herr Schroeder. Is that clear?'

Without another word, Pickering marches to the office door and lets himself out.

As the door latch snaps closed, Skinner shoves himself away from his desk on his rollaway chair. He stands, looking towards Crampton, hands on hips.

'Derek, we went through police college together. We are colleagues and friends, and I hope neither of those things changes. You are among the best that Scotland Yard has, but you have some blind spots that undermine your talent. But get this straight. You are dismissed from this case. You are, as of this moment, on sabbatical leave. That means you take some time – on full pay – to get your thoughts together. Come back when you're ready to pull your oar in the right direction.'

     R. WILLIAM PLUME

CHAPTER 21

Re-Merits Added to the National Programme

STREICHER'S MAN AT THE NUREMBERG SEWAGE WORKS

As Gauleiter of Franconia, Streicher has been informed that the Enlightenment Programme is starting up in Nuremberg just as it is throughout Germany. The local programme is to begin in the Nuremberg Municipal Sewage Treatment Plant. Streicher thinks it an odd place to start but is unconcerned. His interest is Thomas and his role in the Enlightenment Programme.

With some minor pushing and shoving among his contacts, Streicher manages to get a job at the treatment plant for Herr Stoppel. Stoppel starts his employment just as the programme is getting under way.

As it has everywhere in Germany, the programme begins with the singing of 'Deutschland Über Alles'. Stoppel participates in the singing, and, like everyone, he enjoys it.

What Stoppel observes is that the singing has precisely the effect that Thomas intended. The men are happier; they are working harder; they are doing a better job. And yet Streicher has his doubts.

Stoppel delivers reports.

Streicher fires off questions.

In one of these stuck-in-neutral sessions, Stoppel wonders aloud, 'Is there anything beyond singing? Where's the enlightenment?'

'Good question,' agrees Streicher.

Soon they get their answer. Throughout Germany, the Doctrinal Study Programme begins.

The character of Stoppel's reports begins to change.

'This morning we're doin' this training unit on Nazi Party structure. Herr Trainer asks the class if anyone knows what year the Party was formed, see, and some noodle brain says 1889! Well, the class falls about larfin', and Noodle Brain gets a little embarrassed and pissed off. Herr Trainer is tryin' to be all leader-like, see, but can't help snickering a little. He says, "Well, that was the year the Führer was born." Well, Noodle Brain, who maybe isn't such a noodle brain after all, says, "I know that. As far as I'm concerned, the year the Führer was formed was the year the Party was formed. Did you ever think of it that way, you smart farts?" Then he stomps out of the room.'

Over the following weeks, Stoppel brings back reports that describe frequent discord in the classroom sessions. Disagreements often enough lead to confrontations, which occasionally deteriorate to physical violence.

Streicher begins to think he has spotted the pattern he has been looking for. *This is very clever*, he thinks. *Schroeder knows that there will be disagreements, and maybe he is deliberately setting things up to encourage them.*

Soon Stoppel returns with a report of a new development. A demerit system has been introduced.

Streicher approves, but what he is interested in is the effect the programme has on morale. He instructs Stoppel to be vigilant.

Streicher hears rumours that Schroeder had set up a training programme in a ball-bearing factory in Munich. *How did that get started?* he wonders. He goes to Munich and starts sniffing around.

Soon he finds the bearing factory where it all started. What he finds, though, *was* a bearing factory. It has closed down. The entire staff, terminated. The operation became so dysfunctional that it was thought best to start over.

What happened to the manager, this Klausen guy? He was fired along with everyone else. *Does anyone know where he is?*

Streicher finds Klausen unemployed and destitute. Streicher stands Klausen lunch and probes for information while Klausen eats.

'Herr Schroeder insisted on starting the programme, and he wouldn't take no for an answer. He was going to have his programme come hell or high water. And, at first, it was wonderful. The singing was inspired; I'll grant him that. The men were sceptical at first. Who wouldn't be? For heaven's sake, who wants to sing "Deutschland Über Alles" first thing in the morning?

'But sing it they did. Gott im Himmel! Did they what? Everything improved. Everyone was happy. If Schroeder had just done that – the singing, I mean – and nothing else, we would have been the sweetest little bearing factory in Deutschland.'

'What went wrong? How did the whole business go from so wonderfully good to so horribly bad?' Streicher asks.

'Schroeder wanted demerits levied against the men who didn't sing properly, and later he added other things that accrued demerits. Then he insisted that pay should be docked if someone had too many demerits. Then if someone got even more demerits, they could be dismissed. That did not go down well.

'Schroeder moved the programme into the part where they were studying party doctrine, party history, *Mein Kampf,* that sort of thing. That's when the difficulties began to appear. There was some kind of confrontation at every meeting. Often enough, there was blood involved.

'Schroeder was unconcerned. He saw it as the inevitable result of competition. Just as it's laid out in National Socialist canon, he would say. And merit points started about then. Somewhere in there.'

'Where did the idea for the Affirmation Box come from?' asks Streicher.

'Herr Schroeder planted the idea for that.'

'Was the name his –'

'No, the name was my idea. But, please, I don't need to be told how silly it is. I've heard that enough, thanks. I was very proud of it when it started – the box, not so much the name – but it was a bizarre nightmare from the start.

'When the men realised that demerit points could be offset by dobbing in a workmate for this or that deficiency, things turned very nasty very quickly. Some of the men even started agitating for bonuses if they had enough merit points, points they had managed to accumulate by getting other men fired. It was horrid.

'Then, somehow, inward and outward deliveries got messed up. Orders went to the wrong addresses and had to be resent. Then the delivery of supplies, basic things like chromium steel – and you can't make bearings without chromium steel – was late. And then – how? – shipments started going to the wrong places. We couldn't deliver on time; contracts were cancelled. And now, the whole plant has been shut down.'

Full comprehension settles upon Streicher. *It was a trial run! Now he's going to do the same thing countrywide!*

He sees with uncharacteristic clarity the devious simplicity of Schroeder's plan: If power, water, and sewage utilities fail, everything else must soon grind to a halt.

Streicher is a dyed-in-the-wool Nazi. Nowhere in all of Deutschland is there a more devoted acolyte of Adolf Hitler. But even Streicher, for whom Nazi doctrine has biblical solidity, now sees how Schroeder has brought about this catastrophe. He has deployed Nazi philosophy against itself, and it has wrecked a small but important bearing factory in Munich.

Streicher is exultant. He now knows he has Schroeder dead centre under the cross-hairs, and he is thrilled. *I've got him!* He plops an obligatory but mechanical 'Thank you, Herr Klausen' on the table, even as he stands and moves towards the door of the café.

Back in Nuremberg, Streicher anticipates, with relish, Schroeder's certain and calamitous fall from grace. *When Himmler knows what Schroeder is really doing, he'll be in prison, quick as a wink, and then I'll make his life a misery; you can be sure of that!*

 R. WILLIAM PLUME

But Streicher knows his limits. In Nuremberg, he is rat-smart. In Berlin, he is out of his league. *I'm only going to get one shot at this, and trying to nail Schroeder through Wagner is doomed. Wagner will leap to Schroeder's defence if only to cover his own arse.*

To bring Schroeder down, Streicher must meet with Himmler. *That guy sends sweat down my back. He's a walking inflammation. He looks like such a weed, but he can be so-o-o-o-o shitty, and he has the power and the inclination to turn shitty into seriously nasty. Truth is, I'd like to do to Himmler what Röhm did to Himmler, but that'll never happen. I'm going to have to convince him of Schroeder's real intentions.*

If he wants to corner Schroeder, Streicher has no choice but to meet with Himmler and convince him that Schroeder isn't what he seems to be. On the plus side, there are vague rumours that Himmler isn't as obsessed with the programme as he once was.

Meeting with Himmler is not the most enticing prospect, but it's that or nothing.

RE-MERITS BEGIN NATIONWIDE

Thomas writes the re-merit directive. He sends it to Wagner for his approval. Wagner has some questions and comments and calls him in for a pre-release meeting.

'Herr Schroeder, I have read your re-merit directive. I have a question for you. But first, I must say that this directive looks like Herr Klausen, at the ball-bearing factory, could have written it.'

'Effectively he did,' Thomas replies. 'At that time, I was looking in the direction of merit points, but I wanted the idea to be his, so I steered him as closely to the idea as I could without telling him what to do. His construction of the idea was just what was wanted.'

Wagner says, 'I see that a workman can earn re-merits by having the right attitude and identifying those who don't, or by reporting workers who arrive late or leave early or do not get back to their station soon enough after the lunch break, or by reporting departures from or behaviours inconsistent with the Aryan Standard. All good so far.'

'The system is designed to give workers the opportunity to cancel out their demerits. I think they will be pleased,' adds Thomas.

'No doubt they will. One last thing, though. When I read on, I find that workers are to make their observations known to the Enlightenment trainer, in confidence, by writing them on a piece of paper and putting them into a box in the dayroom called the Affirmation Box. Is it really called the Affirmation Box?'

'Think of it this way: People are affirming that so-and-so did this or that.'

'You don't think that perhaps it might end up as a target of ridicule, as in, "Ohh look, Herr Snitchy is affirming that Herr Wanker was basting Wilhelm in the loo!" followed by uproarious laughter?'

'It's possible,' says Thomas blandly.

'You don't seem too concerned.'

'I'm not,' says Thomas with a small shrug.

'Perhaps I'm being too careful. Send it out.'

THE RE-MERIT PROGRAMME ARRIVES AT THE SHOP FLOOR

Monday morning. The workers, gathering for the singing of 'Deutschland Über Alles', find a robust wooden box with a slotted lid bolted to the countertop in the dayroom. Somebody asks, 'What's this?' and gets an answer from Gavriel Weinstein, who is standing by the bulletin board.

'Hey, everyone! I think you all need to have a look at this,' says Gavy, as he is known. 'Finally, someone's got the right idea! There is now a re-merit system that goes alongside the demerit system. This is a way to cancel demerits by doing the things listed here.'

Gavy, the installation larrikin, sees an opportunity to perform. He removes the sheet of paper from the board and turns to address the workmen crowding around him. He calls for space. The men, anticipating another entertaining show from Gavy, move back to create a semicircle around him. He reads the requirements one by one and then repeats them aloud with commentary.

'Regular good attendance with a consistently tidy appearance.' He smirks. 'Tidy appearance! Hah! Some of you guys are a walking demerit.'

People standing around laugh, and someone yells, 'Yeah! And as for good attendance, Schmidt is on his way to the dog box!' The man laughs at his own joke, but other people standing around are already listening to Gavy reading the second item.

'Displaying a positive attitude and identifying those who don't.'

The mood changes to something a little more serious. Someone says, 'I'm all in favour of a positive attitude, but what does it mean to identify those who don't?'

'I'd like to know that too,' says another.

'Maybe it has something to do with that suggestion box on the counter,' someone says.

Gavy interrupts and says, 'It's not a suggestion box. It's an *Affirmation Box* apparently. Who's ever heard of such a thing? Shall I continue?'

There is silence, so he does.

'Reporting workers who arrive late or leave early or who do not get back to their station quickly enough after the lunch break and suchlike.'

The silence continues. Gavy sees nothing humorous and makes no comment.

He reads the last to himself. 'Reporting departures from – or behaviours inconsistent with – the Aryan Standard.'

But he doesn't repeat it aloud. He turns, pins the directive back on the board, and leaves the room.

'What's up with him?' asks Rudi.

'Read the last one, Rudi.'

Rudi is pleasant and friendly but slow, and it takes him a little while to read the item. When he's finished, he says, 'I still don't understand. What's up with Gavy?'

'He's a Jew.'

'How do you know that?'

'From his name! Don't you know anything, Rudi?'

'I know what I need to know to do my job. Besides, I don't understand what being a Jew has to do with anything.'

A week and a few days pass.

As the men are gathering for the singing, Rudi asks, 'Where's Gavy?'

'Rudi, he's been dismissed.'

HANS READS THE DIRECTIVE

Hans has read the directive. His arrangement with Herr Trainer for avoiding accumulating demerits has worked well for them both, but it seems a little pointless now, and he considers alternatives. How, he wonders, can he extract the most benefit for himself from the new system?

Hans buttonholes Herr Trainer at the Gasthaus, and they have another meeting in the dark booth in the corner. Hans starts things off, saying, 'You know, I reckon you still need "administrative assistance", Herr Trainer.'

'How so? What you've been doing is passing me bits of paper. Why don't we just end our little deal, and you just put the paper in the Affirmation Box?'

'Affirmation Box, hah! What a goofy name for a suggestion box. Who thought that up, I wonder? It's more of an aspiration box – *I hope this guy gets a box full of demerits*, or *I hope that guy gets dismissed*. Well, that right there, puttin' paper in the inspiration box, is the problem. If people see me puttin' things in there, they're gonna think that I'm dobbing someone in, and I'll end up bein' the special guest at a blanket party. Know what I mean?'

'So then, it sounds like I'd be doing you a favour by keeping with the arrangement of taking paper backhanded from you, right?' the trainer replies.

'Could look at it that way, I guess.'

'Well, I do look at it that way, and I'm wondering what you are going to do for me to make it worth my while to take the risk of dealing with you directly. It wouldn't be too long before I get reported to Berlin for going outside the system,' the trainer says.

Clandestine discussions setting up such schemes are rife throughout the country.

As the programme continues, workers are dismissed, which causes installation managers to submit to Berlin even more strident complaints about interference from Enlightenment trainers.

Workers can't understand why they've acquired demerits that put them near the point where their pay is docked or they are dismissed. They don't understand when the man who works next to them starts bragging about the pile of re-merits he has against his name.

The whole business becomes an administrative nightmare for trainers everywhere. There seems to be no way out of the mess. The workplace becomes sullen and suspicious.

The singing stops. It's too dreary to bother with. Camaraderie and common purpose are things of the past.

Berlin is not listening. Wagner has left everything to Thomas. Thomas is travelling from city to city, from installation to installation, but only to satisfy the prying needs of pairs of SS men who follow him everywhere. But he never enters any installation. He's allowing things to fester. *It can't be long now before things start to go wrong.*

A PUMPING STATION FAILS IN HANOVER

The water supply for a large part of Hanover fails because the main pump at the Hanover Municipal Waterworks has ground to a halt. The botch-up is the result of a simple human oversight. The timer on the main pump has not been reset.

The engineer responsible for resetting the timer has somehow accumulated too many demerits and has been dismissed by the Enlightenment trainer despite the forceful objections of the installation manager.

It takes some time before other staff can even find the timer, and when they do, resetting it is found to be more challenging than expected. No one can find the instructions, so the plant manager tries to entice the engineer back to show them how to reset the timer.

The engineer, nursing a powerful resentment brought on by the trainer's high-handed and deceitful treatment, is having none of it. He point-blank refuses.

Other engineers feverishly try to figure out how to set the timer so the start-up motor can be engaged to get the main motor going, which will bring the pump back to life. An engineer suggests removing the timer's cover so they can decipher how it works from the internal wiring. The cover is removed, and the screwdriver is immediately pressed into service, pushing wires around.

The screwdriver interferes with engineering plans by spectacularly shorting out the timer's wiring, now reduced to a charred and smoking mess.

The motor that starts the motor that runs the pump spools to a halt.

Emergency calls are put through to the timer supplier with the aim of securing a replacement timer together with instructions for installation and use. The supplier asks for the model number, and when told what it is, informs the engineers that the model they have went out of production years ago. Worse, the supplier also informs them that the new timers are incompatible with Hanover's out-of-date pumping equipment.

The manager of the Hanover Municipal Waterworks calls Hanover's mayor to let him know that the problem will take some time to fix. The mayor wants to know if that means days or weeks or months or worse. He is told that it would be a good idea to organise an alternative water supply.

HIMMLER HUMILIATES STREICHER

'Herr Streicher, I have agreed to meet you only because I'm told the reason for you coming here is alarming. I hope for your sake that you are not wasting my time,' says Himmler with thinly disguised distaste bordering on contempt.

'Thank you, Herr Himmler –'

'Reichsleiter Himmler to you, Herr Streicher.'

Gauleiter Streicher to you, Herr Himmler, thinks Streicher. *But if I say it …*

If he wants to bring down Schroeder, he has no choice but to hold his nose, swallow hard, and comply. 'Thank you, Reichsleiter Himmler.'

Streicher sets out his suspicions about Schroeder's role in the Enlightenment Programme. He gives a step-by-step account of the progression of events at the bearing factory in Munich, emphasising the cleverness of binding the men together with the singing, only to then tear them apart with the initiatives that follow.

The demerit programme followed by a delayed re-merit programme sounds wonderful, but it is the meanest sort of underhanded trickery. Before long, the men are at each other's throats – literally, in some cases – and failure of the plant is inevitable.

'And now we have the serious failure of the Hanover Waterworks, which is obviously related to the dismissal, by the Enlightenment trainer, of the only person who knew how to manage the timer on the pumping equipment. It's clear that the common thread in these two disasters – the bearing factory and the waterworks – is Thomas Schroeder and his so-called Enlightenment Programme. I recommend that the programme be terminated immediately and that Herr Schroeder be arrested –'

'Stop!' Himmler cuts Streicher off with a slashing wave of his hand. He stands and bends over his desk, adopting his most menacing posture. 'I've heard enough! It is you, Herr Streicher, who needs to acquire a better understanding of Nazi Party doctrine! Do you not understand that it's all about survival of the fittest and the best? The best people, the best ideas, and the best bearing factories will survive, and others will fall away.

'The failure of one unexceptional, mismanaged bearing factory in Munich is no bad thing! It will be replaced by a better bearing factory. That's the genius of Nazi Party doctrine. Herr Schroeder understands that, and *that* is the genius of his programme!

'And as for the waterworks in Hanover, that failed because a bunch of idiot engineers were messing around inside the electrical workings with – Gott im Himmel! – a screwdriver! What the hell do you expect?

'As for Herr Schroeder, he has an impeccable pedigree and an unblemished record as a member of the Party since early 1921. He is Alter Kämpfer. The depth of his knowledge and understanding of the Nazi Party and its doctrine is second only to the Führer himself! He was on the street in Munich on the ninth of November 1923, and I'm aware that he has been nominated for inaugural membership in the Blood Order!

'You, on the other hand, Herr Streicher, have a pedigree that is highly questionable, to say the least. I have held your mother's birth certificate in my hands. I have had it examined forensically, and I find no reason to doubt its authenticity.

'Your attempts to undermine Herr Schroeder are sad and pathetic. He is a great lion among lions, and I can't help but think that you are motivated more by envy than you are by a desire to save the Reich! The Reich will survive for a thousand years without your help.

'You should fall down upon your knees and thank your lucky stars that you have the favour of the Führer. Were it not for that, you might well have found yourself in Dachau before this day's end. There is nothing more to discuss! Now, get out of my office!'

　　　　R. WILLIAM PLUME

CHAPTER 22

Nuremberg

MAY 1934. VON HINDENBURG IS DYING

Reichspräsident Paul von Hindenburg is close to death. Vice Chancellor Franz von Papen is shown into the President's office.

'Ahh, von Papen, how good of you to come. Forgive me if I don't stand. It's become such an effort these days. Please sit down.'

'You have made such a sterling effort to stand for Germany over so many years, my friend, that no one will grudge your preference to sit today. How are you feeling?' von Papen says.

'If you are asking after my physical well-being, I'm on the wrong side of my eighties, so I'm no worse than I have a right to expect. If you're asking how I'm feeling about the state of the nation, that's a different answer. Not so sanguine. My dear von Papen, how did this great country of ours come to such a dreadful state?'

'Herr Reichspräsident, the country has, indeed, come to a dreadful state. Now you are the only person who has the way to bring things back to normal. The Office of Reichspräsident is the only constitutional power that can bring an end to the Nazi anarchy.'

Von Hindenburg thinks about von Papen's remark for a moment before replying, 'I am old, and I am tired. But I am still the President. I have the power to invoke martial law, and I may yet do it. I have considered it more than once. Between the two of us, von Papen, you know that I have little time for Herr Corporal and that gang of thugs he has gathered around himself. But I have no time for the arbitrary use of presidential power, either. If I am to invoke martial law and remove Herr Hitler from power, I need a solid reason to do so.'

A drawn space of silence intervenes.

'I'm told that you are preparing to return to your estate at Neudeck, Herr Reichspräsident,' von Papen eventually says.

'The doctors don't see a long future for me, von Papen. It will be something of a miracle if I see another Christmas. Yes, I'm going home, but I'll not stand aside from my post. I will continue to act as Reichspräsident.'

'I underestimated him, Paul. I thought as long as we had positions in Cabinet, we could control him. Now I see how wrong I was. He has outsmarted everyone.'

'When I die, von Papen, there will be an election for a new president. The new president will have that authority. Perhaps you should stand for the office yourself. In the meantime, I cannot take constitutional steps to curb Herr Corporal simply because he has turned out to be inconvenient. I need more than that before I can legitimately invoke martial law or dissolve the Reichstag.'

'Of course, I understand, Herr President.'

'Things are going badly, von Papen. See what you can do to put them right. And I expect to enjoy your company again at Neudeck. You will come soon! That's an order, Herr Vice Chancellor!'

THE NUREMBERG SEWAGE DISASTER

Nuremberg's wastewater reticulation system combines stormwater and sewage, and hence, the water entering the sewage treatment system contains sediment. The sediment load must be removed before the sewage can be treated. Wastewater is directed through an assemblage of large, rapidly rotating sieves that remove progressively smaller grains from the inflow.

Sieving cannot be delayed or circumvented. To fail-safe the operation, there are two sieving trains. The final direction of flow is determined by a single valve that channels the entire flow into one sieve train or the other.

Right or left. Couldn't be simpler.

To prevent interference with this important valve, it is enclosed in a small lockable box of heavy-gauge steel. A lockable shed has been built around that. Changing the position of the valve is done by hand, and the job is entrusted only to the most senior and experienced workmen.

Over time, primary, effectively exclusive, responsibility for the valve has fallen to Herr Melzer.

Melzer is a capable and reliable worker, but he is not very agreeable. His hygiene leaves room for improvement. He rarely changes his clothing. He seems not to need, and does not seek, human company.

The Enlightenment trainer at the Nuremberg Sewage Plant is the diametric opposite: a poster boy for the Aryan Ideal. He sports wavy blond hair and bright blue eyes. He is tall and powerfully built, immaculately presented, and ambitious.

And he is more than a little irritated that he has been assigned to a sewage treatment plant. He despises Melzer at first sight. The slovenly dress, his lumbering gait, and a closed personality all draw loathing from the trainer, who begins to devise a way to rid himself of the repellent Melzer. The demerit system, when it appears, is like an answer to his prayers. It's just what's required.

Demerits are levied against Melzer for the *suggestion* of some form of infraction. To move things along, the trainer occasionally records two demerits instead of the usual one. Before long, Melzer has accumulated enough demerits to make his dismissal inevitable.

Slovenly and lumbering though he may be, Melzer is not stupid. He sees what is coming. He has seen others sacked in a brutal, standover fashion in which the trainer personally escorts the unfortunate dismissed to the exit.

Melzer begins to carry with him a key ring holding two keys that resemble the keys required to change the position of the inflow valve. Every morning, he goes to the tool room where the key cabinet is kept. He puts the fake keys in place of the real valve keys and puts the real keys into his pocket. At the end of his shift, he reverses the process, leaving the real keys and taking the replica keys home.

On the day Melzer is dismissed, he is instructed by the trainer to gather together his personal things and leave the site immediately. Melzer tucks his tool belt under one arm. His remaining belongings he stuffs into a small knapsack that he slings over his shoulder.

The trainer escorts Melzer to the exit. Without a word, Melzer leaves the building and shuffles along the tree-lined footpath that leads up a long, gentle slope to the main gate.

The path closely parallels a sieve train in full, clattery operation.

When he is adjacent to the coarse-gravel sieve, Melzer pulls from his tool belt his largest hammer and flicks it into the rapidly rotating sieve. Just for the hell of it, he throws in the real valve keys as well.

He carries on shuffling towards the gate.

———

'What the hell was that?' yells the installation manager, bolting out of his chair. He runs to the front door and yanks it open. The sieve train has stopped! The entire flow of raw sewage is spilling out of the pipe over the sieves, uncontrolled, and flooding in every direction. It is spilling over the footpath into the trees and heading towards the office door.

Slamming the door shut, he yells to his assistant, 'Get the fucking valve keys out of the key cabinet! NOW!' He quickly pulls on his sludge boots.

'Where the hell is Melzer?' he yells. Then, grabbing the closest person, 'You! Go! RUN! Find Melzer and get him out here. NOW!'

The assistant returns with the keys. The workman sent to find Melzer returns a moment later, saying that Melzer has been dismissed.

    R. WILLIAM PLUME

The manager grabs the trainer by his tie and jerks him face-to-face. 'What the fuck have you done, you snivelling little shit?' He doesn't wait for an answer and heads for the valve shed.

To get there, keys in hand, he must now open the door. When he does, raw sewage floods into the office. His entire attention is directed towards changing the position of the valve. If the valve isn't changed to direct the flow into the other sieve train, he knows that there is no way to stop the unconstrained flow of sewage. By heroic effort, wading through already knee-deep untreated sewage, he manages to gain the valve shed.

His emotional state is bordering on panic, but he finally manages to get a key into the lock on the shed door. It doesn't work. *SHIT! Two keys, a fifty-fifty chance. I got it wrong. The other one must work!*

But it doesn't. 'FUCK! What the HELL is going on?' he yells.

He tries the first key again. Same result. The only thing he can do now is go back to the office and check the key cabinet in case the assistant got the wrong set of keys.

But when he gets himself back to the buildings, he sees there is now a higher priority. The flow must be directed away from the buildings and the electrical equipment.

'ALL HANDS ON DECK!' he bellows. 'We need to move this shit NOW!'

'You too, Herr Fucking Enlightenment Fucking Trainer!'

'No! Not me!! I'm not doing that!'

'Like hell you're not!!' yells the manager, pushing a yard broom into the trainer's hands and shoving him out the front door.

EMMELINE SEES PHILIP'S PHOTO

Derek Crampton, back in favour at Scotland Yard, is scanning the extraordinary headlines in the *Illustrated London News*:

'You've seen the news. It's awful, isn't it, sir?'

'Good morning, Miss Stephens. Yes, it is. What's on your mind?'

'The International Criminal Police Commission has been in touch. There has been a call from a Fräulein von Etting … zz … Ettings … showser … shauser –'

'Ettingshausen,' enunciates Crampton.

'Oh, I see. The "n" looks like an "r". Quite a name, isn't it?'

'Yes, it is, Miss Stephens. You said that she had called the ICPC?'

'Yes. Would you like me to patch you through to her number?'

'Yes, please.'

'And the Commissioner has seen the ICPC calls list for the past twenty-four hours. He's aware that she has called. He wants to see you as soon as you've spoken with her. Apparently, the Bank of England is turning up the heat.'

———◆———

'Fräulein von Ettingshausen, good afternoon. Thank you for your call. Do you have news for me?'

'Yes, Inspector, I think I do. I see that Philip is on the cover of that American news magazine. What is it called? *Zeitung*? *Leben*? I have it here somewhere …'

Crampton hears paper being shuffled around.

'Yes, *Time*. It's called *Time* magazine. *Life* magazine is the other one, less news, more photos. Very popular in America, apparently, though I cannot understand why,' she says.

'Fräulein. Fräulein, please. I think you'll find that if you look carefully, you will see that the article in *Time* magazine is about Herr Thomas Schroeder and that the photo on the cover is of him.'

'I do beg your pardon, Herr Inspector. I think I know Philip when I see him – no one better than me – and the person on the cover of that *Time* magazine is without question Philip von Stauffenberg.'

'Please don't be offended, Fräulein, but have you been drinking?'

'Ach, mein Gott im Himmel! Don't be impertinent, Inspector. Yes, I've been drinking, which is none of your damn business, but I know Philip when I see him. That is *not* Thomas Schrader, Schacter, Schroeder – whatever, whoever that is. That other person. The person shown on the cover of this magazine, this *Time*, is without a shred of doubt Philip Albrecht Graf von Stauffenberg.'

'How can you be sure that it isn't his brother, Thomas?'

'For a start, Herr Inspector – and I would have thought that by now, you, of all people, would know this – Philip does not have a brother named Thomas. Philip's parents had only one child, and that was Philip. This person, the person in the photo on the cover of *Time*, is Philip. Period.'

'How can you be so sure, Fräulein?'

'Because he has a mole on the right side of his chin.'

'And you are familiar with this mole … because?'

'Because I used to put my tongue on it when we were … kissing.'

The pieces of Crampton's 'Philip Puzzle' assemble themselves before his mind's eye. The handpiece finds its own way into its cradle.

He *is* Philip! *There is no Thomas!*

'Hah!' he exclaims aloud.

Defrauds the Bank of England. Goes into hiding in Meersburg. Works as a night-soil man. How bloody brilliant is that? Seeking a member of the German nobility, who would look among the night-soil men? You might go look around the Côte d'Azur or Rio, but nobody would ever go to Meersburg to check out the night-soil man.

Lives alone in an out-of-the-way and lovely house that belonged to his parents. Charms and marries the lovely Lillian, wherever she came from. Discovers he is Jewish. Sets up the hyper-Nazi Enlightenment

Programme. Deliberately constructs it to create destructive dysfunction. And he succeeds!

Crampton slaps his thigh and laughs. He stands.

'Now there is a man with some *proper* gonads. I salute you, Philip Albrecht Graf von Stauffenberg! Well played, sir! Well played! My full respect. Enjoy the spoils. For you, sir, I take this information to my grave!'

———

'Inspector Crampton, come in.'

'Thank you, Commissioner.'

'You've spoken with Emmeline von Ettingshausen, I understand.'

'Yes, sir. I have. Just finished a few minutes ago.'

'And?'

'Not much to report, sir. She was drunk.'

'Did she have anything to say?'

'She thought she was calling room service. She asked for another bottle of gin.'

R. WILLIAM PLUME

CHAPTER 23

Marburg

'You are scheduled to speak at the University of Marburg three weeks from today, Herr Vice Chancellor. That might be a suitable place to draw a line in the sand,' suggests Edgar Jung, a lawyer and von Papen's speechwriter and close advisor.

After a brief period considering the matter, he says, 'I think you might have the right idea, Herr Jung. I'll give that some thought. In the meantime, write up something that you think might be appropriate.'

Two days before the speech, Jung presents von Papen with a draft. It is titled 'How Best to Rein in Hitler's Government?'

Von Papen scans the text. 'A little dull, don't you think, Herr Jung?'

'Dull as ditchwater, Herr Vice Chancellor, but you've given me no guidance on what you want.'

'Didn't we talk about this recently? It was you, wasn't it, who suggested drawing a line in the sand at Marburg?'

'That was my suggestion, sir. You said you'd give it some thought, but you didn't tell me what you had concluded.'

'My apologies, Herr Jung. It's been a busy time. But let's do that, shall we? Draw a line in the sand, I mean.'

Von Papen hands the speech back to Jung. 'File that. Start again. I'm sure you can do something before Sunday.'

Jung has been directed to write the speech he's been itching to write. He goes back to his office, pitches the first draft into the wastebasket, and throws himself into his work.

Jung finishes his work in the early hours of Sunday morning. He is pleased. So pleased, in fact, that when he reviews his title, he decides that it is not up to the occasion.

He winds page one back into the typewriter. After carefully manoeuvring the paper into position, he repeatedly smacks the X key until his draft title is obliterated.

He replaces it with 'The Aims of the German Revolution'.

Now Sunday afternoon, minutes before von Papen is to speak, he is standing offstage, fretting. 'Where is Herr Jung? The speech – where is my speech?'

'He assured me that he would be here in good time, Herr Vice Chancellor. Ah! Here he is now,' says von Papen's secretary.

Von Papen receives the speech into his hands. 'Cutting it a little fine, aren't we, Herr Jung? There's no time for any kind of review.'

'My apologies, Herr Vice Chancellor. I was delayed.'

'Ah, well, couldn't be helped, no doubt. I am to be introduced to the content at the same time as my audience. So be it. But your work, Herr Jung, has always been astute and well-judged, so I will put my faith in that. You haven't written anything that will land me in the cart, have you?'

'The German people will be the judge of that, Herr Vice Chancellor.'

After being introduced, von Papen appears on stage and walks to the podium. He places his speech on the lectern. While removing his glasses from his jacket pocket, he scans the auditorium, gratified to see it filled to standing room only.

The expectant faces of the graduating students are, for von Papen, an inspiration. *And some uniformed Nazis in attendance,* he observes.

Looking at his speech, typewritten, closely spaced, four or five, perhaps six, pages. *A lot of speech here,* he thinks.

Trivia intrudes when he notes, with approval, that the lectern is wide enough to accommodate two pages. His preparatory fussing around plays out for him in slow motion.

On the point of speaking, he knows by intuition or premonition that his future, for good or ill, will be defined by the words on these bits of paper, and he doesn't yet know what they are.

When he finishes, the auditorium erupts. The Vice Chancellor's words are marked with a whole-hearted standing ovation.

But his words are not everywhere received with the same enthusiasm.

VICE CHANCELLOR FRANZ VON PAPEN RESIGNS

Vice Chancellor Franz Joseph Hermann Michael Maria von Papen, dressed in his most formal attire – cane, black tie, top hat and tails – strides through the outer office, through the door held open, and into Hitler's inner sanctum.

Hitler is seated at his desk. When he sees von Papen so powerfully dressed and in high dudgeon, he wonders if he should stand. He expects a tirade from von Papen about the suppression of his university speech, the Marburger Rede. Hitler also wonders if he should perhaps adopt a conciliatory mood or something more forceful. *Von Papen is not nearly as powerful as he likes to think. Perhaps it's time to let him know where he stands.* He decides to be guided by von Papen's opening salvo.

With a gesture, Hitler offers a chair.

Von Papen remains standing. 'It's outrageous! Intolerable, I tell you! That a junior minister should take it upon himself to ban the content of my speech at the University of Marburg,' announces von Papen without preamble.

'You are referring, I take it, to Herr Goebbels, the Reich Minister of Propaganda?'

'Indeed, so. I must demand that the content of my speech be released. I was speaking in my role as Vice Chancellor of Germany and as a trustee for Reichspräsident von Hindenburg, whom I will be advising of this matter immediately.'

At the mention of von Hindenburg, Hitler sees the potential danger to his government. *I have the numbers in the Cabinet. Von Papen can do nothing directly there.* But von Hindenburg and von Papen, both sons of the nobility, Hitler knows, are close friends.

In recent times, von Hindenburg has made numerous suggestions in the direction of declaring martial law. *Perhaps he could be swayed in that direction by an insistent von Papen?*

Hitler chooses conciliation but decides to first show his teeth.

'Herr Vice Chancellor, I understand your disappointment with the behaviour of Herr Goebbels, but you really should have cleared that speech with me before you delivered it. It was an open challenge to my authority, and were you not the Vice Chancellor, as you have just reminded me, you might now find yourself in some difficulty.'

Von Papen flares. 'I'll save you the trouble of asking for my resignation.' He withdraws an envelope from his inner breast pocket and pitches it, with deliberate insolence, in front of Hitler.

Hitler is visibly surprised. *Where did von Papen find the gumption?*

Hitler does the calculus and sees that if von Papen takes the trouble to go to Neudeck, he might be able to steer von Hindenburg towards martial law.

He puts off tolerant aggression and replaces it with appeasement.

'Herr Vice Chancellor, I know how important this is to you, and I have some sympathy for your position. I think the two of us working together can find an appropriate solution to this difficulty. But to do this, of course, you will have to withdraw your resig—'

Von Papen ignores Hitler, turns on his heel, and heads for the door. Hitler's adjutant sees von Papen approaching and opens it. Von Papen passes through the inner door, by which time the outer door has also been opened. He is joined by his adjutant, and together they walk through the outer door.

When von Papen hears the door closing behind him, he says in a low voice, 'Go. Get the car ready. Warn Herr Doppelgänger to be ready for the clothes. Go!'

Hitler now shifts mental gears. He shrugs off all pretence and returns his attention to the possibility of von Papen going to Neudeck. *He is a lazy sluggard. He won't do that … But if he* did … *my career is once again hanging by a gossamer thread.* He growls at his adjutant. 'Have him followed! I want to know exactly what he does and where he goes after he leaves here! Go! Now!'

Hitler must forestall, and quickly, any possibility that von Papen intercedes with von Hindenburg to advocate for martial law. Hitler punches the intercom button on his desk. 'I will fly to Neudeck at the earliest possible opportunity! Make the arrangements!'

VON PAPEN LEAVES THE CHANCELLERY

As von Papen enters his Chancellery office, he is removing his clothing, even before the door closes behind him.

Herr Doppelgänger, von Papen's body double, is waiting, alarmingly even if sensibly, in his underwear. Von Papen's adjutant assists von Papen out of his clothes, passing them to another staffer who is assisting Doppelgänger Papen to dress.

Within seconds, Doppelgänger Papen is fully dressed in the same clothing that Real Papen was wearing when he swept out of the Führer's office minutes ago.

Doppelgänger Papen matches Real Papen in height and build. Even the facial characteristics are similar, but no one familiar with Real Papen would mistake him for Doppelgänger Papen.

Real Papen looks at the approximation of himself. 'It's the best we can do on short notice. You understand that if you are caught, it won't go easy for you?'

'Yes, Herr Vice Chancellor,' the doppelgänger replies. 'I'm honoured to have been asked.'

'Alright then. Do the best you can. And thank you. And one last thing. When you get to my home, please make sure you don't dig up the lilies. You know what a lily looks like, don't you? Frau von Papen will kill us both if you do.' Herr Doppelgänger nods and smiles. They shake hands, and von Papen pats Doppelgänger on the back as the door is opened.

Doppelgänger leaves von Papen's office on his way out of the Chancellery building to von Papen's car waiting on Wilhelmstrasse.

If he makes this simple journey alone, anyone who might be observing the comings and goings at von Papen's office will likely find this unusual. They would also see that the formally dressed man looks similar to, but is not, von Papen. Therefore, to distract attention from the doppelgänger, a gaggle of support staff is organised to accompany him to von Papen's official automobile. The doppelgänger keeps his head down in animated conversation with the support staff swarming around him. The group moves out of the building and to the waiting car. The door is held open, and Doppelgänger Papen is swallowed up by the car, which is already moving into traffic as the door closes.

Another car, much less grand, pulls onto Wilhelmstrasse at some distance behind von Papen's car. Taking care not to be seen to notice, one of the gaggle says in a whisper, 'And the SS is on the case …'

Meanwhile, Real Papen is transformed into Plumber Papen. His moustache is shaved off. He examines the result, thinks it an improvement, but cannot dwell on it. He pulls on a grimy pair of overalls. His hair is ruffled, and his cheeks are smacked to blushing rose. A cloth cap is shoved down on his head, leaving hair sticking out all around. The collar of his overalls is half turned up; the sleeves are turned down to cover his soft hands. Tortoiseshell spectacles are slipped over his ears. An old pipe wrench is put into one hand and a small wooden tool tray into the other.

Von Papen is keen to leave as soon as possible. The moment comes.

Von Papen, alone, must leave, for the last time, his Vice Chancellor's office. He must descend two flights of stairs to the ground floor and find the tradesman's entrance at the back of the building. He does not know where it is. He must find it without appearing to be looking for it.

Outside the building, there is a small, open courtyard he must cross before he reaches the tradesman's van waiting on a side street that joins Wilhelmstrasse.

'Are you ready, sir?' asks an assistant.

'As I'll ever be,' replies von Papen.

'Good luck, sir. It has been a great honour for me, for us, to work for you, sir. God go with you,' the staffer says quietly as she opens the door.

Von Papen walks through into the hallway, casts a casual glance this way and that and sees no one. The staffer, now standing in the doorway, says with a smile, 'Thank you, Herr Schmidt. I'm not sure what we would have done about that pipe if you hadn't come as promptly as you did.'

Von Papen elevates the pipe wrench as acknowledgement, turns and shuffles towards the stairs. He arrives at the landing at the top of the two flights of stairs that will bring him to ground level. He hears voices on the lower flight. He hears his name when one voice says to the other, 'Now that old fool von Papen has gone, we shouldn't have any trouble securing his office.'

Old fool, is it?

Von Papen cannot see the people below and knows only that they are ascending. He has no option but to continue down the stairs but moves to one side of the staircase, hoping to avoid the people coming up. He crumples himself over enough to appear slightly arthritic.

As he turns at the middle landing and begins descending the lower flight, he sees that he has chosen the wrong side. There are two smartly uniformed SS officers ascending the stairs, approaching him head-on. He shuffles towards the centre of the stairs to avoid the two men.

When he looks up from his feet again, he sees that they, looking to avoid him, are also moving towards the centre. He shuffles back towards the rail. And again, the SS men, still concentrating on their own conversation, have taken the same evasive action.

These blundering efforts to avoid each other instead bring Plumber Papen face-to-face with the two SS officers. For a moment, no one moves. Plumber Papen shrugs his hands outward, a gesture that says, *I tried, but I'm sorry. I have failed to move out of your way.* Both men correctly interpret the gesture and begin moving around him. One of them says, 'We'll make it easy for you, old man!' Plumber Papen acknowledges the backhanded courtesy by tipping his cloth cap with the pipe wrench.

As they are passing, the SS man nearest to von Papen stops. He reaches down the single step that now separates him from von Papen and puts his hand on von Papen's shoulder.

'A moment, please, Herr Plumber, if I may.'

He backs down a step and looks into Plumber Papen's face. 'Do you have any relatives who work in government service?'

Von Papen shakes his head but says nothing.

'Well, now, that is most interesting because –' He turns to his companion and says, 'Herr Stäben, come. Look at this.' He puts his index finger across von Papen's upper lip and says, 'Remarkable. You know, Herr Plumber, if you had a moustache, you could be the ex-Vice Chancellor's twin brother. Except, even with those glasses, you are much more handsome than he is!'

He clucks at his own jest and starts again up the stairs. As he passes, he pats von Papen on the shoulder, adds a courteous and genuine 'Guten Tag' and continues on his way.

Von Papen, now outwardly calm but inwardly rattled, continues down the stairs. *Old man, old fool, and ugly. We'll see about that.* At the bottom of the stairs, he finds himself in the familiar, spacious lobby. There are a few people chatting or making their way here and there. In more usual times, as Vice Chancellor von Papen, he would be heading towards the front doors. Today, as Plumber Papen, he is heading towards the back of the building.

 R. WILLIAM PLUME

No one pays any attention to him, but von Papen is nevertheless relieved when he finds, without noticeable confusion, the room that is used for staging tradesmen into and out of the building. He must walk through the room like he owns the place. *Look neither right nor left. Acknowledge no one. Say nothing.* He ignores the few people there and passes through the room and then through the outer door.

As he steps into the small courtyard, he hears behind him the clattering of footsteps running down the stairs. *It must be one of those SS men. Now that I'm out of the building, I might as well run!* And he does. He sprints through the courtyard, slings the tools into the tray at the back of the small utility van marked 'Blitzen Commercial Electricians', and jumps into the passenger seat.

Being the passenger in this vehicle is a soft spot in this deception. But there is no other option. Von Papen has never, not once, not ever, driven a vehicle of any kind, and now is a bad time to start learning.

As the van pulls away, Stäben's fist bangs on the roof, and he yells, 'STOP! I order you to stop!' Von Papen turns and sees rather than hears Stäben's final remark, 'FUCK!'

Meantime, Doppelgänger Papen arrives at the von Papen villa.

The car pulls over. A passenger in the front seat gets out and opens the rear door. Doppelgänger Papen emerges from the car, tips his hat to the footman, and strides towards the house. Another diversionary gaggle of assistants appears from the house and escorts him through the front door, which is then closed and locked.

Doppelgänger Papen is already stripping off the clothes he wears. In a matter of moments, he is reborn again, but this time as a gardener. He is led to the garden shed at the back. The majordomo reminds him to avoid the lilies and, to be certain there is no mistake, directs him towards the dahlia beds, where the doppelgänger sets to work lifting bulbs.

The two SS men, watching this charade from their car, observe that von Papen has gone into his house and that his official car has driven away. They reach the obvious conclusion that von Papen is home and has no intention of leaving. Having successfully completed their mission, they return to the Chancellery.

Plumber Papen is already heading northeast towards his first stop near Weissensee. The driver pulls in behind the residence of von Papen's chief adjutant, and the two men make their way into the house. Von Papen changes his clothes, again transforming himself, this time back into himself, dressing in what is, for him, casual clothing.

He puts through a telephone call to Neudeck and asks to speak to General von Blomberg.

'Von Blomberg,' says a sleepy voice.

'*Hammerkopf* is away,' says von Papen and hangs up.

He and the driver now get into another car, an open-road car that has been prepared for the long, non-stop drive to Neudeck. The driver reckons they will be there soon after midnight.

The SS men assigned to follow Doppelgänger Papen after he left his office arrive back at the Chancellery and report to Hitler that von Papen left his office and went straight home. The crucial information that he shows no signs of leaving is included in their report.

'We are watching the house, and if anything happens, you will be the first to know.'

Hitler chortles. 'What did I tell you? Lazy and as stupid as an ox!'

Stäben rejoins his colleague in von Papen's office. He steers his partner aside and discreetly informs him that von Papen has escaped.

'Won't look good for either of us,' Stäben says.

Electric silence follows.

Whispering, Stäben adds, 'I caught up with Herr Plumber, and that's what he was, a plumber. Agreed?'

'Agreed.'

R. WILLIAM PLUME

CHAPTER 24

Realisation

STREICHER'S REALISATION ABOUT THOMAS

After his abortive meeting with Himmler, Streicher starts over.

He reviews everything he knows about the Enlightenment Programme, the bearing factory, the apparent collaboration between Schroeder and von Mörsbach, and the Hanover Water Crisis.

In his mind, he has arranged a meeting with Hitler, but if the topic of the meeting is the Enlightenment Programme, then both Himmler and Wagner, if not Schroeder himself, will be there. *If I can't get beyond where I was when I met with Himmler … not good.*

The phone rings. It is Stoppel at the Nuremberg Municipal Sewage Treatment Plant.

'It is a complete fucking disaster!' Stoppel yells into Streicher's ear. 'There is shit everywhere!'

When Streicher manages to recover from the initial shock, he sees that this is another version of the Hanover Water Crisis. Streicher jerks the phone from its cradle and calls his mates in the military who have risen through the officer ranks since the war.

'What is going on?' 'Who is von Mörsbach meeting with?' 'Why are they meeting?' 'What are they planning?' His stream of questions overwhelms them.

The best he can drag out of his active-duty military contacts is that something hyper-secret is going on. Nobody is saying anything.

Some days later, Streicher and Kunigunde sit down to their evening meal.

As Kunigunde puts Streicher's dinner in front of him, she ventures, 'I don't know why you're so concerned about that Hitler. You were right there beside him at that half-arsed Putsch of his at Bürgerbräukeller, and what's he done for you in the meantime?'

Streicher leaps out of his chair, knocking his untouched dinner from the table, smashing the crockery, and sending Spätzle and Sauerkraut skidding across the kitchen floor.

Ignoring the mess, he bangs his fist on the table and says, 'That's it! It's a Putsch, a coup d'état! Oh, thank you, Kunigunde!' He squeezes her face between his hands and forces a sloppy kiss onto her mouth. He grabs his coat from its hook by the door and runs from the apartment.

Kunigunde, now alone, sits at the small kitchen table. She surveys the mess, the wasted food, the broken dishes and begins to weep.

She sags back in her chair, scrubbing the back of her hand across her mouth. *If he ever kisses me like that again, I'll clock him! I swear I will! … What now? Eat? Go to bed? Clean up the mess? He sure isn't going to do it.*

She can't decide. Dragging herself from the chair, she shuffles to the bedroom and slumps down onto the bed. She turns her head and looks once again at the gritty, out-of-focus school photos of her two sons, Lothar and Elmar, both forced into the Hitler Youth and then the Reichswehr by their father.

Will I ever see you again? she wonders.

This is it?

WAGNER AND THOMAS ARE SUMMONED TO HITLER'S OFFICE

In a rage, Hitler turns to his adjutant. 'Send someone to the Enlightenment office! Bring Herr Wagner and Herr Schroeder here now! Drag them

     R. WILLIAM PLUME

from their beds if you must. Now!'

It is approaching one in the morning when Thomas and Wagner arrive at the Chancellery.

Both Wagner and Thomas note the presence of two out-of-place, armed SS guards standing alert in the outer office.

Wagner's mind is traversing possible reasons why they have been called with such urgency into a meeting with the Führer. *Something else gone wrong? Something, somewhere, has gone off the tracks?* Wagner's mind is racing.

He realises that while he has been preoccupied with these thoughts, he has been, together with Thomas, directed into Hitler's inner office. He sees that Hitler is seated in the red leather chair. Facing him at the opposite end of the table is Julius Streicher.

Why is Streicher here? What is going on?

The Nuremberg Sewage Catastrophe is a bleeding wound for Hitler.

The international press has turned his discomfiture into a cabaret gag. Bathroom humour is the snickering tone of choice in newspaper reports throughout Europe and America.

Hitler stands, bringing Streicher to standing, and advances on Wagner and Thomas.

Hitler is furious. He is purple with rage. His anger has been intensified by Streicher's insinuations that the failures in municipal installations have been deliberately brought about.

'Now, Herr Streicher, go through what you have just told me again. And get on with it. I don't have much time.'

Streicher lays out his suspicion that the Enlightenment Programme has been designed to produce a situation of such gravity that President von Hindenburg will be forced to impose martial law and dismiss Hitler's government.

He cites the Hanover Water Calamity and the Nuremberg Sewage Catastrophe as the most recent and worst instances of infrastructure failures that can be linked to the Enlightenment Programme.

'And your recommendation, Herr Streicher, is that the Enlightenment Programme should be terminated?' asks Hitler.

'Yes, mein Führer,' replies Streicher.

Wagner is stunned. *What the hell is Streicher on about? Where the hell did this come from? Yes, there have been some hiccups, but production is up, and membership and income are up. What the hell is going on?*

'Reichsleiter Wagner?' asks Hitler.

'Yes, there have been difficulties, but let's be frank. The crisis at Hanover was brought about by nothing less than engineer stupidity with a screwdriver. And Nuremberg is, without doubt, a deliberate sabotage. A large hammer has been recovered from the sieves. How did it get there unless someone threw it in, knowing that it would jam the sieve?

'There's no doubt in my mind that the success of the programme speaks for itself. There have been a few problems, but what initiative doesn't have them? My recommendation is that we fix them and move on. And I would remind you, Herr Streicher, that we are getting requests for assistance from companies in England and America. For heaven's sake! How much more successful does it need to be?

'Furthermore, I am shocked. I am shocked that we seem to have arrived at the brink of terminating the Enlightenment Programme without ever informing me that there are concerns.'

Hitler barges over Wagner's remarks.

'And you, Herr Schroeder. You are Jewish! Yet I have, until this moment, been prepared to overlook that deficiency in your character. But no more! Herr Streicher would have me believe that you deliberately set out to create a programme that began wonderfully but would end by bringing down ruin on Germany by destroying our public utilities.'

Hitler draws himself into Thomas. 'I should have you shot! I am being ridiculed in the international press. This was brought about by you! You! You Jewish bastard! I should shoot you myself!'

Hitler returns to the lampstand on the right of the red leather chair. He jerks open the drawer. The drawer comes completely away from the

R. WILLIAM PLUME

stand. A Luger pistol flies out of the drawer and flops onto the chair. Hitler picks it up.

He turns on Thomas. 'Have you anything to say for yourself, you fucking Jew?'

Thomas is silent.

Holding the Luger at arm's length, Hitler closes the space with Thomas until the barrel of the Luger is touching Thomas' forehead above the bridge of his nose.

'Speak!'

Thomas says nothing. His mind sets before him the crisp winter moment in Hagnau am Bodensee, when he realised that Lilli wanted him. Hitler's rasping demands are like the crackling frost beneath his boots. He couldn't move. Immobilised by a lovely woman, spellbound, frozen to the spot.

Hitler sees the pleasure in Thomas' face.

'You fucking Jew. You think this is amusing?'

The adjutant comes forward and whispers to Hitler, 'If you kill him now, in this room there will remain a stain of Jewish blood that cannot be removed.'

Hitler slowly lowers the pistol and hands it to the adjutant.

'Herr Streicher, thank you. I will be travelling tomorrow, but keep yourself available for further discussions. For now, you are dismissed.'

Streicher salutes Hitler and leaves the room.

'Colonel von Stauffenberg, take these two into house arrest. We will examine this matter closely, much more closely when I return to Berlin.' Hitler steadies his breathing, trying to regain his composure.

'Herr Schroeder,' Hitler continues, 'I will deal with you personally. And you, Herr Wagner, are on your way back to the rank and file.'

Hitler turns and walks to his private rooms. As he is walking away from the three men still in his office, von Stauffenberg signals that Wagner and Thomas should remain silent and still.

When Hitler has closed his apartment door, von Stauffenberg quietly bolts the main doors into Hitler's office. He points to the service entrance and whispers, 'Quickly! Through that door and down the stairs. Move!'

Thomas is first through the door. He immediately realises that Wagner will need help to get down the stairs. He descends the first two steps and waits. Wagner moves onto the upper landing.

Von Stauffenberg closes and locks the door.

'Hold my hand,' Thomas says to Wagner.

Carefully, Wagner takes the first step down. Von Stauffenberg, seeing that Wagner will have difficulty moving, quickly moves behind Wagner and takes his other hand.

'Gentlemen, we need to get down these stairs now! Sometime yesterday! There are three flights. Is it possible for you to move any faster, Herr Wagner?'

'I'm moving as fast as I am able. Where are we going?'

'Don't concern yourself with that. Just get yourself to the bottom. Now!'

Wagner lumbers down the stairs, half stepping, half hopping. By the time he arrives at the bottom of the first flight, he is already heaving for breath.

Von Stauffenberg is behind, urging the two men on. 'Move, move, move!' he demands.

In the middle of the second flight, Wagner missteps on his artificial foot. The foot twists, the shoe is stripped off, and the prosthetic leg slips along the step and jabs into the next step down. Wagner lurches forward and down onto Thomas.

Now, to prevent all three men tumbling together to the lower landing, Thomas must push Wagner upward. Von Stauffenberg assists. The three men, barely standing, stumble down onto the next landing.

'Keep moving!' orders von Stauffenberg.

Wagner, now exhausted, says, 'I can't –'

Von Stauffenberg barks, 'You can! You will! Move!'

At the bottom of the third flight, Wagner falls against Thomas, and the two men together fall against the door.

Now there are two bodies, one of them effectively disabled, jamming the door shut. Von Stauffenberg shoves Wagner into a corner and helps Thomas to move away from Wagner.

Von Stauffenberg says, 'I'm going to open the door. Don't say a word. Do exactly what I tell you.'

He opens the door.

'Turn left! Left again. Black car! Get in!'

A black sedan is waiting in the darkness. A man is standing beside the open rear door.

'Get in!'

Thomas steps aside and shoves Wagner into the car. Wagner sprawls onto the seat and drags himself, as much as he is able, to the far door. Von Stauffenberg pushes Thomas into the small space that remains and shoves the door shut.

Von Stauffenberg then gets himself into the front seat. Closing the door, von Stauffenberg says over his shoulder, 'Blood is thicker than political affiliations, cousin! We're all fugitives now.'

The car dissolves into the night.

VON HINDENBURG SIGNS PAPERS

When von Papen arrives at Neudeck, midnight just gone, he is ushered into the house.

The immediate consequence of his phone call to von Blomberg earlier in the evening is that the entire household, including von Hindenburg himself, are awake and about. Von Papen is directed to von Hindenburg's study.

General von Blomberg and some staff officers are already there. Von Hindenburg is sitting at his desk, reading one of the several metropolitan dailies. The headline shrieks:

Germany's Municipal Utilities are Failing! Why?

Von Papen walks into the room, accepting various acknowledgements in a perfunctory manner, for his attention is on von Hindenburg. He approaches the President and surprises even himself when he says, somewhat operatically, 'Herr President, I bring news from Berlin.'

Von Hindenburg snaps the broadsheet newspaper in half along its width. He looks over the top and replies, 'Ahh, von Papen, you've arrived. How good of you to bring news – important, I'm told by General von Blomberg – from Berlin at such a late hour, no, early hour as it now is.' He pauses and looks again more closely at von Papen's face. 'What happened to your moustache?'

'That's a story for another time, Herr President, but now there are important matters that we must address. First, though, I must tell you that I have no official entitlement here. This afternoon I resigned the Vice Chancellorship.'

'Did you now?' replies von Hindenburg in an offhand manner joined with a gentle smile. Setting the newspaper aside, he continues, 'Well, that was a good move, my friend, for Herr Corporal has been looking to rid himself of you. You've lost your warrant, but you are alive. You have chosen your moment well, my friend. Now, I have another question for you, and for this I will require an answer.'

'I'm listening,' says von Papen.

'Well then, tell me, my good friend, what is going on with Germany's municipal utilities?'

Von Hindenburg picks up the newspaper and smacks it with the back of his hand.

'It's in all the papers. This or something like it. The Great Nuremberg Sewage Catastrophe is on the front page of every daily. There are editorials in every paper, agonising over the sudden and widespread failure of power, water, and sewage facilities. Everybody's wondering how this could happen and what is being done to get things working again. What is going on?'

'Sir, it appears to be connected somehow to an Enlightenment Programme that was initiated by Herr Himmler,' replies von Papen.

'Yes, I've heard of this Enlightenment Programme. Tell me more.'

'Herr Himmler – inspired by two men springing from Munich – hatched an idea that the workforce should be trained to understand National Socialist doctrine and philosophy. He named it the National Socialist Enlightenment Programme. His aim was to have a programme in every workplace in Germany, but for some reason, as yet obscure, he decided to start with municipal utilities. In the early days of the programme, it looked very good. Production soared, workers were happy, and absenteeism was down. Everything looked very positive, and the Enlightenment Programme was credited with the improvement. The Führer was delighted.

'But then things started to fall apart. The early positive results were replaced with widespread and serious troubles. Although the two worst problems were the Hanover Water Crisis and the Great Nuremberg Sewage Catastrophe, there were numerous less damaging but still very inconvenient calamities throughout the country.'

'Was this Enlightenment Programme approved by Herr Hitler?' asks von Hindenburg.

'Yes, sir. It was.' Von Papen nods in confirmation.

'I must also tell you, sir, that the Nuremberg catastrophe was front-page banner headline news in *The New York Times*. The article showed a political cartoon which depicted a melancholy Führer standing chest-deep in reeking sewage. We are told that the street hawkers were yelling, "Read all about it! Glorious German Führer up to his baby blues in number twos!" *The Times* also treated the story as a joke, and the papers in London ran similar themes.'

'So, Germany is now an international laughing stock?' von Hindenburg says.

'It seems so, Herr President.'

'And how is Herr Corporal taking this news? One of those precious little purple rages, is it?'

'He is much displeased.'

'Soon, he will be more so,' says von Hindenburg, leaning back in his chair.

'Germany is skating on the edge of anarchy. Herr Corporal, through the SA and the SS, is outlawing all opposition to his regime. The SA – that collection of contemptible street thugs – is now out of control. They are talking openly of a *Second Revolution*, whatever that might mean. And still! *Still!* I keep hearing these rumours of Röhm and possibly others collaborating with the French to overthrow the government!

'If it were only these things, I might be convinced to give Herr Corporal one last chance to straighten it out, get things under control. But this latest failure, this … this Enlightenment Programme, is a bridge too far. The effect it has had on the German people is bad enough, but to have Germany ridiculed in the international press because of a sewage disaster is utterly unacceptable!'

Von Hindenburg brings both fists down hard on his desk and shoves himself up to standing, flushed and glaring, his glorious recurve handlebar moustache quivering.

'The Germany of Frederick the Great and Otto von Bismarck mocked and scorned! And why? Because there is shit – for God's sake! SHIT! – running in the streets! How?' he thunders, accentuating the final word with a knuckle-busting punch to his desk.

'How, gentlemen, how is it possible that such a repulsive thing could happen in Germany? In any civilised nation on this blessed earth?'

'Will you declare martial law?' asks von Papen quietly.

'I cannot, von Papen, in good conscience allow this instability to continue.'

Von Hindenburg sits. He turns to von Blomberg and asks, 'General von Blomberg, do you have the papers?'

'Yes, Herr President,' says von Blomberg, who is standing beside and a little behind von Hindenburg's chair. Von Blomberg places a folder on the desk. He leans over, opens the folder, places a pen on the paper, and points to where von Hindenburg is to sign the document.

Von Hindenburg sits back in his armed chair, pen in hand, looking at the paper on the desk. For a moment he considers the absurdity of the situation. By doing nothing more than fixing his signature to this scrap of paper, he will dismiss Hitler's government and invoke martial law throughout Germany.

'For my entire life, my purpose has always been to do what is right and what is best for Germany. This may well be the most important thing I ever do for my country. That is for history to decide, a history, gentlemen, which will not include me. This will be my final official act for Germany. May the Lord, in His great wisdom, guide my hand!' A moment passes. He reaches out and scribbles on a newspaper to start the ink run.

When he brings himself forward in his chair, he is enlarged.

He *is* Generalfeldmarschall Paul Ludwig Hans Anton von Beneckendorff und von Hindenburg, Reichspräsident, heir to Frederick the Great and Otto von Bismarck.

Without hesitation, he signs the paper. He watches the ink dry in its own good time. His signature blends into the paper. The paper blends into history.

He closes the folder and hands it back to von Blomberg. 'This matter is now in your hands, Herr General. And, von Papen, I should probably tell you – that document names you as Interim President. Now. I am finished. I would prefer to be alone. Please excuse me, gentlemen.'

Von Blomberg snaps to attention and salutes. 'Herr Generalfeldmarschall, to serve you has been my greatest honour.' He turns and leaves the room.

Von Papen takes von Hindenburg's hands and bows deeply before him.

He leaves von Hindenburg to his final peace.

CHAPTER 25

Hammerkopf

OPERATION HAMMERKOPF

Barking orders, von Blomberg spins into his rooms, converted into a compact but serviceable field headquarters. 'Get General von Rundstedt on the phone. Now! And get Colonel Wahlberg to my office!'

'Colonel Wahlberg is in your office already. General von Rundstedt is on standby. I'll have a connection very soon.'

Von Blomberg spins into his office, issuing orders as he does so.

'Colonel Wahlberg, *Hammerkopf* is away. The Führer flies from Berlin tomorrow. ETA 1030 hours. You know what to do. Move!'

Wahlberg leaves as von Blomberg enters.

The phone rings, and from the outer office comes, 'General von Rundstedt on the line, sir!'

'General von Rundstedt, *Hammerkopf* is away! All possible haste!'

Wahlberg rejoins his unit and issues the order to capture the entire SS detachment assigned to guard von Hindenburg's residence. Wahlberg has planned this small but crucial operation in great detail. The detachment must be detained to ensure they do not raise the alarm. Just as important, tomorrow, when the Führer arrives, everything must look normal, as if nothing has changed.

The telephone lines into the SS communications hut are disconnected. Power to the radio equipment is cut off. All SS communications equipment is secured. The telephone and radio operators are arrested and removed. They are replaced with surrogates who know SS communication protocols, the jargon, and the conversational patter that will be required when Hitler's pilot contacts the facility.

The equipment is reconnected, and the surrogates wait on full alert.

The guards on the barracks are taken without resistance. The barracks themselves are surrounded. The occupants are, one by one, roused and notified that they are under arrest. The barracks are inspected for anything hidden – weapons and so on – that might create difficulties.

The two SS guards assigned to meet the Führer's plane are identified. They are interrogated to determine if they had any special instructions regarding the Führer's arrival. Their uniforms are passed to the army detachment.

The entire SS detachment, shoeless and in their night clothes, is herded into troop trucks and moved well away from Neudeck, where they are secured and placed under heavy guard. The SS clothing and equipment are distributed among the men of Wahlberg's detachment. Two soldiers are dressed in SS uniforms and given the weapons that someone knowledgeable would expect to see in the hands of a rank-and-file SS man assigned to stand guard over the Führer.

It is still the dead of night, and all they can do now is wait.

HITLER FLIES TO NEUDECK

Hitler is driven to Tempelhof Airport. He boards his private aeroplane, a Junkers Ju52 tri-motor.

At 0802 hours the plane rises from the runway and turns to the north and east. The pilot reports to Tempelhof control that he is departing Tempelhof airspace and that he expects to touch down at Neudeck at 1026 hours.

The news of Hitler's departure makes its way to the telephone of General von Rundstedt, who then orders the seizure of the German federal government.

First, the radio operators who handle the communications with Hitler's aeroplane must be replaced. The replacement operators must give no impression that anything out of the ordinary is occurring on the ground.

———

Hitler knows that his government is on the razor's edge. He is alone, ungrounded, staring at Germany as it passes beneath him.

I am Chancellor, head of government. But von Hindenburg is Reichspräsident, head of state. He outranks me. The one and only person in Germany who does. He has the power to cast me aside. Now is the crossroads. The last time I stood here, I was in Landsberg Prison. Herr Franz Hemmrich. I've never had many true friends, but he was one of them. He was so masterful. What would he tell me to do now? He would know.

At times of self-examination, Adolf is always drawn to his time in the war. It is painful, not for what was done, but for what should have been done, what could have been done …

I survived, yes. But what else? Herr Streicher was awarded a field commission. Herr Wagner lost half a leg. Herr Göring, a true hero, was awarded the Pour le Mérite. Herr Röhm led from the front, and his body shows the cost. And Herr von Hindenburg, in his time, marched through hell. He earned his bars.

And what was I? A messenger boy … and not a brave one … never promoted beyond the rank of corporal. Should I do what Hemmrich suggested and go back to painting? But my only real talent is speaking. I can speak, but … well … the truth is … I am a … I'm not keeping Germany alive. I'm keeping myself alive. What choice do I have now? Where is Herr Hemmrich when I need him?

The airfield at Neudeck is a simple grass strip. At 1023 hours the radio crackles with the voice of the pilot calling in his imminent arrival and asking for landing instructions.

He is told that the wind is northerly at six kilometres per hour and that he is to approach the runway from the south. The surrogate radio operator adds that there is a heavy dew on the grass. The pilot thanks the operator, notes that he will touch down at 1026 hours, and signs off. On the dot of 1026 hours, the plane's wheels touch the grass and throw up a spray that transforms the landing aircraft into a powerboat skimming across water.

General von Blomberg is waiting.

The plane rolls into the tie-down bay and stops. The three engines are shut down, and the aircraft door is opened from inside. An armed guard emerges from the plane and stands to attention beside the stairs.

Von Blomberg moves forward and stands at the base of the stairs.

Hitler is the next person to appear. He receives the salute from von Blomberg. They shake hands and exchange pleasantries. Von Blomberg, with a hand gesture, directs the Führer towards the house.

Hitler has been here many times and knows where they are going but allows himself to be guided.

As they mount the stairs leading to the entryway, both doors simultaneously open wide. Hitler and von Blomberg are ushered into the house. The doors are closed. And bolted. A departure from usual practice.

A startled look appears on Hitler's face.

He is taken from behind. His arms are pinned back. His nose and mouth are covered with a thick cloth, tied at the back of his head.

A loaded derringer and its holster are detached from his belt at the small of his back.

He is carried – struggling to free himself, struggling to yell – to a back room. He is handcuffed, his hands in front.

A handler unbuckles Hitler's belt and passes its free end over the chain that joins the cuffs. The belt is refastened. The buckle is moved to the middle of Hitler's back. The belt is tightened so that Hitler cannot move his hands away from his stomach.

His shoes are removed. His feet are shackled.

A mask is placed over his nose and mouth, forcing him to breathe chloroform. It takes a time, minutes, before he passes into unconsciousness. His mouth is examined, and the implanted cyanide capsule is removed.

In this inert and bound state, he is bundled into a small van waiting behind the house. Soon, the now ex-Chancellor of Germany is on a narrow, unsealed secondary road, travelling eastward.

Meanwhile, all the occupants of the aeroplane, including the pilot, have been taken into custody, their weapons confiscated, and their footwear removed. They are transported to join the other SS troops in the stockade.

The Ju52 that was Hitler's private aeroplane is searched and tied down.

Wahlberg reports to von Blomberg that the area is secure. As they are speaking, Signal Corps trucks begin to arrive at the front of the main house.

'They're here,' von Blomberg says, 'to set up a broadcast station. Colonel, could you please welcome them? Thank them for being so prompt and get them started setting things up. Herr von Hindenburg wants to make his broadcast to the nation this evening.'

Von Blomberg tells his adjutant to get von Rundstedt on the line.

'General von Rundstedt?'

'Speaking.'

'Von Blomberg here. The primary target is secured and away. Update me, please, on the operation.'

'It's all going like clockwork, General von Blomberg. The Reichstag and the Chancellery are now surrounded and secure. Everyone who was in either building at the time has been detained. The main government buildings are secure. Detachments have been set at all major Bahnhof. They are stopping traffic on all major intercity routes. All international

     R. WILLIAM PLUME

traffic – rail, air, sea – has been halted.

'All army barracks, naval yards, and air force airfields have been secured. Loyalist general staff are all in custody. We have placed the right people in the appropriate places in the Signal Corps to ensure their equipment is not used or destroyed.

'All major radio stations are under our control, as are the publishers of the major daily newspapers. No one will be allowed to make unauthorised statements using known radio transmitters or printing facilities.

'The entire Cabinet – apart from the obvious exceptions – has been detained, as have all Reichsleiter. Herr Röhm is in custody. All the SA and SS weapons caches have been captured and are under heavy guard. We are now separating weapons from ammunition. As near as we can determine, most, if not all, of their weapons are held in those caches.

'A curfew, 1900 hours, has been set for the entire country. There has been some resistance but surprisingly little. People seemed more relieved than indignant.'

'You've done all of that in four hours?' General von Blomberg says, impressed.

'General, the credit goes to Reichswehr Berlin. They have done a brilliant job of planning every detail.'

REINHARD ARRESTED

Frau Gretel's Gingerbread Café is the very heart of cosy, wholesome goodness. It's about as far as it's possible to get from anything like confrontation. People come here to get away from struggles. They come here to feel as if they've floated into a fluffy bathrobe and slippers when they settle down with a cup of Frau Gretel's delicious and rejuvenating coffee.

Customers are surprised and alarmed when two SS officers, dressed impeccably and carrying holstered pistols, stride into Frau Gretel's.

They advance with grim determination on the table where Reinhard is enjoying coffee and Kuchen.

The two officers stop beside the table, and the ranking officer says, 'Herr Reinhard von Mörsbach, you are under arrest for high treason. You will come with us, please.' There is a gasp from other customers and even from Frau Gretel herself.

Reinhard looks up. 'And who are you? And by whose authority do you arrest me?'

'We are the SS, and we arrest you by order of and under the authority of Reichsleiter SS Heinrich Himmler.'

'Gentlemen, please. Perhaps if you sit down, this conversation will be easier.'

The two officers sit.

'Now, gentlemen, perhaps you have not caught up with this morning's news, but Heinrich Himmler is no longer Reichsleiter SS Heinrich Himmler. He has gone back to Herr Himmler, chicken farmer. As of one o'clock this morning, Reichspräsident Paul von Hindenburg has declared martial law and dismissed Herr Hitler's government. The SS no longer exists. You have no authority to arrest anyone.'

The ranking officer snorts. 'I've heard a lot of reasons why someone thinks they shouldn't be arrested, but that is by some stretch the most original ever.'

'I have a suggestion,' says Reinhard, 'that will save you a lot of embarrassment. You go call your office and find out if what I'm saying is true. I will stay here with your companion. If what I've said isn't true, I will go with you. How does that sound to you?'

The officer says to his partner, 'Make sure he doesn't go anywhere. You have a pistol. Use it if you have to. Understood?' The partner nods.

The officer leaves. Reinhard signals to Frau Gretel that she should bring a coffee for their guest.

An hour later, the now ex-SS officer returns. He sits down at the table, drops his peaked cap on the floor, and says to Frau Gretel across the room, 'I'll have a coffee, please.'

Arms folded, he puts both elbows on the table and says, 'You were right. Herr Himmler is, once again, a chicken farmer.'

21 JUNE 1934. VON HINDENBURG ADDRESSES THE NATION

By noon, the Signal Corps has set up and tested the field radio station. It is arranged so that its output signal will be broadcast on all the standard German domestic and military frequencies.

At 1300 hours and every half-hour thereafter until 1730 hours, a message is broadcast telling the German people that at 6.00 pm President Paul von Hindenburg will broadcast an important message to the nation.

The word spreads. At 6.00 pm everyone in Germany is near a radio.

Von Hindenburg begins.

'Good evening to all citizens of Germany, wherever you are. This is President Paul von Hindenburg speaking. This evening, I have some very important news to share with you. The years since the conclusion of the Great War have been a difficult time for all Germans. There has been a succession of upheavals and important changes in the life of this country.

'The Hohenzollern monarchy came to an end and was replaced by the Weimar Republic. Pestilence in the form of influenza and the famine of the Turnip Winter tested the endurance of this nation. It has also been a time of great political upheaval during which politicians of every hue and persuasion have struggled to control the government of this great nation.

'It is well known to all of you that last year, in January 1933, I appointed Herr Adolf Hitler to the role of Chancellor. The performance, actions, and policies of his government during the intervening eighteen months are the reasons for this broadcast.

'In recent times I have become deeply concerned about the direction of our great country. My concerns are manifold. The government of Herr

Adolf Hitler has been unable to control the illegal, often brutal, activities and pretensions of the Sturmabteilung. All political parties except the Nazi Party have been banned, which is inconsistent with the principles of free and open democratic government.

'The government of Herr Hitler has failed to make a clear distinction between party and state, and as a result, Nazi Party doctrine and ideology have been imposed on and inserted into every facet of German life. Local administrative boundaries have been rearranged to suit the needs of the Nazi Party rather than the needs of the German people as a whole.

'Finally, the recent widespread failure of municipal infrastructure, in particular, the breakdown in the supply of fresh water and the repugnant failure in the treatment of wastewater, is a miscarriage of government which I cannot allow to pass.

'For these reasons and more, early this morning I signed an executive order that dismisses Adolf Hitler's government and instigates martial law throughout Germany. The dismissal was effective as of one o'clock this morning. The dismissal will have the following effects, which will remain in place until such time as elections can be organised.

'Germany – as of 1.00 am on the twenty-first of June 1934 – is under martial law. General Werner von Blomberg will assume the role of Interim Chancellor. The military government will have as its purpose the peaceful reconstruction of a civilian government. Herr Franz von Papen will assume the role of Interim President. I ask you to support these two gentlemen in the mammoth task that lies before them.

'The Schutzstaffel – the SS – and the Sturmabteilung – the SA – and all their offices, groups and divisions are by this order disbanded. All weapons, ammunition, flags, uniforms, and other paraphernalia held by these two organisations are forfeit and will be confiscated.

'Administrative names and boundaries will return to what they were on the twenty-ninth of January 1933. All Nazi government and Nazi Party political appointments – including all mayors – are by this order declared invalid. Where possible, the person or persons who held the position on the twenty-ninth of January 1933 will be reinstated.

'The ban imposed by Hitler's government on all political parties other than the Nazi Party is by this order declared invalid. Parties affected by the ban are free to begin again if they wish. The Nazi Party will not be banned, but if it chooses to remain active, it will be expected to operate on the same terms as all other political parties and fully within the law.

'Herr Hitler is alive and unharmed. He is being held at a location that will remain, for the time being, undisclosed.

'I ask all Germans to now join together to rebuild our great nation. I ask you to support the two men who have been appointed to lead the process of reconstruction. I most fervently ask you to look to, and work towards, a brighter future and not to dwell on the past.

'I have been blessed and honoured to have served Germany over many years. My purpose has always been to do what is right and what is best for Germany. This Executive Order may well prove to be the most important thing I have ever done for my country. That is for history to decide, a history, ladies and gentlemen, that will not include me. This is my last official act as Reichspräsident. May God, in His great wisdom, guide Germany to a bright, just, and prosperous future!

'Thank you. Good night and goodbye.'

Epilogue

After being captured at Neudeck, Adolf Hitler is moved to a small, purpose-built outpost in Eastern Prussia. He struggles with the overnight transition from German Chancellor to private citizen, and it shows in his behaviour. He falls into a deep, prolonged and truculent fug. Staff decline to feed him when he behaves like a child. The purple rages stop when he comes to understand that no one cares.

Stalin is made aware that Hitler is not far away and that, at need, he, Hitler, could be discreetly moved to Leningrad. Hitler discerns that Stalin knows of his proximity. His attitude improves.

He voluntarily submits to dental work which reconstructs his entire mouth, replacing his teeth with dentures. The procedure makes it much easier to be near him.

His primary guards, both Jewish, invite him to join them in pinochle. After throwing the cards around the room a few times and kicking the card table over once or twice, he calms and learns to lose with dignity. He takes up painting again. By way of a close examination of his simple but subtle surroundings, he begins to see and appreciate the grace of his circumstance.

He writes a book entitled *Mein Frieden* (My Peace). Hitler is no poet, but he tries his hand. The text includes knobbly but sincere lyrical poetry about the unpretentious place where he now lives. As time passes, he comes to realise that the world has moved on. His mark has been erased. How did that happen? he wonders. For a short time, he is confused by his own lack of interest in the transition.

One morning, at breakfast, Adolf Hitler chokes on the yolk of a hard-boiled egg. His funeral is simple and brief. No speeches. Dust-to-dust blessing. Done. The grave is filled, the grass restored.

The outpost, no longer required, is decommissioned. Everything – every paper and pencil, every stick and nail, every spoon and cloth – is removed.

No mark remains.

Staff return to Berlin for reassignment.

The End

Postscript

With the dismissal of Hitler's government, the Night of the Long Knives, the annexations of Austria and the Sudetenland, the invasions of Czechoslovakia and Poland, Kristallnacht and the Holocaust, the invasions of Russia and France, the attempted invasion of Britain, and the war in the European Theatre do not occur.